She was just wondering where Madam Barrington had gotten to when her mentor reappeared, having made a full circle of the house. Lily opened her mouth to ask what they were going to do next when there came a clicking sound at the back door. To her complete astonishment, it opened a crack to reveal the thin, pale face of a man in a tartan dressing gown and fuzzy house slippers. His sandy hair stuck up in all directions while a bristling mustache adorned his upper lip like a bad-tempered caterpillar. Firmly attached to his left ankle was none other than Sir Kipling. The triumphant feline had the most obscenely smug smirk on his face. As soon as he spotted Lily he meowed a "look what I found" at her.

"This—this cat. Is it yours?" the man asked, his words sharp and his expression extremely put out.

Lily, while horrified at her cat's lack of decorum, fought down a giggle of mirth. "He is, sir. I mean, yes, sir. Please forgive me—I do apologize—" She started forward to peel her errant feline off the poor man's ankle, but he held up a hand.

"I would prefer you stay. That is, right where you are. Just call it—call the cursed thing off."

Also by Lydia Sherrer:

THE LILY SINGER ADVENTURES SERIES

Love, Lies, and Hocus Pocus Book 1: *Beginnings*
Love, Lies, and Hocus Pocus Book 2: *Revelations*
Love, Lies, and Hocus Pocus Book 3: *Allies*
Love, Lies, and Hocus Pocus Book 4: *Legends*
(books 5-6 coming in 2019!)

The Lily Singer Adventures Novellas:
Love, Lies, and Hocus Pocus: *A Study In Mischief*
Love, Lies, and Hocus Pocus: *Cat Magic (coming soon!)*

Dark Roads Trilogy (Sebastian's Origin)
Book 1: *Accidental Witch*

OTHER WORKS

When the Gods Laughed: Part 1

Hope: A Short Story

LOVE, LIES & HOCUS POCUS

⊶ ALLIES ⊷

The Lily Singer Adventures
Book 3

LYDIA SHERRER

Chenoweth ❦ Press

LOVE, LIES, AND HOCUS POCUS
The Lily Singer Adventures Book 3: Allies

Copyright © **2017 by Lydia Sherrer**

ISBN 13: 978-0-9973391-5-4 (paperback)
ISBN: 978-0-9973391-6-1 (ebook)

Published by **Chenoweth Press 2017**
Louisville, KY, USA

Cover design by Molly Phipps: wegotyoucoveredbookdesign.com

Chapter illustrations by Serena Thomas

1046092

*To my fans, whose expectations of a sequel saved me from
the "binge-watching Netflix" monster*

3.14.19

Acknowledgments

Many overflowing thanks to the people who made this book happen. There were my faithful beta readers who met ridiculous deadlines, not to mention my ever-loyal super fans who give me motivation to keep writing with their unabashed enthusiasm. Then there's my wonderful editor, Lori Brown Patrick, who still seems to think I'm worth her time. Much thanks to my exceptionally skilled and patient cover artist, Tony Warne, and illustrator, Serena Thomas. Both of them have to put up with my picky perfectionism and, believe me, I'm fortunate they haven't kicked me to the curb yet. Huge, huge thanks to the vibrant and positive writing groups I'm a part of on Facebook who share so much advice, aid, and encouragement. I've grown exponentially in the midst of such amazing fellow authors. I'm also indebted to Pat and Cindy Tinney, Stephen Logsdon, Tony and Kae Thompson, David and Jun Mcinteer, and Ted and Beth Thomas whose generosity helped make this book happen. Most special thanks to my wonderful parents, who brag on me shamelessly, and sisters, who only roll their eyes a little bit when I start talking about books. And lastly, to my beloved husband, my best friend in the world and the most faithful and hard-working partner I could ever ask for.

Contents

Episode 5
The Economy of Force

Episode 6
Of Wheels and Deals

Episode 5

THE ECONOMY OF FORCE

Chapter 1
THICKER THAN BLOOD

WHAT KIND OF MUSIC DO CATS LIKE? UNDER NORMAL CIRCUMSTANCES, this would be a difficult question to answer—one which scientists and cat experts have, no doubt, puzzled over for decades. Lily Singer, on the other hand, didn't have to puzzle. In fact, she didn't even have to ask. She was informed, loudly and unequivocally, that cats prefer jazz, specifically ragtime. This was the obvious answer, she was told, because country was too whiny, rock too angry, pop too undignified, and classical too boring—though it was an acceptable substitute. The expert in question? Sir Edgar Allan Kipling, magical talking cat extraordinaire. What, exactly, made Sir Kipling an expert on cats' taste in music Lily had no idea, but she'd learned it was best not to argue with one's cat. At least, not if you disliked losing.

So it was that she spent the first half hour of their drive shuffling through radio stations until she found one that met

Sir Kipling's exacting tastes. How he even knew about jazz, or ragtime for that matter, was a mystery to her. Up until several weeks ago, he'd been a normal cat. At least, as normal as a wizard's cat could be. For Lily Singer was not just the archives manager of Agnes Scott—a private women's college in Atlanta, Georgia—she was also a wizard. And being a wizard meant odd things often happened. In Sir Kipling's case, a mysterious entity had gifted him with human intelligence and the ability to be understood by, but only by, his mistress. That same entity had helped Lily, her mentor Madam Barrington, and her witch friend Sebastian Blackwell stop the theft of a powerful magical artifact, with the side benefit of defeating a greater demon intent on eating them.

Yet Sir Kipling hadn't been the only one to come away changed. The entity's otherworldly touch had made her ward bracelet—the wizard equivalent of body armor—more powerful than any magical artifact she'd ever seen. She'd been told the bracelet would protect her, and protect her it had. Not just against demons, but against her estranged father, John Faust LeFay.

She'd spent years searching for him, allowing a rift to form between herself and her mother and stepfamily in the process. Yet in the end it was *he* who found *her*. She discovered, too late, why her mother had left him in the first place. A powerful wizard in his own right, her father showed his true face when he attempted to use her in a magical experiment that could have driven her insane—if it had worked. Rescued at the last minute by her friends, Lily was left devastated, wishing she could erase the knowledge of who her father really was: an egomaniacal sociopath. The truth may have freed her, but with that freedom came a burden of responsibility. It was, in fact, the reason for her current road trip with her musically opinionated cat.

They were on their way to Bertha, Alabama, to see her family for the first time in seven years. This reconciliation or "strengthening of the ranks," as her mentor called it, was the first step in preparing Lily and her allies to stop John Faust's insane plan to repopulate the world with wizards so they could "benevolently" rule mundane society. Completely aside from her father's questionable ethics—the ends justify the means, all is permissible for the greater good—she was quite sure any wizard interference in mundane affairs, or vice versa, would end in disaster and bloodshed. Even if John Faust's desire to preserve the dwindling wizard race was a worthy cause, his methods and ultimate goal were untenable.

Of course, stopping John Faust was easier said than done. Besides being exceptionally intelligent, highly skilled, and downright rich, he was also a respected member of the wizard community—well, respected by some, feared by others. Any attempt to recruit allies against him would be met with scoffing or outright hostility.

Lily hadn't known any of this herself, unfortunately. Her mother, Freda, had spent the past seven years colluding with Madam Barrington to keep Lily as far away from other wizards as possible, all in an attempt to keep her hidden from her father. Their attempt had backfired rather spectacularly, of course, but as angry as it had made Lily, she couldn't blame them for trying to protect her. The dynamics of current wizard society were something her mentor had only recently explained, now that the cat was out of the bag, so to speak. It made their prospects look pretty bleak, though when Lily made a comment to that effect, Madam Barrington had cryptically implied they weren't as friendless as it might seem. But before they did anything else, she first insisted Lily go visit her family.

It wasn't that Lily didn't love her stepfather and stepsiblings. She was just so…different. She didn't fit into their country way of life. They were perfectly content to drive tractors, raise crops, and enjoy the simple but rigorous life of Alabama farmers. Lily, on the other hand, disliked working outside. Knowledge was her milk and honey, and all she'd ever wanted was to read, study, and be left alone. Growing up on a small peanut and cotton farm with four younger siblings to take care of didn't afford much alone time. She'd been happy to leave and was apprehensive about returning.

Even so, she missed her family more deeply than she cared to admit and was worried how they would react to her visit. What if they wouldn't forgive her long absence? How was she going to explain about wizards and magic? Should she even try? What if they thought she was abnormal? What if they rejected who she'd become? These doubts, and more, were why she'd never come home. It was easier to keep her distance and bury her loneliness than to deal with the possibility of rejection.

"You know," came a silky meow to her right, "you really should stop worrying. It only makes you cranky." Sir Kipling twitched his whiskers, not lifting his head from where he lay curled up in the passenger seat. He was quite the picture, his large, fluffy gray body taking up a good part of the seat while his white-tipped tail hung over the side, slowly flicking back and forth.

"How in the world would you know if I'm worrying?" Lily asked, annoyed.

"You smell different."

"I smell—" Lily stopped herself, and sighed. She should know by now not to try to fathom her cat's maddening ability to know far more than he ought. He claimed it was all part of being a cat, which was hogwash, in her opinion. She was sure the entity who had given him human-like intelligence had given him far more than that, but so far Sir Kipling was playing dumb. So Lily simply grumbled about his "cat magic" and left it at that.

Silence returned to the car. Lily had turned off the radio to give herself room to think—all right, worry—and she stared blankly at the road. The passing scenery, a mix of coniferous woodland and verdant peanut and cotton fields, offered no comfort. It was only a three-and-a-half-hour drive from Atlanta to Bertha, and they were approaching the end of the journey. As familiar landmarks became more frequent, her apprehension grew, exacerbated by Sir Kipling's exaggerated sniffs and whisker twitches. Of course, such behavior didn't make him appear quite as disapproving as he probably thought it did, owing to the white circle of fur around his right eye and the splashes of white on his nose. They made him look like a crotchety old gentleman with a monocle, twitching his mustache, an amusing picture if Lily could have looked at it instead of at the road ahead.

In no time they were passing Eufaula. The sight of it recalled vivid memories of her and Sebastian's "virtuous" break-in of the Shorter Mansion museum during their attempt to undo the Jackson family curse. And, of course, of Sebastian's theatrical "escape" kiss. It had been suspiciously enthusiastic for being only a ploy to throw off the security guard. At the time she'd put it down to his generally over-the-top nature, but ever since he'd helped save her from her father's clutches, she'd wondered. Of course, it wasn't the kiss itself that made her blush now as they drove past the quiet Alabama city. It was the memory of how it had made her feel. Feelings she had promptly, and appropriately, quashed.

"You should have asked him to come with us." Sir Kipling commented, once again out of the blue.

Lily pushed her glasses further up on the bridge of her nose and kept her eyes fixed on the road. Sometimes she wondered if her cat could read minds. "I have no idea what you're talking about."

"Oh please. Don't insult me," Sir Kipling meowed. "Your body temperature just shot through the roof and you're blushing. You're thinking about Sebastian." It was not a question.

"That's ridiculous," Lily protested, attempting a casual tone. "I could be thinking about any manner of embarrassing things." Self-conscious but trying to hide it, she reached up to tuck a wayward strand of her chestnut hair behind an ear. Most of it was caught up in the usual bun at the back of her head, but there were some strands that just refused to stay put.

"I suppose you could be," Sir Kipling admitted. "But you're not, because you also smell—"

"Alright, fine!" Lily interrupted, having no desire to know what she smelled like when she was thinking about Sebastian. "So I was thinking about him. But only because I'm relieved he's not here. He would just make things worse. Imagine trying to keep him out of trouble *and* deal with my family at the same time. What a disaster."

"Mmm," Sir Kipling murmured, obviously unconvinced. "Of course, his absence also conveniently lets you avoid confronting your feelings."

Lily looked away from the road long enough to glare at her cat. "Who elected you matchmaker? I'm dating Richard, for your information—"

"You mean that lawman who suspects you're lying about everything? At least Sebastian already knows you're a wizard."

Sir Kipling's comment earned him another glare as Lily's insides squirmed. "Sebastian is an uncouth reprobate with entirely too many secrets of his own. In any case, he's taken up with that witch, Tina. If you ask me, they deserve each other." Lily knew her words were harsh, but Sir Kipling's barb had stirred an uncharacteristic defensiveness in her.

"I see. So, since when does one coffee translate into 'dating'?" He asked, eyes still closed.

"Well, there would have been more," she pointed out, "but things got in the way." Things like being kidnapped by her father, to be precise. She'd only just recovered from that fiasco when Agent Grant got back in touch, hoping to schedule another date. They'd settled on next Friday evening. Or at least she thought they had. She'd written it down on a slip of paper by the phone but hadn't been able to find it the last time she'd looked. She would look again when they got home. That is, if she survived the weekend with her family.

"If you say so," her cat said, dropping the matter, much to Lily's relief. Faced with the dubious task of navigating familial relationships, this was no time to face the complicated tangle of emotions that were her feelings for her troublemaking friend.

The sudden ringing of her phone was startling in the heavy silence, and she almost dropped it in her rush to answer.

"Hello?"

"Hi, honey." Her mother's voice sent a comforting warmth through her tense shoulders, and she relaxed.

"Hello, Mother," Lily replied, lips lifting in an unconscious smile. Though her father's schemes had done plenty of harm, they'd had one unexpected benefit: reconciliation with her mother. It had been such a relief to finally make things right. She still felt a tinge of resentment, but she knew her mother had only hidden the truth to protect, not hurt, her.

"How far away are you?" Freda asked. After staying with Madam Barrington for a week and visiting Lily every evening, she'd left Atlanta the night before to prepare the house, and the family, for her daughter's visit.

Lily checked her map. "About thirty minutes or so."

"Good. Supper's in the oven and Tom and the others can't wait to see you."

At the mention of her stepfather's name, Lily's smile faltered. "Alright. I'll be there soon."

"I love you honey. Bye-bye."

"I—love you too. Goodbye." The words caught in Lily's throat, but she forced them out anyway. Unlike her mother—who wasn't shy about speaking her mind—Lily had never been good at showing affection. The words felt clunky and alien on her tongue. She was almost embarrassed to let them escape her lips.

After recent events, however, she knew it was foolish to take anything for granted. She'd let resentment steal seven years from her relationship with the people she loved and wasn't planning on giving it any more.

If only she could figure out what to do with all those people now that she'd gotten them back.

The dirt road leading to her childhood home was just as bumpy as she remembered. No doubt it had been leveled and repacked at least once since she'd left, yet the typical ridges and washouts had simply reformed. It was like driving over a washboard, and she hoped her aging Honda Civic could handle it. A mix of pine, maple, and oak trees lined one side of the drive, with a ripening field of peanuts on the other. All over, the reddish, sandy soil ubiquitous to the South peeked through sparse undergrowth, and a dust cloud of the stuff rose into the hot August evening, marking their bone-shaking progress. Her teeth rattled as they drove along, a fitting counterpoint to the jitter of butterflies in her stomach. Not even the sight of Sir Kipling's alarmed expression as he gripped the seat with all eighteen claws could ease her nervous tension.

When they finally rounded the last bend, a two-story farmhouse came into view, its long-ago whitewashed walls now chipped and fading. Yet despite its aged appearance, there were signs of repair, newer boards and paint contrasting sharply with the original construction. There was even a new room built onto one end of the house— probably an additional bedroom. Lily noticed the front porch steps had finally been replaced, much to her mother's relief, she was sure. Broken-down cars and one aged, rusting tractor populated the yard, each surrounded by a ring of weeds and tall grass. Growing up, her stepfather had always talked about repairing them. He probably still did, for that matter. Their working farm equipment was tucked into sheds behind the house, alongside the chicken coop and various other outbuildings her family used in their peanut and cotton farming.

As she pulled up to the house, parking beside her mother's dented car and her stepfather's dust-covered pickup truck, the yard erupted with life forms. The first to reach the car were the family dogs, two mutts that barked and leapt in excitement, their claws making scratching sounds against the car door. Lily had only a moment to register Sir Kipling's reaction—back pressed to the seat and ears flattened against his skull—before her attention was pulled toward the crowd pouring out the front door. Her mother led the charge, with her stepsiblings close behind and her stepfather bringing up the rear. In typical southern fashion they swarmed her as she opened the car door, pulling her out and enveloping her in one hug after another, all exclaiming and talking over one another. Of her siblings there was Dru, the oldest and tallest, a more youthful version of his tanned and weathered father. Then came Sally, blonde hair bleached almost white by the sun that she loved to work in. Third was Becca, only a year younger than Sally but as different from her as night was from day, with dark brown hair and a fiery temperament to match her sister's easygoing one. Last was little Jamie. Or at least, he'd been little when she'd left seven years ago. Now he was a lanky, chestnut-haired young man of fifteen. Of her four siblings, he was her only half sibling, the others being stepsiblings—offspring from her stepfather's first marriage.

Surrounded by chaos, smiles, and voices, it felt for a moment like she'd never left. Despite their differences, her stepfamily was still her family—the only one she'd ever known. Amid the rush of loud and crushing goodwill, she belatedly recalled the defining mark of their relationship: their good-natured disregard of her personal space. Ah, well, one couldn't expect too much as an introvert in a family full of extroverts, and southerners to boot.

Yet as they surrounded her, pelting her with one question after another, she could tell by their sideways glances that all was not as idyllic as it seemed on the surface. That was when she finally noticed Jamie had not joined the throng. Before she'd left for college, he'd been as rambunctious as any eight-year-old boy, always in the thick of things. But now he hung back, solemn face unreadable as he stared at her with grey-blue eyes. There was something odd about him, a sort of presence she couldn't recall being there when he was a boy. She'd practically raised him, with Freda busy helping her stepfather on the farm. But he'd grown so much since then. He looked, and felt, like a completely different person.

Freda finally took control of the chaos, shooting off orders like a general deploying her troops and breaking Lily's concentration. She sent Dru to the car for Lily's bags, Sally to round up the dogs—they were sniffing excitedly at Lily's open car door, undeterred by the furious hissing coming from within—and the others inside to set the table for supper. Lily watched Jamie as he retreated, trying to figure out what was so different. But her mother distracted her as she began to pull her toward the house and the waiting food.

At a plaintive meow from inside the car, Lily came back to herself, regaining her head for the first time since the swirl of chaos had descended. "Really, Mother, it's alright, I remember how to get to the kitchen. I'll be along in a moment," she said, extracting herself from her mother's hold and turning back to the car.

With the offending canines now safely tied to the front-porch railing, Sir Kipling had ventured down from his perch on the passenger seat headrest where he'd taken refuge from their frenzied yapping. He looked distinctly ruffled. Though the fur along his back now lay flat, his fluffy tail still resembled a bottle brush. If cats could frown, he would have. "While your confidence in my capacity for self-preservation is refreshing, I would prefer, in the future, to be forewarned of threats upon my life," he said in his most disapproving tone.

"I do apologize, it slipped my mind." Lily tried only half-heartedly to hide her grin. She *was* sorry, it *had* slipped her mind, and she wasn't one to laugh at another's misfortune. That was Sebastian's purview. Yet only a complete stick-in-the-mud would pass up a chance to chuckle at the expense of her annoyingly smug cat.

Sir Kipling shot her an irritated look. "If you expect me to put up with these mongrels for two whole days, you had better be prepared to pay the price."

"The price?" Lily asked with a raised eyebrow, the urge to smile still threatening to betray her.

"Salmon. Every day. For a week," Sir Kipling said decisively.

"I see. Well, that depends on whether or not you behave yourself."

He sniffed. "Behaving is for dogs."

"Behaving is for troublemakers, like you. Now, are you going to walk to the house or shall I carry you?"

"Humph. I have my dignity," he said, jumping down to the dusty ground and glaring in the direction of the two dogs, both of whom sat at quivering attention, eyes following his every move.

"You know, you could just stay in the house. They're outside dogs."

"And let them think they have the upper hand? Inconceivable. These are *dogs* we're talking about. Besides, I'll need to inspect things, get the lay of the land."

"If you say so," Lily said, giving up the fight with her facial muscles and letting a grin spread across her face. "I'll leave you to it, then." Closing her car door, she headed for the house, feeling in better spirits. At least she wasn't the only one with problems.

Suppertime at the Singer house was just as she remembered: loud, chaotic, and delicious. Her mother hadn't been much of a cook before she remarried. Lily remembered living off grits, fried cabbage, and cold chicken for most of her early childhood. But once Freda had four new mouths to feed, all used to the delights of traditional southern cooking, she'd finally bitten the bullet. With help from enough cookbooks to choke a herd of horses, she'd done what she always did when she put her mind to something: succeeded. Freda could now cook with the best of them and had taught Lily to do the same. Admittedly, Lily's cooking had become much more cosmopolitan since moving to Atlanta—unlike her mother, she preferred not to smother everything in grease and butter. Thus she was slightly overwhelmed by the abrupt return to all things southern, with a dinner of pork chops, fried chicken, fried okra, collard greens, mashed potatoes, and corn pudding, topped off with a chess pie so sweet you could feel your insides crystallizing as you ate it.

During the meal she fielded question after question about her job, house, love interests—which she deftly sidestepped—and life in Atlanta. It was similar yet different in important ways from Ursula's busybody grilling a mere two weeks ago. Her grandmother had only cared about what advantage Lily brought to the LeFay name. The Singer clan, on the other hand, wanted to share in her life, so she made an effort to remain open. Of course, there was the teensy matter of her being a fully-fledged wizard that she had to keep tiptoeing around, glancing toward her mother the whole time.

Despite some initial awkwardness, she felt herself warming to these familiar strangers, so grown and changed over the years. Their eager joy in every detail she divulged made it clear that they had truly missed her. She'd left her siblings a group of obnoxious adolescents, who'd since blossomed into young adulthood. Dru was as loud and

country as you might expect, but well rounded, with a
healthy dose of manners no doubt pounded into him by his
father, with whom he worked on a daily basis. Sally was the
mature one, obviously having taken Lily's place as their
mother's primary helper. Her good-natured words were
employed liberally to keep peace in this family of hard heads
and quick tongues, the quickest being Becca's. She'd broken
from the family tradition of farming and was attending the
local community college. While Becca had certainly grown
out of her snotty brat stage, her new personality as a sarcastic
teenager wasn't much better. Lily decided she and Sir
Kipling would get along very well, if only they could
understand each other.

But the most changed was Jamie. The fun-loving boy
she remembered was gone. Oh, he joked readily enough
with his other siblings. But he barely said a word to her and
didn't ask a single question. Perhaps it was because he'd
been so young when she left, he wasn't used to her now. She
hoped the explanation was that simple. Of all her family,
she'd been looking forward to seeing Jamie the most. He'd
been her little pal, her Jammy boy. While the others had
been off raising hell around the farm, she and Jamie used to
curl up in a cool corner together while she read to him. Even
as he grew into the energetic eight-year-old she remembered,
he'd always preferred hanging around Lily and asking
incessant questions to climbing on tractors or hunting down
frogs in the creek. But now he shied away from her gaze and
only murmured responses to the few questions she was able
to work in amid the storm of conversation. And that strange
feeling kept bothering her. She couldn't put her finger on it,
but it reminded her of something.

Once supper was over, she tried to help with the dishes
but was rebuffed by Sally. "You go rest yer feet now, hear?"

Sally said, busily gathering up dishes and silverware to take to the kitchen. While Freda had instilled in Lily the importance of "proper" English, she hadn't managed the same with Lily's stepsiblings. They took after their father, southern twang rolling off their tongues like honey. So while Sally did the dishes and Tom and Dru headed outside to finish up the evening chores, Freda showed Lily to her room.

Her room wasn't technically a bedroom, it was the attic. Being a family of seven in an old farmhouse, they'd had to make do. Growing up, her siblings had shared two of the three bedrooms, her parents occupying the third. Above one end of the house the eaves peaked to make a small attic that got dreadfully hot in the summer but was vastly preferable to sharing a room with her overloud siblings. Now, at least, her parents had moved to the new bedroom downstairs, which meant Dru and Jamie each had their own rooms, with Sally and Becca sharing the third. But the little attic room had been left untouched. As her mother opened the door, she could see all her things were just as she'd left them, though they'd been joined by several piles of boxes. It was an attic, after all.

"I dusted things up and washed the sheets," her mother said. "I thought you'd prefer your old room. Though if the heat's too much, you're welcome to change your mind. I could make Jamie sleep with Dru and you could have Jamie's room, or the couch downstairs."

"No, this is fine," Lily assured her, staunchly ignoring the beads of sweat already forming on her forehead. It was worth it for some privacy. Looking around, she saw Dru had already laid her bags on the bed, though Sir Kipling was nowhere in sight. She briefly wondered if she should go looking for him—she hadn't heard a peep out of the dogs, so she had no clue what he was up to—but decided against it. If he was going to accompany her in what was quickly becoming a bona fide adventure, she couldn't constantly worry about him. Either he could take care of himself or he couldn't. So far he'd handled demons, crazy wizards, a mechanical crow, and more besides with signature grace, so she doubted a couple of excitable dogs would pose much trouble.

"Well, I'll leave you to unpack," Freda said after a moment of awkward silence.

Lily stopped her with an outstretched hand and a look. "Not so hasty, Mother dear." She closed the attic door and pulled her mother to the bed, taking a seat beside her. "You aren't going anywhere until you explain to me why you haven't told them yet."

"Told them what?" her mother asked, avoiding her gaze.

"About *us*, that's what!" Lily said, thoroughly exasperated. "I understand why you kept it from me all those years: to protect me. But now John Faust knows who I am and can easily figure out where I'm from, if he hasn't already. We need to tell them, for their own safety. What if John Faust shows up one day looking for you, or me? They need to know, and we need to ward the house."

Freda opened her mouth to protest, but Lily raised a hand. "I know any magic in a backwater place like this will shine out like a beacon, but he can find us easily enough without it, so there's no point hiding anymore. You didn't really stop using magic because you feared it, did you? That's what *he* said happened…"

"No, of course not." Freda's sigh was deep and long. "I only stopped to keep us hidden. Since then I've grown positively rusty. But I doubt you'll accept that excuse." She smiled faintly at her daughter, who smiled back.

"Not a chance, Mother. I saw you flinging enough magic at that…that man, to know you remember your Enkinim well enough. Madam B. gave me a full rundown of wards to use on the house, and, one way or another, you're going to help me cast them."

"Yes," Freda said with another sigh, "she warned me she would do that. She agrees with you, of course. Better to tell the truth. I just don't know *how* to tell them…after so many years. They won't believe us."

"Of course they won't, but we have to tell them all the same. And *you* will be the one to do it, not me. You're the one who decided to keep it a secret in the first place, and you're better at explaining things anyway."

"I suppose. Perhaps in the morning—"

"No. Now," Lily insisted. "No more waiting. No more lies."

"Well…about that…"

"What?" Lily asked suspiciously.

"I didn't know for sure, not until yesterday when I got home after using magic for the first time in years. My senses weren't what they used to be. I felt it as I approached the house, and as soon as I saw him, I knew…" Freda trailed off, worry creasing her brow.

Lily's skin tingled in sudden realization and her eyes widened as she stared in disbelief at her mother. "No."

"Yes." Freda insisted with a resigned nod. "Your little brother is a wizard."

They agreed it was best not to reveal that particular bombshell just yet as Freda gathered the various family members around the dining room table. Their expressions ranged from curious to confused. The exception was Jamie.

His eyes were alight with a keen interest and she caught him staring at her again, though he looked away when their eyes met.

Once everyone was settled, Freda looked around at each of them, then glanced to the side at Lily. Lily could see her own apprehension mirrored in her mother's eyes. Without a word, she reached under the table and took hold of her mother's hand, grasping it firmly. Freda squeezed gratefully, then took a deep breath and began.

"As I'm sure you guessed after I rushed off unexpectedly to Atlanta, some…interesting things have happened recently. While we're all thrilled to have Lily back with us, I realize the time has come to tell you all some things I've kept secret for a very long time, though your father knows parts of it." Freda exchanged a look with her husband, who smiled back encouragingly. Lily felt a sudden and unexpected wash of love for her stepfather. He was just a simple farmer, more concerned with the weather than with philosophical discussions or current events. He had no grand words or great intellect, just a solid work ethic and a kind heart. Lily had never truly understood him, but she could see that he loved her mother, and his family, with a selfless depth that a man like John Faust would never comprehend.

"You all know that I left my first husband—a man named John Faust LeFay—when Lily was very young, then later met and married Tom. What you don't know is that I left because John…abused us." There was a sharp intake of breath from Becca, and Dru's eyes flashed in outrage. But Freda ignored them and went on. "I feared for our lives, so I acquired false identities and hid us for several years, never staying in one place for long.

"I knew John would never stop looking, so even though

I met your father years after, I decided we had to keep living under our assumed identities. I never breathed a word about it to anyone but Tom, and then only after we'd married. He wanted to track down my former husband and have him arrested, but I convinced him to let the matter go." She smiled faintly in reminiscence, but Lily could only shiver, imagining what John Faust would have done to her stepfather had the man shown up on his doorstep. "Not only would it have been impossible to prove the abuse, as we never reported it at the time, but there was the small matter of living under a false identity for almost a decade. I knew that if John ever found Lily before she came of age, he would be legally entitled to full custody, and I would likely go to jail." Lily's stepsiblings looked at each other, brows creasing in confusion, but Tom simply looked weary. "I *did*, technically, kidnap you," Freda said in way of explanation, looking at Lily apologetically, who simply shrugged.

"Once she turned eighteen, she was safe, at least legally, from John," Freda continued. "But I still never told her the truth. I thought it was for the best, to keep her safe. But, of course, the truth never stays hidden forever. Two weeks ago John somehow found Lily and made contact with her. Having no idea the kind of man he was, because I'd never warned her, Lily went to meet him and he...he abused her much as he had when she was a child. I went with some old friends to get her out and we spent the past week getting reacquainted.

"Now the truth is out. John knows Lily's assumed identity and can easily find out mine, as well as where we live. I have no notion what he will do about it, but there's a possibility he might come here looking for...I don't know, revenge? Reconciliation? Legal redress? According to the state of Georgia I'm still married to him under my...well my old name, and I just…I don't know what will come of it." She let out a long sigh and bent her head forward, resting it in her hands as she massaged her temples.

Everyone around the table made sympathetic noises and Sally began to rise as if to come over and comfort her mother. But Freda stopped them all with a raised hand. "That isn't all." The table fell silent again. Lily glanced at Jamie, whose sharp eyes were locked onto Freda's face. "Unfortunately this isn't just a simple matter of spousal abuse and legal complications. Because, you see, John Faust is a very powerful…well he's a…" Freda halted, at a loss for words, and looked desperately at Lily.

Lily grimaced, knowing what she had to do even as she cringed inside. Desperately trying to organize her thoughts, she imagined she was giving a lecture on magic to a young child. If she fixed her eyes on the cross-stitch of their farmhouse hanging on the wall behind Sally's head, maybe she could get through this. "I know this will be hard to believe, but what Mother is trying to say is…um…well, certain people can do…oh dear."

Lily took a deep breath. She just had to say it. "Some people are born with the ability to manipulate a form of energy that is most commonly known as magic." There was complete silence around the table, and from her peripheral vision she could see growing disbelief on everyone's face. All except Jamie's. He was leaning forward in his chair, gaze intent. Lily swallowed, mouth as dry as sandpaper.

"While it may seem far-fetched, the best way to understand it is that magic is a form of science that modern technology hasn't yet developed enough to explain. After all, a thousand years ago, primitive people would have considered planes, cell phones, and computers to be magic. But today they are commonplace tools that operate within the laws of nature. The point is, some people are able to sense, and use, this energy to do some rather...magical-seeming things. These people are called wizards. I"—she faltered for a moment, heart pounding, but then forged onward—"I am a wizard. So is Mother. I've spent the last seven years learning how to use magic. John Faust is also a wizard. A very, very powerful one. He's not afraid to use magic to get what he wants. That's why, I assume, mother never went to the police. In any case, he used it on us a long time ago and did so again last week." Lily's vision was starting to blur, she was staring at the cross-stitch so hard. Freda took their joined hands from where they rested on her lap and laid them on the table, putting her other hand on top of Lily's.

"He plans to do some bad things, and I have to figure out a way to stop him. I don't know what will happen. But he might come here and try to hurt you all, so Mother and I are going to put protective wards on you and the house. I can imagine how confusing this must be. I couldn't believe it either when I first found out. But you will have to trust us. Our lives may depend on it." She finished, feeling very hot and prickly. She couldn't bring herself to look at anyone, so kept her gaze on the opposite wall.

Tom was the first to speak. "Well...I can't rightly say I understand this hocus pocus stuff you're talkin' about, but in this here family, we look out for one another. You and your momma do what you gotta do. Any fella thinks they can mess with us has got another think comin'."

Lily was finally able to tear her gaze from the wall and dare a glance at her stepfather. He gave her an encouraging nod and reached across the table to rest his large, calloused hands on top of her's and Freda's. Dru and Sally both reached forward to join him, murmuring words of solidarity. Becca, however, leaned back in her chair, incredulity written all over her face. Lily looked to her left, expecting to see excitement on Jamie's face. She was surprised to see his brow furrowed in hurt and disappointment as he looked back and forth between her and Freda. Finally he fixed his gaze on his mother.

"Prove it," he said sharply.

Though she'd been expecting a demand for a demonstration, Lily's mind still scrambled to think of an appropriate spell. Most spells, contrary to how they were portrayed in mundane pop culture, were not flashy. Though she could "see" magic, so to speak, in her mind's eye, it wasn't visible to mundanes. Much like electricity, gravity, or magnetism, the only visible aspect of magic was the effect it had on the world around them. She glanced at Freda, who had the same deer-in-the-headlights look she imagined was on her own face.

Casting around desperately, she finally spotted a sheet of aluminum foil left over from supper preparation. That would work. Aluminum was the easiest metal to manipulate, as it was the most conductive to magic. She retrieved it, laying it on the table and sitting back down to calm her mind, forcing herself to breathe evenly as she considered the words of power she would need to complete the spell. When she was ready, she started speaking that ancient tongue, using words and will to shape the magic as it compressed the foil, looking for all the world as if an invisible fist were crushing it into a ball.

Everyone but Freda jumped in shock. Becca actually jerked back so hard she capsized, her chair making a raucous clatter as it made contact with the worn wooden floor. She quickly picked herself back up, swearing in colorful southern fashion.

Ignoring her stepsister, Lily focused on her spell. The foil crackled as it shrank, and Lily felt the tingle of energy coursing through her as she concentrated on the trickiest part. Instead of simply crushing it into a rough ball, she spoke again, upping the pressure and adding heat as she crafted her tennis ball-sized lump of crumpled foil into a marble-sized ball of solid aluminum. The air grew cool around them—the heat had to come from somewhere—and finally it was finished. As she ended the spell and cut the flow of magic, the aluminum marble dropped to the table with a clink and rolled toward the edge, toward Jamie.

To Lily's surprise, he scrambled back, eyes wide with disbelief. She couldn't understand why he seemed so startled when, before, he'd been hanging on their every word as if he already knew what was coming. Whatever the reason, he shot her a bewildered look, then took off out the front door. Freda called after him and made to follow, but Tom put a hand on her arm.

"Let him go, Mary."

Freda smiled weakly at him. "Well, Freda LeFay, legally, but I guess we'll stick with Mary Singer for now."

"You'll always be my Mary," he said, standing to wrap her in his arms.

"This is just freaky. I can't do this. You're all freaks," Becca declared shakily, and headed upstairs.

Dru and Sally exchanged looks. While they appeared as shocked as everyone else, they seemed to be taking the news a bit more calmly. With a nod from their father, Sally rose and headed after Becca, while Dru got up and started for the front door.

"No, I'll go." Lily said, rising abruptly. She didn't know why, but somehow she knew she had to talk to Jamie, alone.

Dru shrugged and stepped aside as Lily headed out the door, scooping up the still-warm aluminum marble as she went. She knew exactly where Jamie had gone.

***

The farmyard barn was a piece of history, as old as the farmhouse itself. Its boards were weathered grey with age and the tin roof was brown with rust. Back when her stepfather was a mere boy and his father and grandfather ran the farm, they'd had a few head of cattle, goats, and some horses. Thus the hayloft had been full of old-fashioned square bales: hay for fodder and straw for bedding. Nowadays the barn was used more for equipment storage, but some of the bales remained, slowly disintegrating as they sat, unused. Well, unused for farming. It was the perfect play place for enterprising children, and her stepsiblings had spent many an hour building straw forts and otherwise getting covered in the stuff. She'd preferred to watch from afar—straw dust was a nightmare to get out of your hair. But in the cool of the evenings, when the barn was empty and quiet, she loved to climb up and sit in the open hay door where long ago they'd loaded bales into the loft. With feet dangling over empty air, she would read her books and watch the sun sink behind the green hills. Once he was old enough to climb the wooden ladder to the loft, Jamie had often joined her, and it had become their special place.

Seven years later, she climbed the loft ladder once again, hands automatically finding its worn rungs in the semi-dark of the old barn. It smelled just as she remembered: musty and dry with a hint of motor oil. As her head crested the lip of the loft floor, she could see Jamie's hunched shape in the open hay door, silhouetted by the setting sun. Moving quietly, she completed her climb and headed toward him, loose straw shifting softly beneath her feet. Jamie didn't turn as she approached, and she hesitated behind him, building up the nerve to sit down.

"You know, it was never the same after you left." Jamie's voice was low, and he didn't turn to face her.

Lily sighed and finally sat, leaving a few inches of space between herself and her half-brother. Not sure what to say, she remained silent, staring at the crimson sky.

"The others picked on me more without you there to tell them off, 'specially Becca. I never really fit in. It wouldn't have been so bad if you'd just come back once in a while. But you never called, never visited. You didn't even return my letters. It was like you didn't love me anymore." He still didn't look at her, but his words were filled with a bitterness that sent stabs of guilt straight to her heart. She wanted to protest, explain that she hadn't realized the envelopes addressed in her mother's handwriting had contained letters from him—she'd taken one look at the handwriting and thrown them in the trash, unopened.

"It hurt for a while. I kept asking mom why you didn't come back, but she would never give me a straight answer. Finally I stopped trying. I thought maybe I'd done somethin' wrong, been a bad brother. But finally I realized you were just a selfish jerk who didn't care enough about her family to give a darn what they felt." He finally turned toward her, eyes burning.

She opened her mouth to defend herself, then shut it again, looking away. He was right. Not that she would have admitted that several years ago, or even a few months ago. But now, in light of recent events, her shortcomings crowded in, burning with the same accusation that was in Jamie's eyes.

Closing her own eyes, as if to shut out the accusing stares, she steeled herself to do what she should have done years ago.

"You're right, I *was* a selfish jerk," Lily finally croaked, forcing the words out of reluctant lips. Daring a glance to the side, she saw a flicker of surprise on Jamie's face. That brief softening of expression gave her the courage to continue. "I was an absolute butt-head to you and the others, and I'm sorry. But please, don't think it was because I didn't care. I was just so angry, and hurt, and stubborn, and a little afraid, too." The words started spilling out, and she let them. "I thought about you all the time, in the beginning, but I tried to suppress my feelings and stay as far away as possible to take revenge on Mother." Lily looked down, feeling a flush of shame as she realized how petty her words sounded. But she had to explain. "You know how Mother would never talk about the past? About who my father was? Well it hurt more than I realized, and, after I left, I just wanted her to know what it felt like to be kept in the dark. I'm sorry. I was too focused on my own feelings to consider how my actions must have affected the rest of the family.

"And then...well, then I found out I was a...a wizard. I thought if I came back Mother would yell at me for finding out what she'd been hiding all this time. I thought it would just be easier for everyone if I stayed away." She glanced up and saw her brother's eyes flash with the same intense curiosity he'd shown at the dinner table. But he quickly hid it and returned to scowling, obviously not done being mad at her.

"Easier for you, maybe," he growled. "Did it ever cross your mind that I might want to know too? I *am* the only one in this family besides Mom who's actually related to you."

"No," Lily replied, honestly. "I never imagined you would..." she trailed off, distracted by the sudden realization that she could see his magic. The aura was subtle, which was why she hadn't been able to pin it down before. But now that she knew what to look for, she kept catching glimpses of it. It wasn't the blaze of her father, nor the soft glow of her mother, nor the cloaked majesty of her mentor. It was faint and ethereal, like the shimmer of heat in summer that shivered in the currents of hot air rising from the ground. She wondered how her own magic appeared to him, or if he could even sense it, untrained as he was.

Though he still scowled stubbornly, his expression began to soften around the edges as she finally met his gaze, staring as intently at him as he had at her not hours before.

"When did you..." she began hesitantly.

"About a year ago. At least, that's when I started noticing it as more than just a vague, undefinable feeling."

"Like an—"

"—itch in your soul," he finished for her. "Yeah. Like you know you can do more, but you have no idea what it is."

"And the blur?" Lily asked, fascinated.

"Like you have something in your eye, but only when you look at certain things?" Jamie nodded.

"Did you ever guess?" Lily was curious. She'd had no idea, just a feeling of difference, a restlessness that had driven her to seek answers.

Jamie considered for a moment, scowl lines now replaced with a thoughtful scrunch of the brow. "Not really. Not magic. But I knew something was up, what with the way you left and Mom acting like a clam. But now you're back, and it's all out. You can teach me, show me. I want to know everything." The excited light was back now, and he leaned toward her, eagerness written in every line of his body.

Lily hesitated, unsure. "I don't know if I'm the one who should explain things. I've never taught magic, and I've only been studying it for seven years. In any case, I'm leaving tomorrow, as soon as we're done with the wards. I'm sure Mother will show you."

"What?" Jamie exclaimed, looking hurt. "Leaving? You can't leave. You just got back!"

"I'm sorry." She shrugged helplessly. "I have a job, not to mention a psychotic father to deal with."

He leaned forward, eager once more. "Then let me come with you. You can teach me on the way. I can help!"

"No. Absolutely not," Lily said. "You're too young. And you don't learn magic 'on the way.' It takes years of study to even do your first spell. Plus, it's dangerous. Magic can kill you if you don't do it right, and the further you stay away from John Faust, the better."

"That's not fair!" Jamie protested. "I want to help. I want to go with you. Anyway, you can't just waltz in here, tell me I'm a wizard, then leave!"

She hadn't done anything of the sort, but decided it wouldn't help to point that out. "Look, I know it doesn't seem like it, but Mother is just as good a wizard as I am and can teach you everything you need to know." That wasn't quite true, but the things Freda couldn't teach him were years ahead in his magical education anyway. "I'll make sure she promises to teach you before I leave. The only reason she kept everything a secret before was to protect our family from John Faust. But there's no need for that anymore. She'll open up now."

"But...but I just got you back," Jamie whispered, a desperate look in his eyes. It was suddenly as if the past seven years had never happened and he was eight again, begging her not to leave. Something squeezed her heart and she felt moisture gather in the corners of her eyes. Scooting closer, she wrapped her little brother in a tentative hug, unsure at first, but gripping more tightly as he leaned in and hugged her back.

"I'm sorry," she murmured into his hair. "I promise I'll

come back this time. And I'll give you my phone number. You can call any time you want."

He snorted, now pushing back against the hug. "Hey, it's not like I need to *talk* or anything mushy like that. I just want to learn magic. What do you think I am, sensitive?" He stuck out his tongue at her, a teasing twinkle in his eye.

"Ah, yes, now I remember," she drawled back. "You're a teenager. Heaven forbid you have a meaningful relationship with your sister. You'd lose all your hard-earned street cred for sure."

"Something like that." Jamie grinned and stood up. "You coming?"

"In a little while." Lily said. "I want to enjoy the sunset, and the memories."

Jamie nodded, but as he turned to go Lily stopped him with a gesture. Getting up, she took his hand and dropped the aluminum ball into it, closing his fingers around it. "Don't fool yourself with silly fantasies. Magic is glorious and terrifying in equal measures. It's dangerous and difficult to control and can do just as much damage as good. Which one it does is up to you. Be careful, little brother."

Eyes shining in the near darkness, he nodded. "I will," he said, then turned and climbed down the ladder to the dirt-covered floor below.

Chapter 2
THE SUPREME ART OF WAR

I T WAS FULLY DARK BEFORE LILY FINALLY GROPED HER WAY DOWN THE LOFT ladder and headed back to the house.

Once outside the barn she could see a little better—the stars were bright above and patches of light spilled out from the farmhouse windows. She was just crossing the barnyard, contemplating the evening's events, when a dark streak shot out from some bushes and charged straight at her. A cry of surprise was halfway to her lips before she realized the streak was Sir Kipling, the white tip of his fluffy tail bobbing with every stride. He skidded to a halt by her feet, back arched and fur standing on end as he gazed toward the house, ignoring her presence.

"Sir Edgar Allan Kipling, you are an absolute terror! Don't scare me like that." Lily scolded.

"What? Oh, sorry. I was just, you know, practicing." He sat down, now completely at ease, and started cleaning himself.

Lily sighed but couldn't help smiling. She'd read somewhere that a house cat's habit of randomly racing from room to room was how they exercised and practiced hunting. It made sense, then, that Sir Kipling would need practice. Before his transformation to a talking cat, the largest thing he'd ever hunted was a moth.

With an inward grin at the picture, she bent down and picked up her ferocious hunter.

"Unhand me, woman!" he yowled, struggling.

"Kip," Lily said, a warning growl in her throat. "If you scratch me you will not live to regret it. I'm taking you inside. The dogs will make less of a fuss if I'm carrying you. Now sit still. Or else."

He quieted, though not without protest. "Humph! I'm not worried about the mongrels. They've been shown their place. It's the simple indignity of it. As if I couldn't walk on my own four legs."

Lily rolled her eyes. "I'm sure you'll recover. Wait, what do you mean they've been shown their place? What did you do to them?" They *had* been unusually quiet.

"Nothing permanent," Sir Kipling said airily.

Apprehensive, Lily looked for the dogs as they approached the house. She could see their ropes still tied to the railing, but the dogs were nowhere in sight. Following the line of the ropes in the semi-dark, she saw that they curled around the edge of the porch, low to the ground, and then disappeared...

"Kip, why are the dogs hiding under the porch?" she asked accusingly as she mounted the steps.

"How should I know? Am I their keeper?" Her cat took no pains to hide his smug look, even as he protested his innocence.

Shaking her head, Lily entered the house. "It's a good thing we're only staying one night."

***

With the extra supplies and prefabricated wards Madam Barrington had provided, it took less time to outfit the house than Lily had feared. Even so, they were constantly interrupted by various family members, not to mention the dogs. Every half hour or so they would go into a barking frenzy, pulling and tugging at their ropes. After ensuring Sir Kipling was snoozing safely upstairs, Lily finally untied them so they could run off after whatever varmint they were so eager to catch and give her and Freda some peace and quiet. They made a beeline for a large white oak at the edge of the yard, circling its trunk and barking up at its branches.

Worse than the dogs, of course, was Jamie. He got into everything, asking question after question, looking over their shoulders, interrupting their concentration. Freda had to banish him to his room. He went, but only after Lily made their mother promise to teach him magic.

By that evening, she and Freda had finished their spell casting, including personal wards for each of the family members. These they strung on cords for everyone to wear around their necks. It took threats from both Freda *and* Tom before Becca would wear hers. Even then she looped it around her wrist like a bracelet instead of around her neck, grumbling about how dorky it looked and shooting them baleful looks. While the wards wouldn't hold up against any serious magical attack, they would provide enough of a buffer and early warning for them to get help should John Faust appear with malicious intent.

With no small amount of effort, Lily managed to decline another southern supper, insisting that cold leftovers were sufficient. She really needed to get home at a decent hour. The goodbyes were brief but heartfelt. Jamie was still disgruntled about not being allowed to go with her, but he hugged her just the same, making her promise to come back and teach him some "cool spells" sometime soon. Lily rolled her eyes at that. Becca stayed in her room, which hurt a little, but Tom assured her she would come around, given time. All in all, four out of five mundanes accepting the existence of magic without a fuss had to be a record of some kind. Well…technically three out of four mundanes, since Jamie was a wizard even if he hadn't known it until now.

While some part of her was sad not to spend more time with her family, the constant worry of wondering what John Faust was getting up to spurred her onward. At least her family accepted her—well, mostly. They were a solid wall at her back should she ever need to retreat. It was a comforting thought, especially since, up to that point, she'd felt more or less alone in the world. It was good to have allies.

As she drove away down the bumpy dirt road, she could see her family's silhouette in the rearview mirror, Tom's arm around Freda, her mother waving sadly. As she was about to look away, she noticed something else: a tiny, dark shape taking wing from the oak tree at the edge of the yard and the dogs racing futilely after it, barking at the sky.

Lily rang Madam Barrington's doorbell, then waited, carpetbag in one arm and a stack of books in the other, as Sir Kipling sat primly by her feet. It was Thursday evening and Lily had been coming over to her mentor's house after work every day that week for training. It had taken some wrangling on her part to get away from the library, of course. Fall classes had started that week at Agnes Scott and she was supposed to be holding extended office hours. Well, there was no rule saying she couldn't extend them *earlier* instead of *later* in the day—one of the perks of being a salaried, rather than hourly, employee. The workaround elicited a raised eyebrow from her boss, but the library director had let it stand. Just because students didn't like getting up early didn't mean they couldn't.

It was a good thing, too, since Lily had a great deal to learn herself, now that Madam Barrington was no longer colluding with her mother to keep her in the dark. They'd spent the past two days working on advanced magical theory and its practical application, with Lily memorizing fresh combinations of Enkinim and dimmu runes—the spoken and written language of power.

Madam Barrington had also finally shown Lily the *proper* way to use her eduba, that ancient, magical archive of knowledge she'd passed down to her student while only telling her enough to use its most basic knowledge. The cursed thing had an index, for goodness sake. Not that Lily hadn't looked for one before, but not knowing the proper words to call it forth, she'd simply been wasting her time. Seven years of looking things up the hard way when there'd been an index all along. Honestly. It was a wonder she wasn't emotionally scarred from all the extra effort she'd been put through. And then, of course, she had to go back and properly index all her own entries, now that she knew how. She was still sore about it.

At least today they were going to get to the meaty bits. Madam Barrington had promised to explain what she knew about John Faust, Morgan le Fay, and wizard politics in general. With that happy prospect ahead, Lily was able to summon a polite smile when her mentor finally made it to the door. The older woman was wearing a neatly starched apron over her austere, high-necked blouse and full skirt—all in shades of grey and black. She must have come from preparing tea in the kitchen.

"Good evening, Lily, and you as well, Mr. Kipling," Madam Barrington said as she held open the door and nodded them into the house.

Sir Kipling meowed a polite greeting as he passed, making a beeline for the kitchen and his waiting saucer of milk.

Lily shook her head at the sight of the swiftly disappearing feline. "Good evening, Ms. B.," she said and stepped inside. After the fiasco with John Faust and her subsequent rescue, Madam Barrington had finally started addressing her as "Lily" instead of "Miss Singer," and had tried to get Lily to call her by her first name as well. While Lily appreciated the closer friendship they had developed, she simply couldn't bring herself to drop the polite address. It just felt wrong. Maybe someday when Madam Barrington was no longer her teacher. For now, "Ms. B." would have to do.

Heading down the dim, cool hall, Lily enjoyed the soothing relief from the sweltering weather outside. She laid her belongings on the dining room table, then proceeded to the kitchen to help with tea. There she found Sir Kipling cleaning his whiskers of sticky whiteness, having already scarfed down his allotted bowl of milk. She wished Madam Barrington wouldn't spoil him so. Before she knew it, he'd be expecting *her* to feed him milk, and pet him on demand, too, no doubt. Nothing good ever came from spoiling a cat. They already thought they were gods. It was unwise to feed into their fantasy.

Ah, well, Lily thought. The Madam's house, the Madam's rules.

By the time preparations were done and everything carried out to the table, Sir Kipling had vanished to wherever cats went when they weren't sitting on your lap or demanding food. He would reappear when it was time to leave.

While it was a bit more work than making a sandwich or warming up leftovers, high tea with Madam Barrington was entirely worth the effort. Not to be confused with afternoon tea—held earlier in the day as a bridge between the midday and evening meals—high tea evolved as the working class's evening meal. Unlike the privileged upper class, who had nothing better to do in the afternoon but socialize on low, comfy sofas over a lovely pot of tea, the working class didn't get home until the evening, and so drank their tea with the evening meal at a normal, "high" table. Thus the name, high tea. Of course, the upper class developed their own variation, and nowadays the terms were often confused. Many establishments such as hotels and teahouses used the terms incorrectly so as not to bewilder the happily ignorant tourists.

Madam Barrington's high tea, however, hearkened back to the old days. Though she rarely discussed her early life, Lily knew she'd been born in Aylesbury, England to a family of note, and so had probably grown up with servants. Since immigrating to America, however, she'd obviously learned to take care of herself while still maintaining her English traditions. She had prepared steak and kidney pie, pickled salmon, crumpets, potatoes, and a cheese casserole. This delightful spread was accompanied by copious amounts of Russian Caravan, an aromatic and full-bodied black tea blend with a smoky taste that Madam Barrington had only recently introduced to Lily. One could only drink so much Earl Grey, after all.

Their dinner conversation covered the generalities of wizard society and politics, some of which Lily was familiar with but most of which she'd been dying to know for years. For instance, there was no formal international wizard political system. Attempts had been made several times throughout the nineteenth and twentieth centuries but had always come to naught. Nationally, there had been a bit more success, and most countries had at least a semi-formal conglomeration of stewards whose job it was to preserve what knowledge they could and resolve disputes. But, by and large, the wizard's way was to keep to one's self. The only universally agreed-upon rule was: never meddle in mundane affairs. There was a second, unspoken rule, of course: don't reveal magic to mundanes. Any non-wizard family members—initiates as they were traditionally called—were expected to keep the family secrets.

Lily took a long sip of her tea as she digested all this information, finally putting down her cup to finish the last bites of her pickled salmon. "So," she ventured, "if the stewards of the American territories knew John Faust was plotting to multiply the wizard race so as to rule mundane society as benevolent dictators, they would be displeased, to say the least?"

"To say the least," Madam Barrington agreed, taking her own sip of tea.

"So why don't we just tell them and let *them* deal with my insane, egomaniacal excuse for a father?"

Her mentor sighed and put down her teacup. "Because half of them would secretly agree with him, and the other half would be too afraid to do anything about it. You must understand that, traditionally, no wizard has accepted the, shall we say, oversight of any formal body. None are likely to start now. The stewards are more caretakers and mediators than enforcers. In the past few hundred years, anyone foolish enough to indulge in wild schemes has ended up dead by their own hand long before they could do any public damage. That was not always the case with some of our more ancient ancestors, which is why mundanes have legends of wizards like Flamel, Merlin, Morgan le Fay, Ptolemy, and others.

"No, Lily," she continued, "wizards deal with things internally. It is the responsibility of the family to manage its members and keep things quiet. So that is what we must do."

"But you're not family," Lily pointed out.

Madam Barrington smiled serenely "Perhaps not by blood. But I am your teacher, and your mother's before you, and—"

"You taught Mother?" Lily asked, aghast. "She never said a word!" Her lips thinned slightly and she raised an eyebrow. "No wonder you two were in cahoots to keep me away from John Faust."

"Yes, our connection as teacher and student played a part, but it certainly was not the only reason." Madam Barrington's voice was dry, but amused. "A greater factor was my impartiality to the situation. I do not care for politics, nor am I part of either family's social circle. I am also one of the few wizards in the area whom John Faust would hesitate to cross."

"Fascinating," Lily murmured, wondering if she would ever know how much she *didn't* know about her mentor. "And speaking of John Faust, I believe you promised quite a tale where he is concerned. I must know my enemy if I am to defeat him."

"Indeed," Madam Barrington agreed, pushing away her plate and dabbing at her mouth with a napkin. "But before we venture into that topic, might I suggest—"

She was interrupted by a raucous commotion outside as a cacophony of yowling, hissing, and cawing set Lily's hair on end. They hurried over to the parlor window to see Sir Kipling, perched precariously on a lower limb of the backyard maple tree, swiping furiously at a large black bird. The bird was fighting back, pecking aggressively at her cat's eyes as it beat its wings. When Sir Kipling attempted to back up to escape the onslaught, his back paw slipped and he tumbled out of the tree. Lily almost screamed at the sight, but managed to swallow it as Sir Kipling twisted in mid-air to land on all four paws in fine feline fashion. He wasn't out of danger, however. His attacker dropped from the branch in a dive-bomb that her cat barely dodged.

Lily had seen enough. Not only were ravens not native to the area, but she recognized that diving attack. It seemed John Faust had sent his magical raven construct, Oculus, to spy on them.

Turning from the window, Lily rushed out the back door followed closely by Madam Barrington, both of them readying spells. They needn't have bothered. As soon as Oculus caught sight of the humans, it broke off its attack and winged high into the air, disappearing quickly among the neighboring trees with one last caw of defiance. Leaving her mentor to keep an eye on the skies, Lily hurried over to Sir Kipling, who crouched, panting, on the grass. She dropped to her knees, hands fluttering in distress as she saw blood on his nose. The aluminum and leather ward collar around his neck was only spelled to protect him from magical, not physical, attacks.

"Kip, you're bleeding! Are you hurt? Should we go to the animal hospital?"

"Calm down. It's just a scratch." Sir Kipling had gotten his breath back and was sitting up now, grimacing, though just as likely in exasperation as in pain. He licked his paw and made to swipe it across his nose, but drew it back involuntarily before it had barely touched the cut. Obviously it was sore.

"Just a scratch? There's blood all over your nose, you stubborn cat. Why in the world did you attack that nasty construct? Why didn't you just warn us it was there?"

"Psh, and let it think it could get away with eavesdropping? You seriously underestimate my truculence. Now quit trying to wipe my nose. It will heal perfectly fine without your interference." He expertly dodged her attempt to pick him up, then sauntered toward the back door, though a slight limp in his gait belied his air of nonchalance. Lily sighed and gave up. Animals were notorious for hiding sickness and injury, so she'd just have to keep a wary eye on him.

Standing, she went to join Madam Barrington. The older woman's eyes were closed and her brow furrowed. Lily guessed she had magically enhanced her hearing and was listening for signs of the construct. Normally, searching the area for magic would do. But the mechanical bird hadn't tripped any of Madam Barrington's perimeter enchantments, and Lily hadn't felt even a whiff of magic off it in the brief moment before it had fled. All of which meant it was protected by a very effective cloaking spell.

"It is gone," her mentor finally said, opening her eyes and heading toward the back door. "If you will help me straighten the kitchen, I suggest we retire to the Basement to continue our discussion."

"An excellent idea," Lily agreed. Despite Madam Barrington's assurance, she eyed the trees around her one last time before going inside, wondering where else Oculus had been spying and how long he might have been following her.

On the way to McCain Library, Lily called Sebastian. Though she suspected Madam Barrington would be more than displeased at the prospect, Lily decided her witch friend needed to be there when they discussed John Faust, Morgan le Fay, and how to stop the former from finding the latter. After all, as troublesome as he was, he was still her closest ally in this fight...or at least, she thought he was. He sent mixed signals sometimes, and her feelings toward him were one, big, complicated mess. But he'd always been there when she needed him, even if he was less than forthcoming about a great many things.

The phone rang five times, then went to voicemail. Lily growled under her breath, hung up, and called a second time. He'd better not have broken his phone again, she thought darkly.

On the third try he finally answered, though it sounded as if his head were turned and he was talking to someone else. "Just gimmie a second, okay? Sheesh—Hey, sorry, is this quick? I'm kinda in the middle of something."

Lily suppressed her annoyance. "Well, if it's not of vital importance, I suggest you bring your 'something' to a swift conclusion. Madam Barrington and I are meeting in the Basement to discuss a certain odious wizard and how we're going to foil his nefarious plans. You should be there when we do."

"My, my, my, Lily. Are you actually *encouraging* me to stray onto your women's-only campus? I thought I'd never live to see the day."

Though he wasn't there to see it, Lily still rolled her eyes. "Men are technically allowed on campus as long as they're accompanied by a chaperone. You just never bother with that."

"That's because my sterling reputation is all the chaperone I need."

Lily snorted, glad she wasn't drinking anything since she probably would have choked on it at a statement like that.

Sebastian ignored her. "I agree, I should be there. But what I'm doing now is pretty important too. Can we meet later?"

"No, we can't. And what could be more important than figuring out how to fight John Faust?"

"The supreme art of war is to subdue the enemy without fighting," he quipped.

"What's that supposed to mean?" she demanded, no longer trying to hide her annoyance. It didn't help when, glancing self-consciously to the side, she saw Sir Kipling watching her from the passenger seat with half-lidded eyes.

"Weeell, it's kind of obvious, you know, to win without having to—"

"No, no. I meant, what are you *doing*? What in the world would subdue John Faust?"

"Uhhh…I'll tell you about it later. Let me wrap up what we're doing here and I'll—"

"We?" Lily demanded sharply, now annoyed at both her friend and at her own inexplicable nosiness.

"Yeah. We. Tina is helping me dig up some…well, she's helping me out."

"I knew it! You shouldn't associate with that witch, Sebastian. She's a disaster waiting to happen." Though a part of her mind was silently begging her to shut up, she plowed on anyway. "Not that you aren't your own disaster in the making, but you should be surrounded by sound judgment, not someone who will compound your foolishness."

"Foolishness, huh?" His voice sounded cool but amused. "Foolish, like running off to the private compound of a suspicious stranger who has already threatened you once? That kind of foolishness?"

She closed her mouth, very glad he wasn't there to see

her blush. Half of her was furious at him for pointing out her mistakes, the other half was humble enough to admit he was right. But why did he always have to be so vexing?

"Look, never mind," he said, perhaps sensing her conflict. "I'll come. Just give me twenty minutes."

"Fine," was all she could manage.

There was an awkward silence. "See you then, I guess."

"Good day," she said, and hung up.

Having arrived at the library, she pulled into her usual parking space, turned off the car, and rested her forehead on the steering wheel. She staunchly avoided looking at the seat next to her, but for once Sir Kipling held his tongue, allowing her to sort out her thoughts. The cool surface of the steering wheel against her forehead helped soothe the heat raging inside. How did that man always manage to tie her in such knots? She was usually even-tempered. But something about Sebastian Blackwell, professional witch and troublemaking reprobate, got past all her carefully constructed defenses.

Heaving a deep sigh, she sat up and got out of the car just as Madam Barrington pulled up. While her mentor parked, Lily opened the door for her cat, who jumped down and disappeared into the bushes beside the tall, red-brick building. He would find his own secretive way inside. Cat magic, she was certain.

Together with Madam Barrington, Lily headed into the shadowed coolness of McCain Library. Besides being the library of Agnes Scott, it also happened to be her office. She was the library's administrative coordinator and archives manager, which was just a fancy way of saying she kept everything organized. The job suited her neat nature and attention to detail, not to mention her obsession with books. For a bibliophile, working in a library was like dying and going to heaven. The job also provided a convenient cover for her duties as caretaker of the Basement—a magical archive hidden underneath the library proper. It was accessed through a portal in the broom closet of the library's own basement archive where all the fragile, high-value, and out-of-rotation books were kept.

As the Basement's original caretaker, Madam Barrington didn't need to be shown the way. She made straight for the archive stairs, Lily following with her armful of books. Despite the fact that Lily hadn't spotted hide or hair of Sir Kipling as they moved through the library, somehow he'd beaten them to the basement and sat, tail twitching, by the closet door. This made Lily grumpy. She was dying to know how the stinker did it, but he would only spout some vague cat-ism if asked.

Her grumpiness quickly faded as they entered the Basement and she refocused on the task at hand. She kept a surreptitious eye on Madam Barrington, wondering what the older woman thought of her improvements to the decor. When her mentor had been caretaker, the enchanted room had sported only hard wooden chairs and little or no ornament. Now, in contrast, it was populated with comfy chintz chairs, tastefully arranged artwork, and many more light globes. Lily had even put a glamour on the ceiling to make it resemble the vaulted heights of the reading room above. The effect was much more airy, light, and aesthetically pleasing. Beyond a raised eyebrow and a slight twitch of the lips, however, Madam Barrington offered no opinion on the matter.

Choosing the least poofy chair, Madam Barrington sank gracefully onto it, though she sat straight-backed rather than leaning back into its comfortable embrace. Old habits died hard, Lily supposed.

"Now, where were we?" Madam Barrington began.

"Actually," Lily said, depositing her books on the large

oak worktable, "could we wait a bit to discuss John Faust? I thought—um—well, I think…" she hesitated at the hawk-eyed look her mentor gave her and gulped inwardly. "I think Sebastian should join us," she forced out in a rush.

Madam Barrington's expression morphed into a frown of distaste. That was good. Usually her nephew's name elicited a scowl of severe disapproval. He must have really impressed her when he'd helped rescue Lily from the LeFay estate.

"That is inadvisable." She held up a hand to cut off Lily's protest. "Were he the most upstanding and responsible person of my acquaintance, I would still advise against it. Never has a mundane set foot in this archive. It is a sanctuary for those who commune with the Source."

"But by custom, not by necessity," Lily pointed out. "Sebastian isn't exactly a mundane, if we're being technical. I don't know if you've noticed, but he's been using some powerful fae magic of late, a fact I intend to nail him down and grill him on, soon. Just because he doesn't have direct access to the Source doesn't mean he has no respect for it."

Her mentor's lips remained pursed, but she looked more resigned than upset.

Lily pressed the advantage. "I think you should give him a chance. We're going to need him, whether you like to admit it or not. John Faust was talking a lot about the fae in connection to Morgan, and I have a feeling Sebastian is just what we need to get one step ahead of whatever that man is planning."

"But can he be trusted with dangerous and powerful knowledge?" Madam Barrington asked steadily, looking Lily in the eye. "You know very well the company he keeps."

Now it was Lily's turn to purse her lips in disapproval, though at least she managed not to blush. It was hard to stand up for someone you yourself had doubts about. But though she doubted his decision-making skills, she didn't doubt his loyalty.

"He would never intentionally do anything to harm our cause. And besides, only wizards can access the Basement, so it's not as if he or his friends can waltz in uninvited."

Madam Barrington sighed. "Not exactly. It is true that a non-magic user would have no way of entering the portal. But another magic user, whether wizard or not…magical doors can be forced just like physical ones. That is why limited knowledge of its whereabouts has always been the Basement's best defense. Wizards do not share knowledge willingly, especially not with witches. By the simple fact that witches gain magic from outside forces, they are influenced and often manipulated in ways they do not understand. They are not autonomous, but linked to those through whom they operate."

Lily frowned, wondering how much of her mentor's opinion on witches was founded on personal experience and how much of it was cultural bias. Of the three witches she knew, one had tried to kill her, one had tried to steal something from her, and one was her best friend. Then again, her own wizard father had tried to use her for a potentially fatal experiment, so calling witches untrustworthy seemed a case of the pot calling the kettle black. The corruptive quality of power did not discriminate between wizard, witch, or mundane.

"It comes down to whether or not we trust Sebastian to act in our best interests. I do, and I think you do as well, deep down. I also happen to be the Basement's current caretaker. So I believe the decision rests with me."

Her mentor gave her a level look, face unreadable. "That is correct."

"Good. Because I already asked him to join us." Lily

gave a tight smile, thoroughly disliking the role she'd been forced to take as peacemaker between nephew and aunt. Sebastian had better behave himself, she thought, or Madam Barrington will be the least of his worries.

"Kip," she called, and saw him poke his nose around one of the bookshelves. "Please go watch for Sebastian and let me know when he gets here. I'll have to let him in."

Her cat flicked his tail in acknowledgment and disappeared again.

"In the meantime," Lily said, finally taking a seat herself, "would you mind filling me in on the Basement's history? I've always wondered."

"I suppose it wouldn't hurt," Madam Barrington admitted. Her smile was stiff, but at least it was a smile. "The history of this magical archive is quite the story. I chronicled it in full in that eduba some twenty years ago." She pointed to the red leather-bound volume sitting in the stack of books on the oak worktable. "You can read the details under either the Gregory Rosenberg or Leslie Wilbourne entry, it is cross-referenced in both.

"Leslie Wilbourne was born in 1885 and attended Agnes Scott in the early 1900s," she began in a tone that harkened back to the days when she spent hours lecturing Lily on the subtleties of magic. "She was a middle-class wizard, though the Wilbourne family had higher origins in England before they immigrated to America. In any case, it was a dying line, as many have been in the past century. She was the only wizard out of five siblings, but she received a good education. She was fascinated by the design of things and was a pure soul, intensely focused on helping others. At Agnes Scott she studied architectural drafting and later became one of only two Georgia women in this field previously dominated by men. In contrast to most women of the day, Leslie was very entrepreneurial and became a successful architect, focusing on designing family homes and apartment buildings. She combined her love of architecture and her education in magic to develop innovative spells that she worked into her architecture, preserving the buildings and protecting their residents from disease, fire, and other harm. In contrast to centuries of non-interference, she believed that a wizard's skill in magic was meant to be used for the benefit of all mankind. She tried to start a movement to that effect but was strongly opposed on all fronts— mundanes tend to destroy what they fear and do not understand, so the wizard community's reluctance was understandable. In any case, many of her buildings still exist today and are historical landmarks in Atlanta."

Lily nodded, fascinated. She vaguely remembered reading about Leslie somewhere before, perhaps in a history of Agnes Scott.

"At some point in the 1920s," Madam Barrington continued, "Leslie met Gregory Rosenberg, a much older wizard born in mid-nineteenth-century Germany. He had immigrated to America in 1911 to escape the brewing disaster in German politics as it continued its arms race with Great Britain. He was not alone." Madam Barrington shook her head sadly. "Many wizards fled Europe in the years leading up to the Great War. They could see as well as anyone what was coming and, being much longer-lived than mundanes and in love with their privacy, went to extra efforts to avoid being involved in the conflict. But that is another story for another day.

"Gregory Rosenberg was one of the last descendants of that great thirteenth-century philosopher and wizard, Albertus Magnus." For some odd reason, Madam Barrington glanced to the side at the antique card catalog cabinet when she said his name. Lily couldn't fathom why, the only thing over there was a stone gargoyle and a bunch of dusty old files. It quickly slipped from her mind, however, as her mentor continued. "Leslie and Gregory became good friends, for Gregory was sympathetic to Leslie's goals, though he stopped short of supporting a movement. He did, however, help her develop her architectural magic, using his considerable collection of texts and artifacts passed down in his family line.

"Leslie maintained close relations with Agnes Scott, even helping design some of their school dormitories. So when a new library was set to be built in 1936, she had an idea: to build a wizard's archive as a resource for future generations and to preserve Gregory's legacy. He had, wisely, brought every magical document and item he possessed with him when he left Germany. But he was a single man with no children or even nieces and nephews. So, together, Gregory and Leslie built this archive, and he bequeathed his entire collection to it. It has since grown, as a few other collections of dying wizard lines have been added, including Leslie's. I myself have contributed a few texts over the years, though my most valuable possession is now yours." She glanced tenderly at the beautifully embossed eduba, an object that had been in her family for centuries before she'd given it to Lily.

They fell silent, Madam Barrington having reached the end of her story, and Lily still trying to process the glut of new information. Foremost in her mind was the sober weight of so much history that seemed to settle on her shoulders. With many wizard lines dying out, who would be left to preserve their legacy? The implications were depressing. To distract herself, she asked the first question that popped into her head. "If most prominent wizard families pass down an eduba, then where is Gregory Rosenberg's eduba?"

"Why, with Mr. Rosenberg, I expect," Madam Barrington replied, looking amused.

"You mean he's still alive?" Lily asked in astonishment. She knew wizards were long-lived, but had never asked exactly how long.

"As far as I know. He left many years ago, after Leslie died prematurely in 1967. They had...deep feelings for each other, though Leslie was too focused on her vision to settle down and marry. But he left a will, which shall make itself known once he passes."

"Make itself known?"

"Yes. A simple enchantment involving a magical seal on a legal document. The seal is linked to the owner's connection with the Source. When the owner dies and the link is broken, the document is unsealed. There is usually a secondary spell that delivers it to a predetermined recipient."

"Oh," Lily said, voice very small as she contemplated what might comprise a magical will. Considering she'd already survived several life-and-death encounters, it might be time to make one.

Her thoughts were interrupted by a rubbing sensation on her ankles and the sight of a fluffy white tail tip bobbing back and forth around her knees. Leaning forward she gazed down into the monocled and mustached face of her cat, who meowed at her.

"Sebastian's looking for you."

Lily's brow creased in confusion. "Looking for me? I told you to get me when he arrived. How long has he been here?"

"Five minutes or so. I thought it was funny to watch him stare in confusion at your locked office door. He kept asking me where you were, as if I would tell." Sir Kipling blinked slowly, amusement exuding from every pore.

With an exasperated noise, Lily hoisted herself up from the chintz chair and headed for the Basement door, shooting a brief explanation and apology over her shoulder at Madam Barrington. Hopefully, Sebastian stayed put and waited for her instead of snooping around and getting in trouble.

Through the portal, out the broom closet, and up the archive stairs she went. She paused, however, at the door, hand hovering over the handle. She thought she heard a faint scratching sound coming from the other side. Opening it in a rush, she found Sebastian, frozen in mid gesture as he crouched, lock-picks in hand.

"Sebastian!" Lily exclaimed, aghast. "What in heaven's name do you think you're doing?"

Straightening his tall frame, he hid his hands behind his back and gave her an I-totally-meant-for-this-to-happen look. "Well, you weren't in your office, and I know you always disappear down here when you're working on magic. So I figured this was where your bat cave was."

She spluttered for a moment, not knowing what to yell about first: illegal breaking and entering or his apparent habit of spying on her.

Obviously wanting to prevent an explosion, Sebastian slipped his lock picks into a pocket and started down the stairs, drawing her with him. "I'm sorry, alright? Sir Kipling was hanging around but you weren't in your office, so I thought maybe you couldn't come meet me. Calm down. I won't do it again."

Lily took a deep breath, self-conscious again now that her moment of high dudgeon had passed. When would she learn to not let him set her off? It didn't help that his arm was still around her shoulders, putting her dangerously close to that attractive face, dark tousled hair, and charming expression. She felt uncomfortably warm and prickly, every point where his body touched hers hyperaware.

At the bottom of the stairs she disentangled herself and took a step back, collecting the shreds of her dignity. "I apologize for not being more prompt in meeting you. In future, however, please keep your picks to yourself. This library is private property and if a door is locked, there is a reason. You may come across situations in your..." she paused with exaggerated delicacy, "line of work that lend themselves to less-than-savory behavior. But I won't have any of that here. Do you I make myself clear?" She hated sounding like a teacher scolding a child, but what else was she supposed to do?

"Yes ma'am," he replied meekly.

"I—what?" She was thrown off by his reply, having expected a snarky quip or a roll of the eyes. "Did you just agree with me?" she asked, suspiciously.

Sebastian chuckled, brown eyes twinkling with mirth. "Yes, I did. Now, weren't we going somewhere?"

"Well...yes...I..." she stared at him, still trying to regain her train of thought. Why was he acting strange all of a sudden?

"Your bat cave..." he offered helpfully.

She pursed her lips again, but without any real bite. "It's nothing of the sort. It's a priceless treasure and resource of learning for wizardkind. You, in fact, will be the first non-wizard ever to set foot in it, and I need you to promise you'll respect it like..." she paused, flummoxed. She had been about to say "another man's house" but realized that might mean nothing to a ne'er-do-well like Sebastian.

Sebastian chuckled. "Give me *some* credit, okay Lil? My parents brought me up respectably. I know how to behave. It's not very fun, so I don't do it often, but that doesn't mean I can't. This place is important, I get it. I'll be very careful,

I won't touch anything, and I'll never tell a soul. Does that just about cover it?"

"Yes…it does," Lily said slowly, eyeing her friend. He was still smiling at her, but it was a sincere smile, not a flippant one, so she supposed it would have to do.

"So…is the ol' bat waiting for us?"

Lily tried to look stern, but was hard put to cover her smile. "Don't you dare say that where she can hear you. We're trying to work *together,* remember?" She poked him in the chest with a threatening finger, then turned toward the closet, motioning him to follow. As she opened the door, she suddenly realized what she had to do and fought back a blush.

"Um, Sebastian?" she said.

"Yup?"

"I, um, need you to hold my hand."

"I thought you'd never ask," he joked, winsome smile making her heart skip a beat.

She scowled at him. "I meant, you need to be touching me or else I can't take you through the portal."

"Well, if you're sensitive about your hands, there are plenty of other parts of you I could touch," he suggested, face straight but eyes dancing with glee.

With a ferocious scowl—which did nothing to hide her bright red cheeks—Lily grabbed his hand and marched through the portal, pulling him unceremoniously after her.

Men, she grumbled to herself.

As they emerged into the Basement, Lily heard a "Wow!" from Sebastian. She glowed inside, trying not to be too pleased. Then she spotted Sir Kipling, curled up in her recently vacated chair.

"You, Sir, are in trouble," she warned.

"For what? Teasing Sebastian? I assumed you'd give me an award for that."

Lily paused, considering. He had a point.

"Um, Lily?" Sebastian spoke beside her. "It's not that I don't enjoy it and all, but could you let go of my hand so I can sit down?"

"Oh!" Lily dropped his hand like a hot coal, mortified. He chuckled as he passed, heading to the far end of the room to look around.

Avoiding Madam Barrington's sharp gaze, Lily went straight to her chair, began to sit down, then jumped up in alarm at Sir Kipling's hiss of protest. "Good grief," she grumped at him, picking him up and settling him on her lap as she reclaimed her seat. It took him a moment of ear flicking and tail twitching to decide if he was going to jump down in a huff or stay and get petted. He chose the latter, and Lily was grateful for his comforting warmth.

Sebastian soon returned, face alight with interest. It clouded over, however, when he noticed the only vacant chair was right beside Madam Barrington. Lily returned his plaintive look with a steely expression. The message was clear: get over it. He did, though not without a dark look of his own.

"Now that we are all present," Madam Barrington said crisply, interrupting the youngsters' glaring contest, "let us get right to the point. As we have recently learned, John Faust LeFay is studying wizard genes in hopes of finding a way to make more wizards. How he imagines he can accomplish that, we do not know. But we do know he is seeking out Morgan le Fay, one of his ancestors, in hopes that her power and knowledge will help him achieve his goal of preserving the wizard race and ruling mundanes.

"To give you both some background, the LeFay family is very rich, very powerful, and very old. They were one of the most prominent wizard families left in England in the early 1900s. Some saw their move to America in the 1950s as a step down in the world. If the rumors are to be believed, it was Ursula who convinced Henry to do it. Something about being closer to her side of the family." Lily glanced at Sebastian, suddenly remembering that her father had mentioned the Blackwoods in relation to the Blackwells, something about a murder or a feud. She wondered if that was the side of the family her mentor referred to. "In any case, I suspect John Faust's aggression and ambition are partially connected to his desire to regain his family's prestige. There are rumors of threats and deals."

"You can say that again," Sebastian muttered.

"Excuse me?" Madam Barrington's sharp ears did not miss a thing.

"Oh, um," Sebastian paused, noticing that all eyes were on him. "Well, I've been doing some digging. You know, milking my, erm, contacts." He laughed nervously, no doubt trying not to wither under his aunt's disapproving stare. "The point is, Mr. Fancypants isn't just active among wizards. I don't have any specifics yet, but I think he's got his fingers in the whole magical community, not to mention the, er, illegal side of things, both magical and mundane. Sorry," he finished with an apologetic glance at Lily.

So that's what he'd been up to with Tina, she thought, slightly mollified. "No need to apologize. It's not as if I didn't already know he was a scumbag."

"Hm," Madam Barrington agreed. "It is not exactly a shocking revelation. The question becomes, have you learned anything useful?" She arched a critical eyebrow at her nephew.

"Um…not yet," he admitted, glancing at Lily again. "But we're working on it."

"Do let us know," her mentor said dryly, then continued. "John Faust was largely educated in England and so still retains considerable connections there. I know his wizard teacher by reputation, and he is the best there is, at least on this half of the hemisphere. Fortunately for us, the man is a virtual hermit and the epitome of conservative, so it is unlikely he would aid John Faust in his plans. That is probably why John Faust seeks to discover the resting place of Morgan le Fay: a lack of allies or like-minded individuals in his own circle of influence. We wizards may not be paragons of virtue, but our culture runs deep. We are scholars, not rulers. We do not interfere."

"Except when we do," Lily muttered.

"Yes," Madam Barrington agreed, tiredly. "Except then."

They fell silent, each lost in their own dark thoughts.

"So, tell us about Morgan le Fay," Lily finally prompted.

Her mentor's eyes lost their focus as she cast her memory deep into the past. "She was a real person, that much is known, though most of her exploits in mundane literature are not to be believed. She lived in a time when mundanes were unusually tolerant to the idea of magic. During the time of King Arthur, several prominent wizard families became entangled in the politics of the time after having foolishly intermarried with the ruling elite. What may have begun as simple family rivalry turned into a struggle for the kingdom, and things went downhill from there. While Morgan le Fay may have been the most notorious, she certainly was not the only one. Merlin, bless his heart, tried to mediate, but nobody much wanted to listen to reason back then."

"But what is so special about Morgan that John Faust thinks he will gain by finding her?" Lily asked. "Why isn't he looking for Merlin, or some other great wizard?"

Madam Barrington nodded thoughtfully. "A valid question. I believe it is a matter of influence. We have very little primary source information about Merlin, but all writings agree that he was a conscientious man. I doubt he would agree to help John Faust, and he is too powerful to be coerced."

"Wait a minute," Sebastian broke in. "You're talking as if Merlin is still alive. That's impossible."

Madam Barrington was quiet for a long moment, staring at the both of them. Lily knew that look. It was the one her teacher got every time she was trying to decide how much to tell and how much to hide.

"I thought we weren't hiding things from each other anymore." Lily spoke, trying to keep any hint of hurt or petulance out of her voice.

Her teacher's gaze turned to her, and it held a depth and authority that Lily shrank back from. "Knowledge is a gift, not a privilege. It is a responsibility—a burden—not some prize to be won. And without wisdom, it is as deadly as any out-of-control spell. It will kill you just as quickly. I am trying to balance your healthy growth with the danger involved in knowing. I have seen too many wizards destroyed by it. I do not wish that for you."

Lily's mouth snapped shut with a clop, and she sank back into her chair, thoroughly chastised. Just when she thought she was getting a grip on things, she was reminded how inexperienced she actually was.

After an appropriate pause, Madam Barrington continued. "While no one can prove that Morgan le Fay or Merlin are still alive, there are rumors. Their bodies have never been found, and then there is the legend of Avalon. While mundane myths are far off the mark, they had to originate somewhere. If it exists, Avalon is most likely a reinforced time loop"—Lily and Sebastian glanced at each other in trepidation—"with a portal allowing subjects to enter and leave without halting the loop. Legends of such a refuge existed long before Arthur's time. One would gain a great deal of power from knowledge of this place, and John Faust must hope Morgan will lead him to it. Being Morgan's descendant, he obviously thinks she will be inclined to help him.

"What makes the matter complicated is Geoffrey of Monmouth, a Welsh cleric and author of *Historia Regum Britanniae*, from which most mundane legends of King Arthur and his time stem. What is not known to mundanes, of course, is that Geoffrey acquired several primary-source wizard texts, which is why he knew more of the actual story than many give him credit for. Geoffrey's problem is that he was mundane himself and was not able to understand what he found in context, leading to the creation of a "*Historia*" that was only half truth and half creative interpretation. Our problem today is that we don't have the original texts Geoffrey used and so must guess, based on other secondary and tertiary sources, what actually happened.

"There was rumor, however, of one text found in the LeFay family's collection that spoke of Morgan's exile from Avalon after the events of King Arthur's reign. If the rumor holds any truth, it means Morgan's grave might be found. Whether she is dead and rotted in it, or else found a way to preserve herself, I have no notion. John Faust, obviously, hopes for the latter, but either would suit him."

"So who has the text now?" Lily asked.

"John Faust, I would assume."

"Then how are we supposed to stop him? Break into his house and steal it?"

"Nothing quite so dramatic," Madam Barrington assured her. "No, there may be another way to find out what the text says, and that is to find someone else who has read it."

"Henry?" Lily asked, thinking John Faust's soft-spoken and sympathetic father might be inclined to help them.

"Oh, no. He might have acted to save your life, Lily, but he is still a LeFay. In any case, he probably never read it. He has only a passing interest in magic, having focused mainly on the family business. No, we are going to pay a visit to Allen LeFay."

"Who?" Lily asked, confused.

"John Faust's younger, and much less well-known, brother."

Sebastian's mouth dropped open and Lily's eyes grew wide as saucers. It was a moment before she found her voice. "What? He has a brother? I mean, I have an uncle?" The possibilities sent her reeling, imagining another egomaniacal jerk like her father. But Madam Barrington just smiled.

"Never fear. He is nothing like your father, the darling child of Ursula. Allen takes more after Henry, though he has an eye for magic his father never had. They sent him with John Faust to England for his education, but he had health problems and they brought him home halfway through to finish his studies in the warm South. I was a part of those studies, since I had already tutored both boys until they were old enough for boarding school."

Lily still couldn't believe it. She had an uncle. And he might be halfway decent. She felt a flicker of hope. "So where is he? When do we go see him?" she asked, leaning forward in her chair. The motion disturbed Sir Kipling, who yawned, threw her a perturbed look, and jumped down off her lap.

"That," her mentor said, "is the problem. I do not know where he is anymore. As you might imagine, he was not very close to his older brother. John Faust was always trying to pull him into interfamily politics, using him as a pawn while constantly showing off to prove his superior ability. All Allen wanted was a quiet life. He left about twenty years ago and I have had little contact with him since. I thought you or perhaps"—she paused, lips pursed—"Sebastian might know a way to search via mundane databases on the Internet. I may not be familiar with the most modern mundane technology, but I can not deny its usefulness."

Lily smiled, remembering her mentor's utter loathing of the McCain Library's online database and how she'd spent years avoiding it, only to dump the out-of-date and disorganized system into Lily's lap when she took over. Lily had spent months working with the head librarian to update it.

"I have a better idea," Sebastian offered. "We're short on time, right? I mean, Mr. Fancypants could be taking over the world as we speak, right?"

Madam Barrington arched an eyebrow at her nephew's exaggeration but nodded in agreement.

"Okie-dokie. Well, I think I can find him in a matter of hours, but I'll need something of his. Something that has his scent on it."

While Madam Barrington thought, Lily gave Sebastian a hard stare. He was about to whip out fae magic, and she had yet to pin him down and get any straight answers out of him.

"I have a letter he sent me about five years ago," Madam Barrington finally said. "Would that do?"

"Perfect!" Sebastian rubbed his hands together, eyes alight with an adventurous gleam. "Now, this might involve a little, erm…" he slowed, realizing what he'd been about to say.

"Yes, Sebastian, please do tell us all about your fae magic. You know, those abilities you've been hiding up your sleeve for years? I'm sure it will be fascinating." Lily enjoyed the moment as Sebastian squirmed under her and Madam Barrington's unyielding stares.

He didn't look happy about it but finally threw up his hands in defeat. "Fine, whatever. Just don't tell anyone. I already have enough people gunning for me as it is, alright?"

Lily and Madam Barrington nodded, though the older woman's lips turned downward in a frown. "I might point out, nephew, that had you simply followed my advice a decade ago, you would not have such a problem."

"Yeah?" He turned and addressed his great-aunt directly for the first time since Lily had met him. "Actually, if I'd followed your advice I'd be dead."

Lily's eyebrows shot up, but her friend didn't elaborate, barreling on instead as he vented feelings he'd probably kept bottled up for far too long.

"I'm sick of this whole 'wizards are the superior race and witches are a disgrace' stuff. It's bull and you know it. I'm an adult with my own skills and responsibilities. It's time I got a bit of respect from you, even if you don't agree with how I do business. Maybe I didn't turn out the way you'd hoped, but Mom and Dad would have accepted me for who I am. They taught me to find my own path and help where I could, and that's what I'm doing." He glared at her defiantly, and Lily waited with bated breath.

Ethel Mathers Barrington looked steadily at her great-grandnephew, and Lily could only wonder what was going on behind those dark eyes. Perhaps memories of him as a boy, his parents' death, and his struggles since then. Perhaps she was weighing opinions against facts, cynicism against charity, and seeing which came out on top.

"Very well, Sebastian," Madam Barrington said in a cool, composed voice. "I have seen too much damage done by witches to ever think favorably of them as a whole, but I am willing to be shown why *you* are not like the others. However, if you ever attempt to summon a demon, associate with them, or use their power, I will have no choice but to seek your destruction. They are the most vile, foul beasts in the heavens above or the earth beneath, and they destroy everything they touch. I would sooner cut a branch from the tree than see the whole tree fall into the flame."

Sebastian nodded in agreement, looking pale but determined. "I'm not an idiot, Aunt. Thanks to you." He flashed her a humorless smile, then got up from his chair, muttering, as if to himself, "In for a penny, in for a pound."

He walked to the center of the room and turned to face them. "I'm not positive she can hear me here, but I'll try anyway. Stay there, and no magic. You might scare her." Raising his voice, he spoke in a melodic, flowing tongue foreign to Lily, yet somehow familiar-sounding. "*Elwa, Pilanti'ara. Ihki naroom?*"

There was silence for a long moment. Then, from a great distance, Lily heard tinkling laughter so high-pitched it was nearly a squeak. The sound repeated, louder this time, and suddenly there was something small zipping around the room. In her mind's eye Lily could see its magic. It trailed out behind the tiny creature like a green comet. The little thing finally came to hover near Sebastian's head, moving ceaselessly as it twitched up, down, back, and forth in hummingbird-like bursts. The squeaking laugh was replaced by a high-pitched chatter that Lily thought *might* be English, if it was slowed down about four times over. So, she thought, this was the little creature who'd helped rescue her from the LeFay estate. She hadn't gotten a good look at it then, being drugged and half conscious at the time. Lily glanced over at Madam Barrington to see her reaction. The older woman looked intensely interested—the equivalent of wide-eyed wonder in a normal person.

"This is Pip," Sebastian said, grinning at their expressions. "She's a pixie. Pip, remember these guys? We helped them a few weeks ago."

Pip bobbed and squeaked, then flashed over to Lily and tugged gently on her ear before zipping up to do several loop-de-loops above her head. Lily was so startled she simply froze, not sure if she was being attacked.

Sebastian laughed. "She likes you. She just said she's glad you're alright. That ear tug is a sign of affection."

"Oh." Lily relaxed and smiled tentatively. Then she spotted Sir Kipling crouched on top of one of the bookshelves, bright yellow eyes following every movement of the tiny fae.

"Sir Edgar Allan Kipling!" she exclaimed, voice startling her feline out of his predatory trance. "Don't even think about it, not for one second." She glared daggers at him, and he flicked his ears back in consternation.

"It's not like I want to *eat* it," he protested mulishly. "Just...play with it."

Sebastian and Madam Barrington looked at each other, nonplussed, as Lily carried on a conversation they could only understand half of. Pip, either oblivious to the danger or else foolishly unafraid, went to fly figure eights over Sir Kipling. The cat seemed mesmerized by its movements, head swaying back and forth and mouth opening to chatter at the pixie as if it were a bird outside his window at home.

Alarmed, Lily began to rise from her chair. Her movement startled Sir Kipling and his head snapped down, wide yellow eyes and dilated pupils fixed on her. "Quit it," she warned him, ominously. "If you can't control your instincts, I'll have you sedated. You take one swipe at any pixie or fairy or whatever we come across, and you're grounded. For life. They're our allies and the last thing we need is for your stupid cat instincts to mess that up. Understand?"

He didn't reply, but laid his ears flat in submission, hopped down from the bookshelf, and slunk off into the shadows, shooting her dirty looks as he went.

"Sorry about that," she apologized to Sebastian. "You should probably warn your friends to stay away from Sir Kipling, just in case." It was then that she noticed he was shaking with suppressed laughter.

"That was hysterical," he managed between snorts. "Seeing you assert your authority as head of the pride—ha!—priceless."

"Well excuse me for helping," she huffed, attempting to sound stern as she went cross-eyed in an attempt to look at Pip who had just perched on her nose.

"Don't worry about it. If Kip is foolish enough to go after a fae, he'll learn pretty quick that claws and teeth are no match for magic. They can take care of themselves, believe me."

Mollified, Lily eased back into her chair, trying not to disturb the pixie, who was now poking around in her hair-bun and giggling with glee.

"So…" Madam Barrington prompted, having watched the whole show with arched brows.

"So, yeah, I might just happen to be a friend of the fae. How I got involved…well that's a long story for another time. The point is, I know a few, and they usually help me out when I need it. For a price of course, but it's a price easily paid."

His aunt looked skeptical.

"Mostly alcohol and specially-aged pizza." He grinned at her. "Minor fae are creatures of simple comforts. Ain't that right, Pip? A glass of rum with a few candied cherries and you're all set."

The pixie abandoned the nest she'd been making in Lily's bun and zipped over to tug at a lock of Sebastian's hair as she chattered something unintelligible.

"No, no, that's alright. I just wanted you to meet them. Come by my place tonight and I'll give you something for your trouble. Okay?"

The pixie squeaked in reply and zoomed off. Lily twisted her head, trying to follow the tiny thing, but by the time it had disappeared she couldn't even tell which direction it had gone.

"So, that's me, a witch who gets his magic from the fae. Technically a druid, I guess, but people haven't used that term in centuries. Believe me, I know demonology is bad business. I swore off it after—" he broke off, glancing at Lily.

Feeling guilty, Lily looked away, not wanting to admit she knew secrets about his past that he hadn't chosen to tell her himself. But then Madam Barrington spoke and made it a moot point. "Lily knows. I told her." The older woman met his furious stare levelly, without remorse. "I felt she needed to know what sort of person she was risking her life with. Yet your past did not seem to matter, in her eyes. She was focused on who you had become, and convinced me to do the same. For that you should thank her."

For a moment Sebastian seemed torn between anger and…something else. He dropped his gaze to the floor, fists clenching and unclenching, body tense. But finally he relaxed and shrugged. "So," he said, turning to his aunt, "about this letter from Allen."

"Wait a minute," Lily protested. "What about everything else? Your tattoo? That staff? Who is Thiriel? Don't think I've forgotten what happened at the museum."

Sebastian winced at the name. He wouldn't look at Lily as he replied. "Please, don't say her name. It's not safe. Fae names have power, just like demon names do. That isn't her full name, of course, but still, I'd prefer not to attract her attention if I can help it."

"But who *is* she?" Lily insisted, determined to get some answers.

"A high fae. A being you don't want to get involved with unless you have a really, *really* good reason. They don't like dealing with humans, and they get pretty cranky if you go around bothering them willy-nilly."

"And that, I would think, is all that needs to be said," Madam Barrington spoke, forestalling Lily's next question with a tone of finality. Lily scowled but let the matter drop. "Sebastian, the letter is at my house. Can you meet us there tomorrow evening around, say, six o'clock?"

"Make it nine," he said. At his aunt's questioning look, he explained: "The fae I use for tracking prefers the dark. Not that he can't stand the sun, but it makes him grumpy. I have a feeling this is going to be a tough job, so I need him in a good mood."

Momentarily tense, Lily relaxed. Tomorrow evening, Friday, was her date with Richard Grant, and the last thing she wanted to do was flake on him. Since it was only their second date, she doubted he would be offended if she insisted on an early night, so nine was doable.

"Very well, nine o'clock," Madam Barrington agreed.

"Lily, I do not know how long this will take, but it might be several days. Pack accordingly."

"Jeans and boots," Sebastian said, and both women looked askance at him. "Hey, don't look at me like that. It might be a rough trip. Don't you want to be prepared?"

Lily wasn't sure if she even owned a pair of boots—one without fashionable heels, that is—and doubted Madam Barrington had worn a single pair of pants in her entire life.

"I am sure we shall manage," her mentor said dryly.

They would have to, now wouldn't they, Lily mused. She decided it was high time to assemble a fashionable adventure outfit. Being up to her eyeballs in adventure, she was sure she'd get her money's worth out of it.

Chapter 3
GARDEN CITY

Lily sat stiffly on her living room sofa, scorning the inviting cushiness she normally succumbed to. It was five minutes to six, the agreed-upon time Richard would pick her up for their date. She was too nervous to do anything but sit and wait. Besides, Sir Kipling lurked underneath her desk, yellow eyes fixed on her every move. She wanted to give him no fodder for the sarcastic quips he was so fond of when it came to her dating life.

Resisting the urge to glance at her watch again, she shot a glare at Sir Kipling instead. He'd retreated to the desk after she'd scolded him for rubbing on her freshly laundered—now-no-longer-cat-hair-free—dress. Though he'd always turned up his nose at strangers, he seemed to have a particular dislike for Richard, despite only having met him once when the FBI agent and his partner had questioned her after she returned from Pitts. Normally, she trusted her cat's judgment. But since he'd gained the ability to vocalize his opinions, he'd worn out his welcome in the matchmaking department. In this case, she was sure Sir Kipling was just biased. Richard, as it turned out, was a dog person.

The sound of the doorbell interrupted her internal fretting, and she jumped in surprise. It was six o'clock on the dot. Wiping sweaty palms on the sleeveless, '50s-style dress she wore, she hurried to answer the door, pausing to compose herself before turning the knob.

Pulling it open with a polite smile, she was momentarily thrown off by the sight that greeted her. Richard—tall, dark, and handsome in a crisp button-down shirt tucked into spotless slacks—stood there with an enormous bouquet of roses. "Good evening, Miss Singer. May I say how lovely you look tonight?"

"Th—thank you!" she stuttered, cursing inwardly at her awkwardness as she reached to take the bouquet.

Richard only smiled, eyes twinkling. "My pleasure. Mind if I come in while you put those in some water?"

"Oh no, don't bother yourself," came her automatic reply. She wasn't sure why, but somehow it felt like she was being watched—well, by someone other than Sir Kipling, whose eyes were currently drilling holes in the back of her head. She didn't want anyone in her house just at the moment, so she scrambled for an excuse. "They're, um, so pretty, I'd rather take them with me," she said, mentally cringing. "Besides, I have some work to do tonight so we can't stay out too long. They'll be fine." She gave him an awkward smile, sure he could see right through her.

But Richard simply shrugged with an easy smile and held out an arm for her. "Whatever works for you. Shall we?"

Mute and trying desperately not to blush, Lily took the

proffered arm gingerly and kept her eyes on the ground as Richard led them down the steps. It would be just like her to trip over her own feet at a moment like this. Plus, focusing on her feet kept her mind off the electric tingle emanating from their joined arms. Leading her to his car, he opened the door and helped her inside in the most gentlemanly manner.

The drive to the restaurant—a cozily vintage diner called Majestic—began in awkward silence. But Richard soon had her laughing and smiling with his easy nature and intriguing conversation. She found it was easiest to focus on the conversation and not on her surroundings, lest she remember she was on a legitimate date and do something embarrassing.

They were seated by the far wall, which, instead of being covered with cute signs and vintage photos, was one gigantic mirror. Lily avoided looking at herself, aware of how overdressed she was for a casual date and wondering nervously if Richard thought she was prissy. She had always been one to dress up, rather than down, but perhaps she'd gone a bit overboard.

Richard seemed not to notice, distracting her with questions about her favorite food and the choices on the menu. Once the waitress had taken their order, they lapsed into silence, and Lily felt a desperate urge to say something. Anything.

"How has work been?" she blurted out, immediately regretting her choice of topic. How inane, she thought. Surely she could do better than that.

"Work is…work." Richard attempted a smile, eyes showing the first hint of discomfort Lily had seen. "And you? How are things at the library?"

"They're…fine." Lily gave her own, equally unconvincing smile. What a pair they were.

"Speaking of the library," Richard said, "I just finished a book I thought you might enjoy. It's called—" And they were off, once again speaking easily now that the conversation had turned to safer waters.

Their food arrived—ribeye for him and spinach feta omelet for her—and they were just digging in when Richard's phone started a quiet but insistent buzzing. With a quick apology, he rose and stepped away from the table to take the call. Though his back was turned, she could tell that, whatever it was, it wasn't good. Her heart sank.

After only a minute of clipped conversation, he turned back, his face a mix of apprehension and apology. "I'm so sorry, Miss Singer. The last thing I want to do is stand you up again, but, well, it sort of comes with the territory. I hope you'll forgive me. Here"—he placed several bills on the table, more than enough to cover the meal and tip—"use the extra for a cab. Again, I'm so sorry." He looked anxiously into her face, and she could tell he was genuinely distressed.

"Duty calls. And what higher calling is there, than duty?" Her lips moved numbly, uttering a brave reply even as her heart sank further. Was one good date too much to ask? But how could she blame him? He was an FBI agent. It *did* come with the territory.

"I'll make it up to you, I promise," he said, laying his strong, warm hand on her bare arm and giving it a squeeze. Her heart thudded in her chest and she nodded, not trusting herself to speak. She watched him hurry out of the diner, his brow furrowed and expression distant as he turned his mind to whatever matter he was rushing off to attend.

Forlorn, Lily ate her meal alone, barely tasting the delectable omelet as Richard's food grew cold across from her. Well, at least Sir Kipling would be pleased at the outcome of her date, though she didn't look forward to his snarky remarks. Sometimes, having a talking cat wasn't all it was made out to be.

To Lily's annoyance, but not surprise, Sir Kipling was waiting for her on the low wall in front of her apartment when she climbed out of the taxi.

"Hmm, where's your knight in shining armor?" he meowed as she approached.

"Catching criminals and saving lives," she replied, as dignified as she could manage. "Now stop being a nuisance, I have to get ready for our, um, mission." Funny, she hadn't thought about it in such terms before, but she supposed it *was* a mission, of sorts. A mission to save the world. She almost laughed at the absurdity. From a romantic—but failed—date to life-and-death adventure.

It didn't feel like an adventure, though. It felt like a punishment. The last thing she wanted was to go gallivanting across the countryside, not to mention fight a powerful wizard. A wizard who happened to be her father. But she didn't have a choice. Well, she did, but she was too aware of the consequences to choose inaction.

Sighing, she continued up the steps and into the house as Sir Kipling—blessedly silent—followed behind.

Full night had fallen, swallowing the summer twilight as two wizards, a witch, and a cat assembled in Madam Barrington's small backyard. The back-porch light provided faint illumination so that the three humans could see each other. Sebastian wore his usual messy ensemble, though he'd added a black leather jacket. Why he needed such a thing in the heat of summer Lily had no idea. She herself had agonized over what to wear. Normally, she would have defaulted to her neglected—though more recently oft-used—casual clothes she donned when Sebastian got her involved in his wild schemes. Yet never in her entire acquaintance with Madam Barrington had she appeared before the elder matron in less-than-formal attire. She cringed at the thought of being seen in jeans and t-shirt but had no other practical wardrobe options—a situation she was determined to remedy as soon as she got the chance.

As for Madam Barrington, she wore her customary blouse and full skirt, though Lily noticed they appeared especially plain and no-nonsense. The older woman also had on sturdy, lace-up leather boots that looked straight out of the 1920s. Perhaps they were.

Fashionable or not, they were now assembled and had a job to do. Both women stood slightly apart from Sebastian, who held a box of pungent, moldy pizza. Though she eyed it with distaste, Madam Barrington didn't question her nephew's methods. Lily, of course, knew what to expect. She and her mentor looked on as Sebastian began calling for Grimmold, the mold fae he'd befriended and whose supernatural sense of smell he used to track down his prey. But after a good five minutes, and despite the tantalizing smell of specially aged pizza, the fae had not appeared.

"Lily," Sebastian said, turning to her with a frustrated look. "I think it's Sir Kipling. I know Grimmold is here, I can feel the little bugger, but he won't show his ugly mug with a cat around. I don't think he's afraid per se, just being a pain. You're going to have to carry Kip anyway once we're moving. Is there something in the house you can use for a sling so your hands will be free?"

Sir Kipling was none too pleased at the change of plans, but when Lily told him his choices were either be carried, or be left behind, he grudgingly submitted. Madam Barrington produced a large, thick woolen shawl, which Lily tied around her chest and over one shoulder to create a sling. She had to reposition her small pack containing supplies, clothes, and her eduba, but finally things were settled. Warning her feline against the use of claws, she picked him up and maneuvered his fluffy form into the folds of the shawl. Only his head poked out, yellow eyes narrowed and ears laid flat against his skull, as he suffered the indignity in mulish silence.

Once the cat was tucked away, Sebastian resumed his calling and coaxing, and finally Lily saw a small, squat figure shuffle out of the dark. It shied away from the ring of light cast by the porch lamp, but even so, some reflective light glinted dully off its warty, slimy skin, showing a wrinkled form in the darkness.

Lily was glad this was not her first meeting with Grimmold the mold fae; that first encounter had been quite shocking. She was surprised to feel a fondness for the little creature. She'd rather deal with a fae over a human any day and wondered if Sebastian felt the same. The thought brought a smile to her face as she eyed their grumpy guide. He looked especially ugly and ominous in the dim light, though the faint shimmer around him—what she now knew was his fae glamour—lessened the effect.

She turned to Madam Barrington to gauge her reaction but found her mentor still peering about, trying to locate whatever thing Sebastian was talking to in low tones. "He's right there," Lily pointed helpfully, wondering if her mentor was in need of spectacles. "Can't you see him?"

Madam Barrington gave her a sharp look. "What *are* you talking about, Lily?"

Lily only stared, trying to fathom why she could see the fae and Madam Barrington could not.

Before she could come up with a satisfactory answer, Sebastian straightened from his murmured bargaining and came over, tucking the letter from Allen back into his pocket. "He'll do it, but it's going to be a long shot. The scent is pretty old, and he says the source is far away. Oh, and the way he's taking us…let's just say it's not exactly the yellow brick road. But it's that, or trekking for days on foot. He doesn't do cars."

"What do you mean by—" Lily began, a nervous twinge in her stomach.

"I believe my nephew is trying to imply that speed comes at the cost of safety," Madam Barrington interjected, looking displeased.

"More or less." Sebastian confirmed with a shrug. "But don't worry. This isn't my first rodeo."

"I should certainly hope not," Madam Barrington said dryly.

"But how will we get back once we're there?" Lily protested.

Her mentor seemed unbothered by the dilemma. "Leave that to me."

"Excellent! So it's settled." Sebastian rubbed his hands together. "Might I suggest we get a move on? Grimmold isn't the most patient of fae."

Madam Barrington raised an eyebrow. "By all means, lead the way."

"Right…" Sebastian was suddenly nervous, but he covered it with a cough. "So, um, we'll be traveling through the fae realm, or at least the twilight between realms. You only need to do two things: keep moving, and don't let go. Got it?"

Lily opened her mouth to ask a question, but was struck temporarily mute as Sebastian grasped her hand firmly in his. The sudden warmth of his grip sent her mind reeling off in an entirely inappropriate direction and she completely forgot her question. How could his hand be so soft, and yet so strong?

"Yoo-hoo, Lily?" Sebastian's voice—half amused, half impatient—brought her crashing back to earth. "Take Aunt B's hand. That's it. Now don't let go, got it? Whatever you do: Don't. Let. Go."

Dazedly, Lily complied, gripping her mentor's bony, cool hand in her left and Sebastian's warm, strong one in her right. "But what should I do if—" she began, but was cut off by a sharp jerk as Sebastian started forward.

Lily was supremely glad she'd worn her chucks, one of the few shoes she possessed without a heel. She was used to wearing heels all day at work, but there she did nothing except sit and stand. There was a good reason girls took off their heels in the movies when they were going to run. Those who didn't usually got eaten by the monster.

Stumbling forward at the unexpected start, Lily fought to get her feet back under her and keep up with Sebastian's increasingly swift pace—an impossible task had she been in heels. Sir Kipling, seeming to understand the danger of the situation, hunkered down in his scarf sling and tried to be as still as possible.

They'd only been moving for a few seconds, barely enough time to reach the edge of Madam Barrington's yard—in fact, they were headed on a collision course straight for her fence—when the world around them began to fade. Before Lily had a chance to blink or even scream, they'd run straight through the now-almost-invisible fence and out onto the street. But the street, too, was fading, as were the houses and trees around them.

Though she longed to gaze about at the strange phenomenon happening before her very eyes, she barely had enough energy to keep moving. She was no runner, especially not when carrying a certain fluffy monstrosity that added considerably to her load. As she huffed and puffed, she could faintly see the low, gray shape in the twilight ahead of Sebastian that shuffled along at an alarming pace despite its stubby legs. Grimmold used his long arms like a gorilla to launch himself forward with each step, making it a challenge for the humans to keep up.

The journey devolved into one long, dimly lit nightmare. The air had grown cold and silent as a winter's night—Sebastian's jacket now made sense—but Lily was too out of breath and focused on running to care. She had no idea how Madam Barrington was keeping up, but apparently the older woman was more fit than she let on. Her strong, cool grip never faltered. In the mad rush, Lily was barely aware of her surroundings, only catching sight of dim shadows and shapes out of the corners of her eyes. They seemed to be moving through a dark place filled with the ethereal possibility of both the human and fae realms. She saw a gigantic, shining tree smack dab in the middle of the towering shadow of an office building. The hazy shapes of cars and people intertwined with tall grass, piles of boulders, and an occasional deer. All around them lights sparkled in the air, zipping this way and that.

Lily had no time to dwell on the ethereal beauty around her, because her right hand, despite Sebastian's firm grip, was slipping. It was so covered in sweat and she was so out of breath, she didn't know how much longer she could hold on. She tried to shout, to beg Sebastian to slow down, but there wasn't enough breath in her lungs for more than a tiny squeak. She wondered desperately what would happen if she lost her grip. Would she be lost forever in this twilight world?

Just when she thought she could hold on no longer,

Sebastian slowed his pace and the shapes around them began to solidify. The air grew warmer and the fairy lights faded, but for some odd reason the trees did not. They became more and more real, turning into giants towering above, their crooked fingers crisscrossing the sky. Sounds returned, too, filling the eerie silence with the rustle of leaves and the slapping thump of feet on pavement.

Sebastian finally stopped, and Lily stumbled forward to lean desperately on his shoulder and pant, her brain too oxygen-deprived to worry about propriety. She was dimly aware of Madam Barrington's loosened grip, and of Sir Kipling poking his head cautiously out of his woolen sling. But all she cared about was how nice it felt to rest against something solid and warm.

"Well, that was a lovely jaunt," came Madam Barrington's voice behind them. Lily turned her head just enough to see her mentor brushing off her skirts in a businesslike manner. Though the older woman's forehead glistened in the light of a nearby streetlamp and her breath was uneven, she maintained a dignified grace that Lily had completely abandoned in her winded state. Feeling her mentor's eyes on her, Lily finally straightened with a suppressed groan and took in her surroundings.

She was quite surprised to see the shapes of stately, historic buildings rising on all sides, interspersed by the gigantic trees she'd noticed earlier. Judging by the Spanish moss dripping from every branch like slate-green hair, these were probably southern live oaks. Turning to look behind them, she noticed a well-tended grassy square surrounded by trees and adorned with various monuments and historical markers. While she'd never visited here herself, the scenery made it pretty obvious where Grimmold had taken them: to the historic downtown district of Savannah, Georgia, the

Garden City. She wished they'd come to the city at a less urgent time. Savannah was legendary for its beauty, history, and culture. She'd have liked to look around. Maybe some day when she wasn't busy saving the world.

Noticing movement on the sidewalk, Lily brought her mind back to the task at hand. Their guide was scuttling furtively around the edge of a three-story, tan-colored townhouse on the street corner. He was obviously nervous about being out in the open, but the streets were empty. Lily looked around, wondering what time it was. With a jolt of surprise, she noticed the sky was no longer star-filled but grey with the approaching dawn. How long had they spent traveling? It had felt like forever, but it couldn't have been more than ten or fifteen minutes, not with her legs. How could it be dawn already?

Just then her arm jerked forward and she realized Sebastian still had her hand in a death grip and was towing her toward Grimmold and the tan house. Though their journey through twilight had ended, Sebastian's words— *Don't. Let. Go*—still echoed through her mind, and she felt a strange reluctance to let them fade. So, instead of protesting, she tightened her grip and trotted to catch up.

"What's he doing?" Lily whispered, once she'd caught her breath.

"Trying to find the scent, I assume." Sebastian's brow was creased in concentration, but then he did a double take. "Wait a minute, you can see him?" He looked back at the mold fae, as if checking something. "Huh…you sure you can see him? Butt-ugly face, warty skin and all?"

Lily nodded.

"Well, I'll be." Sebastian scratched his head as Grimmold crept through some bushes by the side of the house, heading toward the vine-covered fence that surrounded its tiny back yard.

"What?" Lily hissed.

"Well, unless you're a fae, or you're looking through one of these"—he tapped the triangular seeing-stone on a leather cord around his neck—"you shouldn't be able to see him right now. He's using fae glamour to stay out of sight, seeing as how we're in the middle of a city."

"But you can see him," Lily pointed out, noticing as she did that Madam Barrington was examining the front of the house, a strange look on her face.

Sebastian shrugged. "I'm different." When he didn't elaborate, Lily cleared her throat and elbowed him firmly in the ribs.

"Fine, fine," he grumbled, rubbing the spot with his right hand. His left still held Lily's, as if they were in a silent contest to see who would let go first. Lily's heart fluttered at the idea—like a silly schoolgirl, she thought in consternation—but still, she held on. "A certain, erm, individual, thought that if I was going to be hanging around the fae, I deserved to know what they really looked like."

Lily pursed her lips. Getting information out of Sebastian was like prying candy from the fist of a toddler. "And who was this individual?"

He didn't reply because at that moment Grimmold returned. The squat creature shuffled up and attempted to hide behind Sebastian's boot, clutching his pant leg and eyeing the empty street suspiciously. Sebastian crouched down, prying the nervous fae from his leg one-handed and keeping a firm grip on one warty arm as he questioned him.

"Is this it?"

"Grimmold want pizza."

"And you'll get it, once we find the wizard. Is this it?"

"Smell right."

"You mean it smells like the letter?"

The grimy fae nodded, a scowl of impatience making his already loose, wrinkled skin droop over his eyes in a comical fashion.

"But how do we know the wizard is here?" Sebastian insisted.

"Smell right."

"Can you smell the wizard?"

The mold fae glared at him. "Grimmold want pizza."

"And thus we return to the crux of the matter," Sebastian sighed.

"Are you two inseparable, or might I borrow my student for a moment, Mr. Blackwell?" A dry voice came from behind them, and Lily jumped, turning. At the sight of Madam Barrington's severe stare, she dropped Sebastian's hand like a hot coal.

Sebastian was just opening his mouth to retort when his phone rang. The shrill beep split the quiet dawn air, and he scrambled to answer it, letting go of the truculent fae and looking around almost as nervously as Grimmold had. On the way to putting it to his ear, he glanced at the caller ID and cursed under his breath. Shooting Grimmold a warning look, he hissed, "If you ever want another scrap of pizza in your life, you'd better stay put."

Grimmold stuck out his tongue in response but nonetheless retreated to the bushes and plopped down in the dirt, long arms crossed over his ugly chest.

"This had better be good," Sebastian growled into the phone, now standing to his full height and turning his back on Lily and Madam Barrington.

Lily couldn't make out the reply, but it didn't sound happy.

Sebastian backtracked, his shoulders hunching and his voice lowering as if to exclude his onlookers from the conversation. "Okay, okay. Sorry. You're right, you deserve a medal. But I'm kind of busy at the moment. Can you get to the point?…Oh, really?…Hmm…That's good news. I don't suppose you could, uh, do this one solo?"

He suddenly held the phone away from his ear, wincing at the yells coming from the other end. "Okay, okay, calm down. I'll get there as fast as I can," he said, then hung up, cutting off the angry reply. "Okay, people," he said, turning, "change of plans." He deflated slightly at the looks on both his female companions' faces.

"Don't you even *think* about running off," Lily warned him, arms crossed as her stomach clenched in worry.

"Look, we're here," he protested, gesturing at the tan house. "Grimmold says the scent leads to this house."

"But he wouldn't answer when you asked if he smelled the wizard himself. Sounds to me like he's trying to trick us."

"No, no, it's nothing like that. Formal agreements are sacred to the fae. You can be sure the letter came from here, no doubt about it. As for Allen, we know he's not *outside* the house, or else Grimmold would smell him. So he has to be *inside*, right?" He looked to the bush for confirmation, and the grumpy fae underneath it grunted in agreement.

"There you go. He's here somewhere, so you don't need me any more."

"What do you mean we don't need you any more?" Lily began, voice rising in alarm. At a hush from both Sebastian and Madam Barrington, she lowered her tone and stepped closer, hands on hips. "You aren't here to twiddle your fingers and then disappear. You're part of…well, part of our team. We need you. Here. I—I need you." She finally said, the last words a bare whisper as she fixed her eyes on his collar, too chicken to look up.

A moment of stunned silence greeted her pronouncement, and then Sebastian cleared his throat. "I...I want to be here, really, I do. But remember how I said Tina and I were working on—"

"That witch again!" Lily exclaimed, now glaring readily up into Sebastian's face as she took a furious step backward.

"It's not like that," he hissed, moving close once more. She crossed her arms but stayed put. "I'm serious, we're working on something, something to take down John Faust in case the...other stuff doesn't work. Well, more like to make the other stuff unnecessary. Supreme art of war and all that." He gave her a weak smile. "I've got to go take care of this, or the chance will be gone. I promise I'll come back as soon as I can. It's not like you don't have my number, right?"

Lily was furious at him and had no idea why. Everything he said made sense, and it wasn't as if they really *did* need him. And yet, she didn't want him to leave.

She felt a light hand on her shoulder as Madam Barrington joined them. "Go, nephew. Take care of your business, and be quick about it. But expect to give a full explanation when you return. After all, are we not working toward a common goal? There is no call for secrets among allies."

Sebastian nodded mutely and turned toward Grimmold. "You want pizza? Take me back to the house, it's all there."

The fae grumbled but got up and started off anyway, casting a nervous look over his shoulder at Sir Kipling as he did. The cat had remained still and quiet throughout, but nonetheless followed the odd creature with his large yellow eyes.

Waving an apologetic goodbye, Sebastian trotted off after the fae, and both faded into the grey dawn, disappearing like mist in the shadows.

Madam Barrington wasted no time. She made a beeline

for the ivy-covered gate that opened into the house's tiny backyard.

Now that Grimmold was gone, Sir Kipling started squirming, attempting to extricate himself from the folds of the shawl. "Hold still," Lily scolded as she reached into the woolen cocoon and lifted him out. As soon as his paws touched the ground, he was off like a dart, twining between Madam Barrington's legs and slipping inside the gate as it was opened. Apparently Sir Kipling and Sebastian had more in common than she thought: neither of them wanted to stick around. Expression downcast, she trudged after her mentor's disappearing form.

She caught up with Madam Barrington on the back steps of the house as the older wizard examined the lintel and doorpost. Seeing her approach, her mentor explained in a quiet voice. "This may very well be the origin of Allen's letter, but I can not detect a single sign of habitation or magic within. It is as if the entire house is devoid of life."

"So you think he's not here?"

"I did not say that," Madam Barrington continued, stepping back to examine the second-story windows. "While it certainly appears to be abandoned, I suspect it does so at the command of its owner. Remember, Lily, things are rarely as they seem, especially when it comes to magic."

"Of course." Lily nodded. "Do you think he's watching us?"

"Most probably."

"So why doesn't he open the door?"

"I suspect he does not want to be disturbed," Madam Barrington commented in a dry tone, brow furrowed as she inspected the doormat.

Lily didn't blame him. Backing down the steps, she stared up at the house while Madam Barrington went to check for other entrances. In the growing light of dawn, its seamless, tan walls took on an amber hue. The house was devoid of excessive adornment, though it did have a nice sort of covered porch and garden between it and the next house. It would have looked decidedly plain except for the finely carved shutters and lintels of its sparse windows. While all the shutters were open, curtains inside each window were firmly shut, providing no insight into the depths within. All in all, it seemed to have little to recommend it in comparison to the fancier historic buildings around it. Of course, if this was Allen LeFay's home, then it had probably been selected precisely *because* of its plainness.

She was just wondering where Madam Barrington had gotten to when her mentor reappeared, having made a full circle of the house. Lily opened her mouth to ask what they were going to do next when there came a clicking at the back door. To her complete astonishment, it opened a crack to reveal the thin, pale face of a man in a tartan dressing gown and fuzzy house slippers. His sandy hair stuck up in all directions while a bristling mustache adorned his upper lip like a bad-tempered caterpillar. Firmly attached to his left ankle was none other than Sir Kipling. The triumphant feline had the most obscenely smug smirk on his face. As soon as he spotted Lily he meowed a "look what I found" at her.

"This—this cat. Is it yours?" The man asked, his words sharp and his expression extremely put out.

Lily, while horrified at her cat's lack of decorum, fought down a giggle of mirth. "He is, sir. I mean, yes, sir. Please forgive me—I do apologize—" She started forward to peel her errant feline off the poor man's ankle, but he held up a hand.

"I would prefer you stay. That is, right where you are. Just call it—call the cursed thing off."

"Is that any way to greet your niece, Allen?" Madam Barrington, previously out of the man's line of sight, now came to stand by her student. She gave Allen the same look of disapproval she reserved for naughty children. And Sebastian.

Allen froze and his eyes widened in shock, staring at them dumbly for several long moments. Then he heaved a very deep, very long sigh. "Oh, bother."

"Indeed." Madam Barrington's voice couldn't have been dryer if she'd been standing in the Sahara Desert. "Are you going to invite us in, or shall I explain the situation on your doorstep?"

"No, no. Come in. Quickly." He cracked the door a bit wider, motioning sharply as he looked back and forth to ensure the street was still empty. They hurried inside, Sir Kipling relinquishing his grip on Allen's ankle to follow Lily as she passed.

Lily felt the familiar whisper touch of wards as she crossed the threshold, but hardly even noticed it next to the sudden, blinding presence of magic all around her. It wasn't that the magic was literally overwhelming the light receptors in her eyes. It was that the sheer surprise of so much magic in one place, magic that was completely invisible from the outside, was startling. She marveled at the range and complexity of the spells as one thing after another caught her eye: a ticking clock with no moving parts, its hands suspended in midair; a hall mirror that, instead of showing their faces, showed their backs; being able to see clearly out of every window, despite their drawn curtains; and, most curious, a flock of mechanical hands that circled lazily about the ceiling, looking for all the world like glittering vultures.

They appeared to be some sort of construct, perhaps similar to her father's raven.

How her uncle managed to keep all this a secret, smack dab in the middle of a popular tourist town, was beyond her. One thing was for sure: no mundane would ever be allowed to set foot over this threshold, not with all these disembodied hands floating about.

Allen led them along the hall toward the front of the house. The rich mahogany of the polished wood floors complemented the antique cream wallpaper nicely, both colors accented by elegant artwork in gilt frames. Light globes above their heads softly brightened and faded as they passed, enchanted to automatically detect their presence. Lily wondered if their detection parameters were based on movement, body heat, or something else entirely. She didn't dwell on it long, however, being much more interested in the rooms they passed: a cluttered library followed by a spotless kitchen. Lily wondered at the contrast. Most doors were closed, however, perhaps indicating unused rooms.

Reaching their destination, Allen motioned them into the front sitting room. It was strikingly similar to Madam Barrington's parlor in Atlanta, at least as far as antique taste was concerned. It seemed rather more finely decorated than an eccentric such as Allen would have preferred, but being one of Savannah's historic homes, perhaps it had come that way.

The women took seats on a richly embroidered settee while Sir Kipling crouched at its side, eyes following the slowly circling hands that seemed to follow Allen from room to room. Allen himself did not sit but paced nervously, stopping occasionally to stare at Lily and mutter. As he moved back and forth, Lily marveled at the difference between this man and her father. He was John Faust's polar opposite in stature, looks, and demeanor, though Lily thought she could detect the same hungry intellect in him as she saw in her father. Obviously, the famed LeFay prowess in magic hadn't passed Allen by, as evidenced by his abode and the wonders in it.

For a long time they sat in silence, waiting for Allen to speak. Or at least, speak to them. But he seemed to have forgotten their presence, pacing back and forth and carrying on a muttered conversation with himself, mustache dancing as his lips moved. Finally, Madam Barrington tired of his antics and addressed him sharply. "Allen!"

The slight man jumped in surprise, recalling their presence.

Madam Barrington continued in a stern tone. "While I'm pleased to see my tutoring in magic was not wasted on you, I am quite sure I taught you better manners than this."

"I do—um—apologize, Madam…Miss…I don't…well, it's been a long time…you see, I'm not accustomed. To visitors, that is," he muttered, looking down in contrition. His words were abrupt, almost staccato, as if he were a bird pecking at seeds.

"Then this will be an excellent opportunity to practice," Madam Barrington said, back straight, eyes piercing. "Allen, allow me to present your niece, Miss Lillian Singer. Lily, Mr. Allen LeFay."

Lily was torn, not knowing if he expected her to rise and embrace him—being a family member—or if that would be terribly presumptuous. She opted for a bow at the waist from where she sat, painfully aware of her informal attire. Fortunately, Allen didn't seem to notice. He gave a jerky bow in return and muttered, "Pleased. Quite pleased. Miss."

Silence fell again, though now, instead of pacing, Allen simply stood and stared at her. He still twitched nervously, muttering to himself and looking over his shoulder every now and then, but she could tell his curiosity was getting the better of him.

With a sigh of forbearance, Madam Barrington broke the silence again. "Well, I suppose that was as good as could be expected. Now, Allen, I'm sure you have questions—"

"Yes! Yes, yes," he interrupted, suddenly resuming his pacing and wringing his hands. He seemed extremely upset about something. "Questions. I do, in fact. Most urgent. I don't suppose. Could it have been possible? Do you know if…J—j—j…" unable to continue, he stopped himself, closed his eyes, and took a deep breath, visibly controlling his tremors. Opening his eyes again, he glanced back and forth between them. "Do pardon my, my little quirks. They are, hmm, courtesy of my d—dear brother." He looked about to start twitching again but rallied himself and continued. "I am usually quite, yes, quite calm. Your unexpected appearance…it put me to mind…most distressing…"

He trailed off, and Lily and her mentor looked at each other, both wearing a similar look of concern. The fact that this brilliant man was clearly terrified at the mere mention of his brother's name boded ill for their quest. Yet Lily thought she understood, and she felt a pang of sympathy for her poor uncle. She knew what it was like to suffer under the manipulative and brutal control of John Faust, and she'd only had to endure a few days of it. Imagine spending a lifetime under John Faust's, not to mention Ursula's, thumb. But what had John Faust done to his brother to make him so frightened?

Madam Barrington must have had similar thoughts, because she spoke in a soothing voice. "Do not worry yourself, Allen. We came by means of fae magic. There is no way John could have followed us. Your secret is safe."

With a whoosh of air, three mechanical hands dove from the ceiling towards one of the sitting room's chairs, pushing it behind Allen just in time for him to collapse limply onto it. They immediately returned to their slow hover around the ceiling, moving so fast Lily barely had time to process it. She wondered how in the world her uncle was controlling them without speaking.

Allen drew a hand across his brow, but he looked considerably better already. "I had assumed, no, hoped, that you—being familiar with the family—would take precautions. Silly of me to doubt, no doubt." He smiled weakly at his old teacher, who pursed her lips in reply, though in that way you do when you're trying not to smile.

"If you had left any way to contact you, we certainly would not have disturbed you so unexpectedly," Madam Barrington said, half in apology, half in reprimand.

"No, no, not safe. My brother has eyes and ears everywhere. I needed to disappear. Find a place of my own. Somewhere I could be, well, myself. So sorry, Madam. Couldn't be helped. You can imagine…rather disturbing to—to be found. I'd be very interested to know how you, hmm, did it. Fae magic, you say? Fascinating! How exactly—"

"Perhaps at a later time, Allen," Madam Barrington cut him off, firmly but politely. "At the moment, we have more pressing matters to attend."

"Indeed?" Allen asked, one of his eyelids twitching, almost as if he knew what was coming.

"Yes. I'm sure it won't surprise you to know that your brother is making a nuisance of himself again."

Lily thought that was the understatement of a lifetime, and apparently Allen agreed. His barking laugh, tinged with nervous hysteria, rang out in a startling burst, then cut off abruptly, as if he only had so much mirth to spare. "Of course. Of course. Always my brother. And I thought, well, I thought I might…shall we say, be rid of him. But no. I suppose that was a foolish hope." He glanced at Lily as he said this, and she felt a flush rise to her cheeks. Did he mean her? Did he fear and hate his brother so much that he didn't even want to associate with his niece?

He must have sensed the direction of her thoughts, or at least noticed her red face, because he backtracked quickly. "Not that I don't…I mean to say, the rest of the family, that is…" He took a calming breath and leaned forward, guilt plain on his face. "Your mother was the bravest woman I've ever had the pleasure to, well, meet. We thought she might, hmm, soften J—John's"—he forced the word out—"rough edges, shall we say. Alas, his edges are not exactly pliable, but she never, hmm, bent either. Stood up to him. I admired that. Wished her well when she, when you, um, disappeared. It was her actions that, well, gave me the courage to do the same."

At his confession, Lily felt the same flash of anger she'd felt toward Henry and Ursula when she discovered they'd turned a blind eye to her father's abuse. Yet, she had forgiven them, however grudgingly. The least she could do was extend the same courtesy to her uncle. With an effort, she smoothed her expression and nodded in mute thanks to Allen's tribute.

Relief passed over his face, and he leaned back. "So, dear Madam. What is, hmm, J—Johnny up to this time?"

Madam Barrington's mouth twitched in a smile, "If I recall correctly, he tried to curse you any time you called him that when you were boys."

"Quite," Allen agreed. "Though, after Mother punished him for withering my tongue, he discovered better, hmmm, more subtle ways to deter me."

Gripped by a horrified fascination, Lily found herself leaning forward. When Allen didn't elaborate, she asked, "What did he do?"

"Ah, hmm. Many things. But the straw that broke the camel's back—my back, so to speak—was the live spiders."

"What happened?" she asked, not sure if she wanted to know.

"Compelled me to eat them. Not very, well, pleasant."

Lily recoiled in horror.

"Indeed," Allen agreed. "He could be a perfect angel. So courteous, so generous and, hmm, kind, when it suited him. Buttered you up, made you feel important. Never malicious without reason. But as soon as you crossed him..." he trailed off with a shrug.

A chill washed over her at Allen's words. Dark memories rose to the surface and crowded around so that when she tried to speak, her breath caught in her throat, frozen in echoes of dread.

Sensing her distress, Madam Barrington smoothly took up the slack. "Well, as you might imagine, he has not changed for the better. In fact, I believe he has grown a good deal worse..."

For the next half an hour as the sky lightened, the birds twittered, and the streets stirred with life, Madam Barrington told Allen the whole story. Lily chimed in when needed, filling in the gaps and adding insight to John Faust's actions. Allen listened avidly, occasionally exclaiming or muttering to himself. When they came to the part about Lily's imprisonment, he became very agitated, especially when Lily told him of the enchanted shackles that had suppressed her ability to use magic.

"Hmm...bad, very bad," he muttered, rubbing his wrists in a nervous fashion.

"You're telling me," Sir Kipling meowed sarcastically,

giving a tail twitch that Lily had come to realize was the cat equivalent of an eye roll. "Careful, don't mention the spying raven or he might have a heart attack."

Lily shot her cat a suppressive look, unable to scold him properly with a stranger looking on. Given the unprecedented nature of Sir Kipling's abilities—supernatural even to a wizard—she and Madam Barrington agreed it was best to keep them under wraps, passing her impudent feline off as unusually smart and nosey, but nothing else.

Fortunately, Allen seemed not to notice. He was too busy muttering to himself, occasionally consulting a small book bound in midnight blue leather that he'd conjured up from somewhere. It looked to be an eduba, and Lily wondered where it had come from, since John Faust undoubtedly possessed the family eduba passed down the LeFay line.

"So," Madam Barrington prompted, when Allen showed no sign of resurfacing from his own little world, "*do* you know of the text we are looking for? Or rather, did such a text ever exist in the LeFay collection?"

"Hmm? Oh, yes, sorry. I mean, no…wait, what was the question?"

With a look of consternation, Madam Barrington repeated herself. "As I said earlier, we need to find out more about Morgan le Fay, so as to stop John Faust from finding her and acquiring her powers. There was a rumor the LeFay family possessed primary-source material on her history and location. Are you aware of any such book in your family's collection, and if so, have you read it?"

"Ah, yes. I was just, hmm, checking my library. I can't quite find…that is, rather jumbled…it might be best to, ah, do it the old-fashioned way."

Lily couldn't help but smile at the wizard's apologetic look. She knew well the difficulty of keeping records organized and properly indexed, and she was a neat freak. She couldn't imagine how much harder it would be for someone as scatterbrained as her uncle.

"Yes, well...shall we?" He gestured politely, clearly making an effort. When the two women simply looked at each other in confusion, he realized his mistake and jumped up to lead the way, his pale face flushing pink. Lily's heart warmed, feeling an odd rapport with her newly met uncle. She'd always assumed she'd gotten her awkward nature from her father, because it certainly wasn't from her mother. That was, until she'd met her father. Her new theory had been that Henry was to blame, the trait having skipped a generation and manifested in her. Apparently Allen had gotten a healthy dose of the same gene.

Sir Kipling was the first to rise, trotting forward with his fluffy tail held high, followed in turn by Lily and Madam Barrington.

Chapter 4
BACHELORHOOD AND ITS PITFALLS

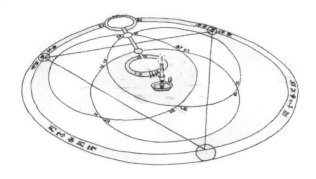

THEIR HOST LED THEM BACK DOWN THE HALL AND TO THE RIGHT, INTO THE library. In contrast to the rest of the house, the library was a jumbled mess of stacked books, papers, and bric-a-brac, most of it covered in a liberal layer of dust and cobwebs. Lily noticed that the hovering constructs didn't follow them into this room, their fluttering process halted by an invisible barrier. Allen must be more obsessive than she'd thought, if he didn't want his magical housemaids touching all this carefully arranged mess. Her own fingers itched to organize. She felt an almost physical pain at the sight of precious books and documents being treated in such a haphazard manner. It was scandalous. No book deserved such treatment, especially not ones that looked as old and fragile as some of the ones she spotted around the room.

The system seemed to work for her uncle, however. He moved through the stacks with an odd, stork-like grace, weaving between piles of books while deft fingers gently flipped through papers and poked around objects in his search. Again, she was reminded uncannily of herself: so awkward in social situations, yet completely sure and steady in her natural environment. Now if only she could figure out how to maintain her surety in all situations, like Madam Barrington did.

Allen delved further and further into the labyrinth of books, finally disappearing behind one of the massive, freestanding bookshelves near the back.

"Ah-ha!"

The cry of triumph was soon followed by a head poking out from behind the bookshelf. Allen carefully extracted himself from the mess and wound his way back to them, his tartan robe and slippers now liberally smudged with dust.

Back at the library door he held up the ancient volume for them to see, his eyes bright with that inner fervor which drove all scholars. "Here we are. But, it might be best, yes, to retire to the kitchen. As you can see, the library is a bit, hmm, cramped." He waved a vague hand at the room in general, which indeed only had enough space for a single person amid all the clutter.

As they filed out, Lily noticed Sir Kipling had not entered, but set up post by the door, back straight and eyes bright as he surveyed the goings-on both inside and outside the room. She gave him an odd look as she passed. He flicked his ears at her and meowed softly in distaste. "There is entirely too much dust in that room. I thought it more prudent to guard the door."

Lily held back, letting the other two pass, then bent down to scratch her cat's ears. "I thought cats *liked* to roll around in the dirt?" she murmured softly.

Sir Kipling didn't reply; instead, he leaned into her

hand, relishing the ear scratches. When she stood, he jumped up and put his front paws on her leg, begging to be picked up. Lily rolled her eyes but obliged. It would be easier to carry on a conversation this way in any case.

As she headed after the other two, Sir Kipling elaborated. "We enjoy dirt baths well enough when we need a good scratch, or when it's hot. But dust is an entirely different matter, not to mention cobwebs. Nasty, sticky things they are."

She nodded gravely, humoring him. She knew that mere dust and cobwebs wouldn't stop him if he were curious. It was probably just his excuse to keep an eye on the floating hands, which he was obviously dying to chase.

Speaking of floating hands...she entered the kitchen just in time to see a group of them dive-bombing Allen, all armed to the teeth with brushes and dust cloths. They must have taken offense to him entering their clean kitchen covered in dust. He cursed, flailing his arms and batting away the offending appendages until they retreated, rising to hover about his head in a cloud of quivering indignation, still clutching their cleaning implements.

Madam Barrington, mouth quirked in amusement, reached out to gently take the book from Allen's hands. "Might I suggest you retire to freshen up before we get down to business? And, perhaps, some clothes might be in order."

"Ah, yes. An excellent suggestion, Madam," Allen muttered, blushing and clutching his tartan robe tightly about him as if he suddenly remembered that was all he had on. He beat a quick retreat, followed closely by half of the hands. The other half put away their cleaning implements and got busy preparing breakfast.

Lily watched in fascination. There was no reason why you couldn't enchant objects with the same command spells and intelligence as you might build into a humanoid construct, but it was still unnerving to see the disembodied hands at work.

Busy staring at the pair of hands frying an egg, she was startled by a sharp clapping sound. Sir Kipling clawed his way out of her arms and jumped to the floor, glaring behind him before slinking out into the hand-free hallway. Lily saw that the hand-clap had come from a pair of hand constructs which had pulled back a chair for her to sit in at the kitchen table. They motioned insistently, and she obeyed, not wanting to find out what they would do should she refuse. She and Madam Barrington sat watching as the hands brewed tea, fried eggs, and buttered toast. It was all laid before them in an orderly fashion, and they tucked in without a word. Lily was surprised to taste malty undertones in her tea—she hadn't pegged Allen as a Scottish Breakfast sort of person. Perhaps it was in rebellion to his mother, whom Lily had heard declare during her recent sojourn at the LeFay manor: "Only *foreigners* break their fast with anything but English Breakfast."

About halfway through the meal, Allen reappeared wearing a very rumpled white shirt and brown corduroy pants held up by slender suspenders. His house slippers had been replaced by rather scuffed-looking leather loafers that nonetheless gave him the air of an English gentleman. He ruined the image by plopping down in the chair proffered by his enchanted hands and gulping down his fried egg whole as if it were a fish and he were a heron. Lily's horror deepened when he withdrew a small flask from his pocket and added a healthy dose of golden liquid to his tea— whisky, no doubt. Picking up the cup to drink, he noticed both women staring at him, scandalized. He flushed.

"Ah, yes, um, do pardon my table manners. The drink, it helps calm my, er, nerves and, you see, I don't often…well, that is, I never entertain guests." His speech became rife with awkward pauses, as it seemed to do whenever he got nervous.

They finished their meal in silence, the mechanical hands clearing away everything with flawless efficiency. Madam Barrington had placed the ancient volume in the middle of the table, where one of the hands carefully dusted it while they ate. Now Allen pulled it gently toward him, hesitating before reverently cracking its weathered cover. If this book was truly primary-source material, possibly written by Morgan herself, it would date back to the sixth century. As all books of that time were individually constructed, there was no uniformity as far as size or shape. But still, this volume was much smaller than the stereotypical tome, about as tall and wide as Allen's hand. Its pages were made of parchment—specially prepared animal skin—and its cover was two slender boards sewn together with sinew, then covered in fine leather.

Lily was surprised at first that the tome appeared so plain. Most books of that time were heavily decorated, tooled, and even inlaid with precious materials. But this one had only a single symbol in the center of the cover: the ouroboros snake perpetually eating its tail, though in the shape of an infinity loop instead of a simple circle. While detailed and quite beautiful, the symbol—like the cover—was surprisingly simple. Perhaps its author wanted the book to escape notice, rather than attract it.

Lily held her breath as Allen turned the first few pages, afraid lest she distract him and cause his hand to shake. But the wizard's hands were sure, his devotion to preserving the written word evident in his motions. Such an ancient book ought to be in a museum, really, not collecting dust in the back of a cluttered library. But she supposed this wasn't the sort of thing they wanted to fall into mundane hands.

Allen bent down, peering at the neat rows of tiny

writing on the first page. Unable to contain themselves, Lily and Madam Barrington crowded around, eager to see for themselves. To Lily's surprise, however, the writing was unintelligible.

"Is it in code?" She asked, confused.

"Ah, no." Allen's face had fallen. "I, hm, forgot. Apologies. Silly of me. I know I have a dictionary around here somewhere…" he trailed off, patting his pockets and drawing out his blue eduba.

Lily looked at her mentor, eyebrow raised in question. Then it struck her. People didn't speak English in the sixth century. Modern English didn't start to take recognizable shape until the thirteenth and fourteenth centuries, around the time of Chaucer.

"Remind me," Lily asked Madam Barrington while Allen searched. "When did the Romans abandon Britain?"

"Around 430 AD, I believe."

"Right, and they left it to the Celts, who were driven west and north by migrating tribes of Anglo-Saxons. They would have been left with Scotland, Ireland, Wales, and Cornwall."

"That sounds correct." Madam Barrington agreed.

"I know English evolved from the various German dialects spoken by the Anglo-Saxons, but what would the Celts have spoken? Gaelic?"

"No, Old Brittonic. It was the root language which split and evolved into modern-day Welsh, Gaelic, Cornish, and Breton."

Lily nodded in understanding. This was going to be interesting.

Allen spent a moment muttering over his eduba, calling forth page after page of text to its open leaves, but rejecting each one after a skimming glance. Finally he jumped up, startling both women. Oblivious to their surprise, he tore off toward the library. Exchanging a glance, Lily and Madam Barrington sat back down at the kitchen table to await his return.

He soon burst back into the room, once again covered in dust and cobwebs. His trailing flock of constructs descended in a desperate attempt to keep their domain clean, and her uncle fought a brief but furious battle. Finally, the hands retreated, clicking mournfully. One enterprising appendage tried to sneak a quick brush of his back, but Allen whirled, batting at it and knocking it clean across the room. Following its flight, Lily watched in horror as it headed straight toward the doorway where Sir Kipling crouched, watching the commotion. Yellow eyes alight, he jumped four feet straight up, twisted, and plucked the unfortunate hand out of the air as if it had been a bird in flight.

Before Lily had a chance to scold him or demand its release, her cat had disappeared. Halfway into rising from her chair, she halted, torn between pursuing her errant feline and examining the pile of papers Allen was now spreading across the table. Unsurprisingly, the papers won. She just hoped Sir Kipling didn't damage the device…or the device, him.

Joining her mentor and uncle, she bent over the dusty pages covered in lines of bold, neat script. She jerked back at the sight, as if burned. It was her father's writing.

Allen didn't seem to be bothered by it, however, because he picked out one page in particular and began to read. "*By my hand and by my blood is this written, Morgen of Avalon, a true account, that my inheritance may know the way and prepare for my return.*" His words rang out into the silence, as smooth and powerful as his own speech was weak and halting.

"Well…" Lily trailed off, unsure what to say. Everything about this felt unreal, like a dream. The idea that Morgan le Fay had been a real person, that she had written an account of her time, was beyond belief. The image of a seductive, red-headed enchantress, clad in clinging green velvet, popped into her head, and she almost snorted. That image of Morgan was a modern construct, twisted and exaggerated over centuries of storytelling. The original account of her in Geoffrey of Monmouth's writings was of *Morgen*, a benevolent ruler of Avalon, a healer and a scholar, not the vindictive enchantress found in pop culture. Historically, in fact, she would have been better educated than King Arthur himself. Lily knew from her study of history that princes in that time were more commonly schooled in the art of war and politics, not reading, writing, and science.

"My return?" Madam Barrington mused, thoughtful. "Does the text elaborate on that point? Were her descendants supposed to enact her return or did she stipulate under what conditions she would reappear?"

Allen shrugged, taking off the spectacles he'd donned to read. "I've only ever read the, hm, first few pages. This was J— Johnny's obsession, not mine. I spent years trying to, well, escape. My family, that is. This book…this translation…I possess them out of spite, not interest." Lily gave him a questioning look, so he elaborated. "After years of being under, well, my b—brother's thumb, you learn to go along. Quietly. I watched. Waited. For my chance to disappear, you see. When it came, I left a, hm, parting shot, as they say. I burned down h—his" he paused, taking a breath. "I burned his…workshop. T—terrified me to death to do it, but the revenge was sweet. I took the books in it with me, of course. They weren't to blame, after all. I believe he had just, er, finished the translation when I…yes, well, you know," he finished lamely, shrugging.

Lily stared, wide-eyed, at her uncle. He had actually burned down her father's workshop? She could sympathize with the feeling, of course. Her mother and Madam Barrington had taken great relish in leaving John Faust's workroom a ruined mess when they came to rescue her. But still… "Weren't you afraid he'd come after you? To punish you and get his books back?"

"Oh yes!" Allen laughed nervously, looking over his shoulder. "Absolutely t—terrified. Why do you think I take such, well, precautions? But it was, shall we say, worth it."

"Well," Madam Barrington said, voice businesslike. "At least John did the difficult work for us. We shall need to read through these notes, first of all. We don't know if they are a complete translation or only partial. Second, I should like to compare them to the original for accuracy. Finding a reliable lexicon for Old Brittonic will be tricky, but I have a few acquaintances at Oxford. They will know where one can be found."

"In the meantime," she turned to Lily, "I will transfer all of this into your eduba so we have a copy at hand."

Both Lily and Allen opened their mouths to protest, but Madam Barrington held up her hand. "I know you are perfectly capable of doing it yourself, Lily. But your time is better spent with Allen. I am not sure how long we shall be able to stay, and, despite his outward appearance, your uncle is a powerful wizard with plenty to teach, should he choose." She eyed the slender man, a question in her voice.

Allen looked uncomfortable, but nodded nonetheless. "I'm not, er, accustomed to, haha, teaching. But I'd be honored to, hm, exchange knowledge, niece? Though, before I forget, um, Madam, you will find it quite impossible to copy the book. It has been warded to prevent the magical reproduction of its contents."

"Indeed? What have you tried?"

"Transference, duplication, replication, visual conveyance, even essence fascimilification." He ticked each one off on his fingers, spouting magical technical terms like they were ice cream flavors.

"Hmmm." Madam Barrington's brow furrowed, considering. Finally, she sighed. "There is one other thing I might attempt, but it is possible we shall have to copy it by hand."

"Ahem, if I may?" Lily cleared her throat, cutting through the intellectual shroud. Both older wizards stared at her with that unconsciously condescending look of elders who were humoring a favored child.

With a slight smile, Lily withdrew her phone from her pack and carefully opened the cover of the ancient book, snapping a picture of the first page with the camera imbedded in her phone. The image immediately popped up on the screen, and she showed it to the two stunned wizards. "You know, mundanes have some pretty impressive 'magic' themselves. I'm sure if Morgan had created her wards in the modern day, that wouldn't have worked. There are spells to shield against light reflection, or she might have invented a spell to disrupt electrical signals, if she'd known what they were. But since cameras use the same stimulus as the human eye—light reflection—if the wards allow you to see it, then it will allow a camera to take a picture."

For a brief moment, Lily thought Madam Barrington actually blushed. But perhaps it was just her imagination. "I see." The older woman cleared her throat. "Well done, Lily. Perhaps I should spend more time learning these modern contraptions. I assumed a *normal* camera would work, but I did not know if we had one on hand."

Allen just stared at the phone in her hand, amazed.

"Where did you get that thingamajig, now, niece? It is, well, quite fascinating, I must say. What did you say it was? How does the internal transference function work?"

Lily rolled her eyes. "Really, uncle, you should spend more time learning about mundanes. Their technology is advancing quite rapidly and doing things that even magic can't. Or at least, things we haven't created spells for. Who knows, perhaps one day they'll discover the science behind magic. If they ever find out about it, that is." That was a disconcerting thought, and she recalled John Faust's grand schemes of wizard-mundane integration. Which, translated, actually meant mundane subjugation. Not that she thought mundanes would take that lying down. The thought of such a war made her shudder.

"Very well, then." Madam Barrington's voice broke through her thoughts. "If you will lend me your cellular phone and show me how it is used, I will make pictures of the book after I transfer John Faust's translation."

Dipping back into her pack, Lily handed Madam Barrington her eduba and then showed her the basic operation of the phone's camera, all the while having to work around her uncle's curious interference. His clever fingers poked and prodded the device with childlike glee.

When she finished, Madam Barrington shooed them off before sitting down at the kitchen table to get to work. Out in the hall, Lily and Allen looked at each other in silence, wide eyes reflecting the same panic of suddenly being required to interact. But after a moment, Lily began to relax, and she saw Allen do the same. They were so alike, after all. Perhaps it wouldn't be so bad.

"Well, hm," Allen cleared his throat. "Perhaps we should, um, retire to my study?" He motioned above him, and Lily nodded, following him down the hall and up the stairs at the back of the house. They were trailed by his flock of hands—Lily couldn't tell if they were still one short. Where was that cat of hers?—who attempted to straighten Allen's disheveled hair as he walked. He let them, for once, though Lily could hear him muttering things like "blasted busybodies" and "nefarious Nazis of neatness."

As they reached the upstairs landing, she could no longer contain herself but simply had to ask. "If they annoy you so much, uncle, why did you make them?"

He turned, a chagrined look on his face. "Ah, yes, well…you see, the state of bachelorhood is, for most men, a deplorable state. Yet we endure it cheerfully, ignorant or undesirous of the order created by, hm, well, the feminine presence. Thus I am, yet not only a bachelor but a hermit as well. I haven't the pressure of, ahem, social mores or occasional visits to recall me to the basics of decent living. Consumed by my studies, I devolved to a state of, shall we say, base existence not fit for any man. My mother taught me better, bless and curse her meddling heart. When I first made my helping hands"—he gestured toward the circling flock—"I endured a period of calibration. Too meddlesome and they drove me to distraction. Too lax, and I found mold growing in my mustache." He twitched the aforementioned appendage, and an unexpected giggle burst from Lily's lips. She immediately slapped a hand over her mouth, mortified and blushing, but Allen only grinned.

He led her down the hall and into the second door on the left. The single window of the room let in the bright sunlight of a cloudless August day, despite the fact that its thick blinds appeared drawn to anyone outside. In addition to the natural light, the ceiling was liberally populated with light globes, though at least half of them were dim or out. She suspected Allen wouldn't remember to renew the light spells until it got so dark he had trouble reading.

This room was considerably less cluttered than the library below, though not by virtue of Allen's "helping hands." The constructs were once again halted by an invisible barrier at the door. The empty space came from the large spell-casting circle that took up almost half the room. Its irregularity caught her eye and she stepped closer to examine it.

It was not, in fact, a single casting circle, but four. The outermost was a powerful containment circle, obviously meant to limit the influence of any spells that got out of hand. Based on the numerous scorch marks marring the floor within its circumference, Lily guessed Allen did quite a bit of experimentation. Inside the containment circle was a triad of three smaller circles laid out in a Venn diagram— a triangular shape made by overlapping the three circles with each other. Peering at the dimmu runes around each, she guessed the circles created different parameters and environments in which to experiment. Depending on where you stood, you could either be outside all three, inside one, two, or the whole set in various combinations. It was an excellent layout for spell work.

While she examined the floor, Allen rummaged around on the other side of the room, shifting piles of books, strange contraptions, and an exquisite model of the solar system to uncover a chair for her to sit in. It was a large armchair, probably used for sitting at one time, but having since succumbed to its usefulness as a flat surface upon which to stack things. The only other chair in the room was a high stool by the worktable where Allen now perched, rocking back and forth as he muttered. Lily lowered herself gingerly onto the weathered armchair but jumped up again with a squeak of alarm. She'd sat on something pointy and *moving*.

Peering suspiciously at it from a safe distance, Lily saw another construct, this one resembling a cross between a crab and a spider. Its body was the size of her palm, rounded, and disk-shaped, with four pairs of legs positioned for optimal scuttling. At its front was a fifth pair of legs, these crowned with three claws for grabbing. Currently, it was waving those claws in her direction, clicking them threateningly as if scolding her for squashing it.

"Oh dear. I do apologize. That is Egbert. I haven't really, that is, manners are not his forte. Shoo!" Allen made a flapping gesture at the diminutive creature, and it scuttled away down the side of the chair and across the room to hide underneath a pile of boxes. Though out of sight, Lily could still hear its clicking, low and irregular. It sounded so much like Allen's disgruntled muttering that she had to choke back another giggle.

This time she examined the chair carefully before perching gingerly on its edge. "Are there any other, um, critters about that I should be aware of?"

"Eh? No, no. That is, I *was* working on a, hm, sort of miniature octopus. For extra hands, you see, at the crafting table."

Lily recoiled, horrified yet fascinated. "What happened?"

"Flexibility versus, hm, stability. Crafting requires a, well, steady hand."

Silence fell, but it was a considered silence, making room for thought. Lily was content to examine the room while Allen decided what to say next.

"So. Madam Barrington has, erm, given you a thorough education?"

"As thorough as we could manage in the space of seven years. Since I became aware of my father, she's been filling in some gaps."

"I see." Allen stared, mustache twitching from time to time as his brow furrowed in consideration.

"Mostly defensive and offensive spells," she added helpfully. "Though we only had time to scratch the surface of battle magic."

"Hmph." Allen's snort surprised her. It sounded rather condescending.

"You disapprove of battle magic?"

"Fighting is, ahem, for children. Wizards ought to rise above such vulgarities."

Despite heartily agreeing with him, Lily found herself arguing anyway. "The world, and wizards, are not as they should be. I suspect such an ideal is a sure way to get killed." She'd been hanging around Sebastian too much.

"If one were sensible, one would avoid such situations," Allen argued back.

"I see. So we should just forget about John Faust and let him do whatever he wants?"

Allen's face flushed. "Well...not exactly...not what I was...that is, alternative methods could be sought. Brains are mightier than, ahem, brawn."

"So, what you're saying is, there's nothing useful you can teach me to help us stop John Faust," Lily prodded.

"I—that is—not—" Allen spluttered.

"Alright, so if not that, what *can* you teach me?"

He pursed his lips, making the hairs of his mustache bristle out at odd angles. "Discipline. Control. Finesse."

Lily didn't even try to mask her incredulity. How could this awkward, stuttering man teach her control and finesse?

Yet he didn't seem offended, simply gave her a knowing look. "Appearances can be, er, deceiving." Without a word, look, or glance from Allen, all the light globes above suddenly shone with brilliant light, blinding Lily. She fell back into the chair, shielding her eyes with a cry of surprise.

The light faded as quickly as it had come and Allen hurried over, attempting to help her up as he muttered apologies. "Ah, a bit too vigorous. Do pardon me."

Straightening from her undignified sprawl, Lily blinked rapidly, clearing her vision so she could stare at Allen again, mouth open. "How did you do that? You didn't say the renewing spell. And so many at once?"

Seeing she was alright, Allen returned to his chair as he replied. "Why should I, hm, say anything? Does the Source have ears? Do sound waves trigger its power? Magic is controlled by, well, the will. Speech is simply training wheels. A crutch to the mind."

Lily shut her mouth, considering. It made sense, to some degree, yet it went against everything she'd been taught. "But words are precise. They help guide and control the magic to make sure it doesn't get out of hand."

"Yes, yes, of course. Words are quite crucial. Magic follows, well, rules just like the rest of nature. But speaking words versus thinking them"—he raised a finger, tapping the side of his nose as he winked at her—"only a crutch."

"But Madam Barrington—"

"An estimable wizard," he said, cutting her off. "And no doubt capable. But modern wizards have become, hmm, complacent. No longer threatened by superstitious mundanes…or older brothers, in my, ahem, case. Must you talk in order to think?"

"You do." Lily pointed out, a bit mulish.

Allen flushed. "Ah, hmm…a result, perhaps, of my isolation. My point remains. The Source responds to the, ah, mind of wizards, not their mouths."

"Alright…so how do I do it?" Lily asked, curious and willing, if a bit skeptical.

In response, he led her over to the casting circle and—again without a word—activated the outermost ring's containment shield spell. Then he activated the three interlocked ones in the center and had her stand in one as he stood in another, placing an unlit candle in the space shared between herself and the third, empty circle. "These," he explained, pointing to the three central circles, "are highly customizable wards. Your personal ward, of course, is your, ahem, first line of defense, and will protect from most failed spells. But I can tweak these wards', hm, sensitivity levels, based on the object, or, er, direction. Your circle will allow energy to leave, but not enter. The candle's circle will allow energy to enter, but not leave. Thus you are doubly protected from any possible, well, mishap while still being able to affect the item in question."

Lily nodded, understanding. It was simple, but ingenious. They definitely needed one of these in the Basement. She'd have to remember to ask for a blueprint of the runes involved so she could make one herself.

"Now, light it." Allen pointed at the candle.

It was a simple enough casting, though that didn't translate into easy. Like all magic, the spell didn't defy science, simply manipulated energy to raise the wick's temperature until it reached its kindling point and caught flame, the same thing that happened when you held it in a lit match. Minus the match, of course.

Forgetting and opening her mouth to speak, she was immediately shushed by Allen, who gave her a stern glare so reminiscent of Madam Barrington that she giggled, more from the image of her mentor with a mustache than anything else. Suppressing her mirth, she concentrated on the wick, tapped her link to the Source, and thought the necessary words of power, imagining the candle catching flame.

Nothing happened.

"Again," Allen said, seemingly unconcerned.

She tried several more times, but the candle remained cool. Finally, she gave up, wiping a thin film of sweat from her forehead. "I can't do it. Saying the words in my head distracts me from shaping the magic with my will. Either the magic responds but does nothing, or I get the right command but my magic ignores me." She puffed out a breath, discouraged.

"You, ahem, meditate?" Allen asked, still unfazed.

Lily nodded. "Before and after my weekly yoga sessions."

"Ah. Not enough. You need, I should think, daily practice. Just like any skill. Wizardry is an art and, well, science. Of the highest order. Mental casting requires, hm, complete and minute control of the mind and body."

Well, at least Sir Kipling would be happy, she thought with a sigh. He liked to sit in her lap while she meditated, which wasn't strictly proper, but his purring helped her relax.

"Your mental voice is, ahem, weak," Allen continued. "If you spent your whole life whispering, well, you can imagine. Weak lungs. What you need is brain training. Your brain is a, hm, muscle. You must strengthen it."

Lily felt like she was a beginning student again, having been exposed to a whole new level of wizardry. Allen took her through several exercises and made her promise to practice every single day, morning and evening, along with regular meditation.

As they discussed magic, Allen's speech became more fluid, with fewer *ahem*s, *hm*s, and *well*s. She wondered how long it had been since he'd carried on a conversation of more than a few sentences. They became quite comfortable with each other, and her lesson devolved into many eye-opening discussions of magical theory and a few experimental castings. He showed her more efficient ways to combine Enkinim in spell casting, and how a few simple word choices could make her spells that much safer. He was a bottomless pit of knowledge, and she grew to admire and respect him more and more with each passing minute.

Most of all, she felt safe with him. He didn't look at her as if she were something to be used or manipulated. He didn't show disappointment or condescension upon learning the gaps in her knowledge. She was not a project to him, like she'd been to John Faust. To Allen, she was simply herself, and he delighted in their shared love of knowledge.

The sound of a clearing throat came from the doorway, interrupting their argument over the relative advantages of various aluminum alloys in crafting. Lily looked up and was astonished to see that it was dark outside. Where had the day gone?

Turning, she saw Madam Barrington in the doorway, surveying them with a ghost of a smile. Sitting at her feet was Sir Kipling, looking around curiously. Despite having no respect for rules or boundaries, he was smart enough to proceed with caution when it came to wizards' domains.

"I hope your time together has been profitable?" Madam Barrington asked with raised eyebrows.

Lily nodded vigorously, noticing Morgan's journal and a neatly organized sheaf of papers in her hand. She must have finally finished making copies.

"It is past ten and I, at least, should like to retire for the night. We hesitate to impose on you, Allen, but I suspect you would rather we stay here than be seen coming and going?"

He blinked for a moment, then seemed to recall himself. "Of course! Of course, Madam. Let me see. Yes, yes. There are two spare bedrooms on this floor. Never, ahem, been used, of course. May be a bit cluttered. But I shall have them cleaned at once."

He hurried from the room, no doubt sending silent commands to his constructs. The hands made short work of preparing the rooms, seeming glad to have something to do. Lily was just getting ready for bed when she realized she hadn't seen Sir Kipling since she left the workroom. *Uh-oh*, she thought.

Just then she heard a rapid clicking sound, growing louder and louder. Looking up from the bed where she was brushing her hair, she watched in astonishment as Egbert scuttled past her open doorway, racing down the hall, pincers clicking madly. Seconds later, Sir Kipling raced past in hot pursuit.

As she stared, torn between mirth and concern, she heard a hiss, a yowl, and the rapid patter of feet coming back the other way. Her ferocious hunter raced past the doorway once more, hair standing on end, followed closely by a furiously clicking Egbert.

Lily smiled and decided to leave Sir Kipling to his own devices. As he had pointed out to her on multiple occasions, he could take care of himself.

Sir Kipling's frantic pawing woke her. For a moment she thought she was back home in bed, and her cat was demanding she refill his food bowl.

"Leavemelone." She moaned, rolling over. "Feedyou ina mornin…"

Sir Kipling added claws into the mix.

"Ouch!" Lily yelped and sat up, rubbing her arm.

"Shut up!" he hissed, ears flat against his skull as he crouched low, pressing his quivering body against hers.

Lily was instantly on the alert. Something was wrong. Casting about in a panic, she tried to orient herself. This wasn't home. Where was she? Oh wait, of course. Allen's house. Her pulse slowed slightly but still pounded in her ears as she slipped her feet out from under the covers and crouched on the floor, putting her mouth next to her cat's ear.

"What is it, Kip?" she breathed, voice barely a whisper.

"Intruders," he hissed back.

She could feel him vibrating, a subvocal growl rumbling through his body.

"How many?"

"Not sure. At least two, coming down the stairs from the third floor. I didn't see them myself, a little voice warned me."

Lily's heart rate picked up again, thumping so loudly she was sure it was audible out in the hall. What did he mean, little voice? No, that didn't matter now. What should she do? Scream? Hide? Her mind raced. She was no good at this. All she could think was how much she wished Sebastian were there.

Taking a deep, calming breath, she tried to slow her heart. What would Sebastian do? Not scream, of that she was sure. Perhaps try to surprise the intruders? But what would she do to them? She'd never learned hand-to-hand combat, nothing but a two-hour self-defense class all the girls at Agnes Scott were required to attend their freshman year. No, she had to hope she'd be able to hold them off with magic.

Running through spells in her mind, she began to rise, but froze. Was that the creak of floorboards in the hall? Bending back to Sir Kipling's ear, she whispered, "Go warn Allen and Madam Barrington."

"I'm not leaving you," he growled, digging his claws into the covers as she attempted to push him toward the doorway.

"You have to," she hissed, tone fierce. "They'll be able to protect me better than you can. Now go! Go!" She dared not raise her voice, but she put every ounce of will and authority she possessed into her command.

Reluctantly, he slithered down off the bed and toward the doorway, a shadow in the night. But before he could reach the door, he was no longer the only shadow in the room.

She only saw it because she was looking right at the door. The darkness from the hallway was briefly blotted out by a deeper darkness, and she heard the faintest rustle of cloth on skin.

Her whole body froze in panic. She couldn't breathe, even as her mind screamed at her to do something, *anything*.

With an earsplitting yowl, Sir Kipling launched himself at the intruder, latching onto them with all four sets of claws as he tore into them with a vengeance. His frenzied attack kicked Lily into action and she let loose her own bloodcurdling scream, hoping that would wake everyone in the house if her cat's yowl hadn't already.

As the shadow cursed and struggled with Sir Kipling, Lily finally gathered herself enough to remember the illumination spell, and the room was flooded with light. The sudden brightness was blinding, and she covered her eyes, backing into a corner. She could make out a dark shape whirling in the center of the room, grunting and punching Sir Kipling who was making bloody mincemeat of their side. She saw a glint of metal and screamed "Kip, jump!" just before the knife descended.

Her cat twisted away from the blade, flinging himself off of his victim and landing between them and her. He arched his back, hissing, spitting, and yowling ferociously. Lily had never seen him so angry. It was as if hell itself had been let loose in the form of her cat.

With her vision finally adjusted, Lily assessed the situation. Her attacker was clad all in black, his loose garments wrapped tightly at the wrists, waist, and ankles, with soft-soled shoes and a black mask completing the menacing ensemble. His now-mangled shirt revealed pale skin, torn and bleeding from Sir Kipling's attack. Even as Lily took this in, shouts and sounds of battle filtered in from other parts of the house. She wondered desperately if her friends were alright.

Her attacker slowly drew twin curved blades from sheaths on his back, and Lily realized she couldn't afford to think about anything but her own survival. She threw up a shield wall between them and charged it with energy. It would shock her assailant should he try to pass through. Maybe not enough to knock him out, but enough to deter him. Then she prepared to throw energy bolts should he approach. She'd never had much practice fighting with magic before, but at this point it was fight or die.

As he took his first step forward, however, a shouted command from the hallway made him pause. Then he turned and rushed from the room, sheathing one sword and holding the other down at his side as he ran. More shouts, crashes, and the crackling of magic echoed through the house and Lily hesitated, unsure if she should try and help. Would she be in the way? But she couldn't sit there while her friends were in danger.

Dropping the energy shield, she moved cautiously forward.

"Don't!" Sir Kipling hissed, trying to block her progress. He wanted her to stay where she was safe.

"I'm not staying here. We have to help. Come on!"

He didn't look happy, yet still turned and raced to the doorway, slowing to peer carefully around it before twitching his tail at her to follow. She crept after him, heart pounding in her throat and spell at the ready.

Lily poked her head around the doorway and saw that the hall was empty. But flashes of light came from the room two doors down where Madam Barrington had been sleeping.

Lily jumped as something thumped into the ceiling above her head. She'd forgotten that the townhouse had three floors and, in growing horror, she remembered that Allen's bedroom was on the third floor. Even as she thought this she heard his frightened cry of pain that was suddenly cut off.

Torn, she paused in the doorway. What should she do? Who should she help? Her mind scrambled and she cursed. Where was Sebastian when she needed him? Madam Barrington's cry from the bedroom down the hall made up her mind. She hoped Allen was alright, feeling guilty as she ran toward the second bedroom.

Skidding to a halt in the doorway, she saw her mentor locked in a furious battle with another wizard, a young man she'd never seen before. Not giving herself time to think, she shouted her spell, pulling on the Source with all her might and pushing it out of her in a massive bolt that crashed into the young man's back. Crackling energy flared all around him, a personal ward, no doubt, taking the brunt of the blast. Yet the force of it still made him stumble forward, his singed shirt smoking.

Lily sagged as the magic left her, catching hold of the doorway for support as Sir Kipling raced between her legs and leapt onto the man's back, clawing and biting. The wizard screamed in pain and fury, whirling to grab the cat as Madam Barrington took him out with one well-aimed shot to the head. The spell knocked him unconscious and his eyes rolled back in his head as he collapsed.

Sir Kipling jumped free of the man's inert form and trotted over to Lily, nuzzling her drooping form in concern.

Panting, Madam Barrington hurried forward as well, grabbing Lily under the arm and helping her up as they headed down the hall toward the stairs to the third floor. Lily hoped briefly that all the light and commotion would attract the city's finest, but then realized that Allen had obviously spelled the whole building to be sound and lightproof. No one outside would know what was going on, even if they'd happened by at this time of night. Or morning, she had no idea which.

By the time they reached the stairs, Lily had gotten her feet back under her, though they felt like jelly. She definitely needed to practice casting battle magic, whether she liked it or not. "Kip," she whispered, "stay behind and warn us if anyone comes up the stairs. That man might wake up."

Sir Kipling mewed a soft reply and took up a post on the first step, keeping an eye on both the second-floor hall and the first-floor stairs.

The two women crept cautiously up the stairs to the third floor. Lily wished they had light, but that would make them a target. As they crested the stairs, they saw two dark shapes silhouetted against the window at the end of the hall, one of them dragging a third, limp form.

Knowing they couldn't sneak up on the intruders, Lily started swiftly towards them, activating the light globes as she went, Madam Barrington close behind. But what she saw at the end of the hall stopped her in her tracks. John Faust stood holding open the door to what she supposed was the attic as the fighter in black dragged Allen's limp, unconscious form toward it. The shock of seeing her father again sent her reeling, his patrician features and ice-blue eyes so familiar and yet deeply disturbing. She stumbled back into her mentor's arms, feeling the ghost of iron bands on her wrists, tasting the foul potion in her mouth. The helplessness, the hurt crept out of dark holes, filling her limbs, freezing her heart...No! She wouldn't let him do that to her again. She was *not* helpless.

"Stop!" she yelled, steeling herself and striding forward. She was terrified, but the warmth of Madam Barrington's presence behind her gave her courage, and she knew Sir Kipling had their back. If her mother could stand up to this bastard, so could she.

John Faust LeFay had seen them as soon as the lights went on, having glanced up and scowled. But he ignored their presence, instead urging his accomplice forward with an impatient command. They must have come in through the roof, Lily realized, perhaps where the wards were weaker, and were attempting to escape the same way.

"Leave Allen alone!" Lily called again, breaking into a trot. She had to step around singed mechanical hands littering the floor, their gears bent and crushed as if they'd been shot out of the air and then stomped on. Those brutes, she thought. If only she could think of a distraction, surely Madam Barrington would know a way to stop them.

As she approached, she realized in surprise that the one clad in black was a mundane. She'd been too scared for her life to notice before when he'd crept into her room. With the fighter's hands full of Allen's limp form, she focused her attention on her father, the greater threat. With a final jolt of horror, she spotted Morgan le Fay's journal and its translation in his hand.

She'd reached the pair, but too late. The man in black was already dragging her uncle up the attic stairs and John Faust was backing up, a dangerous glow emanating from him as he prepared for their attack.

"Well, well. Hello, my darling Lilith," he said, his smooth voice sending chills down her spine. "I must congratulate you for accomplishing what I've failed to do for twenty years: finding my dear brother."

"You bully! Leave him alone!" Lily clenched her fists, furious but unsure what to do. She couldn't rush him, and wasn't sure she had enough concentration left to send a spell after him.

"I do not suppose I should be surprised, LeFay." Madam Barrington's ice-cold voice came from behind as she moved up to stand beside Lily. Her face was tight, disgust in every line. "You have already proven yourself to be a craven, dishonorable lout of a man. Attacking and kidnapping innocents in their home in the dead of night is just what I would expect of you."

A spasm of anger flashed across her father's face, but he quickly smoothed it with a smug smile. "Insults are the weapons of small minds. Though why you're angry with me, I can't imagine. After all, if it wasn't for Lilith's help I never would have found this house." His eyes glinted maliciously as Lily's mouth opened in astonishment.

"What do you mean?" She demanded, stomach dropping like a rock.

"Why, the potion I gave you at my estate, of course. Did you think I would just let you leave without ensuring I knew your whereabouts?"

Let her leave, indeed, she thought huffily, trying to distract herself from the wave of nausea sweeping through her. She should have known he'd do something like that.

Should have looked for the spell. What a fool she was. This was all her fault.

"When you disappeared from Atlanta two nights ago, I immediately took notice. I knew that witch"—he pointed a lazy finger at Madam Barrington, who stiffened at the insult—"would seek out my brother's help. So I knew that must be where you'd gone. It was simple enough to find you with my tracking spell. He was clever to hide in plain sight. I've been to Savannah multiple times since he disappeared, walked past this building even. Never detected a trace. He really is extraordinary, you know. If only he were a bit less foolish, thinking I wouldn't find him, in the end."

"Don't you touch him," Lily said, taking a step forward without a single notion of what she would do.

"Ah, ah, ah!" John Faust warned, holding up a finger. "I don't *really* need him, you know, now that I have these." He held up the papers in his hand. "If you make trouble— such as, for instance, trying to stop me—I will, hmm, hurt him. And you, of course. And that would be such a pity. Despite your betrayal"—he spat out the word like it was a foul taste in his mouth—"you are still my daughter. My firstborn. I would hate to have to…damage you."

The menace in his voice made her heart flutter in fear. How did he have such control over her? He was nothing to her! At least, that's what she desperately told herself.

Madam Barrington put a bony hand on Lily's shoulder, drawing her back. When she spoke her voice snapped like a whip, its iron strength bolstering Lily's trembling legs. "You obviously have the upper hand, LeFay. For the moment. I suggest you turn tail and flee like the coward that you are, and hope to heaven we do not find you."

John Faust threw back his head and laughed, but it was a hollow sound. Lily could tell that Madam Barrington's words disturbed him. "Forget Allen. This is a matter between brothers and none of your business. Stay out of my affairs and I shall let you be, though by all rights I should challenge you to a duel for your insults against my family."

"You would lose," Madam Barrington said simply.

"If such a delusion comforts you, then you are welcome to it. For now, I take my leave. I warn you, do not try to follow. I will know, and I will hurt him."

Madam Barrington didn't flinch. "Are you not you forgetting something, LeFay? We have one of your own prisoner."

They didn't, actually, but Lily hoped John Faust would fall for it.

Her mentor continued. "Who is he, I wonder? Some misguided son of your peers whom you blinded with promises of adventure and reward? Which family is he from? The Johnstons? The DuPonts? Or perhaps a Blackwood? I promise you, his parents will not be pleased when we bring him home."

Her father really did laugh this time. "Your threats are as empty as your hands. Besides, he can take care of himself. Much like me." His eyes shone with pride as he boasted, and he finally started to back up, reaching for the knob of the attic door. "Remember, do not try to follow." He slammed the door shut behind him and they heard his footsteps running up the stairs.

Lily started forward, but her mentor tightened her grip on her shoulder, holding her back. "Stay, Lily. He has won this round. Lacking the element of surprise we cannot rescue Allen without risking his harm."

Legs finally giving up their effort to keep her upright, she sank to the ground, leaning against the wall. "I can't believe he got away with that," she murmured in a daze. "I should have known, should have expected. It's all my fault."

"It is nothing of the sort," Madam Barrington corrected her sternly. "If there is any blame, it is on myself. I know him better; I should have anticipated him. But that is all in the past. We should—"

She stopped abruptly at the sound of rushing paws on the hall carpet. Sir Kipling ran up, skidding to a halt and doing a quick visual check to make sure neither of them were hurt. Then he moved forward, bracing his paws on Lily shoulder as he licked her nose in concern. "The other wizard is gone. He woke up and left through the back door. I followed him outside. He helped the sword man carry Allen away. They're all gone now."

"What happened? What did he say?" Madam Barrington asked, peering down the hall suspiciously.

"They're all gone. The man we knocked out left through the back door," Lily relayed her cat's words dully. She was so tired. So very tired.

Sir Kipling stopped abusing her nose and crawled into her lap, snuggling down and purring loudly, trying to comfort her in the only way he knew how.

She'd failed. John Faust had everything: a hostage, the diary, the upper hand. How could things be any worse?

A ringing and a clicking sound behind her brought her head up, and she glanced over her shoulder. Egbert was coming down the hallway, picking his way through the ruined hand constructs, bravely holding her ringing cell phone high over his head even though the weight of it threatened to topple him. Sir Kipling bristled as the crab-spider neared, but stayed firmly in her lap. She shifted to face the little creature and took the phone dumbly, putting it to her ear.

"Lily?"

"Sebastian! Good grief, where are you? We ne—"

"Hold on, hold on! Wait a minute, Lily" he spoke over her, voice tight. He sounded more nervous than she'd ever heard him before.

Getting a grip on her raging emotions, she took a deep breath and asked, "Are you alright?"

"Um…not really. I'm, um, in federal prison, actually. I need you to get me out."

Things had just gotten worse.

Epilogue

THEY DID THEIR BEST TO RE-WARD THE HOUSE AS THEY LEFT. NOT BEING THE creators of the wards, they couldn't do it as well as Allen would have, but at least the house would be undisturbed by mundanes. They left Egbert to guard it, Madam Barrington having cast a conveyance spell on him so that they would know should something happen.

The morning light was just peeking over the moss-draped trees as they closed and locked the back door, letting the final ward settle into place behind them. The streets were still deserted, probably because it was a Sunday.

Lily moved in a distracted daze, trying to control her anxiety at the situation they were in. She wavered back and forth between worrying about what to do and trying to forget that it all existed.

Once the house was secure, Madam Barrington reached into her bag and withdrew a glass bottle of something liquid and silver. She shook it vigorously for several moments, then unstoppered it and dipped in a brush she'd also withdrawn from her bag. Lily watched in silence as her mentor painted dimmu runes on the lintel and threshold of Allen's back door in what she realized was aluminum paint. Then she quietly cast a spell that caused the air between the runes to shimmer, rippling like water before settling once more.

"Come." Madam Barrington motioned her forward. "This is a temporary portal. Take Sir Kipling and step through. The spell is linked to the Basement's entrance and you will appear there. I shall be right behind."

Too tired to be astonished or even question her mentor

about the mechanics of this unfamiliar magic, Lily gathered her cat into her arms and stepped through.

Despite how exhausted she felt, there was no time to rest. After they returned to Atlanta via the Basement, the first order of business was to get rid of John Faust's tracking spell. It wasn't a complicated process, but she had to remove her ward bracelet to do it and afterwards take copious amounts of iron salt tablets just in case any last vestiges of the spell remained. It left her feeling woozy and for several hours afterward she had trouble sensing her connection to the Source, blocked by the iron she'd ingested.

Unfortunately, the trials didn't stop there. Once home, Lily washed, changed, and headed right back out the door. Now she stood in front of a cheap apartment in College Park. She was glad it was bright daylight, because she wouldn't have had the energy to be careful had it been nighttime. College Park was not a place for the faint of heart, and she'd avoided it ever since coming to Atlanta. Sir Kipling sat at her feet—he'd flatly refused to let her out of his sight for a single moment since their return, even perching on the toilet while she'd taken her shower. Now he served as a lookout, keeping a wary eye out as his mistress did what she needed to do.

And oh, what a task lay ahead. She hesitated, finger hovering above the doorbell, reluctant to press it. Her other hand was clenched around a piece of paper with an address written on it, the only thing Sebastian had been able, or willing to tell her while on the monitored phone line at the United States Penitentiary, Atlanta.

While she was grateful to be alive, and unharmed, she cursed inwardly at the turn of events. Part of her ire was directed at her father, whom she was quickly coming to not just fear and dislike, but to hate. Yet an even greater part was directed at Sebastian. If he'd just done his part and stayed with them when they'd needed him, they wouldn't be in this mess and she wouldn't be standing here, about to do the last thing in the world she wanted to do.

Something in the back of her head tisked, reminding her that she didn't have all the facts, that surely Sebastian knew what he was doing and it was all going to work out. She ignored it. Sebastian was supposed to be there for her. He was supposed to have her back.

Wait a minute. She paused, realizing something. When had she started caring so much? She was acting like…like a…

No. She shook her head, trying to dislodge the thought. It hung on stubbornly, so she stabbed her hand forward and rang the doorbell, forcing her mind to refocus on the sound of footsteps coming down the stairs toward the door.

She felt Sir Kipling arch his back against her legs and heard him hiss softly as the door opened, revealing a petite, girlish face framed by a pixie haircut.

"Hello Tina," Lily said. "We have a job to do."

INTERLUDE

RED HANDS

One week earlier

WHILE IT CERTAINLY WASN'T BEYOND HIS ABILITY, BEING STILL HAD NEVER been one of Sebastian's favorite things to do. He was a man of action—well, words, at least, but even those required movement. Of course, he could have picked a more concealed spot further out and just used binoculars. Then he could have shifted around as much as he liked. But watching Lily through binoculars would have felt…wrong. Well, more wrong than he already felt, anyway.

Sitting with his back against the brick wall of the apartment building adjoining hers, he had to keep still for his fae glamour to work. Not being a fae himself, simply using gifted power, there was a definite limit to how effective it was. He could not turn invisible, nor completely transform his features. He *could* create a sort of shimmer that copied the pattern and color of an object behind him—

a brick wall for instance—thus camouflaging his outline. If he sat still.

At least he was in the shade, or would be for another hour. He hadn't expected to be there this long. Lily was traveling today to reunite with her family in Alabama, and he'd expected her to leave sometime that morning. Well, it was two o'clock and he was only just seeing signs of life, Lily having emerged a few minutes earlier to load her car. He wondered if she was delaying on purpose, and the thought made his lips twitch in a grin. He certainly didn't blame her. If he was supposed to go see his brother, he would "lose" his watch, then drive around in circles until he ran out of gas as far away from a gas station as possible.

His grin faded, however, as he remembered what going to see her family entailed: leaving Atlanta. Which meant he could no longer keep an eye on her. It wasn't stalking, he told himself, it was counter-stalking. A man like John Faust—powerful, obsessive, controlling—wouldn't just shrug and give up if his prey escaped. Sebastian was sure he was having his daughter followed, probably using that creepy raven thing during the day and who knew what at night.

While he had no way to drive off John Faust's spies— and his suggestion that she go into hiding had been summarily rejected—at least keeping an eye on her from afar kept him from worrying himself to death. And ensured he was on hand should Mr. Fancypants decide to show up.

Not that Lily knew he was there. If she ever found out, she would curse him halfway to next week. But her curses scared him far less than the possibility of losing her. He'd been lax once before, and look where it got him: she'd almost died. And that scared him more than anything ever had. His heart rate picked up and his muscles tensed in readiness at the mere thought of her being in danger. Suffice it to say, he hadn't been getting a lot of sleep lately.

"Merrrow murph meow meow?"

Sebastian almost jumped out of his skin. As it was he fell to the side, away from the sound, and scrambled to his feet. If anyone had been looking it would have appeared that a human-shaped section of the brick wall had just detached and started flailing.

"I swear, Kip, if you scare me like that one more time…" Sebastian glared down at the entirely unrepentant feline sitting primly next to where he'd been reclining, lost in thought.

Sir Kipling just blinked at him.

Besides wanting to head off an attempted kidnapping by John Faust, the fact that Sir Kipling knew he was following Lily was the other reason Sebastian's conscience was clear when it came to his maybe, maybe-not stalking. If the cat approved, then everything must be okay. Sebastian figured Sir Kipling was glad of the help. It was he, after all, who'd led Sebastian to Lily when she'd been held captive at the LeFay estate. Communicating with his partner in crime was sometimes challenging, but Sir Kipling always found a way to get his point across. Sebastian thought he was getting rather good at reading this impudent, devious, very protective ball of fur.

Glancing around to make sure there were no observers, Sebastian resumed his seat against the wall and gave Sir Kipling a good rub behind the ears. "Girls sure do take a while to get ready, don't they?" he observed, and Sir Kipling gave a chuff of agreement.

Sebastian assumed Sir Kipling had just come out to say hello—and wait for his mistress to get ready—and so kept his eyes on Lily's front door as he absentmindedly petted the cat, making sure to rub that favorite spot on his neck where his leather ward collar made him itch. But at a paw from Sir Kipling, he looked down and realized the crafty feline had brought him something: a slip of paper with a scribbled note on it in Lily's handwriting.

"What have you got there, you little snipe?" He picked it up and read: *Richard - Majestic - Friday at 6*

"Hmmm." He glanced at Sir Kipling for elaboration, but the cat obviously had nothing more to say. He simply stared at Sebastian with hooded yellow eyes, enigmatic as a sphinx.

Well, this was certainly interesting, Sebastian thought. Lily's familiar had just brought him the time and place of her date with Agent Doofusface. Was this simply so Sebastian could plan accordingly in his protective shadowing? Or did Sir Kipling have something more…disruptive in mind? With no sign from Sir Kipling himself, only a steady stare, Sebastian figured the decision was up to him.

"Thanks, Sir Bond. Now, go put this back before she figures out it's missing." Giving his partner a last rub, he held out the piece of paper, which Sir Kipling took gently in his mouth before trotting off and disappearing around the back corner of Lily's apartment building.

Sebastian sat in a state of turmoil. He wasn't one to make friends. Allies, certainly; partners, maybe; enemies, most definitely. But not friends. Oh, he helped people, but you didn't need to be friends with someone to help them. In fact, it was better to not be friends. Then they wouldn't get all hurt and indignant when you disappeared after helping them out of whatever mess they'd gotten into.

In his school years it had been different. He'd had a respectable little clique about him, the good-looking, popular boys who got good enough grades to not be grounded but spent most of their time looking for adventure and girls. That was, until his parents died. Everything changed after that. Everything. His so-called friends avoided him like a disease, though a few, such as Cory, stuck around out of the sheer novelty of being "friends" with an orphan.

Orphan. He hated that word. It was largely his hatred of it which had kept him from making new friends: he would have had to explain why his parents never came to school events and why he was never allowed to have parties at his house—Aunt B. was nothing if not strict and refused to allow "young miscreants" into her domicile. So, instead of explaining, he simply stopped talking. It was easier.

After school and his break with the old Bat as his guardian, he was completely on his own. A loner. A survivor. Beholden to no man. It was why he made such a good witch: he liked clear-cut deals and trades. A service for a service. None of this wishy-washy friendship that never held up when you needed it. And, of course, once any person found out he was a witch, there was no danger of friendship anyway. Mundanes feared or mocked him; witches were always suspicious he was after something of theirs, which he usually was.

Then he'd met Lily. Lillian Singer. Even her name was beautiful. And she was smart, no-nonsense, and straightforward. A little awkward, perhaps, but that just added to her charm. And she was a wizard. And she didn't seem to mind he was a witch—unheard of in the wizard community. And she put up with his shenanigans. And, and, and. A handful of years and many "ands" later, he'd finally admitted to himself that he had a friend. Well, probably more than a friend, but he couldn't let himself think about that. She was way too good for him.

Not that she made it easy to keep emotionally distant.

Every time he thought he had a handle on their relationship, she did something unexpected like giving him the benefit of the doubt when faced with suspicious circumstances. Really, who did that? People who got themselves killed, that's who, he grumbled to himself, trying not to think about how her trust in him made him feel giddy with joy.

And she *was* going to get herself killed at the rate she was going. Which was why he was counter-stalking her. She was too stubborn and independent to accept his help—something that had almost proven fatal once already. He wasn't going to let her do it again.

He had the utmost respect for her privacy and rights as an adult human being. Which was why he was *only* counter-stalking her instead of having one of his fae friends hover a foot behind her twenty-four hours a day. He was counting on Sir Kipling to take up the slack on that front. She was his friend and had stuck her neck out for him on multiple occasions. He intended to return the favor.

He told himself the fact that he couldn't keep away, couldn't stop thinking about her, couldn't keep his heart from beating faster every time he laid eyes on her had nothing to do with it. She wasn't interested in him, anyway. She was interested in Agent Doofusface.

Sebastian kept extra still as he spotted Lily emerging from her apartment for the last time. As she turned to lock the door, Sir Kipling trotted down the steps and headed for the car, not giving the slightest tail-twitch, ear-flick, or sideways glance to indicate he knew Sebastian was watching. Good for him, Sebastian thought. He's shaping up to be a real James Bond. The neighborhood lady cats had better watch out.

He waited until Lily's car had pulled out of the parking lot and headed down Ponce De Leon Avenue before standing up and letting the glamour fade. "Alright, Jas, you're up," he said to the seemingly empty air. Yet, at his words, a sort of colorful hologram fuzzed into sight in front of his eyes. He had Jas on a retainer these days. Though more temperamental and mischievous than most pixies, he was darn useful. The little guy was so enamored with light and sound waves that he didn't appear to even have a corporeal form anymore and could mimic any wave desired, creating illusions and noises at will. Having the little squirt on call was costing him a fortune in alcohol—the preferred payment of most pixies—but it was worth it.

"Remember, you're supposed to observe only. Stay as far away as you can and notify me immediately if anything happens. Well, go on," he urged the quivering hologram, waving a hand in the direction of Lily's disappearing car. Jas faded from view and, he assumed, zipped off after his friend.

Sebastian had work to do in the city, or else he'd be following Lily himself. The open road was a dangerous place and the perfect opportunity for John Faust to lay a trap, if he wanted to. Sir Kipling was a formidable foe but wouldn't be enough if he and Lily were ambushed. Jas was a precaution. If something happened, he could report back to Sebastian in an instant. Time and distance meant little to the fae, especially one who could manipulate light waves.

Stiff from hours of sitting, Sebastian suppressed a groan as he stretched and limbered up his muscles. Feeling better, he headed across the apartment complex to where he'd hidden his car, mentally going over the things he needed to get done that weekend while Lily was gone.

Top priority was to get back with Tina to see what else she'd dug up on Rex Morganson. He knew in his gut that Rex and John Faust were one and the same, and he didn't intend to let that sorry excuse for a human being take another swipe at Lily. If he could just find something to connect the two, he could sic the FBI on Mr. Fancypants's fancy pants faster than you could say "you need a new wardrobe." The FBI were awfully interested in Rex, so it shouldn't be too hard. He had a few other contacts to touch base with as well. It was going to be a busy weekend.

It turned out to be not only busy, but stressful. Not the least because he couldn't stop worrying about Lily. But then Monday came around, Lily was back home safe from her family's house, and he could resume his counter-stalking with a sigh of relief. It wasn't as if he had to follow her everywhere. She was relatively safe at McCain Library, and of course at Aunt B's. Even her house was acceptably secure after she redid the wards following her "adventures" at the LeFay estate. It was just in between that made him nervous. However, her love of routine and keeping to a schedule worked in his favor, and he had time to slip away and take care of the few odd jobs and spur-of-the-moment clients, which kept food on his table and gas in his tank. The hardest part was Tina, who, when she wanted you for something, wanted you *now*. As in, yesterday.

Frustratingly, she had not made much progress when he'd checked in with her over the weekend. She was supposed to be tracking down Rex Morganson's criminal records and any information the FBI had on him. He didn't ask her how she did it. He didn't want to know. All he wanted was to know everything possible about Rex's movements and activities so he could try to match that with what he knew of John Faust. So far, however, they hadn't had much luck.

It wasn't until Thursday morning that Tina finally

found something useful, and she'd wanted to show him in person. In reality, she probably just wanted him around as a punching bag for her poltergeist, but hey, appreciation was appreciation.

He rang the doorbell to her apartment and then quickly stepped to the side, narrowly avoiding the egg Percy had just dropped from the second-story window. It splatted on the doorstep and he grinned to himself. He was learning.

Tina glared at the spot when she came to open the door and muttered a few choice words under her breath. Sebastian hoped that meant she would tell Percy off but doubted he would get that lucky. "Come on," she said, gesturing curtly up the steep stairs before mounting them herself. He followed, judiciously not looking up at her ascending backside as he climbed.

Upon reaching the apartment, Sebastian ducked as he went inside, just in case. Nothing happened, and he made it into the living room safely. If only he could see the darn poltergeist, that would be half the battle won. At least anything Percy picked up remained visible, so if he saw a pillow floating through the air at him—

He ducked.

The pillow narrowly missed one of Tina's prized lava lamps, and Sebastian swore inwardly in disappointment. So close.

Percy must have realized what a narrow miss that had been, because the mischief-maker dropped the pillow and the apartment went still. There was a limit to how much he could get away with inside the apartment, and he knew it. As Sebastian turned to survey the living room—currently buried under a mess of papers strewn over couch and floor—he heard glass breaking in the kitchen. Tina drank enough beer and soda to kill an elephant, and Percy was allowed to smash the bottles on the kitchen floor instead of wrecking other, more important things. Sebastian wondered who cleaned up the glass—Percy or Tina.

"So, what's all this?" he asked, ignoring the crashing sounds coming from the kitchen.

Tina, perched on the one clear spot in the middle of the couch, grinned. "This is me earning my keep, loverboy. I finally got my hands on the FBI files. Your Rex Morganson is a busy man."

Sebastian's eyes lit up, and he grabbed the nearest piece of paper. "Excellent! Have you read them all yet?"

"Who do you think I am, your deputy? Our deal was for me to find it, not analyze it. I've just been scanning the juicy bits. You never know when you might need to blackmail someone." She winked.

"Actually," Sebastian replied, looking up from the paper he was reading, "our deal was to help me get evidence against Rex so the FBI could arrest him. You don't get the coin until we have that evidence. So I suggest you start reading a bit more thoroughly."

"Yeah, yeah, whatever." Tina rolled her eyes and stuck out her tongue but then bent back over the papers.

Sebastian settled in and they spent hours reading, only breaking the silence to mention anything useful they'd found. Takeout was ordered, delivered, and consumed. Percy was yelled at multiple times for distracting them—Sebastian's favorite bit. Usually Tina let her poltergeist have his way, but she seemed especially dedicated to this job. Possibly because his truth coin was the promised payment.

He didn't actually intend to give it to her, of course. It was a family heirloom, given to him by his father. But Tina hadn't been interested in money, and he'd made it clear her other payment preference wasn't an option. He hadn't known how else to get her to help. If he was lucky, by the time they were finished she'd let him talk her into taking money instead. Or, as a last resort, perhaps Lily could find someone to reproduce the coin. It was a gamble, but sometimes you had to take risks.

Midafternoon had come and gone before they finally felt like they had a grasp on the whole file. After gathering up the papers, they collapsed on the couch to compare notes. Tina, beer in hand, blew a bit of wayward bangs out of her eyes. "This Rex guy is a slippery fish. I can't believe in all of this mess they don't have a single solid piece of evidence against him. All that work and the FBI are just chasing hunches. And who is this LeFay guy?"

Sebastian nursed his coke, alternating between sipping it and holding it to his forehead. All that reading had given him a headache. Lily would laugh if she saw him. She'd call him a lightweight. "It's not all that bad. I'd hoped for something a bit more solid on Rex, but he's a professional. Why do you think he uses people like Anton? It's so they can't peg this stuff on him in a court of law. They can have suspicions, but they can't prove it."

The next part was tricky. He wanted to protect Lily's privacy as much as possible from someone as nosy as Tina, but it would be hard, what with her name staring up at him from a file on top of the pile. "I think we can conclude that the LeFay guy is who they think is behind the Rex Morganson alias," he said carefully, addressing her question.

He kept his expression neutral, but inside he was nervous. Originally, he'd hoped to gain some points with the FBI by pointing them in John Faust's direction. But that was down the toilet, since they already had their own suspicions. More disturbing, however, was that they'd somehow connected Lily to it all. How in the world they'd done that, he had no idea. He thought it might be due to the missing child report for Lilith LeFay, filed about twenty-three years ago by one Ursula LeFay. Sebastian suspected it was filed without John Faust's knowledge. He didn't seem like the kind of guy to go to the police about anything. So why had Ursula done it? Desperation, perhaps?

But that wasn't all. Also in the file were nine other missing children reports, dated from twenty to about three years ago. All of them followed a similar pattern: the father of the child was unknown; the report had been filed by a concerned relative, not by the mother; the mother could give no information about the circumstances of the disappearance, nor had she told any of her relatives who the father had been.

It was bizarre. You would think the mothers would have been desperate to find their children. But in every single one of the interview reports, the women seemed to suffer from some sort of amnesia, most likely brought on by the trauma of their loss. At least, that's what the psych report said.

The important question was, why in the world did the FBI think John Faust was connected to a slew of child disappearances? Was it just because of the similarity between his case and the rest? Or did they think he was responsible?

Judging by the confused crease on Tina's forehead, she had just as many questions as he did. "But why, though? Why do they think it's the same guy? That's the part I don't get," Tina complained.

"Well," Sebastian began, but was interrupted by a muffled ring coming from underneath him. He ignored it, but instead of giving up, the person called back, setting off another round of rings.

Tina rolled her eyes impatiently. "You gonna do something about that?"

"Nah, they'll leave a message. So, remember the memo

talking about how they'd found illegal activity tied to Rex Morganson—" he began, but was soon interrupted by more ringing. Apparently someone very much wanted to talk to him.

"Hurry up and answer it before your butt rings off," Tina said, glaring in annoyance, "and tell them to go jump in a lake, we're busy."

Digging underneath him, Sebastian extracted his phone from his back pocket, checking the caller ID. Uh-oh. It was Lily.

"Just hurry up, will you?" Tina said. Sebastian could have sworn he felt Percy perk up, perhaps hoping Tina's annoyance would translate into an excuse for him to abuse the guest.

"Just gimme a second, okay? Sheesh—hey, sorry, is this quick? I'm kinda in the middle of something." He tried to keep his tone light, though his heart was pounding as it always did these days whenever he interacted with Lily.

"Well, if it's not of vital importance, I suggest you bring your 'something' to a swift conclusion. Madam Barrington and I are meeting in the Basement to discuss a certain odious wizard and how we're going to foil his nefarious plans. You should be there when we do."

Well, that certainly sounded fun. Minus the Aunt B. part. He couldn't help but grin at the thought of them sitting down to a powwow together. "My, my, my, Lily. Are you actually *encouraging* me to stray onto your precious campus? I thought I'd never live to see the day."

"Men are technically allowed on campus as long as they're accompanied by a chaperone. You just never bother with that," Lily retorted, making him grin even wider.

"That's because my sterling reputation is all the chaperone I'll ever need."

Lily snorted, which made him want to make another joke, but he caught sight of Tina's impatient glare and got to the point. "I agree, I should be there. But what I'm doing now is pretty important, too. Can we meet later?"

"No, we can't," came her brusque reply. "And what could be more important than figuring out how to fight John Faust?"

Well, so much for that, he thought. "The supreme art of war is to subdue the enemy without fighting," he quipped, hoping it would throw her off enough that she would forget to press for details about exactly what he was doing.

"What's that supposed to mean?" she demanded, sounding annoyed.

"Weeell," he hesitated, pretending to take her question literally. "It's kind of obvious, you know, win without having to—"

"No, no. I meant, what are you *doing*? What in the world would subdue John Faust?"

"Uhhh…" His mind raced, looking for a way to delay the inevitable. "I'll tell you about it later. Let me wrap up what we're doing here and I'll—"

"We?" Lily demanded sharply.

Uh-oh. He cursed silently. Now he'd done it. He proceeded as nonchalantly as he could manage. "Yeah. We. Tina is helping me dig up some…well, she's helping me out."

"I knew it! You shouldn't associate with that witch, Sebastian. She's a disaster waiting to happen. I mean, not that you aren't your own disaster in the making, but you should be surrounded by sound judgment, not someone who will compound your foolishness."

Well, that was about as bad as he'd been expecting. She was in full bossy form now. What he couldn't figure out was, if she'd accepted him for who he was, why couldn't she do the same for Tina? It was when she got all high and mighty like this that he remembered why he'd avoided having friends all these years. No matter, two could play that game. "Foolishness, huh? Foolish, like running off to the private compound of a suspicious stranger who's already threatened you once? That kind of foolishness?"

He'd had to pick his words carefully, what with Tina listening in. But based on her abrupt silence, his words had found their mark. Perhaps too well. "Look, never mind," he said into the lengthening silence. "I'll come. Just give me twenty minutes."

"Fine," she said, tone clipped.

He massaged his temples, trying to figure out how to salvage the conversation. It had not gone at all how he'd hoped. "See you then, I guess."

"Good day," she said, and hung up.

He stared at his phone, expression morose. Well, that had been a disaster.

"Lovers' quarrel?" Tina asked, eyebrow raised in interest.

Sebastian's stomach did a somersault at the mere idea of such a word being associated with Lily. "Nah," he waved a hand casually, hoping to deflect her curiosity. Which was completely unfounded, of course. "Just one of my other contacts. They've got some stuff for me, so we really do need to wrap up. So, where was I…right." He collected his thoughts and hurried on.

"Remember that memo? The one about how they'd found illegal activity tied to Rex Morganson popping up in each city *two years* before a kid went missing? And how each of the kids went missing at *two years old*? This LeFay guy was the first one whose two-year-old, well almost two, went missing under the same suspicious circumstances. And then, none of the women could tell the police who the father was. There was no father listed on the children's birth certificates. The mothers could only give a physical description, no name. But the physical descriptions from every woman were very similar, and they matched this LeFay guy. You have to admit, that's pretty suspicious."

Tina was still looking at him oddly, but she seemed willing to get back into the debate. "So, what, this dude is going around getting women pregnant and then kidnapping the kids? That's crazy. I could see a disgruntled dad kidnapping his kid if the mom was trying to lock him out of the picture. But for the same guy to do it nine times? What the heck is he doing with them all? Making a circus troupe? That theory is just crazy. Even if it wasn't, Rex's profile is all extortion and theft. What does that have to do with kids? No wonder the FBI is getting nowhere with this investigation. Whoever's running it is a raving lunatic."

Sebastian didn't agree, but that was because he knew things about John Faust that Tina didn't. And he wasn't about to share them. So instead of disagreeing, he changed tack. "Okay, forget about all the other stuff on Rex. There's no way we can prove he was behind any of it. Instead, let's suppose that Morganson *is* LeFay, and he's somehow involved in the disappearance of the kids. Doesn't it seem suspicious that none of the women could remember anything? If it was just one, I might agree with the shrinks. But all nine? That sounds like magic to me, some kind of mind-control spell or brainwashing. What if we found one of these women? We could interview them and figure out how to break the spell. If we could record a full confession, we'd have solid evidence."

Tina looked skeptical. "That is, *if* there actually is a connection and *if* there is even magic involved. I think the

FBI has its head up its butt on this one. None of this makes sense."

"Well," Sebastian hesitated, not sure how much he should say. "Maybe there's more to the story," he hedged. "It's worth at least trying to track down one of these women, right? We could start with the most recent disappearance. Her contact info is probably still good."

With a sigh, Tina slumped down even further into the couch, taking a swig of beer. "Fine. But not until tomorrow. I think I've worked enough today."

"Tomorrow, then," Sebastian said, getting up and collecting his things. "But no later. We need to move fast on this. Call me as soon as you have something, okay?"

"Sure thing, *boss*," she said, voice dripping with sarcasm. "For someone who enjoys meddling in the affairs of wizards, you sure are a boring person. Work, work, work, all the time. Positive you don't wanna stay and hang out for a while?" She winked suggestively, patting the couch beside her.

"Ah, no. No, thanks."

She looked disappointed but not surprised, and he beat a hasty retreat before she, or Percy, could think of any way to delay him further.

Sebastian was not in his normal counter-stalking spot, mostly because he made a point to stay as far away from badges as possible. Not that he had anything against them. They were a vital part of society. Sort of like dung beetles. If you didn't have them around, the dung would pile up and destroy the world. But that didn't mean he wanted to get caught up in their "cleaning" activities. So that Friday evening, instead of hanging out one apartment building over, he watched Lily's doorstep through a pair of binoculars, sitting in his car a block down the road.

He'd been prepared, albeit with no small amount of subconscious grumbling, to stay out of the way when it came to Lily's choice in men. It wasn't any of his business, after all. None at all. Zip. No matter how protective he felt, it wasn't his place. Okay, so he'd allowed himself a few jokes here and there—what kind of friend would he be if he didn't?—but he had strictly forbidden himself from interfering. Not even when she'd chosen to take up with Agent Doofusface.

What he was doing now, he told himself, wasn't interfering. It was following up on a hunch. If he was right, *then* he would interfere, for Lily's own safety. Now that he thought about it, the list of what he'd done—and was doing—for her safety was growing uncomfortably long. Most of them were things that annoyed her, like not telling her everything she wanted to know, or things that *would* annoy her if she knew, like his counter-stalking. Thank goodness he'd dodged the "Thiriel" bullet, at least for now. He'd learned all too well in his short life that ignorance really was bliss. But Lily would never see it that way. At least their "powwow" last night in the Basement had been informative. And, surprisingly, his aunt had shown him a bit of respect for the first time since he was a teenager. He'd long since stopped caring what she thought, but still, it was nice.

The arrival of Richard Grant's car put an end to his musings, and he watched as the agent ascended Lily's front steps and rang the doorbell. What she saw in that self-righteous, unimaginative, hunk of dung beetle he had no idea. Seriously, roses? Any guy with two brain cells would know to bring Lily a book, not flowers. And if you just *had* to be traditional, at least pick flowers with some character, like daffodils.

Watching the exchange through his binoculars, he saw the FBI agent gesture inside as Lily held the roses and blushed. He couldn't hear her reply—he'd resisted the temptation to have Jas relay the conversation—but it was obvious she'd rebuffed her date's attempt to get inside, instead taking his arm as they headed to the car. Good girl, he thought. At least she had *some* common sense.

As Richard's car pulled away, Sebastian set down his binoculars and waited. He knew where they were going, so there was no rush, and he wasn't stupid enough to try and tail an FBI agent. Not that they were all that observant, the average badge. But there were good ones out there, and Sebastian hadn't seen enough of this particular one to know which he was. Better safe than sorry, that's what he always said. Well, sometimes. Occasionally. In this particular instance.

After giving them a good five-minute head start, he pulled out of his parking space and headed toward the Majestic Diner, mind busy as he mulled over his plan. Yes, he'd intended to keep his nose out of Lily's private life. But that was before he'd learned the FBI had an open investigation on Lily's father, and they knew she was his daughter. The daughter Ursula LeFay had filed a missing person's report on twenty-three years ago. Tonight Sebastian planned to kill two birds with one stone. Well, three, actually, if his hunch was correct.

Parking in a lot across the street, he carefully scanned the diner through his binoculars, hoping he could spot them from where he sat instead of having to creep closer. Lily would roast him alive if she caught him. And he would deserve it. But his well-being, and her feelings, were unimportant when it came to keeping her safe.

Examining the far end of the diner, he hit pay dirt. They were sitting by the mirrored wall, talking animatedly. He waited a few more minutes, giving them a chance to order. Technically, there was no need to delay, but he hesitated anyway, feeling guilty for ruining Lily's date. Despite the fact that he'd like to punch Mr. Doofusface in the face, he knew how hard it was for Lily to muster the courage to voluntarily engage in social activities. It seemed a shame to waste all her hard work. Then again, perhaps it was better not to draw it out.

Sebastian withdrew a recently purchased pre-paid phone from his pocket and dialed the number for the local FBI field office. He ground his teeth as he waited for the automated system to finish telling him his options. It finally shut up and transferred him to the operator, much to his relief.

"FBI."

Pitching his voice low and giving it a gravelly tone, he said: "I've got information on Rex Morganson. I want to talk to the agent in charge of the case."

"Excuse me, sir, who? And what did you say your name was?"

"I didn't. Tell your superiors that I have critical, time-sensitive information on Rex Morganson in connection to John Faust LeFay and that I want to talk to the agent in charge of the case, ASAP."

"Alright," the operator said over the sound of rapid typing. "Is there a number where they can reach you?"

"No. I want to meet them in person, tonight, at"—he glanced at his watch, which read 6:20—"seven o'clock, sharp. Tell them to come alone. I'll be in the abandoned warehouse off Alders avenue," he said, naming a location in south Atlanta.

"Sir, I don't think—"

"Just tell them. They're looking for evidence and I can give it to them. Seven o'clock. Do it," he finished, and hung up. Taking the back off the cell phone, he removed the important bits and set it all in the seat beside him. He'd wipe them down and dispose of them on the way to the meet. Picking up his binoculars, he refocused them on Lily and her date. Give it about five minutes, he thought, for the operator to pass the information up to someone senior enough to know what it meant. Then, if he was right...

Sure enough, after about five minutes Agent Grant shifted, taking out his phone as he stood and turned his back to Lily.

Sebastian punched the air in triumph. He'd called it. Three birds. One stone.

Going back to his binoculars, he saw that Agent Grant had disappeared, leaving only a forlorn-looking Lily. Scanning the restaurant, he just caught sight of the man disappearing out the front door, phone back to his ear as he headed for his car.

Well, that was his cue to skedaddle, Sebastian thought. He started up his old clunker and headed out a different entrance, avoiding Ponce De Leon Avenue. It would take about fifteen minutes, perhaps longer, to get to the meeting place, and he wanted to get there before the cavalry arrived.

The abandoned warehouse was nothing special, just one of the many places in Atlanta that had fallen into disrepair for various reasons: money, pollution, changing demographic, or just the inexorable march of time. It was a popular hangout for kids who liked the thrill of trespassing, and graffiti artists had had their way with it for many years. The surrounding fence and boarded-up windows were in such a state of decay that it wasn't an issue of "breaking and entering." More like "walking in and trying not to stab yourself with broken glass." From his previous forays into the abandoned structure, he knew there was a door off its hinges around the back that made for the easiest entry. He parked several blocks away and sprinted along the back alleys until he got to the derelict fence. Slipping through, he entered the building from the back and set up camp next to one of the front windows where he could see out but not be seen from the outside.

He'd shunned a more public location because his backup didn't like crowds. Despite the fact that Pip was perfectly capable of using fae glamour to hide from the human eye, she still didn't like being around people in general. Sebastian didn't blame her. He wasn't a big fan of people in general, either. In an abandoned place like this, she would be perfectly comfortable. Speaking of Pip…

"*Elwa Pilanti'ara*. You ready?"

He waited, finally hearing a tinkling laugh off to his left. Despite the sound, there was still no sign of her. Darn that pixie. "Look, Pip, this isn't the time for games. Men are going to show up any minute. Now get over here."

Another tinkling, high-pitched laugh, this time behind him.

Grumbling about pixies who didn't understand the concept of "urgent," he crossed his arms, adopting a casual tone. Yelling or getting upset at fae got you nowhere. It just egged them on. You had to know how to push their buttons. "So I guess this means you didn't want that glass of Captain Morgan's Pirate Paradise I was going to make you, huh?" He waited. No tinkling laugh. Pixies were especially fond of mixed drinks, as they couldn't make them themselves, and rum was Pip's weak spot. This particular drink was a mix of elderflower liqueur, coconut water, rum, syrup, and lime juice. He was rather partial to it himself. It was an exquisite drink.

A tug on his ear told him he'd won. "Uh-huh, I thought so," he said to the little slip of a fae hovering at eye level.

She squeaked at him.

"Two? In your dreams. That's extortion, that is."

Tiny arms crossed, a minuscule nub of a nose pointed in the air.

"Alright, fine, you little rascal," he said. "But I have to go somewhere tonight and I may be away a few days. You'll have to wait until next week to get payment."

Pip squeaked in agreement and did several loop-de-loops in excited anticipation.

"Yeah, yeah. Calm down, short stock. Here's what I need you to do." He explained the situation, and she nodded in understanding. It was a cakewalk for her, and nowhere near worth the price of two mixed drinks. But he had a soft spot for Pip and usually let her get away with her extortionist deals. All she had to do was keep watch, make sure no one snuck up on him, and distract the cops if he needed to make a quick getaway. Hopefully none of that would be needed, but he'd been in the game far too long to not plan for the worst.

He settled in to wait as Pip cloaked herself and zipped off to scout the perimeter. They didn't have to wait long. Barely ten minutes had passed before an unmarked yet unmistakably government sedan pulled up in front of the building. Two people stepped out: Agent Grant, accompanied by his partner, Agent Meyers. Sebastian had seen them both for the first time at the Clay Museum when they'd arrived after the fiasco with Veronica. Though they hadn't spoken directly to him, they would probably still recognize his face. Which was why he wasn't wearing his normal face. While he didn't have strong enough fae magic to completely change his appearance, he could subtly alter features, and that was all he needed in a situation like this. He'd worn a baggy shirt and pants to obscure his physical build. A touch of fae magic and his face appeared to morph, brows thickening, chin sharpening, skin sagging in wrinkles on a thin face below dark hair now shot through with grey. He made sure his hands appeared as wrinkled as his face and stooped slightly for added effect. As a last precaution, he changed the color of his clothes.

Since he was playing the part of a nervous informant, he hid behind a stack of old boxes off to one side, waiting patiently as the two FBI agents checked out the front of the building. Most likely backup wasn't far away, ready to swoop in should this turn out to be a trap. It wasn't, of course, but the FBI didn't know that.

As the two agents moved toward the front door, he felt a double tug on his ear, Pip's signal that the perimeter was clear. At least they'd had the sense to not try and jump him. That was a bad way to build trust. Of course, he hadn't given them any time to set up surveillance on the building. Otherwise they'd have had the building bugged long before he arrived.

Agent Grant took point, stepping cautiously up to examine the front door outfitted with bar and lock. Of course, the fact that the bar was hanging off the door, unattached to the surrounding building, made the security measure kind of moot. Agent Meyer peered in the front windows and, seeing no one, gave her partner the go-ahead. She kept watch while Agent Grant pushed and cursed at the door—exactly the reason why Sebastian had come in the back. Rusted hinges did as good a job as locks at keeping people out.

The two FBI agents finally got the door open, both, he was sure, unhappy at the amount of noise they'd made in the process. Looking wary, they peered around the unlit room, bright evening sun outside making it hard to see in the cool dimness. Well, Sebastian thought, I'm up.

"Good evening," Sebastian said calmly, stepping away from the boxes with his hands held unthreateningly out to the sides. The last thing he wanted was to get shot by a startled FBI agent.

Predictably, both agents jumped, surprised. Agent Meyer's hand even went to her holster. But seeing him alone, unthreatening and unarmed, they relaxed. "You the one who called?" Agent Grant asked, approaching.

"I am."

"Good. I'm Agent Grant. I'm spearheading the investigation into our mutual friend. You wanted to talk, Mr…."

Sebastian ignored the question and stepped closer, making sure to keep his back bent and his voice soft and wavering. "I asked to speak with the head of the investigation. Alone."

The two agents looked at each other, probably sharing some nonverbal communication built over years of partnership.

This was taking too long. Sebastian needed to get home to prepare for their hunt tonight with his aunt and Lily. He didn't like this man, with his perfect hair and calm eyes hiding lies behind them. But he had a job to do, so best be about it. "You can pat me down if it helps. I came to pass on information, nothing more. But I will only talk to you." He pointed at Agent Grant, then took another step forward and raised his arms above his head, inviting the agent to check him for weapons.

Agent Grant nodded at his partner, who kept a watchful eye out while he approached and patted Sebastian down. He found nothing, of course, but a large silver coin in Sebastian's right pocket. Satisfied, he stepped back.

"Pardon the precautions. Our mutual friend has proven more dangerous than we expected and people have gotten hurt trying to help us."

"Understood. Now, if you please..." Sebastian waved dismissively at Agent Meyer. She looked annoyed, but, at a nod from her partner, stepped back, going to cover the front door.

Sebastian beckoned Agent Grant closer, lowering his voice even more and choosing his words carefully. "You are investigating the connection between elusive criminal Rex Morganson and upstanding citizen John Faust LeFay, correct?"

Agent Grant nodded, expression carefully controlled to hide any surprise he felt at Sebastian's knowledge.

"I can assure you, they are the same man. I heard Mr. LeFay himself admit to perpetrating several local crimes under the guise of Rex Morganson." That was a lie, but Sebastian wasn't about to give them more reasons to bother Lily, the person who'd actually heard John Faust admit such things.

"Really? When and where was this? Give me details." Agent Grant got out a notepad and pen, poised for writing, though Sebastian assumed he was miked and had agents listening in down the block in some unmarked van.

"I most certainly shall not," Sebastian hissed, making his hands and voice shake even more. "My life would be forfeit. I simply wanted to assure you that your suspicions were correct."

Agent Grant gave a little sigh. "Sir, I appreciate you

risking yourself to tell me this, but you said on the phone that you had critical evidence. Your hearsay, especially if you're not willing to give details and testify in court, doesn't do us a shred of good."

"Well, you certainly are a young whippersnapper if I do say so myself!" Sebastian grumbled, adding in a huff or two for good measure. "Positively ungrateful."

The FBI agent opened his mouth, but Sebastian raised a gnarled-looking hand, cutting him off. "Never mind, young man. I am simply frustrated, you see. My position is precarious. I am, however, committed to the cause of justice. I will get you evidence. Oh yes, such evidence it will be. But on one condition only."

That got him a suspicious look, but Agent Grant nodded. "Go on."

"You must leave Mr. LeFay's daughter completely out of your investigation. Your nosing about is endangering her life. Her father watches her, I'm sure. Who knows what retribution he will carry out, what with you canoodling up to her like you are." He glared sternly at Agent Grant who looked away, carefully controlled face showing a flash of guilt.

But it was only a flash. He masked his movements by pretending to jot down a few notes, then looked back up at Sebastian. "I can't comment, nor make any promises on behalf of the FBI regarding whoever you think you're talking about. This is an ongoing criminal investigation and we can't exclude anyone from it. I promise you, however, that we take the utmost care in ensuring all our sources and witnesses are protected." He gave Sebastian a significant look. "If this hypothetical daughter were in any danger, we would provide protection. But to do that, she would have to come forward and tell us *everything* she knows. We can't protect someone we don't know about."

That. Bastard. Sebastian thought, forcing his jaw to relax lest he clench his teeth and give away his anger. This little pipsqueak knew exactly what he was talking about, but was playing dumb to try and squeeze him for more information. And, based on the warmth of the truth coin in his pocket, the FBI may or may not be as committed to protecting witnesses as Agent Grant claimed.

"I am disappointed that is how things must be," he said coldly, stepping back a pace and giving the agent his best haughty look. "I had thought our law enforcement would be committed to protecting the innocent and bringing the guilty to justice. I see I was mistaken." He began to turn, as if to walk away, but Agent Grant caught his sleeve, holding him back.

Glancing behind him at his partner, he drew closer and whispered to Sebastian, "Look, mister, I don't know who you are or if anything you're telling me is true. But you're wrong. I *do* want to see this man brought to justice, and…his daughter protected in the process. But you've got to give me something to go on. I can't just blindly trust every loon who calls in a tip. Most are high or delusional or making things up to get a reward."

Sebastian's jaw muscles loosened a bit, noticing that his coin remained cool. He had to give the man credit: he did seem to care, even if he acted like a git in the process. Heck, what did he know about being an FBI agent? It couldn't be easy. "Very well," he said slowly, then paused, giving the agent plenty of time to sweat. "I will see what more I can acquire for you. I shall be in touch."

The FBI agent seemed to want more but finally released Sebastian's sleeve, reaching into his own pocket and drawing out a business card with his cell number on it. "Call me directly this time. The sooner, the better."

"I will do what I can," Sebastian replied, pocketing the card and stepping back. "I think I shall wait here while you leave. Until we meet again, Agent Grant." He gave the man a curt nod and stood, waiting.

The man didn't look happy, but he nodded and turned to leave, muttering some words to his partner as he passed. They both exited the building.

"Pip," Sebastian whispered out of the side of his mouth, "Follow them and make sure they leave, then come back and get me. We'll go out the back."

He felt the wind of her wings as she zipped past him, invisible to the normal eye. While he waited for her return, he reviewed the conversation, thinking about where he stood. It had gone about as well as he could have expected. He hadn't *actually* had evidence—nothing that would hold up in court anyway—to give the FBI agent, he'd just wanted to establish contact, confirm his suspicions, and gauge the man's reactions.

Hopefully, though, things would soon change. If Tina could track down one of the women whose children went missing, they could find out if Mr. Fancypants had indeed used a spell to hide his involvement. The trick would be gathering evidence that framed the slimeball without revealing the magic involved. Not out of a fear that mundanes would discover magic—they'd been ignoring what was right in front of their noses for decades already—but because no judge would believe it. They would throw it out on principle.

Well, he couldn't worry about that just now. He had to get home and prepare to track down a reclusive wizard who absolutely, positively did not want to be found.

* * *

Lily really *was* going to kill him now. He couldn't believe Tina had insisted he come right away. It was as if she knew how much trouble it would get him in. But he'd started this thing, so he had to finish it. And Tina had a point: The sooner, the better.

But the look in Lily's eyes when he'd had to leave…she thought he was abandoning her on a whim and being irresponsible, unreliable. It wasn't like that, of course. But he could only hope Lily would understand once he had a chance to explain himself. Which wouldn't be anytime soon. Not until he had proof of his suspicions. Dagnabbit. He really did have himself in a pickle this time.

Yet, all he could do was move forward. He'd already sent Jas back to Savannah to keep an eye on things, though he felt sure Lily would be safe in Aunt Barrington's company. That old bat was a force to be reckoned with. He had to focus on the task ahead: meeting up with Tina so they could go talk to the woman she'd tracked down. He couldn't imagine the lady would be eager to speak to them on a Saturday morning, but Tina had been in no mood to argue. No point in stressing an already tenuous alliance.

Foot to the gas pedal, he pushed his old junk-heap of a car as fast as it could go—an impressive fifty-five miles per hour—roaring down the street in a cloud of exhaust. Several newer cars passed him easily, ruining the brief image he had of himself racing to the rescue in a sleek, sexy ride. Ah, well. You couldn't always be both fashionable and effective, though he suspected Lily would disagree.

It turned out that Tina was in a rush because the woman she'd found, Heather Foster, lived down south in Valdosta, Georgia, a good three and a half hours away. They carpooled from her house, taking her car because she threatened to strangle him if they had to drive at fifty-five miles per hour the whole way.

On the way, they argued about whether or not to call first. Sebastian thought it would be odd to just show up on her doorstep, and she might be more inclined to help if they had the courtesy to call ahead. Tina thought it would just give her more of a chance to turn them away. Plus, what if she were being watched? Calling ahead would give the watchers—whether John Faust or the FBI—advance warning of their plans. Eventually, Tina won the argument.

Sebastian had never been to Valdosta before. It was a good-sized city, with its own mall, university, manufacturing plants, the works. But they weren't there to sightsee. They followed Highway 75 down toward the southern end of town—the poorer end—getting off and paralleling some railroad tracks as they searched for Heather Foster's address. It led them to a small neighborhood bordering a train yard, its narrow, shotgun-style houses in various states of disrepair. Some were lovingly patched and maintained, while others were obviously vacant, with boarded-up windows and tall grass out front. A few children played in the streets, though they stopped to stare as Tina drove slowly by, counting the numbers on the houses.

"Here it is," she said, stopping the car and pointing out the window at one of the nicer-looking houses on the block. Though the paint was chipped and fading, the porch steps had been recently replaced and a small garden out front showed the owner went to pains to keep her domicile looking cheerful.

They parked and locked the car, heading up the steps to the front door. On the way down from Atlanta they'd agreed that Tina should take point. Being small, cute, and female, she would appear less threatening. Both wore nicer-looking clothes than they usually preferred—they were pretending to be reporters for an Atlanta newspaper—and

Tina carried a small, hand-held camcorder. To that, Sebastian had made her add a pocket-sized audio recorder, which she had, already recording, in her handbag. To his great relief, she'd made Percy stay home for this, though she grumbled about the state her house would be in when she returned.

Sebastian stood back, one foot on the porch and one on the first step, as Tina rang the doorbell. She pasted a welcoming smile on her face, looking as bright and cute as she had the first time he'd met her. He had to smother a smile at the thought, remembering how flustered Lily had been at their exchange. He hadn't dared read into her reaction—alright, he admitted, hadn't been *brave* enough to read into it—yet he thought it might have been jealousy. Which was, of course, why he'd shown interest in Tina in the first place, to provoke a reaction. Okay, so maybe that hadn't been the *only* reason, but he'd figured out pretty quickly that Tina wasn't his type. Maybe if he'd met her a decade ago…no, he wasn't that person any more. In any case, that had all been before Mr. Fancypants had entered the scene and kidnapped his best friend. Ever since then he couldn't stop thinking—and worrying—about Lily.

The scrape of an opening door reminded Sebastian to focus, and he quickly tucked away his speculations and smiled politely as a woman in her late twenties or early thirties appeared behind the still-closed screen door. Her clothes were worn, but clean, and she wore no jewelry except a shining silver locket on a thin chain around her neck. Her face looked middle-aged, but she already had a few grey streaks in her dark hair. She stood slightly hunched with arms wrapped around herself as if literally holding herself together.

"Can I help you?" She asked, polite but uncertain.

"Good afternoon ma'am," Tina greeted her smoothly. Sebastian was surprised at the mix of genuine concern and professionalism in her voice. Apparently she was better at this game than he thought. "My name is Stella Smith and this is my colleague Frankie Overton. We're from the Atlanta Daily doing an exposé on the problem of child disappearances and the FBI's lack of attention to these very serious cases. You filed a missing person report for your two-year-old son five years ago and no progress has been made on the investigation. We were hoping you could give us a few brief moments of your time to discuss how you feel about this." She stopped there, giving the woman time to think.

Sebastian watched Heather Foster's face closely, trying to see her expression through the screen door. She hadn't closed the door on their faces—a good sign—but she still seemed hesitant. Time for a little persuasion.

"Ma'am," he said softly, tenderly. "I can't imagine how painful it must be to bring up these awful memories. I'm sure you've already been through hell and just want to be left alone. But we're committed to helping you find your son, and we really think this article will put a fire under the FBI's collective posterior. It's going to make a difference. But we can't do it without you. Will you please help us? For your son's sake?"

His plea did the trick, and he had to push down a stab of guilt at the flicker of hope that crossed Heather's face. What they were doing *would* help the FBI find her son. Just not through a newspaper article.

"Come on in, then," Heather said, holding open the screen door.

They filed into her house, carefully observing the surroundings for any clues. Sebastian thought the interior looked humble but well loved. The furniture was definitely on the battered side, but bright throws covered the back of the couch, and small pots of flowers decorated the windowsills.

As they sat, Heather disappeared into the back of the house, returning with two glasses of iced tea. Surprised but pleased, Sebastian took his and savored its rich, sweet flavor. It had been so long since he'd hung around normal people, he'd almost forgotten the delights of southern hospitality. Not that Lily wasn't hospitable, but she showed it in the form of hot tea and scones, having been turned into a tea snob by his aunt.

They spent a few minutes exchanging small talk. Sebastian could tell from Tina's twitching eyelid that it took all her self-control to keep up the friendly façade. Being polite wasn't Tina's strong point. Taking pity on Tina's waning powers of polite conversation, Sebastian steered the conversation toward the reason they had come.

"Ms. Foster, you don't mind if we record this, do you? So we can be sure to make accurate quotes in the article?"

"I…suppose that would be alright," she said, hesitantly.

Sebastian nodded to Tina, who set up her camcorder and started filming.

"Now, Ms. Foster, I wanted to start out by asking a few questions about the case, to establish the true facts behind the investigation so our readers know what's going on. Any and all names and places can be altered, if you prefer, to protect your identity. Alright?"

Heather nodded, looking even more uncertain.

"Good. Now, can you tell us the name of your son's biological father?" Sebastian asked, watching Heather's eyes very closely.

As he'd suspected, they clouded, taking on an unfocused look as the woman's mouth hung slightly open. "I—I don't remember," she stuttered, uncertainty replaced by a blank mask of confusion.

"Are you sure?" Sebastian pressed, glancing over at the camera to make sure Tina was getting a good shot of the woman's face. "Didn't he give you his name when you all met?"

"I d—don't remember," she said again, forehead creasing in what could have been pain or distress.

"What about pictures? Do you have any pictures of him?"

"No, no. No pictures." Her eyes remained clouded, but her answer was more certain now that she could give a definite yes or no.

Sebastian looked at Tina again, giving her an "I told you so" arch of his eyebrow. She'd argued the whole drive down that they were wasting their time and there was no wizard behind the disappearances.

Tina glared back at him, but nodded curtly, acknowledging the need to move on to Plan B.

Despite endless hours of searching, they had not been able to find a single picture of John Faust LeFay anywhere on the Internet. Without there being time to sneak up to his estate and take a few—an incredibly risky venture in any case—Sebastian had a different plan.

"Ms. Foster, why don't we take a short break? Do you have a bathroom I can use?"

She nodded, eyes clear once more as she showed him to a tiny bathroom off the hall. He locked himself in, taking with him a small knapsack he'd brought from the car. Moving with difficulty in the cramped space, he used fae glamour to change the color of his business slacks from black to grey, and put on a grey suit jacket he'd stuffed into the backpack. Then, he looked in the mirror and slowly shaped his facial features to mimic what he remembered of John Faust's appearance. He knew it wouldn't be perfect, as he'd only seen the man briefly. But he had a good eye for these things. It should be close enough to fool Heather. Unruly black hair appeared to pull into his scalp and spread down his face, giving him a trim goatee and beard. His smooth, boyish features appeared to lengthen and flatten, giving him an older, patrician air and a prominent Roman nose.

When he was ready, he emerged from the bathroom, taking a deep breath and hoping Tina had remembered to stop the recording, change the internal date stamp, and restart it so the recording appeared to be at a later time.

Well, here goes nothing, he thought, and stepped out into the small living room.

Tina, who was facing the hall with her camcorder, jumped involuntarily at the sight of him. She uttered a colorful curse, eyes wide as she let the recording device droop. He'd told her what he could do, to prepare her, but she hadn't really believed him. Until now, of course.

Sebastian cleared his throat and gave her a pointed glare, jolting her out of her opened-mouthed shock and returning her attention to the camcorder, which she dutifully raised to focus on him.

At Tina's exclamation, Heather started to turn, eyes searching for the disturbance. When she spotted him she gave a small scream, hands covering her mouth, eyes like saucers. They were clear.

"Oh my god, Rex! Is that you?"

Several things happened in quick succession. Sebastian opened his mouth to utter his prepared reply, but saw that Heather's mouth had still not closed, though her hands had dropped to her neck, clawing at the necklace which hung there. Only it was no longer hanging. It had tightened, digging into the skin and choking her like a garroting wire.

Cursing, Sebastian let the glamour disappear and leapt forward, hands reaching for the necklace as his mind raced for a plan, a spell, anything that would help. Why hadn't he thought of this? Of course John Faust would have put something in place to silence this woman if the memory spell failed.

As his hands scrabbled on Heather's neck, trying to find purchase on the slender but incredibly strong chain, Tina just sat there, frozen in shock. "Do something!" Sebastian yelled. "Call 911. Now!"

"But—I—what—" she stammered.

"Do it!" Sebastian roared, looking desperately about the room for something slender to stick under the chain and cut it, perhaps a pair of scissors. But there was nothing in sight, and Heather's face was growing bluer by the second, her desperate choking making his mind race in hopeless circles. His fingers were already bloody—his or Heather's he had no idea—from trying to get under the chain.

"Come on Heather, stay with me. Stay with me!" he yelled at the choking woman, trying to avoid her thrashing legs as she struggled in panic. Her eyes rolled in their sockets and her bloody hands were now scratching at his face and arms in desperation, her brain no longer getting enough oxygen to think straight. He couldn't—quite—get—his—fingers—under—

Tina's frightened voice broke through his panic as she yelled into her phone. "Yes, imminent danger, she's dying! He's choking her! I mean the necklace is! Rex—oh never mind, just come! Yes! Right now, we need an ambulance!"

The last thing he heard was Tina rattling off the address, getting it wrong twice before she scrambled in her purse to find where she'd written it down. But by the time she'd hung up—ignoring the operator's order to stay on the line—it was too late.

Sebastian stood, body numb and mind frozen in shock as he looked down at the dead woman. She'd rolled off her chair onto the floor in her mad thrashing and now lay splayed, lips blue and eyes staring blankly at him in death.

"Oh—my—" Tina's voice shook as she stared at the poor woman. Then she seemed to snap out of it. Scrambling across the floor, she retrieved the camcorder, stuffing it into her purse as she made a mad dash for the door.

"Hey, where are you going?" Sebastian exclaimed, catching hold of her arm.

"You couldn't pay me a million dollars to stick around, buster," she said, trying to break free from his hold. "That woman just died. The police will think we did it! This is your mess, not mine. Now let me go!"

"But we can't just leave her here! We have to explain what happened, we have to…"

"Uh-huh," Tina said sarcastically, seeing the realization in his eyes. "Nobody is going to believe you didn't do it. Magic doesn't exist, remember?"

"But you were a witness, you can tell them the truth."

"I'm not a witness. I'm an accomplice, you idiot!" she yelled, digging her nails into his hand. "Even if I was stupid enough to try and tell them a necklace mysteriously choked a woman, it wouldn't do any good. They would just say I'm covering up for you. Now come with me or let me go!" After one last, ferocious dig of her nails, he released her arm with a yelp and she sped out the door.

He stood, helplessly torn between what was right and what was smart. He had caused this. No, it wasn't his fault, it was John Faust's fault, the murdering sack of dung. But he, Sebastian, had still caused it to happen.

Looking back at the horrible scene on the living room floor, he hadn't even begun to decide what to do when he heard the squeal of tires and saw Tina's car speeding away. Well, he thought, I guess now I don't have a choice. Fleeing on foot was a possibility, but the neighborhood kids had already seen his face—his real face—and there would be a manhunt. He could escape, most likely, but the incident would dog his steps for the rest of his life. Better to stay and hope for the best.

He tried to force his mind to consider alternatives, anything to salvage the situation. But all he could think of was his mother's face and her soft, brown eyes as she told him to "be kind, even when the world punishes you for it." It was one of the last things she'd ever said to him before she died, and he'd always tried to live up to it. This woman deserved better than to be discovered alone on her living room floor, the victim of a crime that would never be solved.

As he knelt next to her body, belatedly attempting CPR in case she wasn't completely gone, he berated himself, calling himself every kind of fool. That's where the policeman found him bare minutes later when he burst through the open front door, gun raised.

"Hands where I can see them! Step away from the woman!" the cop shouted, and Sebastian complied, attempting to explain himself.

"Sir, calm down, I'm trying to help. I didn't kill this woman, she was choking and I was trying to help her."

But the policeman didn't want to hear it, yelling at him to be quiet and put his hands behind his back. He was cuffing Sebastian when the ambulance arrived.

Episode 6

OF WHEELS AND DEALS

Chapter 1
BIG GIRL PANTS

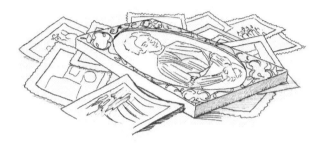

LILY SAT ON HER BED AT HOME, KNEES TUCKED UP UNDER HER CHIN, ARMS wrapped around her knees as she held up a photograph of Madam Barrington. It was a normal enough photograph. Or at least it had been, until her mentor cast a conveyance spell on it and an identical copy they'd mailed to Sebastian first thing on Monday. The spell was for sound only, so it had been odd listening over the past few days while the picture traveled through the mail system and finally found its way into the federal penitentiary in Atlanta.

Judging by the odd bits of conversation she'd caught earlier that day, she knew the letter had been delivered and opened, and Sebastian had been allowed to keep it in his cell—a common practice for inmates who were not high security. She'd been waiting all evening for the call of lights out, so she and Sebastian could converse.

Of course, Sebastian might not know the picture was

enchanted. He'd probably guessed, but Lily hadn't been able to put any sort of hint in the letter, lest a prison guard read it and confiscate the whole thing on suspicion of containing a coded message.

Finally, Lily heard the call for lights out echo through the prison cells. She kept quiet, waiting, assuming it would take several minutes for things to quiet down.

Sure enough, a few minutes later she heard: "I'm assuming this picture has been enchanted, or am I just making a fool of myself by conversing with a photograph?" Sebastian's whisper came through, quiet but crisp, and Lily let out a sigh of relief, despite the fact that she was severely vexed at him.

She was briefly tempted to let him stew for a while. After all, where had he been when she'd needed him? But then Sir Kipling, sitting alert at the end of the bed, gave her a knowing stare and meowed impatiently. A guilty twinge at the thought of Sebastian, alone and friendless in a prison cell, was enough to prompt a reply. With a quiet word—she'd been practicing the non-verbal spell casting Allen had taught her, but hadn't yet made any progress—she activated her side of the conveyance spell so Sebastian could hear her speak.

"Hello." She ought to say more, but couldn't think what. Dominating her thoughts was a jumble of feelings, too tangled to even begin to unravel. Hurt, disappointment, longing, anger, relief, uncertainty, elation. What was she supposed to do with it all?

"Hi, Lily." His whispered reply, surprisingly tender, caught her off guard, and she stared blankly at her cat.

Sir Kipling took the opportunity to meow a greeting, and Lily heard Sebastian chuckle. "Hello to you, too, Kip," he said.

"Um…how are you?" Lily finally asked. It was all her overstimulated brain could come up with.

"I'm doing okay. For being in prison, at any rate. It's not like I couldn't break out if I wanted to. But I'd prefer to not spend the rest of my life on the run."

"Oh." A few months ago, she would have scoffed at his casual assertion that prison bars couldn't contain him. But not anymore.

"Um…right…" Sebastian paused, obviously at a loss for words—a rare occurrence. "Thank Aunt B. for the lawyer, will you? She's seems quite, um, competent."

"Sure," Lily promised. Madam Barrington had, of course, gotten her nephew the best initiate lawyer money could buy. It didn't happen often, but there were, occasionally, situations where magic and the law collided. It behooved the wizard community to have a few of its members—initiates, of course, because what wizard would want to be a lawyer?—in a position to obscure or reinterpret any irregularities caused by magic so as to ensure the best outcome for their wizard clients and the continued ignorance of the mundanes.

It was through the lawyer and at Sebastian's request that they'd gotten the basic facts of his case. He'd been charged with first-degree murder, though the FBI was trying to cut a deal to bring the charge down to involuntary manslaughter if he agreed to cooperate. They wanted information on some random person named Rex Morganson, and Lily had been both annoyed and confused at this news, failing to see the connection all this had with John Faust and their mission.

She'd had time to cool off after her initial, incandescent rage at Sebastian for pulling another one of his irresponsible, ridiculous stunts, getting himself into trouble when they needed him. When she needed him. She'd also had time to reflect on her feelings, specifically how many of them existed that shouldn't. It was time to stop projecting her feelings onto someone who was obviously uninterested, not to mention of questionable reliability.

She reminded herself that any personal feelings of betrayal were irrelevant. There was nothing between them, and she simply needed to come at this from a professional standpoint. As a friend and ally, she would, of course, make every effort to help Sebastian out of prison. But she couldn't let herself get emotionally attached...okay, so it was too late for that. Rather, she couldn't let her feelings, which she was in the process of bringing to heel, get in the way of doing her duty.

To that end, she took a deep breath, cleared her mind, and got down to business. "I'm not sure how much time you have, but I need a detailed explanation of what's going on so we can create a plan of action. I'll be passing everything on to Madam Barrington."

"I may have to go silent if a guard walks by, but we should have plenty of time," Sebastian assured her. "As far as a plan, where's Tina? She knows what's going on and what to do."

Lily's temper flared, as it usually did when the witch's name was mentioned. "Tina slammed the door in my face before I could even begin passing on your message," she bit out, her clipped tone leaving no doubt as to her feelings on the matter. "I've been back several times, but the apartment has been dark and no one is answering the doorbell or her phone."

"Ah. Hm. Well, that puts a wrench in our plans," Sebastian said, sounding guilty.

As he should be, Lily thought, stewing.

"Sebastian Blackwell. You had better tell me what's going on right now or you can consider this conversation

over. I can't help someone who refuses to be frank with me."
She laid out the ultimatum in an even voice, but her heart
was pounding like a drum. At Sir Kipling's reproachful look,
she glared back defiantly, tired of fumbling around in the
dark.

There was a moment of silence. Then Sebastian let out
a long, weary sigh. "Lily…I can't tell you everything right
now."

"Then—" she began, but was cut off by his hiss of
impatience.

"Will you just hear me out? Good grief, relax, woman.
We're on the same side." His voice was full of impatience, a
tone he'd never used with her before. He'd always treated
her in a teasing, good-natured fashion. She withdrew, hurt,
and annoyed at herself for feeling so.

Perhaps he regretted the harshness of his words, because
his next ones were very gentle. "I'm sorry, Lily. I can't tell
you everything because I don't *know* everything." He
sighed. "Tina and I were trying to dig up evidence on your
dad—evidence of his illegal activity—so the FBI could deal
with him and we wouldn't have to. I'm sorry if you felt I
was going behind your back, but I didn't want to hurt you.
That worthless prick has already caused you enough pain. I
didn't want to add his ongoing douchebaggery to that list.
Of course you deserved to know eventually, but I at least
wanted solid evidence before bringing it up. We were
following a lead when, well, you know what happened. I
think our, um, questions activated some sort of spell that
choked the poor woman. But we obviously can't tell the FBI
that. With me struggling to get the necklace off, there's
enough of my DNA on the body for any lawyer worth their
salt to spin me into some kind of woman-strangling
psychopath."

Lily was silent, her mind reeling with questions and her carefully controlled emotions once again a confused tangle. Of course he'd been trying to help. If she was honest about it, that's all he ever did: try to help. But why did he think she couldn't take the news? Did he think she was weak? Of course he did, because she *was* weak. She'd lived an easy, sheltered life. But how was she supposed to help if he refused to be honest with her? What had her father been up to this time? How bad could it be? Her stomach clenched at the thought.

"Uhh, Lily?" Sebastian's whisper broke through her thoughts, jolting her back to the moment. She scrambled to collect herself.

"I'm here. Yes, I suppose the details aren't immediately relevant. Personally, I don't think the FBI can help us. It's not as if they could keep John Faust in prison anyway, unless they knew to use wrought-iron shackles. Be that as it may, getting you out of jail is top priority. We need you here. While you were…gone,"—she resisted the urge to use a more accusatory word—"John Faust managed to track us to Allen's house and kidnap him, as well as steal Morgan's journal."

"I know," Sebastian said miserably.

"I—what? What do you mean *you know*?" Lily demanded.

A quiet cough, probably Sebastian clearing his throat, came from the photograph. "Well…it wasn't like I'd leave you there without any backup. I had one of my, um, fae friends hang around. To keep an eye on things. He warned me as soon as John Faust showed up, but I was already in jail by then and couldn't help, so I sent him to wake Sir Kipling.

So that's what Kip had meant by a little voice. "I see," she said, not sure what to think. At least he hadn't completely abandoned them. He had simply *appeared* to have completely abandoned them. "And how many other times have you left one of your 'friends' to keep an eye on me?" she asked, suddenly suspicious.

"Ummm…weeell…a couple times?" he said very slowly. Tentatively. As if he expected her to explode. It was not an unfounded fear.

Lily pursed her lips, torn between annoyance and relief. On the one hand, he obviously cared more than she'd given him credit for. This made it harder to squash those pesky emotions she was attempting to ignore. On the other hand, he sure had a funny way of showing it. And, she suddenly realized with a blush, if he'd been spying on her, he might know more about her…activities, than she really wanted to share. Did his "friends" eavesdrop on her conversations? Did they follow her around to, say, dinner? Dinner with a particular someone…

"You weren't—that is, last Friday when I was—when I went out, were you 'keeping an eye' on me then?" she asked, attempting to remain calm.

"Um…about that," Sebastian began. "I know it's none of my business, but there's some things you don't know about Agent Grant that—"

"How *dare* you!" Lily exclaimed, cutting him off. Yes, Sebastian should be afraid of an explosion. He deserved it, the nosy, interfering little—

"I would advise against taking your unwarranted indignation out on Sebastian." Sir Kipling spoke unexpectedly. His yellow eyes had never left her face as he listened in on the conversation. "He was only helping me."

"What!" Lily squawked, almost dropping the picture in surprise.

"What is it?" Sebastian hissed, sounding nervous. "What's he telling you?"

Lily spoke a hurried word, muting her end of the conveyance spell, then glared at her no-good, backstabbing, devious feline. He blinked at her, utterly unfazed. She huffed, trying to hold onto her sense of self-righteous betrayal in the face of Sir Kipling's no-nonsense stare.

"Stop being childish," he said, no apology in his meow.

"I—I am not—"

"Yes, you are. First you act like a spoiled teenager mad at her crush for not being at her beck and call. Then, when he tries to help, you get all indignant that he isn't playing by your rules."

"I—he is not—how dare you—" she spluttered.

"Get over yourself and start acting like an adult. It's time to put on your big girl pants."

Lily glared at her cat, trying to stare him down. It didn't work, as she knew it wouldn't. Yet her pride wouldn't let her do otherwise, mostly because she knew he was right. Drat that cat.

"Pride is unbecoming to humans," Sir Kipling pointed out, as if he could read her thoughts. "Only cats and dragons do it justice. You are neither, so I suggest you focus on what you *are* good at. Mainly, using your courage, intelligence, and skill to make the world a better place. By getting rid of John Faust, of course," he amended.

Well, when he put it like that…Lily deflated, letting out a gush of air and feeling her whole body sink into her bed cushions in defeat. "I'm hopeless." She said, burying her head in her hands.

Next thing she knew, Sir Kipling was rubbing on her elbow, his deep, soothing purr reverberating through her body. "Nonsense. You're doing just fine. But it might help if you stop getting so indignant about everything. We've all been worried about you and about what might happen next.

Sebastian was just helping keep an eye out in case your sire decided to pay a visit. I can't keep you safe all by myself, you know."

Lily picked up her cat and buried her face in his fur, wishing his purr would make her confused tangle of emotions disappear. Why did being an adult have to be so hard?

It was Sebastian's whispered "Psst, Lily. You still there?" that prompted her to finally straighten.

"Better now?" Sir Kipling purred, a satisfied look on his face.

She took a deep breath. I can do this, she thought, deciding to ignore Sir Kipling's description of Sebastian as her "crush." She'd have to deal with it eventually, but not now. Not when they were in the middle of a crisis.

She unmuted the conveyance spell and responded to Sebastian's ever more anxious whispers. "I'm here. Everything is fine. Now, what do we need to do to get you out? We can't wait for this to go to court, and you can't take a deal from the FBI. You're innocent and we need you out *now*."

He hesitated, obviously wanting to ask about her long silence, but sensing now wasn't the time. "Well, about the deal with the FBI. I actually *want* to cooperate and tell them everything I know about Rex. But as of right now it won't do them any good. We don't have anything concrete on him, just suspicions."

"Wait," Lily stopped him. "Remind me who this Rex guy is and how he's relevant?"

"What? Oh, er…" Sebastian said, sounding suspiciously reluctant. "We think he's…ummm…an associate of, uhhh, your dad's."

"I see," she said through numb lips, determined not to

let emotion derail her thought process. But it was a losing battle. Was having a normal father too much to ask?

"Er, Lily?" Sebastian's nervous voice came out of the photograph like a quavering shaft of light in the darkness threatening to overwhelm her.

"I'm here."

"Look, let's not get distracted, okay? Right now, the most important thing is to find Tina. We recorded the whole thing. With her and the tape, maybe we can at least convince the FBI I'm not their prime suspect and they'll let me out on bail while they sort out the legal stuff." He didn't, of course, address how in the world they would explain a necklace randomly deciding to strangle a woman of its own accord. That's what they had a lawyer for. "Hopefully the legal stuff will take so long, we'll have plenty of time to find John Faust, save Allen, and get the evidence we need to clear my name. We can do this, okay? Just find Tina."

"But how?" Lily asked, feeling desperate.

"I've got a plan. Here's what you need to do…"

They talked for another thirty minutes until Lily was sure she understood and had finished taking a few notes to pass on to Madam Barrington. When they finished, they said an awkward goodbye and Lily crawled under the covers, stroking Sir Kipling's soft fur as he curled up next to her. She stared dully up at her dark ceiling, feeling nervous and emotionally drained.

"This is not going to be easy," she sighed.

"If it were easy, I'd get bored." Sir Kipling yawned at her, his pink tongue faintly visible in the light from the street lamps outside.

"Humph. Easy for you to say," Lily grumped. "You're just a cat."

"Exactly. It's what I do best." He gave her a lazy stare,

yellow eyes glinting in the dark. "And what you do best is save the world."

"Riiight," Lily scoffed. "But only if it doesn't interfere with tea," she joked.

"Naturally," Sir Kipling agreed, settling his head down on his paws. "Now go to sleep. You need it."

"Yes, Mother." Lily rolled her eyes at him in the dark but did try to relax and clear her mind, helped along by the furry motor at her side. Even so, it was a long time before she finally fell asleep.

Atlas Galleries was located on the bottom floor of a high-end office building on Marietta Street in downtown Atlanta. Lily eyed its glass front, the atmosphere of imposing elegance adding to the nervous butterflies already whipping up a storm in her stomach. She wore her most expensive suit, charcoal grey, made of hand-finished wool, with a black silk blouse underneath. The combination was striking but not very comfortable to wear while standing around under the hot sun. Just because it was the beginning of September didn't mean Atlanta's famous muggy heat was ready to acknowledge the approach of fall.

Straightening her spine and fixing a calm, aloof look on her face, she took hold of the glass door and glided into the art gallery. She was glad Sebastian's instructions had included taking time to actually look at the art before approaching the proprietor, a man named Anton Silvester. It gave her a chance to collect herself. She was *not* good at this sort of thing. Cloak-and-dagger stuff was Sebastian's purview. Yet she had no choice but to do her best. She tried to think of it as just another part of her job. A business transaction. All she had to do was keep cool and not do anything awkward.

The art was actually quite beautiful. She found it easy to lose herself in examining it, enjoying the subtle shades and exquisitely evocative subjects of each piece. She became so absorbed, in fact, that she didn't notice the tall, rail-thin man float into place at her side, silently watching her inspect the paintings.

"Theodore Tresky. An excellent choice, madam."

Lily nearly jumped out of her skin. Somehow she managed to not fall over as she turned to face the silk-smooth voice. "Oh, excuse me. I didn't see you there, Mr…." She let the question dangle.

"Silvester, madam. At your service." He gave the tiniest dip of his head.

Lily arched an eyebrow, playing it cool and imagining herself channeling her inner Madam Barrington. "Pleased, I'm sure."

"If you enjoy Tresky, I have several other exquisite examples of his handiwork. If you would allow me," Anton offered, extending a hand toward the back of the gallery.

Nodding in acquiescence, Lily followed the thin man as he glided past painting after painting, his gait exceptionally smooth for one so angular. Near the rear wall, he showed her two other paintings, each depicting a different scene but both exhibiting the same ethereal style. They really were fine pieces of art, and if she made about four times as much, she just might be able to afford them. The brief thought crossed her mind that, had she joined her father, she could have had any painting she desired. Money would have never been an issue. The thought brought a stab of pain, but she pushed it aside. That wasn't the life she'd chosen, for good reason.

Dragging her mind back to Anton's mellifluous voice, she listened as he extolled the virtues of his artwork. So far, this was going as Sebastian had described. Now it was up to her to take it to the next level.

"They are, as you say, exquisite pieces," she finally interrupted him, keeping her expression uninterested. "But my employer prefers art that is a bit more…unique. A commission, perhaps. Could you arrange such a thing, Mr. Silvester?" She spoke carefully, using the exact words Sebastian had instructed.

Anton stared at her, unblinking, expression like a glass pool: completely opaque, revealing nothing of the depths beneath. Lily felt her resolve quaver. She wanted to look away, duck her head, blush, something. Such a prolonged stare was not only impolite, it was unnerving. But she held as best she could, masking her discomfort with an impatient arch of her brow. "I was told such…custom pieces were available at your gallery, and assured that your service was unparalleled. Were my sources mistaken?"

"Not at all, madam." Anton replied evenly, finally blinking and turning to a small computer terminal recessed in the fine wood paneling of the gallery's back wall. He took a sleek USB drive from a drawer beneath it and handed it to her. "If you would have your employer fill out the necessary paperwork and return it, we can begin inquiries at once. I will need some time, of course, to find a suitable artist. But I assure you, we will provide an excellent fit. Someone with more than enough skill to carry out your…customizations."

Lily took the USB drive, slipping it inside her suit pocket. "I will return within the hour. Time is of the essence," she said, all business. On the outside, at least. Inside her heart was pounding and her armpits felt decidedly damp. At this point she was winging it. Sebastian had given her general guidelines for how to close the deal but couldn't predict exactly what would be said. "My employer has a space in need of decoration for an important event and will pay whatever necessary to make it happen. There is, in fact, an artist he already has in mind. Someone whose work he has seen before. I'll be sure he mentions it on the form."

"While I cannot guarantee any particular artist's availability, madam, I will, of course, make every effort to secure their services. Might I suggest a generous, up-front offer to…encourage their participation?"

She nodded. "Thank you for the suggestion. I'll be sure to pass it on."

"Excellent. I look forward to your return…Miss Singer."

This time Lily really did jump, and blush, her careful façade slipping a fraction. How did he know her name? Forcing herself to look Anton in the eye, she searched his expression for any indication of his intentions.

His gaze remained passive, not helping her in the slightest, and his words confused her even more. "If I may be so bold, madam, as to suggest you advise your 'employer' that he plays a dangerous game and has no business dragging you into it."

"I—I shall. Thank you, Mr. Silvester. Good day." With that, she turned and headed straight for the door, hoping she didn't wobble noticeably—her legs had turned to jelly in relief at finishing her ordeal.

Back at her house, USB drive plugged into her computer, she spent a tense half hour filling out the form with Sebastian's whispered help. He was in his cell, but guards passed at regular intervals and she could sometimes hear conversations carrying over from adjoining cells.

When she told him what Anton had said, he cursed quietly.

"What? What did it mean?" Lily shifted in her chair, anxious.

"Nothing too bad," he whispered back, pausing as the

sound of footsteps grew louder, then faded. "I just didn't expect him to recognize you. But it doesn't matter. He'll deal with anyone who pays. Well, there was that time…never mind," he amended quickly, moving on to forestall questions. "I don't know what kind of game he's playing, but I think he's just warning us to not try anything funny. And we're not planning to, so it should be fine. He'll put out the job, and hopefully Tina won't be able to resist making contact."

"Er, what about the payment?" She asked, addressing what seemed to be the elephant in the room. The amounts they'd put on the form were *very* high.

"Don't worry. I'm good for it. Just use the bank information I gave you. It'll be fine."

Her curiosity burned, but she kept her mouth shut. If she asked how in the world a ne'er-do-well like him could get his hands on so much money, she suspected she wouldn't like the answer. Better not to know.

The return trip to Atlas Galleries went without a hitch. She didn't even speak to Anton, simply walked in, handed him the flash drive with a curt nod, and walked out.

Later that night, her worried fretting was interrupted by an unexpected but welcome call from her mother. Lily gave her the edited version of events, chiding her for not mentioning the existence of Allen.

Her mother had the grace to be contrite. "I know, honey. It just never came to mind when I was with you. There were always other, more important things to talk about. And anyway, I never saw much of Allen. He's not exactly the social type, as I'm sure you noticed. That poor thing," she continued, voice sounding worried. "He and

John never did get along, even as adults. Do you want me to come up and help you look for him?"

"No, Mother. You stay right where you are. You're the only thing protecting the family right now. But since we're on the topic, are there any other family members I should know about?" She'd always been curious about her mother's side; maybe now she would finally find out.

"On your father's side? No. Not that I know of. On my side...well, I haven't exactly spoken to them in twenty-three years, but I suppose it's about time I give them a call."

"Mother! Seriously? Why didn't you contact them as soon as we started talking again? We might need their help, and I'm sure they're worried stiff about you."

"Mh-hmm. Now who's calling the kettle black?"

"Well..." Lily bit her lip, blushing.

"I suppose I never told you they weren't thrilled when I married John. My parents were, quite rightly, wary of John's controlling nature. And they were less than thrilled at the way Ursula looked down her nose at them. But I was headstrong and in love. After...everything that happened with John, I guess I was too embarrassed to reach out, knowing they'd been right about him. And, of course, I was in hiding."

"Well you aren't any more," Lily pointed out. "And after all, *we* worked things out alright, didn't we? You'll call them, won't you?"

Freda heaved a deep sigh. "Yes, I will, sweetie. I've just been putting it off. All the explaining I'll have to do, it gives me a headache simply thinking about it."

"You'll have fun, Mother, I'm sure," Lily said, a teasing note in her voice.

"No thanks to you," she replied archly. Then her voice took on a mischievous air. "I'll be sure to sign you up for the next family reunion, so you can meet *all* our friends and family at a big, loud, fancy party."

Lily gasped, only half feigning the horror in her voice. "You wouldn't!"

"Count on it," Freda promised.

"Humph." Lily was inclined to be grumpy. "At least you asked first. Ursula didn't ask, just threw a ball and tried to marry me off like a painting at an auction."

"Oh, sweetie, that must have been awful."

"You have no idea. It was the first time I yelled at her, too. I completely lost it when she scolded me for being impolite to my suitors and hiding upstairs."

Lily heard her mother chuckle, a warm sound tinged with ruefulness. "Ah, the famous Silvester temper. You have both French and Italian blood, neither of which are known for their—"

"Wait a minute, what did you say?" Lily asked sharply, suddenly realizing what she'd heard.

"Um, that the French and Italians aren't known for their cool-headedness?"

"No, before that. What is your maiden name?"

"Silvester. My father is first-generation Italian."

Lily's skin tingled uncomfortably, wondering what, if any connection, there was between her family and Anton. Was their shared last name simple coincidence? She considered asking her mother but decided that was a question best left for another time. Perhaps at a family reunion.

"Is everything alright?" Freda asked into the silence.

"Yes, everything's fine. How's Jamie?" she asked, changing the subject.

Her mother heaved a great sigh, the rushing air causing static on the line. "He's well enough, I suppose. Just impatient and restless as a caged lion. He pesters me every day to teach him magic. I've tried to start with the basics, but he's so dismissive of learning 'boring stuff,' you know, the foundational things like meditation, mental exercises, and magic theory. I'm afraid he's going to get himself killed."

Lily made a sympathetic noise. She understood what it felt like to just be stepping into the world of magic. She'd felt impatient as well. But she was also naturally meticulous, taking satisfaction in each little step on her way to bigger things. Her brother, apparently, did not share her methodical nature.

"Just make sure he has a good personal ward and never tries magic outside a casting circle," Lily suggested, knowing her mother would have already taken this precaution, but not having anything else to offer.

"Oh, believe me, we've already been over that. His father had to whoop his hide black and blue when we caught him trying to light a candle in his room. Could have burnt the whole house down. He'll be the death of me," Freda finished, sounding weary.

"Perhaps when, you know, *all this* is over, he can come to Atlanta for a while. I'm sure Madam Barrington could frighten some sense into him."

"Perhaps," Freda agreed, then went silent, probably considering how to juggle the mundane and wizard education of her youngest child.

"Well," Lily said, "it's getting late and I should be heading to bed."

"Of course, honey. Let me know if you need anything. And tell Sebastian I said hello. He seemed like such a nice young man, I hope things clear up alright."

Lily rolled her eyes, ignoring the little flutter in her stomach. But she promised to keep her mother updated, and they said goodbye.

***

The next day, after work, Lily picked Madam Barrington up and they headed north. Just because Sebastian was temporarily out of commission didn't mean they could sit back and do nothing for Allen. They'd decided to pay a visit to the LeFay estate, strictly to talk. Madam Barrington was fairly sure that, with Henry, Ursula, and the others there, it wouldn't come to spells as long as they didn't start anything. They hoped against hope to talk some sense into John Faust, a last-ditch effort to prevent open violence.

They discussed casting technique during the drive. Lily had been practicing every spare moment she wasn't at work or trying to unravel Sebastian's mess. It was exhausting and frustrating, but she *was* making progress. She still couldn't get the hang of silent casting, however. When she asked Madam Barrington about it and why she'd never taught her, the older woman thought for a moment before responding.

"Silent casting is of limited utility compared to the difficulty of learning it. Most modern wizards never have need of it. The technique was more prevalent in historical times, when the ability to remain unnoticed by mundanes was the difference between life and death. I had not yet introduced the technique because it was highly advanced and I didn't see the need. In light of recent events, of course, it could certainly be useful. But I would advise you to focus your efforts on perfecting your defensive and offensive spells first."

"But won't John Faust have the advantage? Surely he knows the technique?' Lily asked, brow furrowed.

"Not that I have witnessed. I certainly did not teach it to him, though I'm sure he is capable of learning it himself, if he had the inclination. Allen did, after all."

Lily nodded. "Allen is…amazing. And very odd."

Madam Barrington's face broke into a rare smile. "Indeed. Of the two brothers, the younger is clearly the more skilled. What he lacks in social graces he makes up for in sheer brilliance. I should like to spend a good deal of time with him myself, if we ever get the chance. He has far surpassed my expectations from when I was his tutor many years ago. He always did have a natural intuition when it came to magic that his older brother never displayed. John Faust came at things looking for a way to conquer them, master them, bend them to his will. Allen saw the world as a beautiful mosaic of possibilities that needed to be discovered, nurtured, and understood. He recognized that magic is not simply a servant, or even a tool. Rather it is a part of who we are as creative beings. Both a science, and an art."

They fell into silence and Lily spent a long time digesting her mentor's words. Right now, she saw magic as a raw force to be controlled. Not so much a tool as a wild animal she was still learning to tame. Was she too much like her father? Was she struggling because she tried too hard to control something she hadn't taken the time to understand? It was food for thought. She just hoped they could save Allen before his brother did any…permanent damage.

When they finally pulled up to the LeFay estate's gate, the sun was sinking towards the western horizon. As Lily leaned out the window to push the call button on the gate's control panel, she kept an eye out for a black, raven-shaped shadow. But Oculus was nowhere to be seen.

"Please state your name and business," said a cool, mechanical voice.

Well, here goes nothing, Lily thought, hoping they wouldn't be zapped where they sat as soon as she mentioned their names. "Lily Singer and Ethel Barrington. We're here to see, um, the LeFays." She decided not to be specific, in case that threw up any red flags.

There was a long silence. So long that Lily wondered if the device had even registered her response. Then, finally, the voice said, "Thank you. You may proceed."

Driving forward through the gates, Lily pushed down a rising feeling of panic. This was not like last time. She was going in eyes open, with Madam Barrington at her back. Several deep breaths helped her maintain an outward semblance of calm, but inside her heart was racing and her skin felt clammy. Madam Barrington shot her a worried look at all the heavy breathing but kept her peace.

The LeFay mansion was just as gigantic, imposing, and beautiful as she remembered. Unlike last time, Fletcher, the butler, waited for them on the gravel drive, positioned perfectly to open Madam Barrington's door as soon as Lily pulled to a stop. He helped her out with a bow and a murmured word, then circled around toward the driver's side. But Lily didn't give him a chance. She was out of the car before he'd even rounded the hood.

"Miss Singer," he said, bowing politely. "It is a pleasure to see you again."

Lily eyed him, deciding how to reply. He had helped her escape her father's clutches, yet there was so much more he could have done. She felt mostly ambivalent toward the lot of them—Fletcher and her grandparents. They'd stood silently by, or simply ignored, John Faust's inappropriate behavior. Yet, knowing the kind of person her father was, she couldn't be too hard on them. Sometimes you did your best, and it was not enough. But at least you'd tried.

She settled for a polite nod, then headed around the car toward the front door in Madam Barrington's wake.

Somehow, Fletcher managed to arrive before them both, holding open the massive doors and directing them to the left, into the west wing's parlor.

"Please, right this way. Mr. and Mrs. LeFay are waiting for you."

Lily hesitated before stepping into the house, wondering if it was a trap. Fletcher hadn't mentioned John Faust. Was her father hiding somewhere, waiting to jump out and…no, that was silly. Plus, Madam Barrington was here. They would be fine.

Upon entering the parlor, it took only a second to confirm that John Faust was not present—unless he was hiding behind some sort of cloaking glamour. But looking carefully into all the corners, she didn't see any of the telltales, so she finally relaxed and turned to face her grandparents.

Henry stood behind the settee upon which sat his wife, looking much less fashionable than was her habit. Her hair drooped and she had dark circles under her eyes. For some reason, she wore all black, the harsh color contrasting with the lovely cream and embroidered white of the settee. Henry had his hands resting on the back of the piece of furniture, not on his wife's shoulders. There was a distance between them that spoke volumes. Lily was pretty sure she knew what was coming.

"Where is John Faust?" Madam Barrington asked coldly, scorning the niceties of small talk or even a polite preamble. Every inch of her exuded steely authority.

"Not here," Henry LeFay said. At his words, Ursula gave a loud sniffle, wiping her nose with a wrinkled handkerchief clutched in one bony hand. Ignoring his wife, Henry continued. "I made it clear he was no longer welcome under our roof after what he'd done to our granddaughter, and that it was high time he found somewhere else to live."

"You threw him out, my poor baby!" Ursula sobbed into her handkerchief.

To Lily's astonishment and amused delight, Henry actually rolled his eyes heavenward, letting out a tiny sigh as if praying for patience.

"So, where did he go?" Lily asked.

Henry pursed his lips in displeasure. "I did not ask and do not care to know."

"We haven't heard from him in weeks," Ursula sniffed, obviously struggling to hold onto her semblance of composure. "He could be—be lying dead in an alley for all we know," she said, throwing a dirty look over her shoulder at her husband, whose expression remained stony.

Madam Barrington's lip quirked upward. "I sincerely doubt that," she said dryly. "Your older son is more than capable of looking after himself. Your younger one, on the other hand…have you heard from Allen recently?"

Both of Lily's grandparents looked away, Ursula hiding her face in her handkerchief as she blew her nose, Henry staring out the window with a weary sigh. Her grandfather was the first to look back, the old scars of guilt and sorrow shadowing his eyes.

"We haven't heard from Allen since he left. Why?"

Lily and Madam Barrington looked at each other, coming to a collective decision. "Because John Faust has him," Lily said, weariness creeping into her own voice.

"What?" Henry exclaimed, face more animated than she'd ever seen it. Ursula said nothing because she'd broken down sobbing.

Madam Barrington took up the tale, editing heavily. "We recently paid Allen a visit, so he could meet Lily. Unfortunately John must have followed us there and took the opportunity to rekindle their old sibling rivalry. He seems bent on punishing Allen for things that happened decades ago."

Lily noticed that her mentor hadn't bothered mentioning Morgan le Fay. But then she supposed it was irrelevant at the moment as far as her grandparents were concerned.

"They were such good boys," Ursula wailed, coming up for air. Her tears left streaks through layers of makeup and her handkerchief was stained. "Why couldn't they just get along? What did we do wrong?"

Henry finally sidled over, laying a comforting hand on his wife's shoulder. "John always bullied him. We knew that, Ursula, even if we chose to ignore it," he said, the frank confession only eliciting a fresh wail from his wife. He didn't look much better. His shoulders drooped, and his face was worn and drawn.

As if on cue, Fletcher glided into the parlor, carrying a tray laden with a cup of coffee, two cups of tea, a shot of some amber liquid, and a box of tissues. He offered the cups of tea to Lily and her mentor—they both declined—before turning to present the coffee to Henry. The older man took it gratefully and sipped while his butler coaxed Ursula to take the shot of liquor, blotting her eyes as she sniffed pitifully.

Lily felt a pang of sympathy. Despite their mistakes, they were still human beings who loved and lost, just like she did. It couldn't have been easy, trying to parent a child like John Faust. At least they cared, even if they'd done a terrible job of showing it.

"Do you have any idea where he might be now?" Lily asked, trying to sound gentle, "or where he might have taken Allen?"

"None," Henry said with a shake of his head.

"He never told me anything," Ursula added miserably between hiccups, "just that it was 'business.'"

Sharing another look with her mentor, Lily asked, "Do you mind if we take a look at his workroom?"

Henry shrugged. "I doubt you'll find anything of use, but you are welcome to look. He cleaned it out before he left. Took most of our family book collection with him as well." He scowled in displeasure. "We haven't touched the room since."

They nodded in understanding and headed out of the parlor, leaving Henry and Fletcher to comfort a distraught Ursula.

As they approached the end of the west wing hall, Lily felt her heartbeat quicken as goosebumps tingled across her skin. She took a few deep, calming breaths, reminding herself that John Faust was gone, and with him the ominous feel of the hallway. The doors leading up to the workroom, one of which had held Lily prisoner only a few weeks ago, looked and felt normal. Gone also was the heavy weight of resistance at his workroom door, the fortress of wards having been removed. It was locked, however, so they fiddled with a spell to trip the mechanism, rather than bothering Henry for a key.

As they entered, Lily felt the tiniest brush on her face, like a spiderweb. But it was gone the instant she noticed it.

"Did you feel that?" she asked, her voice echoing in the large, empty space as she stared around the desolate room with its tall windows, vaulted two-story ceiling, and landing in the northeast corner which led to the second floor.

"Yes. A trigger spell, I would guess. Most likely left to alert John when someone entered the room."

Lily felt her stomach churn, nervous despite herself. The place felt eerie, devoid of John Faust's possessions—the crafting materials, books, papers, experiments and equipment—yet still his presence lingered in the odds and ends littering the floor.

The scraps of paper, bits of crafting reagents, and random test tubes scattered around reminded her what the room had been, and it made her shiver.

While Lily examined the floor, Madam Barrington looked upward, scanning the ceiling and walls. Then, abandoning her observation, she drew close to her student, rummaging in her handbag as if to cover her odd behavior as she spoke softly. "If I am not mistaken, and I rarely am, we are being watched."

Lily looked up as well, though she wasn't really looking with her eyes. Reaching out with her senses she, too, could detect the faint pricks of magic, four of them, spaced around the ceiling's perimeter. Though not as adept at recognizing spells as her mentor, she could tell they were in the conveyance category, and what else could they be for if not to spy on the comings and goings of the room?

Taking the proffered handkerchief Madam Barrington had withdrawn from her handbag, Lily blew her nose conspicuously before whispering back, "Do you think he's watching us right now?"

"Possibly," the older woman said. "He rightly assumed we would come looking for him, though I can not imagine what he thinks he will discover by watching us stare at an empty room. Still, let us spend a few minutes carefully checking for anything of interest, and then we can retire and discuss our thoughts in a less...compromised location."

Lily did as Madam Barrington had advised, though she was distracted by the prickling sensation on the back of her neck. It was the feeling of being watched.

After a good ten minutes of going over the room, inch by inch, she'd found nothing of interest and no sign of other spells. The last place for her to check, as Madam Barrington finished her own round of the room, was the landing. The landing where, mere weeks ago, she'd been strapped down, poked, prodded, and studied like a lab rat. By her own father.

She shuddered, hesitating at the bottom of the stairs. The large contraption to which she'd been strapped—a sort of old-fashioned dentist chair in the center of two vertical rings of metal, set perpendicular to each other and welded together, inscribed with dimmu runes—was gone. A device of John Faust's own invention, he'd created it to try to locate Morgan le Fay, probably after Allen had absconded with his primary research material on that ancient wizard. John Faust had enchanted the device with some sort of location spell linked to the LeFay bloodline which would enable him to pinpoint the physical location of Morgan herself. To work, however, it needed to be fueled by a direct descendant. And there was the pesky side effect it had on its subject. Nothing too terrible, just probable insanity and possible death.

Obviously, John Faust couldn't use himself as a subject. He'd already tried Ursula's mother, Vera, hoping her distant relation—most wizard families were distantly related in some way or another—would be enough. It hadn't been, and the device's side effects had been evidenced by the crazed moaning Lily had heard at night when she'd first been a "guest" at her father's estate. Apparently they kept the old woman locked up in a room somewhere. The fact that she had been a willing participant, at least according to John Faust, had not made the revelation any less horrifying.

Now, as she lifted her foot to mount the first step, all Lily could think about was how she'd nearly been the next "subject." Of course her father hadn't *wanted* to damage his own daughter. But when she'd refused to join him, he claimed she'd left him no choice. She would help advance the cause of wizards everywhere whether she wanted to or not. And, he assured her, he'd made the necessary adjustments to make any adverse side effects very unlikely—as if that would make her feel better about being strapped down and experimented on.

"Lily? Are you quite alright?" Madam Barrington's voice came from across the room, snapping Lily out of her gruesome recollections.

Taking a deep breath, she forced her legs to move. "I'm...fine. Thanks. I just want to check out the landing and then I think we can leave."

The landing was empty but for the tables and various bits of debris everywhere. Looking down, Lily could see the holes in the fine paneled wood where the device had been bolted to the floor. She took a moment to glance over and under the tables, picking up each scrap of paper in case it had writing on it.

As she rounded the back edge of the landing that abutted the north wall, she came to the east wall where a door was supposed to open into the upstairs hall of the west wing and thus to the rest of the house. There was an identical door leading to an identical landing on the opposite side of the house where the vaulted ceilings of the family library caught the glorious rays of the rising sun. But unlike that door, this door was shut, locked, and boarded over.

Reaching between the boards, Lily tried it, just in case. It didn't budge, of course, and her hand came away covered in a layer of dust. Much like his brother Allen, it appeared John Faust didn't trust his constructs to come in and clean his precious workshop.

She stepped back, examining the doorframe. It seemed normal enough, but there was something odd about it. It looked much newer than the surrounding wood, almost as if it had been recently replaced or revarnished. Laying a hand on it she closed her eyes and concentrated, reaching out to try to detect any lingering magic.

What she found was confusing, to say the least. After taking one more, good look, just to be sure, she left the landing. She didn't want to give whoever was watching a reason to think she'd found anything.

Meeting Madam Barrington in the middle of the room, she shook her head. "Nothing but trash. Did you find anything?"

The older woman also shook her head. "There is nothing left. This, at least, is a dead end. Let us not waste any more time here. There are other, more promising leads we should attend to."

Lily nodded and they headed out the door. She wasn't much of an actor, and could only hope their little show had been enough to convince John Faust. Well, she wasn't sure they *had* found anything of use, so who knew, maybe the act wasn't an act at all. She would find out on the drive home.

Chapter 2
WHEN ALL ABOUT YOU

THOUGH SHE RARELY HELD OFFICE HOURS ON SATURDAYS, THE START OF A NEW term was always hectic, so Lily usually ended up at McCain Library more Saturdays than not. Today it was to help the beleaguered library staff with the usual start-of-term shenanigans that a host of college freshmen brought into their sacred domain.

Not above grunt work, that particular morning she was hanging notices of library rules and policies in every reading cubbyhole and study space. Each year there were always those few students who thought the library was their personal playground, the librarians their mothers whose job it was to pick up after them. This year it seemed particularly bad. All week the staff had been finding library books strewn about the place, not just in the cubbyholes or desks but even on the floor in between aisles. It was absolutely scandalous, not to mention irritating. And they were the oddest books, too. Not the normal reference material related to freshman classes or the titles on the required reading list. She'd found a book on elementary education and another on basic linguistics. Not even their children's section had gone unscathed, with picture books about Moo the Cow and the *Adventures of Tiny Tim* lying splayed open in front of their shelves. As she hung flyers with many a mutinous grumble, she plotted what punishment she'd inflict on any student she caught in the act. They would be scarred for life when she was done with them.

Once she'd covered every blank wall space on all seven floors with her dire warnings of death and destruction, she returned to her office on the first floor to tackle the growing pile of paperwork and answer a few emails. It was no wonder she was behind. When you were busy trying to stop a megalomaniacal wizard bent on world domination—okay, slightly melodramatic, but true nonetheless—you tended to spend more time practicing life-saving spells than pushing papers. Today, however, she was taking a break from practicing magic. In the case of spell casting, all work and no play meant you got burned out, sloppy, and careless, which usually ended up getting you killed.

After a few productive hours in her office, she headed home to clean the house, do laundry, dishes, and all the other little things she'd been neglecting. Not only did straightening the house help her relax, but she was also expecting a guest that evening.

Ever since their unexpectedly short date last Friday, Richard had been calling her every day, leaving apologetic messages and attempting to reschedule a makeup date. While she appreciated his concern and proactive planning, he obviously didn't know much about interacting with introverts. Pestering was the absolute worst way to get on an introvert's good side. Every time her phone rang and she saw his number pop up, she silently begged him to go away and leave her alone. It wasn't that she didn't want to go on another date, or even that she didn't want to talk to him. It was just a really bad time. Her conflicted feelings about Sebastian, of course, had nothing to do with it. Nothing at all.

Finally, out of common decency and politeness, she'd called him back. Unwilling to venture out again with the possibility of being left stranded, she'd decided to invite him to a low-key dinner at her place: lasagna and salad with a healthy dose of chess pie to top it off. While she preferred foods not battered, fried, or drowned in butter, she was still, at heart, a Southerner. Chess pie was basically in her DNA. One of the most simple yet delicious southern desserts, it was the ultimate pantry pie: an adaptable recipe easily made with common ingredients found at home. It was also insanely sweet. While Lily was a purist when it came to hot tea—only heathens took sugar with their tea—she had a definite sweet tooth where dessert was concerned. She liked making chess pie because it was quick and simple, and she didn't have time to plan anything more elaborate.

While she still felt a nagging discomfort at the thought of Richard in her house, it was a far better compromise than her going to *his* house where she would be completely vulnerable. The fact that she thought of herself as 'vulnerable' around him probably should have raised a red flag or two, but she figured it was normal dating jitters. She didn't exactly have vast amounts of experience when it came to dating, or men, or relationships in general. This was the very first person she'd ever had a second date with, and definitely the only one who looked, and acted, like a man— a fact that made her delightfully warm every time she thought about it. Her online dating profile had seemed to attract an inordinately large percentage of males who either still lived in their mother's basement, or hadn't bothered to learn the basics of English grammar, both of which excluded them from the "man" category in her book.

So her house it was. She studiously ignored her pesky doubts, including Sebastian's words of warning. It wasn't like he'd ever taken her advice when it came to Tina. Besides, having Richard over to dinner at her house killed two birds with one stone. Three, actually. It kept her on her home turf where she felt at ease and in control, and it wouldn't leave her feeling abandoned if he had to leave early. Lastly, she'd decided to broach the topic of Sebastian—getting him out of jail, of course, not her feelings for him. Not that she had feelings for him. At least not feelings that meant anything.

A grain of common sense pointed out that it might not be wise to discuss a murder investigation with an FBI agent without a lawyer present, but if there was any chance he might help, it would be worth it. If the evening went well, and Richard seemed in a generous mood, she would bring it up before he left.

Of course, not being the only resident in her apartment did pose a slight problem, especially since said resident was not her date's biggest fan.

"Kip, I want you to stay in the bedroom while Richard is here," she said with as much authority as she could muster while strapped into an apron and up to her elbows in tomato sauce. "I'd like to have dinner with him in peace and quiet without worrying about you causing a scene." She glared down at the cat who sat at her feet, watching her add the ground beef to the lasagna with an eagle's eye, ready to "retrieve" any piece foolish enough to attempt an escape.

"I promise not to cause a scene," he said distractedly, eyes fixed on her hands as they moved back and forth. "Unless, of course, a scene is needed," he added after a pause, tail-tip twitching.

Lily pursed her lips, finishing with the last layer of noodles, tomato sauce, and cheese before covering the whole dish and sliding it into the oven. Rinsing off her red-splattered extremities, she turned to her cat, hands on hips.

"I shall not require your 'intervention,' thank you very much. You *will* remain in the bedroom, or else. If I catch sight of a single hair or whisker, you'll be getting that long-overdue bath you've been avoiding for weeks now."

With the ground beef thoroughly tainted with tomato sauce and guarded by the fiery furnace, Sir Kipling had turned his full attention to her. At the mention of a bath, he glared daggers, ears put back in feline displeasure. Lily raised a hand, pointing it toward the bedroom as she banished him with a word.

"Shoo."

He didn't budge, but instead raised a back leg over his head to ostentatiously clean his posterior.

"Whatever," Lily grumbled, knowing a lost battle when she saw one. She turned back to the counter, seeing to a few last preparations before shedding her apron and heading to the bathroom for a shower. Calling over her shoulder, she left the room with a warning. "If you're not in the bedroom by the time he's supposed to arrive, I'll carry you there myself."

In retrospect, Lily thought as she let streams of hot water wash away the dust and stress, it probably wasn't wise to telegraph her battle strategy. She wouldn't be surprised if she emerged from the shower and discovered her cat had disappeared, only to reappear at the least opportune moment. She was inclined to worry but comforted herself with the thought that Richard was a skilled and respected FBI agent. He could handle something as simple as a scheming cat. Probably.

To her great surprise, she found Sir Kipling sleeping—or at least pretending to sleep—on the bedcovers when she re-entered the bedroom wrapped in a towel. She eyed him suspiciously, but he ignored her, so she turned her attention to picking just the right outfit. It needed to be casual, yet attractive. But not too attractive. She wanted to encourage Richard's interest, not wave a red flag in his face. Not that she owned any flag-waving outfits. Well, there was that one little black dress, but that was for cocktail parties. Her taste in fashion followed a more conservative bent with a vintage twist. She settled on a demure grey cotton dress with white polka dots. Its simple A-line skirt, cap sleeves, and v-neckline were elegant without being fancy. If the v-neck dipped a bit lower than most of her other outfits, well, she would just have to make do.

She finished her hair—a simple twist with plenty of bangs left loose to curl around her face and neck—and makeup just in time. At the sound of her doorbell, she rushed from the bedroom, giving Sir Kipling one last warning glare before shutting the door and hurrying to the front of the apartment. She slowed as she reached it, taking a deep breath and fixing a smile on her face before opening the door in an unhurried fashion.

Richard Grant stood on the doorstep, once again effortlessly handsome in crisp slacks and a button-down shirt. He even wore a tie this time, though Lily wasn't sure if he was putting forth extra effort due to a guilty conscience, or if he was simply trying to impress her. Either way, it worked. She had to force herself to stop admiring his finely chiseled form, instead fixing her eyes on his face as she welcomed him in with a smile. He held another bouquet of roses, which he presented as he stepped across the threshold.

"To make up for the ones we accidentally left in my car," he said with an apologetic smile.

"They're lovely," Lily said, thanking him warmly. They really were quite pretty, if lacking in the fragrance department—one of the pitfalls of greenhouse flowers bred for sturdiness, not scent. Turning, she led him through to the kitchen, motioning him to a chair as she got out a vase for the flowers. With her back turned to him, she didn't realize he hadn't taken the proffered seat until a few minutes later after she'd finished arranging them and picked up the whole confection to set it on the dining room table.

To her surprise, and displeasure, he'd wandered back into her living room and was now examining her bookshelves with obvious interest. While she was pleased by his interest in books, she wasn't thrilled at the thought of him wandering around her house at will. Why did she feel like she had to keep an eye on him?

Shaking her head, she set down the flowers and joined Richard in the living room, watching with interest as he ran reverent fingers over her leather-bound copies of classics like *Great Expectations*, *The Count of Monte Cristo*, and the collected works of Rudyard Kipling. His hand stopped when he got to Kipling and he carefully removed the book from the shelf, letting it fall open in his hands.

Lily felt a hot flash of annoyance that he hadn't asked permission to handle her books, even if he was treating them with the deferential care they deserved. But she was distracted from this when Richard began to read. His voice was surprisingly smooth and melodic, shaping the words with not just feeling, but a familiarity that spoke of deep understanding.

"If you can keep your head when all about you are losing theirs and blaming it on you, if you can trust yourself when all men doubt you, but make allowance for their doubting too…" he trailed off, brows drawing together in somber contemplation.

Lily took up the recitation. Being an ardent admirer of all things Kipling—as evidenced by her choice in cat names—she knew many of his poems by heart. "If you can wait and not be tired by waiting, or being lied about, don't deal in lies."

As if her words were a magnet, Richard's eyes lifted from the page to her face. His normal look of quiet strength had fallen in a moment of thoughtful distraction, and behind it Lily could see doubt and the heavy weight of responsibility. Looking at her, yet seeming not to see her, he continued, heedless of the open book in his hand. "Or being hated, don't give way to hating, and yet don't look too good, nor talk too wise." He stopped, breath stilled, as though the words themselves had stolen it.

With a pang of pity, she continued the verse for him. "If you can dream—and not make dreams your master; if you can think—and not make thoughts your aim."

Her words recalled him, and he looked at her in wonder as if he really saw her for the first time. Joining her, their voices mingled as they stared deep into each other's eyes.

"If you can meet with Triumph and Disaster and treat those two impostors just the same; if you can bear to hear the truth you've spoken twisted by knaves to make a trap for fools, or watch the things you gave your life to, broken, and stoop and build 'em up with worn-out tools."

They stopped, falling silent as one for an extended moment as they searched each other's face. Finally remembering that she needed to breathe, Lily took in a great gulp of air, breaking the spell. They both laughed as Lily smiled and blushed, feeling silly but oddly not embarrassed.

"You're very well versed in your Kipling, Miss Singer," Richard said. "Not that I would have guessed any different," he added in a rush, smiling sheepishly as he returned the book to its shelf.

"It's an occupational hazard, I assure you," she said, surprised at how relaxed she felt. "Of course, *If* is my favorite poem of all time, so I could probably recite it in my sleep."

"It's one of my favorites as well," Richard agreed, his smile broadening. "It speaks to every person on such a deep level, encapsulating what it truly means to be human, while at the same time giving a fascinating perspective on the idea of manhood and the essence of Britishness during the time of Kipling. It's an inspiration, a conviction, and an education all in one."

Lily's polite smile turned into a wide grin of unabashed admiration. He was speaking her language, and it was divine. How long had she yearned for someone, a companion with whom to share her love of history, literature, and poetry? An intellectual, a lover of knowledge? And here he was, all beautifully packaged and tied up in a gentlemanly bow. It seemed too good to be true. "I couldn't have put it better myself, Mr. Grant. You obviously care a great deal about the written word, and I can give no higher praise."

He laughed. "Please, call me Richard. Nothing makes me feel older than being called *mister*."

"Sorry," Lily ducked her head. "It's rather ingrained. Nothing like a proper southern upbringing to ruin your ability to be casual."

Richard laughed again, stepping forward to gently take her arm and steer them both into the kitchen. She found she liked making him laugh. It made her feel witty and socially adept. A new feeling, to be sure.

"I'm guessing that getting your hide tanned for not addressing an adult properly will do that to you," Richard commented, looking down at her with a crooked smile.

"Something like that," she murmured, once again caught by the depth of those eyes. She hadn't noticed before, but the hazel of his irises was flecked with the most enchanting green.

A loud beeping made her jump, pulling her arm out of Richard's grasp as she rushed to the oven and hurriedly removed the lasagna. Thank goodness she'd set an alarm, or else it would have burned. She'd completely forgotten about it, thanks to Richard Grant's powers of poetry recitation.

She busied herself setting the table, pouring drinks, and serving the food to hide her suddenly resurgent nerves. What if Richard didn't like pasta? What if he were a vegetarian? What if he preferred sliced tomatoes to grape tomatoes in his salad? She mentally kicked herself for not asking such questions beforehand, despite knowing they were just the product of a worrying mind. She knew she was a good cook, she'd just never fed a man a home-cooked meal before. Sebastian didn't count. He would eat anything that didn't move, and some things that did.

"Smells delicious." Richard smiled encouragingly at her, finally able to catch her eye now that she had nothing else to do but sit and eat.

"Oh—thank you. It's all very simple fare, of course. I wasn't sure if you had any food allergies or what type of cuisine you preferred," she babbled, stabbing distractedly at a leaf of lettuce with her spoon. "I mean, if you had a gluten or dairy allergy, then lasagna would be a terrible choice, but I didn't think that likely since—"

"It's perfect," he said, cutting her off as he laid a reassuring hand on her arm.

She twitched ever so slightly, fighting her traitorous instinct to pull back and instead stubbornly forcing herself to relax and enjoy the warm tingle where his skin touched hers.

It was a brief moment, however, since he soon followed his words with action by digging into the meal with gusto. Lily was quite impressed with how quickly, yet neatly, he put away his food. Not once did she catch him speaking with his mouth full as their conversation moved from poetry, to history, to social science.

Despite her worries, her four-footed harbinger of chaos and snark did not appear, seeming to take her threat of a bath seriously enough to stay in the bedroom. She actually managed to relax and enjoy the meal, getting up to serve Richard seconds and even thirds—where did men put all that food?—before he finally raised a hand, swearing he couldn't eat another bite.

"Well, that's a shame," she said with a smile. "Where are you going to put all the chess pie I made?"

"Chess pie? Mm-mmh! Don't you know, I have two stomachs. One for food and one for dessert."

Lily laughed, getting up to retrieve the pie from the refrigerator. "Would you like some coffee with your dessert?" she asked over her shoulder.

"The answer to that is always yes. I stop moving and go into a coma if my caffeine levels get too low."

She thought about pointing out how unhealthy it was to be addicted to caffeine but decided he probably already knew.

"Hey, do you mind if I use the bathroom while you're getting dessert ready?" Richard asked.

"Of course. It's at the end of the hall."

She heard the scrape of his chair as he stood up and headed down the hall while she busied herself with slicing pie and putting on a large pot of water to boil. Opening her tea cabinet, she examined the orderly rows of boxes and bags, trying to choose what to drink with her pie. She decided on an Indian-spiced chai. Not her usual fare, but the creamy blend of honey, milk, black tea, and exotic spices would go well with the simple sweetness of the southern dessert.

Selection made, she began to grind Richard's coffee while the water boiled. Being largely ignorant when it came to coffee, she'd made a quick search online earlier that week to bring her up to at least 101 level. She didn't own a coffee machine, but discovered she didn't need one. Using her pepper mill to grind the beans, she clipped a handkerchief across the mouth of a large mug for the filter and carefully poured the boiled water over her jury-rigged coffeemaker in 30-second increments to keep from scalding the grounds.

For something that tasted so vile, the freshly ground and brewed beans smelled surprisingly delicious. She hoped that meant she'd made a suitable cup of coffee, and put the water back on to reheat for her tea as she cleaned up.

Richard still hadn't returned to the kitchen by the time she'd finished steeping her tea, and she started to worry. Had the toilet stopped up? Had Sir Kipling escaped and somehow locked her date in the bathroom? How he would pull off such a stunt she had no idea, but she wouldn't put it past him.

After carefully arranging their plates of pie and hot mugs of steaming goodness, she headed for the kitchen doorway, intending to poke her head around the corner and see if the bathroom door was still closed. Just as she neared the corner, however, Richard rounded it, moving with uncharacteristic haste, and they collided. Well, actually, Lily bumped into Richard's tall, solid frame, and bounced. She might have fallen flat on her bottom if he hadn't reached out and caught her, pulling her to him in a convulsive grab that seemed to surprise him as much as it surprised her. He quickly let go, apologizing profusely as he checked her over for damage. His look of embarrassed guilt was slow to fade as she shakily brushed off his concern, spouting every politeness she could think of in an attempt to halt the rising flush in her cheeks.

They finally made it back to the table and sat, avoiding each other's gaze as they partook of the after-dinner fare. Lily hadn't put out cream or sugar, assuming Richard scorned those frilly additives as just a distraction from the all-important task of caffeine consumption. Sure enough, he reached for his coffee straight away even before tasting the pie, not pausing until he'd brought it close enough to breathe in the aroma rising from it on swirling tendrils of steam.

"Wow!" he exclaimed, eyes widening in surprise. "This smells fantastic. For someone who thinks coffee is vile, you sure are good at making it!" He beamed at her, raising his cup in salute before drinking at least half of it down in one gulp, unaffected by or simply ignoring the scalding heat.

Lily couldn't help but smile. She sipped her spiced chai primly, trying not to look too pleased. "Oh, don't exaggerate, Mr. Grant. I mean, Richard," she amended at his mock scowl. "I'm sure it only tastes so good because you're used to cheap diner coffee."

"Not true," he argued, putting down the cup and picking up his fork, which he waved about animatedly as he drove home his point. "I happen to be quite the coffee connoisseur. I know what a good cup of joe tastes like. And this"—he pointed to his cup with the fork—"is a good cup of joe."

"You're too kind," Lily insisted demurely, though only because it was polite to do so. Inside she was glowing, feeling that she'd finally accomplished something. For once. "I would save the gushing, though. You haven't tasted your pie yet."

He did, dramatically rolling his eyes heavenward and making sounds of ecstasy as he savored the first bite. "Holy smokes, woman, where have you been all my life? I haven't had pie like this since my Granny's fourth of July picnics back when I was a kid." The pie disappeared in short order, even before the rest of the coffee, which Lily took as a greater compliment than all of Richard's words and dramatic sound effects put together.

Of course, it was possible he was just laying it on thick in an attempt to make up for their last date. But Lily chose to focus on the genuine look of pleasure on his face as he ate instead of dwelling on the possibility of calculated compliments. After all, you couldn't blame a man for trying.

After dessert they retired to the couch. Well, it would be more accurate to say that she attempted to hide behind a stack of dirty dishes, which Richard deftly extracted her from as he gently pulled her toward the living room. She didn't know why, but now that the distraction of food and drink had been removed, she felt suddenly and cripplingly shy. What happened next? Was it too early to ask him to leave? Did she even want him to leave? If he stayed, what would they do? Hadn't there been something she was going to ask him? She couldn't remember.

Fortunately, her ninja worrying skills were no match for his quiet confidence, and he seemed not to mind her abrupt awkwardness as he settled her on the couch and sat next to her: not so close as to crowd, but close enough to lean in for a kiss. Why that particular measurement of distance came to mind she declined to consider, yet she didn't scoot away to a more respectable distance, either. For some reason, though, when Richard rested his arm on the back of the couch—not touching her, just reminding her of the possibility—she felt oddly caged. Hemmed in on all sides. Was that a normal feeling? She had no idea, having nothing to compare it to. She wanted to *want* to be near him. But her traitorous emotions were not cooperating.

She tried to relax, reminding herself that sitting companionably on the couch was a perfectly normal thing to do with one's date. Wasn't it?

Richard, it seemed, had a nervous side, too, under all that calm composure. His posture was relaxed, but Lily could feel tension in the air. "Thank you for the wonderful meal," he said abruptly, probably as desperate as she was to break the silence.

"It was nothing," Lily murmured, staring at the bottom corner of her bookshelf where it met the rug.

"Nonsense, Miss Singer. I—may I call you Lily?"

She nodded mutely, now examining the books on the shelves.

"Lily, it was a delicious example of fine cooking and I'm honored to have been a part of it."

Pleased, but not knowing what to say, she simply didn't answer, eyes absently surveying each title on her bookshelf to make sure it was in alphabetical order. Wait, what was *The Adventures of Sherlock Holmes* doing to the right of *Alice in Wonderland*? It belonged on the left side. Who had moved it?

"Lily? Lily!"

Her head finally turned at Richard's second, more insistent call. She focused on the knot of his tie. A very well-tied knot it was, too. A handsome knot. A handsome man.

"Is there something wrong?" he asked, voice warm but concerned.

"Um…no." Lily said slowly. "I'm just not very good at…well…you see I haven't had much opportunity to…"—she hesitated, paralyzed mind refusing her command for an elegant way to express herself—"date," she finished, blushing.

Richard chuckled, though it had a nervous tinge to it. "Don't worry. Even old dogs like me freeze up sometimes. But I don't see why you have anything to worry about. You're a remarkable woman. Smart, talented, beautiful, well-spoken. Nobody is going to care about a few awkward jitters when you've got all that going for you."

"Really?" She asked, finally daring to look up. His hazel eyes caught hers and he stared deep into them, seeming to forget what he was about to say.

Some inexorable force was pulling at her, drawing her closer to him. The decision-making part of her mind had shut down, refusing to respond to the frantic voice in the back of her head, and she found she was grateful. And terrified. How could one be excited about and yet dread something at the same time? She spent a good few seconds mulling over this question, clinging to the welcome distraction as Richard's face loomed nearer and nearer. He seemed just as mesmerized as she, though there was a hint of something else in his eyes.

His face was so close now that she could feel the warmth of his breath. It sent tingles all the way through her body, down her spine, and to her toes, awakening a fire in her she'd never felt before. It was deep, hot, and made her shiver in delight. She closed her eyes, waiting, breathless.

"MEOW!"

The *very* loud and insistent sound crashed down over her like a bucket of ice-cold water. She felt Richard jump in surprise, and her eyes flew open as she whipped her head around toward the sound's source, thunderclouds coalescing above her head.

"Sir Edgar Allan Kipling! I told you—" She stopped abruptly, gaze falling on the small pile of black somethings at her saboteur cat's feet. "What are those?" She asked in confusion, an uncomfortable chill washing over her skin that only moments before had been so hot.

"Gifts your date left in the hall, bedroom, and bathroom. I suspect there's one in here, too, but I haven't looked yet."

"How in the world did—" Lily vaguely heard Richard's confused voice, but she shut it out.

"What do you mean?" she asked her cat, not caring that there was another person in the room witnessing her one-sided conversation. She started to get up, needing to prove to herself that those small black things were *not* what they looked like. But Richard grabbed her wrist, stopping her. She turned in surprise, and finally saw, looming there plain as day, what she'd only caught glimpses of before.

Guilt.

Her heart skipped a beat and she could hardly breathe.

"Look, I can explain—

"Let go of me!" She bit out, wrenching her wrist from his grip with a sudden viciousness that caught them both off guard. Thoughts and feelings bombarded her, horrified questions she needed, but didn't want, answers to. Getting up from the couch, she bent and gathered the objects, a cold dread washing through her as she stared down at them. She didn't need to be an FBI agent to know that they were listening devices.

The cold dread was replaced by a hot knife. Her chest hurt like she'd been stabbed. First her father, then her best friend, now her date. Was there any man she could trust?

"Get. Out." Her words snapped through the air like gunshots. Was that why her ears were ringing? Or was that the rage?

Richard got up slowly from the couch, hands held up in pleading. "Lily, it's not what it looks like. I mean, it is, but not like you think. Please, let me explain." He tried to take a step toward her, but Sir Kipling arched his back and hissed ferociously, making him start.

"Explain? It seems pretty plain to me, Agent Grant," she said, her words sharp enough to cut glass. Richard winced at each one. "You took advantage of me. You came into my house, ate my food, played with my feelings, all so you could spy on me. Obviously I'm under FBI investigation, though for what I have no clue"—she had some guesses, but wasn't about to voice them—"and apparently it was just too difficult to set up a van on the corner like any *normal* FBI stakeout. No, you had to worm your way into my home and string me along all while pretending to be a respectable southern gentleman.

"Why? Were you bored of sitting out in your van? Did you want a little sport? You make me sick," she spat out. "Well here's your sport. Catch." She threw the handful of electronic bugs at him as hard as she could. He reacted instantly, arms raising reflexively to protect his face so that the tiny missiles bounced off them instead, scattering in all directions.

Arms still raised, he peered at her between them, expression tortured. "Please, Lily. It's not like that at all. I really am interested in you. Everything I told you is the truth. Yes, I originally approached you because you're part of an ongoing investigation and I had to do my job. But that doesn't mean I don't care. There's a lot of stuff going on you don't know about. The FBI is trying to protect you as much as get answers. I'm trying to keep you safe, not spy on you. If you'd just sit down we can talk about it. I'll explain everything."

Lily drew herself up, summoning every shred of dignity she had left. "You will address me as Miss Singer, if you please, Agent Grant. And I am not interested in hearing anything you have to say. You've manipulated me from the start and I want you out of my house this instant. If the FBI has anything to say to me, have them send someone else, because I never want to see you again."

"Please—"

"*Leave!*"

Sir Kipling punctuated her word with a few more hisses and a threatening swipe in Richard's direction.

Richard's shoulders drooped in defeat, and he bent to pick up his surveillance equipment before heading for the door. After he opened it, he looked back, lips parted to voice another plea.

"Out!" Lily almost yelled, desperate to be rid of him as hot tears pricked the corners of her eyes.

He turned and left, closing the door softly behind him.

Lily collapsed on the couch, burying her head in her arms as she wept, heart broken in so many new, painful places she hadn't realized were there.

Fortunately she had all of Sunday to regain enough composure to be seen in polite company. It seemed she'd fallen harder for Richard than she realized, though that wasn't the worst of it. What hurt the most was knowing she had, once again, ignored her instincts in search of companionship. She yearned for someone to be close to, someone who understood her—whether that be a father who shared her interest in magic or a boyfriend who could recite poetry with her. John Faust had been bad enough, but her blindness in that case was understandable. She was desperate to know her real father, and John Faust was a master of lies and manipulation. After seeing the truth, she should have been more careful, should have known better. Well, she *had* known better, deep down, which is what galled her. Richard was an FBI agent, for goodness' sake. Why had she deluded herself into thinking he cared for anything else than to pry into her life?

Copious amounts of tea and chocolate dulled the stabbing hurt but left a bitter ache that plagued her deep into the night. Sir Kipling kept close, rubbing on her ankles and curling up to purr in her lap at every opportunity. He didn't utter a single "see" or "I told you so," proving his undying love for her with uncharacteristic restraint. She was more grateful than words could express, as he seemed to be the only male around she could trust these days.

With that sad commentary on her life to keep her company, she left for work Monday morning in less-than-high spirits. She'd had her phone turned off since Saturday night, not wanting even the possibility of a call from Richard to disturb her. Now, sitting down at her desk, she took a moment to relax surrounded by the comforting smell of books and the soft glow of morning light suffusing her office. Then, taking a deep breath, she turned on her phone and braced for a slew of voicemails she was determined to delete without mercy.

To her great surprise, she had only one, and it wasn't from Richard. She felt both relieved and hurt but tried not to dwell on it as she listened to the voicemail.

"Miss Singer, your commission has been accepted by your first choice of artist. She has agreed to meet this Monday evening at the time and location indicated on your form, to discuss the particulars of your commission. As per our contract, we will be withdrawing fifty percent of the agreed-upon payment from your bank account, with the full amount to follow at the confirmed completion of your commission. If, for any reason, the artist fails to complete the commission, your payment will be refunded minus a ten percent transaction fee. We are at your disposal should you have any questions or concerns. Have a good evening."

The crisp, painfully proper voice of Anton Silvester cut off as the voicemail ended, leaving Lily even more weary than before. Over the weekend she'd done her best to forget about everything—the ploy to find Tina, Sebastian's predicament, her father's machinations. Now it all came crashing back and she wondered how she would get through it all.

There was nothing for it, however, but to do her best. Duty wasn't something you abandoned just because you'd had a bad day. Or weekend. Or life. And despite the fact that, in the throes of hurt and betrayal, she'd lumped Sebastian in with all the other men who'd caused her pain in her life, he was actually the one person out of all of them that she missed. She just wished he'd stop hiding things from her.

The day passed much more quickly than she wanted it to, bringing her inexorably closer to her confrontation with Tina. She wasn't looking forward to it, not least because she was terrible at confrontation, but also because she'd have to talk about Sebastian. Those feelings were still a tangled mess, and it was easier to ignore them.

Through the form she'd submitted to Anton, she'd

arranged to meet Tina at Grant Park, close to the entrance to Zoo Atlanta. It was a public enough place that there would be witnesses about to discourage any foul play, but private enough that they could have a conversation without fear of eavesdroppers. Lily stopped by her house on the way to meet Tina to pick up Sir Kipling, instructing him to watch out the back dash for anyone who looked like they were following them. She took a circuitous route and doubled back a few times just in case. This was not a meeting she wanted the FBI observing.

It was still bright and hot as Lily surveyed the spot where she was supposed to meet Tina. Tina, of course, didn't know she was meeting Lily. Just some unnamed person paying her a lot of money for a "job." Since Lily was afraid Tina might run away as soon as she saw her, instead of sitting on the agreed-upon park bench wearing a blue purse over her right shoulder, she simply left the purse on the bench and retreated to stand behind a nearby row of bushes, shaded by a spreading tree. Sir Kipling crouched under the bushes, surveying all with watchful eyes. It was his job to follow Tina if she ran off.

Close to their meeting time, a middle-aged woman sat down on the park bench, giving the lone purse an odd look. Lily's heart jumped, and she waited with bated breath, hoping she hadn't blown the whole thing. If the lady picked up the purse or looked around to find its owner, Tina might get suspicious. But if only she would sit there and look normal, as if the bag were hers…

Several moments passed and the woman stayed put, busy with her phone. Lily slowly let out her breath but remained tense. Where was Tina? She should be arriving any minute now.

Sir Kipling's soft meow filtered up through the branches

of the bush. "Straight ahead, in the shadow of that ticket booth over there."

Lily peered in that direction and finally spotted her quarry. Tina was leaning against the wall, arms crossed as she watched the bench, waiting. This presented a conundrum for Lily. Should she come out of hiding, giving Tina a chance to see her and run before she was close enough to talk? Should she stay put and let Tina approach the bench? Or should she try to sneak around closer and surprise Tina? Good grief, Lily thought, she was no good at this stuff.

Before she had a chance to decide, however, Tina pushed herself off from the wall and started slowly, casually, toward the bench. Lily let out a sigh of relief, suddenly realizing how tense her whole body had been. She rounded the edge of the line of bushes, keeping them between her and Tina, and waiting so she could come up behind the witch as she puzzled over the purse on the bench. Sir Kipling slunk off to find a good ambush spot in case Tina made a dash for it.

Tina came to a stop in front of the bench, looking around carefully before she turned to the clueless woman still sitting there, eyes glued to her phone. Picking up the pace, Lily hurried to get behind Tina while she was distracted, and just caught Tina's last few words to the unsuspecting mundane, who responded in complete confusion.

Now directly behind her target and only a few paces away, Lily spoke. "I'm the one you're looking for."

The witch whirled, eyes wary and fists rising in a defensive gesture. When she spotted Lily, however, she dropped her hands in disgust, lips forming a sneer. "Well if it isn't Little Miss Perfect. I should have known it would be you."

"Yes, you should have, after you abandoned Sebastian."

Lily said, eyes flashing and suddenly feeling dangerously confident. This good-for-nothing had caused her enough trouble already. It was time to stop being nervous and get the job done.

She stepped forward and took Tina's upper arm in a not-quite-threatening grip, towing her away from the bench and into the shade of some trees. Tina resisted at first, but Lily tightened her hold and hissed a word of warning, sounding almost like Sir Kipling, who had emerged from the bushes and was trotting behind them. Lily was a good head taller than the petite witch, and while she might not have had much bulk or muscle strength, she had plenty of practice frightening careless students who mistreated her books. Where her precious library was concerned, she was as fierce as a she-tiger. Now she focused on channeling that feeling, filling herself with righteous indignation that squelched her timid embarrassment.

Finally spinning the smaller woman to face her, Lily glared down at that pixie face, which was glaring back up at her stubbornly.

"Sebastian needs you, and you are going to get off your sorry butt and help him." Lily declared, arms crossed.

"That idiot friend of yours got into trouble all by himself, and he can get out by himself, too. He already owes me for the investigation I did. There's nothing more in this for me and there's no way I'm sticking out my neck for him without some kind of guarantee. No way, José."

Her ears perked at Tina's choice of words. The witch was willing to help, if only for the right price. But first things first. "Sebastian said you got the whole incident on camera. Is that true?"

"Yeah," Tina shrugged. "I haven't gone back and looked at it or anything. Things got real crazy, real fast"—she shivered in disgust at the memory—"so I don't know what all it caught. But I've still got the camcorder."

A knot of tension inside Lily eased at the news. There was hope. "Then it's simple. Just bring the video in and testify that Sebastian didn't murder that woman and everything will be fine. We have a"—she was going to say initiate, but realized Tina might not understand the subtleties of wizard sub-culture, so chose to fudge the details for the sake of simplicity—"wizard lawyer. She's there to explain away any 'irregularities.' If you need it to be worth your time, we're perfectly willing to compensate you fairly."

Tina stared at her, brows pulled back and forehead creased in a look of incredulity. "You don't get it, do you, Miss Perfect? They're not going to see me as a witness, they're going to see me as an accomplice. They've already been tracking Rex's activities and probably know he was behind the museum job, where I just so happened to be when a valuable artifact was almost stolen. Now I show up at the murder scene of one of Rex's victims, someone who could put him in jail if she had only talked, and she ends up mysteriously dead? There's no way I'm coming in. All that tape will do is get the FBI to start digging into my past, and I ain't gonna let that happen. I don't care what kind of hocus pocus your lawyer thinks she can work, but unless you plan on telling the FBI about wizard strangling spells, there is *only* one thing that could have logically happened: loverboy killed that woman and I watched him do it."

As Tina spoke, Lily's stance slowly deflated, and her arms dropped to her sides. "Wait, wait," she finally said, "You've got it wrong. John Faust LeFay was behind the museum job. So how is Rex Morganson involved? Was he John Faust's partner?"

"Seriously? Sebastian didn't already tell you this?" Tina

threw up her hands, annoyance in every line of her body. "He'd better not get out of jail anytime soon, because if I get my hands on him—"

"You and me both," Lily muttered, and Tina froze, staring at her in surprise. Then she let out a guffaw, slapping her knee in mirth. Lily managed to crack a smile, sharing the brief moment of mutual frustration.

"Look," Tina said, turning serious again. "I don't really know what's going on either, I just read some FBI reports. But here's the gist: the FBI is investigating this guy named Rex Morganson, who's some sort of crime boss wanted for everything from fraud to theft and extortion. Only they think Rex is just an alias for this other guy named John Faust LeFay"—Lily froze at the witch's words, eyes widening in horror—"who they think is connected to a bunch of kids going missing over the past couple decades. It's pretty convoluted," Tina admitted, shrugging as she misinterpreted Lily's expression for confusion, "which is why loverboy and I tracked down one of the missing kid's moms to interview her and try and figure out what was going on. Then your idiot friend uses some sort of gimmick to look like Rex Morganson and trick the woman in to talking, and she freaks out! She yells his name, and before you know it her necklace comes alive and starts strangling her. I stuck around long enough to call 911 and then I booked it."

Lily felt around for a chair to collapse into, realized there wasn't one, and had to lock her knees halfway through trying to collapse into said nonexistent chair. The effort left her feeling lightheaded and clammy, despite the heat, but she gritted her teeth and tried to hide her shock. She shouldn't be surprised, of course. She already knew her father was an insane criminal. But realizing the full extent of his activities—especially when pointed out by someone else—filled her with shame. And then there was Sebastian. She finally realized why he'd been so reluctant to explain his and Tina's investigation. He'd wanted to spare her from this horrible feeling of…taint. How long had the FBI been investigating her father? What had Richard known that she didn't? She felt a pang of guilt on top of everything else, and cast her mind about, trying to think what to do next.

"Hey, you okay?" Tina said into the silence, staring at Lily who stood frozen, body stiff and eyes unseeing.

Lily shook herself, wishing desperately to bury her face in a book and forget about the world and its convoluted mess of humanity. "Yeah," she managed.

"Look, I'm actually sorry about Sebastian," Tina offered, still looking at Lily strangely, but in a you're-a-big-girl-you-can-handle-it kind of way. "It's not like I want him to get in trouble. But it's honestly not my problem. He asked *me* to help him dig up information, and I'm not even going to get the payment he promised for all my work, not with him stuck in jail. If there was anything I could do, I would. But there isn't. So just leave me alone, will you?"

She turned to go, but Lily caught her arm again, no longer assertive but desperate. "Wait! Please, you have to help. I—I can't let you go unless you do." Lily gulped, trying to summon her inner she-tiger as Tina looked at her with a raised eyebrow, eyes glinting dangerously.

"Can't let me go, huh? I wouldn't try that, if I were you, Miss Perfect. I've got friends."

"Well—so do I," she replied with much more bravery than she felt. But then a thought hit her. A thought which she did not like one. Single. Bit. But it was all she had. "In fact, I have friends in the FBI. I can get them to promise you immunity."

Tina stopped pulling away, looking at her suspiciously. "From everything?"

"Everything." Lily gulped. In for a penny, in for a pound, she thought. "I can get them to drop the whole case against Sebastian if we can give them Rex. You know they do this sort of thing all the time, giving immunity to people who rat out crime lords and drug bosses. This situation is no different."

The witch was silent for a long moment, and Lily could see gears whirring behind her calculating eyes. "I still get the payment you promised through Anton?" It was not a question.

The thought galled Lily, but she nodded anyway.

"Fine." Tina jerked her arm out of Lily's grasp, straightening her shirt with a huff. "Contact me the normal way once you have the immunity agreement *in writing*, judge-stamped, on official FBI paper or however they do it. And not before. Got it?"

Lily nodded again, assuming the conversation to be over. But Tina paused, mid-turn, looking at her strangely. Lily felt like she was being evaluated.

"You know, you don't deserve him," Tina said.

"Ex—excuse me?" Lily spluttered, not sure whether to be shocked or offended. Or just confused.

"Don't get me wrong, you're spunky and all. I'll give you that. But your Little Miss Perfect act makes me sick. You can't love him for who he is when you're always expecting him to be like you."

This time Lily really was shocked speechless, staring at Tina with her mouth hanging open.

"Oh, puleeze!" Tina rolled her eyes. "Don't pretend you haven't noticed. I started calling him loverboy as a joke, you know, because that's kind of the hat he wears. And I thought he was after me, at first. But he keeps turning me down. Na, he's loverboy because he's stupid in love with you. I'm talking really stupid. Smart guys get what they can, when they can. But no. He's only got eyes for you, and you haven't even noticed. That's rich."

"S—Sebastian?" Lily asked, so dumbfounded she'd even forgotten to blush.

"No, *duh*, Einstein. Good grief, you really *don't* deserve him. Heck, since the feelings obviously aren't mutual, be sure to send him back my way when this all blows over. Maybe even put in a good word for me," she winked impishly. "Be sure to say you were too busy judging him to even notice. That'll cinch the deal. See ya!"

The tiny witch gave a mocking wave and headed off toward the parking lot. As Lily stared after her, Sir Kipling gave a pained yowl, racing past her up a tree to glare around at empty air from his perch. Percy the poltergeist had finally made himself known, but Lily was too preoccupied to comfort her abused feline.

Sebastian loved her? No. There was no way. He'd never said a word, never made a move. He'd been hanging out with that witch, for goodness' sake. Tina said he'd refused her advances, but she could be lying. Why else would he be acting all cozy with the witch? Not to make her jealous, surely…

She's…kind of wild, and not a very nice person. Not like you. You actually care about people. She only cares what she can get out of you.

Sebastian's words echoed in her head, spoken at her bedside after he'd helped rescue her from the LeFay estate. She blushed at the memory, recalling the tender way he'd looked at her, the way his hand had felt, soft but strong.

You don't deserve him…You can never love him for who he is when you're always expecting him to be like you…You're too busy judging him…

Lily winced, shoulders drooping as she let out a long sigh. Tina was right. And she'd been too busy picking apart every way Sebastian offended her to even notice. Apparently, her self-awareness had some serious blinders when it came to her friend. She suspected it had to do with pride, not to mention her tendency to ignore things she didn't want to deal with. And there was plenty of that where Sebastian was concerned. Such as that word Tina had used, a word which made her want to cringe and whoop with joy at the same time.

Love.

Did she love Sebastian? She had no idea. But maybe it was time to start thinking about it, instead of ignoring it. Time to stop pretending and start dealing. Yes, that sounded nice and "go get 'em."

Lily groaned, remembering the task that lay ahead. This was going to be so much more complicated in light of her new resolution.

"Kip, are you okay?" She called up into the tree where her cat still crouched, looking grumpy.

"Humph. I will be, once my tail stops feeling like it's been used as a bell rope. If I ever get my claws into that poltergeist…"

Making soft noises of sympathy, Lily coaxed her cat out of the tree and retrieved her purse from the bench. It didn't have anything in it, of course, but it was one of her favorite purses, so she was grateful the random lady who'd served as unwitting bait hadn't carried it off.

On the way home she didn't bother looking for a tail. After all, she was about to paint a target the size of Georgia on her forehead, so what was the point? She briefly considered putting it off—perhaps giving things a few days to settle down would be better—but knew that Allen didn't have time for delays. For all she knew, he was already dead. Or driven to insanity. Or being tortured for information.

No, there could be no delay. As soon as she got home, she had to call Richard.

Chapter 3
THE ADVANTAGES OF BEING CRAZY

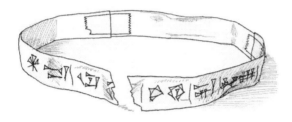

TO SAY THAT SHE DREADED THIS PHONE CALL WOULD BE PUTTING IT mildly. Sitting on her couch, staring at the cell phone in her lap, she procrastinated by thinking of a sufficiently colorful comparison for how she felt about the situation.

She would rather drink bottled green tea than call Richard Grant.

She would rather admit she'd had a crush on her ninth-grade English teacher, whose rendition of Shakespeare's 116th sonnet had always made her swoon, than call Richard Grant.

She would rather be seen walking the streets in a neon-orange vinyl jumpsuit with a feathered mullet than call Richard Grant.

She would rather burn a book…well, alright, perhaps that was going a bit too far.

The point was, he had manipulated her, lied to her, and betrayed her. What was worse, he'd probably done it in an effort to protect her, darn drat his overdeveloped sense of chivalry. And, therefore, the worst part of all: she felt guilty for yelling at him. Not that he hadn't deserved it, but it had been terribly impolite, not at all like her. At least, not like the person she tried to be. She was beginning to realize the two were more different than she cared to admit.

Sir Kipling, who was cat-loafing on the floor by the bookcase and watching her with half-lidded eyes, gave a yawn. "Coward."

"Oh hush," she retorted. "You have no idea, so don't even pretend. Have you ever had your heart broken by a lady cat? Hm? Have you ever even *talked* to a lady cat?"

"I'll have you know I'm all the rage among the local dames," he informed her, whiskered nose in the air.

"Uh-huh. I'm sure."

He gave an indignant huff and shifted, uncurling a paw, which he licked with deliberate care, proving his utter disdain for her unbelief.

Silence fell once again, and Lily's thoughts returned to the issue at hand, namely, thinking of a way to get out of calling Richard. She heaved a deep sigh. No, that was only wistful thinking. She had a duty to her friend; to her uncle; to a world that didn't deserve being inflicted with someone like John Faust. And then there was her recent commitment to "stop pretending and start dealing." Which meant she had to figure out her feelings for Sebastian without letting them obstruct her sound decision-making.

Not that what she was about to do was in any way sound. She was preparing to break the cardinal rule of wizardry: never reveal magic to mundanes. Madam Barrington would absolutely forbid her to do any such thing, which was why she had no intention of telling her until after the fact.

She wasn't even sure how she was going to do it. What

if Richard simply refused to believe what was in front of his very eyes? What if he tried to get her locked up in an insane asylum? He didn't seem like that sort of person, but still. She was about to do something very, very unwise. But her back was to the wall and time was running out. Now that she thought about it, it was a very Sebastian thing to do. The idea made her smile, and she finally got up enough willpower to dial Richard's number.

To her delight, and despair, he answered on the first ring.

"Miss Singer?" His greeting was more of a question, wavering between uncertainty and hope.

"Agent Grant, we need to talk." Hearing his voice again brought back all the anger and hurt, and she fought to keep it out of her voice.

"Thank goodness, Lily, I was so worried. Thank you for understanding. I promise, I'll explain everything—"

"Shut up." Her sharp words cut him off, and there was a stunned silence on the line, Lily being just as surprised as Richard at the words that had come out of her mouth. She hadn't meant to say that. At home it would have earned her a mouth-washing with soap. She hurried on.

"I wish to make it abundantly clear that I have no intention or desire to continue in any capacity but as professional acquaintances. We need to discuss your investigation. I have information you need to know, and I believe I deserve an explanation as well. We have the same goals and can better achieve them if we work together."

"Oh…alright?" He sounded disappointed but rallied himself. "Why don't you come into my office? We can set up an interview with myself and Agent Meyers."

"No. I assure you, you will want privacy for this conversation. Come to my house. Now."

"Well, that's highly irregular—"

Lily snorted, a most unladylike sound, but it made Richard pause.

"Irregular? You're trying to hide behind doing things by the book now, are you? Please, Agent Grant, have some self-respect. You are investigating my father, John Faust, and I can promise that I, more than anyone else, want him to face justice for his actions. If you want my help, and my information, you will come, now, to my house, alone. I'll be waiting." She hung up…and promptly slumped down into the couch's cushions, head back and arm flung over her face.

"That went well," Sir Kipling observed.

"I can't do this," Lily moaned.

"Then I suggest you research prison security, because our next option is to break Sebastian out by mischief and magic."

"Uunngg."

"That last time I checked, 'ung' was not in the dictionary. Pray tell, what does it mean?"

Lily finally sat up, giving her cat the eyebrow. "Last time you checked, huh? For your information, it means keep your snarky comments to yourself."

"Ah. It's all so clear now." He yawned.

Despite everything, Lily couldn't help but smile. After all, what were cats for if not to rescue you from your own self-pity through the liberal application of snark? She tried to remember how she'd gotten by before Sir Kipling could express himself in such salubrious detail. Cat owners around the world had no idea what they were missing.

With a last groan, she hauled herself off the couch and began preparations for her and Richard's "talk."

***

When Richard arrived an hour later, Lily was tired, but

ready. She wore a conservative business suit—just so there'd be no confusion as to her intentions—and had ordered Sir Kipling to watch the man like a hawk, even following him into the bathroom if need be. Not that her cat needed to be told, but it was nice to have him follow orders for once.

She knew the moment the agent arrived, alerted by her cat's pricked ears and soft meow. Opening the door, she motioned him in without a word or glance, noting that he, too, wore a business suit—normal FBI attire. Well, it was nice to know where they both stood.

"Have a seat, Agent Grant," she said, sitting at her desk and swiveling the chair so that she faced him. When she finally looked at him, she was taken aback at how miserable he seemed. While her initial reaction was pity, she stiffened her resolve, refusing to give in.

But as she opened her mouth to begin her prepared speech, Richard raised a hand, stopping her.

"Before you say anything, I want to apologize," he said, voice filled with solemnity, not the pleading she'd expected. "While I promise that everything I did was to try and protect you, I realize I went about it in a very…improper way. I'm very, very sorry for hurting you."

Lily stared levelly at him, considering his words. Inside she vacillated from intense relief to stubborn ire, unsure which should win. She finally settled on something in the middle. "In my family, if one of us wronged another, we were expected to admit, verbally, that we were wrong, and ask the other's forgiveness. Simply being 'sorry' was not enough. You can be sorry all you wanted—sorry you've been caught—yet still be unrepentant and unchanged." She said this without emotion, as though giving a report on the weather. Yet her intent was clear.

Richard cleared his throat, looking away. Lily watched

him closely, wondering if he would choose the high road or the easy one.

"I was—wrong. Wrong for misleading you and taking advantage of your trust. Will you—" He paused, mouth tightening ever so slightly. But then he let out his breath, shoulders loosening. "Will you forgive me?"

Despite herself, Lily was impressed. She felt a tight knot of anxiety loosen inside. Whatever else she thought of Richard, he certainly had a sense of honor, at least when he was called out. That boded well, since he could potentially use what she was about to tell him to ruin her and her whole family. Not just her family, the whole wizard race.

"I forgive you," She stated simply, businesslike.

Richard heaved a deep sigh of relief, face breaking out in a tentative smile "Thank you, I—"

But Lily held up her hand, as he had, cutting him off. "I wasn't finished. I forgive you because you had the humility to ask, because it is the right thing to do, and because the stakes are too high for any animosity to remain between us. However, I have no interest in anything but a working relationship. Treat me as a fellow professional and we will get along fine. I asked you to my house because of some very sensitive, dangerous things I have to show you, not because I wanted you to…renew your addresses to me." She pursed her lips, then continued.

"I am putting a great deal of trust in your skill as an FBI agent and your dedication to justice. I'm trusting you to not take advantage of the information I give you to further your own career, or earn points with your superiors. I promise to speak the whole truth if you promise to treat my secrets as your secrets. I promise to give you information you can use to take down John Faust. But first I have to show you…something. Something you can never tell a soul. Do you understand me?

Do you promise to keep my trust?" Asking that last question she forced herself to look him straight in the eye, unflinching. It was terribly difficult, and her insides felt like they'd turned to a quivering pile of jelly.

The strange thing was, Richard wasn't reacting like she'd expected. At the beginning of her speech, he looked extremely uncomfortable. But by the time she got to the part about showing him something he could never tell a soul, his shoulders seemed to relax and his expression eased.

When she finished, he gave her a wan smile and nodded, though she noted he didn't hold her gaze for very long. "Of course," he said.

Lily sat, stunned. This seemed too easy.

"Of course, what?" She asked, suspicious.

"Of course I won't tell a soul. You can trust me." He smiled again, brighter this time like he was putting some effort into it.

"Are you sure? Doesn't this break some sort of FBI oath or something?"

He seemed confused for a moment, then he backtracked. "I mean, if you were a criminal it would be different, of course. But you're not. You're a good person, Li—Miss Singer. I know you'd never do anything illegal."

"Well," she said slowly, thinking hard, "I've seen people do some pretty terrible things. People I thought were decent." Richard squirmed at her words, looking away. "I have to be sure you're serious, that you're really hearing what I'm saying. *Nobody* can ever know what I'm about to show you. Not your partner, not your superiors, no one. If you tell anyone it could get me and a lot of other people killed."

The FBI agent finally looked her in the eye. Really looked at her. "I know I don't deserve your trust, but I would never, *ever* do anything to hurt you. I promise, I won't tell anyone."

Lily sat back, considering his words. She believed that *he* believed himself to be trustworthy. But he'd already proved once that what he thought was protecting her wasn't exactly the most pleasant of experiences. Kind of like Sebastian.

Why did men always think the best way to protect her was to lie to her? Did all men do it or just the ones in her acquaintance? Suddenly unsure of herself, Lily started to rethink her decision to let Richard in on the whole "wizard" secret. She'd relied on her instincts before, and where had it gotten her? Could she even trust herself anymore? But it was too late to back out now, and how else was she going to get Sebastian out of prison?

"Good grief. Why do I always have to save your proverbial bacon? It's positively exhausting." With a protracted meow that startled them both, Sir Kipling appeared from wherever he'd been lurking. He jumped up on the couch and gave Richard a long, evaluating stare. Then, with a flick of his ears and a twitch of his fluffy tail, he slowly and deliberately climbed onto the man's lap, stretched, and curled up, purring.

Richard glanced at her with a startled look, as if he didn't know what to do about the fur-ball of cuteness that had just inserted itself into his personal space.

Unable to help herself, Lily laughed. "You now have Sir Kipling's vote of confidence. And let me tell you, he gives it out few and far between. I'm surprised, considering he was about to buzz-saw your face off the other day."

"Tell me about it," Richard muttered, tentatively stroking Sir Kipling's soft grey fur. Her cat—a complete pushover when he needed to be—mewed contentedly and rolled to present his tummy for further adoration. Lily arched an eyebrow in surprise. Her cat was systematically wrapping Richard around his furry paw, that sneaky little snipe. It just went to prove that every dog person was just a cat person who hadn't yet met the right cat.

Staring at the two of them, Lily finally made her decision. Right or wrong, she didn't know. But if Sir Kipling thought it was a good idea, at least they'd be in it together. She cleared her throat. "Not to interrupt your make-out session over there, gentlemen, but we have important things to discuss."

Sir Kipling gave her a lazy-eyed stare, completely unconcerned about important things while his belly was being rubbed. Richard looked up with a startled, guilty expression on his face, as if he'd just been caught doing something unmanly. He gave her a pleading look, glancing back and forth between her and her conniving feline in desperation. "Um, how do I get him off my lap? Please?"

Lily smiled. "Normally I would say 'you don't.' But since you asked nicely..." She gave her cat a pointed look. "Shoo."

Grumbling, Sir Kipling rolled over and off his victim's lap, landing on his feet and sauntering unhurriedly to a corner of the room where he began the long process of straightening all his mussed fur. Lily had no doubt that he would demand more pettings later, playing the "you owe me" card.

"So...?" Richard asked, letting the question dangle.

"Yes, um, so..." Lily said tingling with apprehension. How was he going to take learning about magic? At the very least, they already had an established relationship where he saw her as an intelligent, educated person. That should help. Or else confuse the heck out of him. She'd thought long and hard about how to explain it and, after giving herself a splitting headache, had decided to just be blunt and straightforward. Either he would believe her or he wouldn't.

Here goes nothing, she thought, and straightened her

back to give Richard a level look. "Agent Grant, I am a wizard, as are my father, my mother, and many others in our world. Magic is real, and, while most wizards go to great lengths to keep to themselves and never cause trouble, there are, unfortunately, exceptions." Richard's eyebrows rose higher and higher, almost disappearing into his hairline. But she kept going.

"Magic is not some supernatural hocus pocus. You can't wave a wand, say some silly word and make a pineapple tap-dance across your desk. It is science, though our understanding of it is severely limited. Most wizards are not concerned with how it works, simply that it does. But to give you my best explanation, magic is energy, which some people are genetically predisposed to manipulate through word and will. We've spent millennia trying to avoid mundane notice—excuse me, mundane is the word we use for anyone non-magical—and I am breaking a cardinal rule by telling you all this. Unfortunately, I feel I don't have a choice. My father isn't just a petty criminal, he is a brilliant and powerful wizard with plans that could…"—she hesitated, unsure how much to tell Richard at this juncture—"prove harmful to mundanes.

"Since we both want him stopped, I propose an alliance. Myself and my friends, along with you and the FBI. You would be the liaison and sole keeper of our secret. I know this is asking much, but I hope you see that the only way forward is together."

Finally finished with her speech, she closed her mouth with a snap and waited, tense as a wound-up spring. She couldn't decide by the wrinkle of his forehead or arch of his brows if he was incredulous, flabbergasted, or both. She wished he would say something.

"Um…okay…" He finally got out. His expression leaned toward incredulous. Lily was sure that if they hadn't had deep and intellectual discussions on multiple occasions, he would have immediately written her off as insane. Though of course he would have tried to be polite about it.

Sighing, she stood. "It's alright. No one could reasonably expect you to believe me without proof. What do you want to see me do?"

"Can you fly?" came his half-amused reply.

"Not in the manner you are imagining," Lily smiled ruefully. "There are levitation spells that involve creating pockets of neutral gravity, but I've never done them before and would need much practice to do it safely. One misconception that you should get straight right away is that magic is dangerous and requires years of careful study to control. There are simple spells that are easier to master, but when you're channeling vast amounts of energy, a lot of things can go wrong if you aren't good at what you do."

"Lovely," Richard muttered, looking green. "Okay, what about something simple? Can you, um, make a ball of fire?"

"If I want to singe my house, perhaps. How about this: I've crafted my light switches to respond to commands, since mundane friends might start asking questions if I outfitted my house with light orbs."

Lily took a calming breath, focusing her connection to the Source, and spoke a word of Enkinim. The light switch on the wall flipped down and the room darkened. She spoke another word and it flipped back up, illuminating Richard's skeptical face.

"Cute, but you could just have voice-activated lights."

She rolled her eyes. "That's exactly what I *do* have, Agent Grant. Don't think about magic as some unknowable force that defies the laws of nature. Magic is *part* of nature. It is simply science you mundanes can't yet explain. Perhaps, some day, wizards and mundanes will live in harmony, and every facet of magic will be scientifically understood. I don't know, and I doubt it would be wise to try and tell the world about it, since mundanes tend to fear things they don't understand and have a long history of burning us at the stake."

That sobered him up, and Richard started to look less flippant and more thoughtful.

Lily continued. "You use voice recognition software made of tiny metal chips and controlled by a series of zeros and ones. I use metal inlaid runes imprinted to respond to certain verbal commands when stimulated by my channeling of magic, which in very simple terms is just energy."

"So…you're like an alien with advanced technology?" he asked, attempting a smile.

"Hardly," Lily said, pursing her lips. "Wizards are genetically identical to homo sapiens, we just have an extra gene—or so my father believes—that gives us the ability to sense and manipulate magic."

"Your father?"

"Yes, my father is researching wizard genetics. I told you, he is very intelligent and powerful, and not to be trifled with." Lily took a deep breath, steeling herself to go on. "He is, as I believe your investigation has guessed, one and the same as Rex Morganson. Though I was not familiar with that alias until recently, he admitted to me in person that he was behind at least one of the crimes you are investigating Rex Morganson for. Of course, I should have known right away that it was him, what with a name like Rex Morganson."

"But—wait, what?" Richard said, sidetracked from demanding some sort of information.

Lily sighed. "My father has a dramatic flair, and is, I believe, an unadulterated megalomaniac." She squeezed her eyes shut, embarrassed and hoping Richard didn't laugh. "He believes we are descended from Morgan le Fay and is quite fond of the name. I suspect Rex, which means 'king' in Latin, is just more evidence of his narcissism."

When Richard didn't make a sound, laughing or otherwise, she cracked an eyelid to check on him. He was staring into space, a distracted look on his face.

"Shouldn't you be, I don't know, taking notes or something?" She asked, suddenly annoyed.

"Oh! Yes, of course." He pulled out a pad from his pocket and started scribbling furiously, apparently content to use her information as an excuse to delay wrapping his mind around the question of magic.

He looked up. "And would you be willing to wear a wire so we can get that confession on record?" His tone had turned routine, as if he were questioning a witness.

This was not good, Lily thought. He was headed in the wrong direction. So she stepped forward and gently, but firmly, took the pad from Richard's hands.

"Stop, Richard. Just stop. You're not getting it. John Faust is *dangerous*. I don't mean crime-lord, guns-blaring, thugs-on-the-street dangerous. I mean he could kill any of you with a mere *thought*. I mean he can't be kept in jail except with specially designed wrought-iron shackles that would negate his magic. He has…plans. What he's doing he believes is for the greater good, but his reasons don't matter. I think he will end up hurting a lot of people. He's already kidnapped my uncle and could be torturing him to death this very instant. I need you to focus on the big picture. I need you to drop the ridiculous charges against my associate Sebastian—you know he didn't kill that woman, for goodness' sake—and let him go so he can help me and my allies track down and stop John Faust. Because I promise you, you won't be able to do it."

Richard's expression turned stubborn. "I can assure you, the FBI—"

"—has no idea what it's up against, and you will see to it that it never does," Lily finished for him, hardening her own expression. "That's what I and my fellow wizards are here for. We will take care of the magic side of things and make John Faust available to the FBI to prosecute. I am happy to give statements, though I warn you I know very little to nothing about my father's activities, since I only just met him for the first time since I was two. To find and neutralize John Faust, we need Sebastian."

"Is he a wizard, too?" Richard asked, letting the matter go for the moment.

"No, he's a witch. I wouldn't worry about the difference just at the moment."

The FBI agent looked like he was about to go cross-eyed. "So, let me get this straight. You expect me to take you at your word that you and a whole subset of the world population can manipulate some energy source that scientists are completely unaware of. It's dangerous and hard to control, but John LeFay can do terrible things with it. So, of course, we should let a suspected murderer free from jail to join you and your bunch of clueless civilians to go hunt down a powerful, insane, dangerous criminal all by yourselves because the FBI 'can't handle' him. Am I right so far?"

"That is an accurate summation, yes."

"You're crazy." Richard said without animosity, just pure amazement.

Lily smiled. "There are advantages to being crazy, you know. And Sebastian killed no one. John Faust did. I can prove it to you."

"Really?" Richard said skeptically.

"Yes. We have the incident on video camera and a witness who will testify to Sebastian's innocence, in return for full immunity, of course."

"The girl who called 911 I assume?"

"Yes."

"Look, Lily, I can understand wanting to get your…associate…out of jail. But a woman was murdered and there were only two people on the scene. If Mr. Blackwell didn't do it, then his friend did, and I can't promise—"

"You're forgetting about magic, Agent Grant," Lily said, slowly, patiently.

"Yeah, right. Your friend said the woman's necklace came alive and choked her. Like that would hold up in court."

"You don't believe him?"

"Of course I don't, Lily. I respect your beliefs in this magic, thing. Seriously, you're free to follow whatever path you choose. The world takes all kinds. But you can't expect me to believe in it, too, and you certainly can't expect me to think it relevant to a murder investigation." He said all this so calmly, almost bored, that Lily wanted to slap him.

"The name is Miss Singer," she said through gritted teeth, "and if you don't believe in magic then surely you won't mind conducting a little experiment."

Having prepared for this eventuality, she stepped up to Richard, presenting a strip of paper on which she'd already drawn a line of dimmu runes in aluminum-laced ink. She reached up, attempting to put the piece of paper around his neck and tape the ends together to form a collar.

"Whoa, whoa! Hold on a minute," he protested, holding up his hands and leaning back. "What do you think you're doing?"

She smiled to herself. The violence of his reaction

proved he wasn't quite as disbelieving as he tried to pretend. "Showing you the spell John Faust used on the necklace that killed that woman. I'm not sure how he got the dimmu runes on the necklace, since the chain links would be too small to engrave, but the spell itself is straightforward enough. Perhaps experiencing it will convince you."

"So you're going to try and strangle me with a piece of paper?"

Lily rolled her eyes. "Yes, Agent Grant, I'm attempting to murder you with a strip of paper—no, of course not! Good heavens. It's paper. It will rip when it contracts. You'll be fine. You don't believe in magic, remember? So why not let me put this on your neck? Don't tell me you're afraid?"

Richard frowned at the jibe, but it was still several long moments before he let his arms fall and allowed her to tape the piece of paper snugly around his neck.

"Good." Lily stepped back, observing her handiwork. "Now, if it becomes uncomfortable, simply reach up and rip the paper, alright?"

He nodded. For someone who didn't believe in magic, he looked inordinately nervous.

Once again calming herself, she summoned the Source and spoke a command. Though Richard wouldn't have noticed anything, in her magical sight the dimmu runes on the paper glowed briefly, absorbing the energy and its accompanying parameters. Then, she stepped back.

"I assume Sebastian told you the necklace started choking the woman when she said my father's alias?" Sebastian hadn't told *her* that, of course. He'd barely told her anything. But she'd worked it out from Tina's description of events.

Richard nodded, looking even more nervous.

"Good. I've spelled the paper to react to my father's

alias, first name only, voice-activated. It's an uncommon enough name, which is probably another reason he chose it. Go ahead, say the name."

He hesitated, beads of sweat breaking out on his forehead. "Are you sure this is safe?" he asked.

"Come now, are you honestly afraid of a piece of paper?"

The FBI agent gulped, then said, "Rex."

Immediately, the paper began to crinkle and contract, tightening on Richard's neck. With a cry of alarm he scrabbled at it, fingernails digging under the edge and ripping it off with frantic haste. He jumped up off the couch and threw it away, backing up when it only went a foot or so and fluttered down to the floor where it continued to contract until it was a tightly wadded ball of paper. He glared at it.

Lily simply shrugged. "I told you so."

"Okay, okay," Richard grumbled, rubbing his neck. In his haste to get it off, he'd managed to give himself a paper cut. "How did you do that, anyway?"

"I told you, energy manipulation, the same way everything else in the world works. Just because we call it magic doesn't make it unreal—though, to be fair, there are plenty of charlatans or just plain idiots out there who give magic a bad name. You know, if you think about it, people in the Middle Ages would have burned you at the stake for talking on your phone, listening to the radio, and even driving your car. They would have said you were in league with the devil and had demon-possessed objects that gave you unholy power. We fear that which we don't understand." She shrugged again.

"Hmm." Richard made a noncommittal noise, still glaring at the ball as if it were going to jump up and attack him should he get too close. He looked up at Lily. "Even if I believe you, there's no way the court is going to accept this. Even if you show them, they'd..."

"Lock me in a padded room. I know."

"I wasn't going to say that."

"But you were thinking it," she insisted with a sad smile.

"Perhaps. The point is, this doesn't help get your associate out of jail."

"Yes, it does, because the only person I need to convince is you. I don't want to prove Sebastian is innocent to the court, because I want you to drop all charges and release Sebastian without a trial. You've seen yourself what magic can do. You can talk to the witness and see the video recording. Sebastian has no motive and no prior record. If you get him out of jail, we can work together to capture the real culprit. It's the same kind of deal you cut with petty criminals every day to catch the bigger fish."

"Well..." he hesitated.

Lily's gut tightened. She'd come too far to fail now. "Don't tell me you can't because you're not in charge or you don't know the right people. You're the FBI; figure it out."

He laughed, "No, actually, the irony of it is that I *do* have the power. I'm in charge of the LeFay investigation. Through a series of...well, *how* is not important, but I got stuck with this investigation because nobody else wanted it and it had already ruined two other agents' careers. So I got the job and thought for sure I was sunk. But then, well, things started happening, and, um, you showed up. As crazy as it sounds, this is exactly what I've been looking for...I just wish it had come in a more, er..."

"Believable package?" Lily offered, her smile ironic.

"Something like that." He nodded, pursing his lips in thought. "Look, I can't promise anything until I've talked to the girl and seen the videotape. But...if everything adds up like you say...I think I might, *might*, mind you, be able to get the charges dropped. I just have no idea how I'm supposed to explain all this to my superiors, much less write the report." He ran a restless hand through his close-cropped hair.

"That's the point. You don't try to explain it, you find a way to ignore it. We have a lawyer who can help you. Not, officially, of course, but off the books, you might say. She's, um, trained in explaining away unexplainable things."

"That might help," he said absentmindedly, then shook himself. "Let's say Mr. Blackwell *does* get out of jail, then what?" His question sounded oddly casual, and Lily sighed, knowing what was coming.

"Then you wait," she said. "We need Sebastian to help find my father. Once we find him, we'll neutralize him, try to hide the, um, magic part of the equation, then call in your team to take him away."

Richard gave her an uncomfortable look. "You can't seriously expect me to let you walk into a situation like that by yourself? You're...I'm sorry, I don't mean this to be offensive, but you're not in any position to protect yourself."

Lily's eyes glinted dangerously, unsurprised but still stung by Richard's words. "First of all, I won't be alone. I told you, I have allies. Second, I can take care of myself." Feeling reckless, she turned and spoke a word, concentrating all her frustration and anger on the crumpled ball of paper lying on the floor. It burst into brilliant, white-hot flame which lasted only a second before disappearing, leaving a crumbling pile of ash and a singed spot on her living room rug. She knew she would regret the spot later, but right now the look of fear on Richard's face made it worth it.

"I retract my statement," he said shakily, not a shred of

disbelief left in his face. There was, however, still plenty of concern.

"Yes, well," Lily said, straightening her suit and smoothing down her constantly frizzing hair, "now that we are on the same page, might I suggest the time for words is over? I can arrange a meeting with the witness as soon as you can produce some kind of guarantee of immunity—a paper or something—for me to show her. Otherwise, she won't talk."

"I can cobble something together by tomorrow," he said, rubbing his forehead, then murmured as if to himself. "It's going to be hellish trying to explain all this away…"

Lily sighed. "Keep it simple. The fewer people to ask questions, the better. For your sake. Because"—she gave him a hard look—"I promise you, Richard Grant, that if rumors leak out and reporters start showing up at my doorstep, I will deny every single thing I've said and claim you made it all up."

He chuckled, though the sound held no mirth. "Don't worry, Miss Singer. No one would believe me if I told them."

"Yes," she mused, "a fact which has kept wizards safe on countless occasions."

They agreed on a time and place to meet with Tina— Lily insisted on her house over Richard's office, as she knew Tina would refuse to show up at FBI headquarters—and he left, giving Sir Kipling a scratch on the ears as he went.

Lily watched him go with mixed feelings. Mostly relief that the ordeal was over, but also apprehension. Would he betray them? Would he keep the secret? She could only hope, and take things one step at a time.

"He'll be good," Sir Kipling commented by her feet, staring with her after the FBI agent. As usual, he seemed to read her mind. "I have him fully under my feline sway."

"Since when do you have a feline sway?" Lily asked, fighting to keep the grin from her face as she closed the front door.

"Since I was born, of course," her cat informed her, as if it were obvious.

"I see," Lily said, and left it at that. She had plenty to do and no time to argue about her cat's overinflated opinion of his "feline sway."

Things moved quickly after her talk with Richard. Meeting with Tina the next day went smoothly enough, if you ignored the part where Percy gave Richard a wedgie. Having threatened the poltergeist with metaphysical harm should he break a single thing in her house, she considered a minor thing like a wedgie a victory of the highest order. The only hitch was explaining how Sebastian had used fae glamour to appear as John Faust.

Thankfully, after Tina had finished her statement and left, leaving the videotape in Richard's keeping, the agent took the opportunity to discuss in full what the FBI actually suspected John Faust, aka Rex Morganson, of doing, bringing Lily up to speed and enabling them to compare notes. She told him a modified-to-sound-less-insane version of John Faust's plan to "make" more wizards and instigate an age of benevolent dictatorship.

Based on the FBI's report, it looked as if John Faust had used the Rex Morganson alias for all his illegal activities related to the kidnappings and his schemes to raise funds, as well as the theft of multiple artifacts and antiques that Lily suspected were magical in nature.

With all the information on the table, Lily tried to paint

a coherent picture for herself of what John Faust was up to. As best she could guess, he'd discovered some way to find children of wizard heritage, perhaps through ancestry records or maybe some device he'd invented to detect the "magical" gene he was researching. So he was kidnapping wizard children, raising funds, and stealing magical artifacts to do...what? Build an army? The idea made her sick, and even more grateful to her mother for all she'd gone through over the years to keep her away from that horrible man.

Of course, her father wouldn't see it as sick. He would say he was "rescuing" children from a life of ignobility, deprived of their heritage by the ignorance of mundanes. It was all a matter of perspective to him, and the greater good as he saw it. Lily suspected his ego had as much to do with it as anything altruistic. While she considered what had happened to all those children, she realized with a jolt that she might have already met one, possibly two of them: The young wizard who had attacked Madam Barrington at Allen's house, and maybe even the ninja-like fighter who had tried to neutralize her. Why John Faust would keep around a mundane child she had no idea, seeing as how he looked down on mundanes as almost sub-human.

At least between Tina, the videotape, and what both of them knew, Richard was finally and thoroughly convinced. The problem was, they could prove very little.

"In the end, though, it won't matter," Lily assured him, hoping she was right. "Once we find him and stop him, that will lead us to wherever he's keeping these children, not to mention his personal records and effects. I promise, it will all be yours. Well, except anything inexplicably magical. Some things will need to conveniently disappear. Once all is said and done, though, this will simply look like some sort of cult fanatic who went off the deep end. The children will be rescued, you'll have your culprit, and probably a promotion to boot." She smiled at him.

He smiled back, though he still looked green around the edges. "Maybe. I'll tell you this for sure: the paperwork will be a nightmare."

Lily shrugged sympathetically. "Just be grateful you're not the one who will be storming the castle, so to speak."

"Oh, believe me, I'd much rather be doing that," he said with feeling, to which Lily raised an eyebrow. He looked away, probably remembering that little pile of ash on her living room floor. "Alright, so maybe not. But still, I feel like I got the short end of the stick on this one."

Lily could only shake her head in disbelief. She would rather be sitting at a desk, filling out paperwork any day. If she could have given her powers to Richard and hidden from the whole mess, she would. But she couldn't, no more than she could stop being John Faust's daughter. Life didn't let you pick your hand. All you got to do was choose how to play it.

In the end, Richard did finally agree to get the charges against Sebastian dropped, though he insisted she owed him about a hundred chess pies for all the work it would take. His half-hopeful, half-disgruntled look made Lily laugh.

"You'll have me baking until my fingers fall off, at this rate," she accused him.

"That's the idea," he gave her a mock glare. "I figure, if you have no fingers you'll get into less trouble."

She started to smile at his teasing, then stopped, remembering they were supposed to be acting professional. Molding her face into a polite expression, she simply nodded.

He picked up on her coolness, and his own smile faded. He sighed, and Lily sympathized. Richard was an easy man to like. It was too bad she'd decided not to. All it took to strengthen her resolve, however, was remembering that stab of pain she'd felt at the sight of a pile of surveillance bugs on her floor. Yes, he was easy to like, and probably a good man, too. But he was an FBI agent, first and foremost.

Sensing that the time for games was over, Richard assured her Sebastian would be out of jail within twenty-four hours, and they parted ways. He hesitated when saying goodbye, as if he wanted to say more. But Lily kept her expression neutral and he, finding no encouragement in her gaze, let the words go unsaid. If his shoulders sagged a bit and his expression looked defeated, Lily chose not to dwell on it. She'd done what she needed to do, and now things were finally looking up.

She only hoped they could find Allen, and that he would still be alive when they did.

That night, she gave Sebastian a brief update. Worried about the guard's notice, she kept things short, saying only that she'd worked out a deal with the FBI to have the charges dropped. He tried to question her, but she put him off, saying she'd explain it all once he was safely out of the clutches of the United States Federal Penitentiary. She instructed him to call her as soon as he got out, so she could pick him up and give him a ride to wherever they'd been holding his car for evidence.

"Sure, sure," he whispered, sounding a bit distant as if he were checking the hall for guards. Then the sound of his voice drew nearer again. "So you pick me up from jail, we get my car, and then what? What's been going on? Do we know where Mr. Fancypants's lair is yet?"

"Ms. B is working on that. We've got some ideas, but I

was hoping we could try Grimmold first. He worked so well finding Allen, maybe he could do the same with John Faust, or even follow Allen's scent to wherever John Faust has taken him."

"It's worth a try," he agreed, "though you should know he doesn't *always* get it right. And sometimes he just refuses. He's a finicky little bugger."

Lily's heart sank. She'd been depending on Grimmold's tracking skills, as their other plan was tenuous at best. But it was what it was.

"Well, hopefully you can convince him," she said.

A little sigh came from the photograph. "Yeah, hopefully. So…I guess I'll see you tomorrow?"

His words caused Lily's heart to skip a beat as it leapt in excitement, taking her completely by surprise. She was thankful Sebastian wasn't around to see her blush, thinking about the many, many things they needed to talk about. "Yeah…see you tomorrow."

After putting the photograph away in a drawer—nestled between a pair of socks in Sebastian's honor—she let out a breath she hadn't realized she'd been holding. This, she thought, was going to be interesting.

Work that Wednesday was excruciating as she waited for the call from Sebastian. Richard had promised twenty-four hours, but she kept having this horrible feeling that something would go wrong and she would get a call from Richard instead of Sebastian, saying he was sorry but things hadn't worked out. Every little sound made her jump and glance at her phone, until Penny, her assistant, eventually asked if she were alright.

Close to five, the call finally came. Lily hurriedly

checked that everything was settled for the day, then rushed out of the library and jumped into her car. She'd made Sir Kipling stay home that day, saying she didn't want him anywhere near a prison, just in case. There would be electric fences and guard dogs, and she had no desire to tempt fate where her thinks-he's-got-nine-lives cat was concerned.

She drove with a lead foot, honking at traffic and straining every seam of her poor Honda Civic to its limit as she headed southwest toward the Atlanta federal prison. Her nerves were all a-jangle and her emotions a mess, but at least she would be getting Sebastian back where she could fuss at him face to face instead of through an enchanted photograph. Not that she would be scolding him, not with Tina's words still fresh in her mind. Well, she thought, maybe a little. After all, he *was* a reckless, obstreperous excuse for the most amazing man in the world.

Wait…where had that come from? She decided to just stop thinking entirely, since her brain was obviously as strung out as a whole clutter of cats on catnip.

When she pulled into the prison parking lot, she saw him standing on one end—as far away from the prison entrance as possible—body language closed and wary as he leaned against a telephone pole, arms crossed. When he spotted her car he straightened, but she couldn't see his expression and still park safely, so she focused on her driving.

By the time she opened her car door, he was only a few steps away. Since she'd conveniently turned her brain off, there was nothing to stop her jumping out of the seat and throwing herself on him. Wrapping her arms around his lean, firm chest, she buried her face in his neck, breathing in his musky scent. She had no plan, no goal, no thoughts at all. She just missed him and wanted to be near him.

He stumbled slightly as she hit, obviously not anticipating being jumped. But he quickly found his balance and froze where he was, as though afraid any movement would send them crashing to the ground.

It took a few long seconds for him to react, and when he did his voice sounded as confused as it was startled. "Uhhhh...Lily?"

"Hush. Just hush," she said, voice muffled by the fact that her face was pressed against his collar.

He did, carefully raising his arms to rest them lightly around her in a tentative embrace. Maybe he thought if he did any more, she would fuss at him for that, too.

The thought kicked her brain back into motion and she could almost hear the reboot music as she realized what she was doing. She let go as quickly as if he were a scalding hot potato she'd been foolish enough to pick up, stepping back to look down at her feet and blush furiously.

"I...I missed you," she forced herself to say in way of explanation, though really all she wanted to do was melt into a puddle of embarrassment and ooze away to hide under the bushes. This whole "dealing" thing was turning out to be the epitome of "easier said than done."

"I, uh, couldn't tell."

Though she still could not bring herself to look at him, the hint of amusement in his voice indicated he, at least, hadn't been completely scandalized by her brashness—not that he was ever scandalized by anything. While she assumed Tina's description of him as "stupid in love" was an exaggeration, a part of her hoped it wasn't completely off the mark.

She kept her eyes fixed on the ground as she heard him step forward. Then she felt his warm fingers under her chin, a silent request to look up. She did, slowly, reluctantly, afraid of what she would see—whether Tina was wrong or right. Both seemed equally terrifying.

When she finally met his gaze, she felt something inside her melt. She saw some uncertainty, and a guarded shadow that sent shivers down her spine. But overall, they were full of relieved, eager warmth.

"I missed you too, Lil," he said, voice husky.

Gently, giving her ample time to stiffen and withdraw if she chose, he gathered her into a more deliberate but no less sincere embrace, pressing his cheek against the side of her head so that she could feel his breath tickle her neck. She did not withdraw, though she felt as stiff and clumsy as a log. Now that her brain was working again, it foiled her attempts to relax, clamoring about all sorts of inanity while distracting her from enjoying what she now realized she'd been longing for all day. Maybe all her life.

Her mind was so consumed by trying to figure out what to say next that she barely noticed when he let her go.

"So. Can we go now?"

His voice made her jump and she realized in relief that he wasn't launching into an interrogation of her feelings, nor demanding an explanation of her strange behavior.

"Yes," she said, almost laughing with relief. "Yes, let's."

Chapter 4
ALL THE KING'S MEN

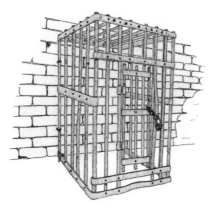

AFTER RETRIEVING SEBASTIAN'S IMPOUNDED CAR, THEY HEADED TO MADAM Barrington's house for a "council of war," as Sebastian put it. When his great-aunt opened the door and saw him on her front porch, her reaction was about what Lily had expected. Her eyes widened in shock, cycling through relief, confusion, suspicion, and finally settling on resignation.

"Well. As glad as I am to see you in good health, nephew, I sincerely hope the next words out of your mouth do not include 'escape,' 'run away,' or, heaven forbid, 'I need somewhere to hide.'" The older woman glanced back and forth between them, eyebrow raised.

Lily gulped down a nervous giggle. Soon enough those disapproving eyes would be focused on her and, for once, *she* would be getting the tongue-lashing, not her obstreperous friend.

"I promise, Ms. B., Sebastian's release was entirely legal.

Perhaps it would be better if I explain things inside?" Lily said, clearing her throat.

Madam Barrington sighed. "Of course, do come in. I'll put the kettle on."

As she stepped aside to let them in, Sir Kipling—whom Lily had stopped by her house to pick up—bounded ahead down the hall, making a beeline for the kitchen. When they arrived themselves, they found him sitting beside an empty bowl by the pantry door, looking disappointed. Madam Barrington had taken to keeping it around ever since the precocious feline had started accompanying his mistress to her mentor's house. But since Madam Barrington hadn't been expecting them today, it was not filled with its usual milk and cream.

Sir Kipling gave Madam Barrington a piteous look, coming forward to rub pleadingly on her ankles and mew. He was somewhat stymied by her floor-length skirt, but he soldiered on, leaning in until he found firm leg to rub against amid the gathers of fabric.

With a small, fond twitch of the lips, Madam Barrington headed for the refrigerator, taking out the milk and giving her supplicant a generous portion.

Lily sighed. "Ms. B., you're spoiling him. If you keep giving him that he'll expect to get it at home, too."

"Nonsense. A little milk every now and then does a pussycat good. Keeps their fur silky and their teeth strong."

Sir Kipling paused in his not-so-dainty consumption of the creamy treat, milk dripping from his whiskered chin as he gave her a smug look. "See, I told you," he said, and returned to the all-important task of cleaning his bowl.

Not dignifying her cat's statement with a reply, Lily simply rolled her eyes and went to help Madam Barrington prepare the tea. They worked in silence, Madam Barrington exuding calm stateliness, while Lily did her best to imitate her. The knot in the pit of her stomach made it rather difficult. Sebastian ignored them both, crouching down by the bowl of milk to get reacquainted with Sir Kipling. Her cat liked that just fine, arching his back and sticking his butt in the air for scratches while he kept his face firmly planted in the bowl. She watched them out of the corner of her eye, wondering what sort of mischief they would get up to if only they could talk to each other. She shuddered. The world wouldn't know what hit it.

When all was prepared—a simple but strong Assam blend accompanied by cheese scones and sliced sausage on rye bread—they retired to the parlor. As was Madam Barrington's habit, they poured and sipped their tea, letting the mood settle in contemplative silence before starting in on whatever would be said. Though Lily noticed Sebastian hesitated when reaching for a scone, he eventually followed through and brought it to his lips, face scrunched up in trepidation as he took the first bite. When nothing happened, he gave a suppressed sigh of relief and dug in with gusto, putting far too much sugar in his tea, as per usual, and drinking several cups to their one.

Lily smiled, remembering the first time she'd come here with him, back when they were trying to unmake Annabelle Witherspoon's curse on the Jackson Mansion. He'd hinted then that his aunt had once fed him hexed food, which was why he'd studiously declined the delectable treats at her house ever since. Prison food must have taken a greater toll on him than she'd thought if he was only now desperate enough to brave the scones.

After a suitable amount of time had passed, during which Lily tried not to fidget or look guilty, Madam Barrington finally spoke.

"Now, Lily, pray tell me how Sebastian has come back to us a free man while the lawyer I hired for him is still working on a defense?"

"Yeah, why did they let me go?" Sebastian chimed in, eyeing Lily with such keen suspicion that he looked distinctly Madam Barrington-like. Only the gravity of the situation kept Lily from laughing.

"Well…I made a deal with the FBI," she hedged, wondering if she could gloss over the part where she told Richard about wizards.

Sebastian gave her the eyebrow and Madam Barrington said, "I see," in that tone of voice that meant she most certainly did not see, and Lily had better explain herself on the double or risk the dreaded Barrington ire.

She explained. They were not pleased.

"Seriously, Lil?" Sebastian was incredulous, and even, it seemed, angry. "How could you do that? You know we can't trust the FBI. In fact, they are the last people on this planet we should be trusting. What are we going to do? For all I know they plan to clap me back in irons as soon as they get what they want! Did you get any promises in writing? Anything signed by a judge? Was there a lawyer present while you had this little tête-a-tête with your boyfriend Richie?"

"Calm down, nephew," Madam Barrington snapped, her own stress showing in the tightness of her voice. "I believe we have much larger things to worry about than mere legalities. If this agent decides to take advantage of this knowledge it could prove disastrous for all wizardkind. I am severely disappointed in you, Lily. What you did was not only foolish but irresponsible."

Lily felt her face grow hot with shame at her mentor's reprimand, not to mention Sebastian's biting jab. Yet she couldn't let it get to her. They needed to be unified, now more than ever. Taking a deep breath, she shoved the hurt aside, forbade herself from tearing up, and spoke in a calm voice. "Look, both of you. I did the best I could given the circumstances. I took a calculated risk and I'm ready to deal with the consequences. What's done is done and we have better things to do than sit here and discuss all the possible disasters that could occur." Stop pretending, start dealing she thought to herself over and over. It was a stupid mantra, but it gave her courage. "Sebastian," she said, turning to him, "Richard is not my boyfriend. I told him I never wanted to see him again after I caught him planting bugs in my house."

At the start of her words, Sebastian's face split into a badly concealed grin until his brain caught up with the second part of her sentence. "Oh, great, just great!" he exclaimed, throwing his hands in the air before getting up to pace around the room, gesticulating as he spoke. "We're trusting a guy already proven untrustworthy who you then summarily insulted. We are totally screwed."

"Despite what you think, Richard was only doing his job and trying to protect me. The same thing you were doing, I might point out, when you so conveniently got yourself arrested and accused of murder, forcing me to take desperate measures. Our and the FBI's goals are the same: to stop John Faust. More than anything, I believe Richard is committed to justice, and he is an honorable man. I trust him with our secret, and he is absolutely right that no one would believe him, anyway. This is the only way, and you know it," she said, glaring at both Sebastian and Madam Barrington, whose lips were pressed together in a line so thin they virtually disappeared. "We need someone in the government who can cover for us. They've already been investigating my father for years, and they aren't going to drop it. He's involved in a lot more than we realized and we aren't going to be able to clean it up ourselves."

Sebastian crossed his arms, looking stubborn, and Madam Barrington's steely expression had not softened one iota.

"Ethel," Lily said softly, turning to face her mentor. "Did you know my father has been kidnapping children?"

The woman's face slackened in disbelief. "What is this nonsense? Where did you hear this?"

"It's complicated and there's no time to explain it all now. I think he's been collecting wizard children to, I don't know, brainwash them or something. He's building an army. Even if we were able to neutralize him by ourselves, what about all those kids? We need to work with the FBI on this one. I don't know what's going to happen or how everything will work out, but my father has done too much harm for us to do this the 'wizard way.' He's hurt too many people. This isn't the Middle Ages, when we could make a few people disappear and everything would be fine. Unless you know about some top-secret "wipe" team we can call that goes around cleaning up after wizards gone bad, the FBI is our best bet."

Madam Barrington did not look pleased, but her expression was more resigned than angry. "Whether or not they are, what's done is done, and we must make the best of it. I sincerely hope, Lily, that your trust in Agent Grant is not misplaced."

"Me, too," Lily said, her insides twisting nervously.

"Just tell me you didn't promise them first dibs or anything?" Sebastian said pleadingly, collapsing back into his chair and rubbing his eyes.

"Give me a little bit of credit," she said, defensive. "After all, everything I know about doing risky, insane things I learned from you. I told Richard we'd deal with my father and clean up anything overtly 'magical' before we called in the cavalry. The only thing that has changed is that now you're out of jail and we have a cleanup crew. You're welcome."

There was a long silence. Lily stared at the floor, mad at both of them and completely out of words. She'd done enough dealing for a lifetime as far as she was concerned.

"Well, you all are as big a bunch of ninnies as I've ever seen. At this rate, John Faust will rule the world before you get your heads out of your respective backsides," Sir Kipling commented from the doorway. At his meow, all eyes locked on him. He sat motionless except for the very tip of his tail, which twitched rhythmically.

"What did he say?" Sebastian asked, breaking the silence.

Lily let out her breath in a great whoosh, then laughed, relaxing as she realized that Sir Kipling was right. After all, the only thing worse than fighting with allies was fighting without them. "He said we're being silly for bickering when Allen is in danger, and I agree. Like Madam Barrington said, what's done is done, and we have work to do. I suggest we get to it."

They all looked at each other, and nodded.

Meowing, Sir Kipling stood up. "Well that's all fine and dandy, but is it going to take long? Because I'm out of milk."

It took a day to set things up. The first task was to test Grimmold and see if Sebastian's fears were correct. Unfortunately, they were. Grimmold took one whiff of John Faust's scent and shut down. He wouldn't track it, not for any amount of specially aged moldy pizza. When Sebastian demanded to know why, all he would say was "baaaaad," before scampering off into the underbrush.

Once that avenue of attack was eliminated, they turned to what Lily had found in John Faust's workroom. On Madam Barrington's recommendation, it was Lily who called up her grandfather. They hoped he would be more agreeable to their request if it came from her.

Once everything was arranged, there was nothing to do but wait for night to fall. Lily tried not to focus on her nerves. It was hard, seeing as how her large and small intestines seemed to be having a who-can-tie-themselves-in-the-most-knots contest, while her stomach felt like it was practicing its bungee-jumping skills. She decided to forgo dinner, instead drinking copious amounts of chamomile with lavender tea. Though not much of an herbal tea drinker, there were always those rare times when she needed a calming drink without caffeine in the mix to make things worse.

When it was finally time to go, she was almost relieved. Better to get it over with. Maybe once her father was safely behind bars she could go back to her quiet life of books, tea, and magic. Well…perhaps not too quiet. Sebastian got bored when things were quiet, and she had to admit life was more interesting with him around.

She drove north through the night, Madam Barrington in the passenger seat and Sebastian in the back with Sir Kipling. Aside from discussing a few contingency plans, none of them said a word, each lost in their own thoughts. Sir Kipling slept, as he was wont to do, unconcerned with the coming confrontation.

As she'd discussed with Henry, the LeFay Estate gate was left open for them, though it swung slowly shut once they passed. Turning off the car lights, Lily navigated by the light of the moon filtering through the branches that overhung the driveway. She pulled off the driveway and parked just on the edge of the estate's expansive yard. They all clambered out, checking pockets and shoelaces to make sure everything was secure. Lily had finally bitten the bullet and gone out to purchase some stand-in "adventure" clothes. They weren't at all fashionable, but at least they were sturdy and quiet—a black turtleneck, black jeans, and sturdy black boots. She promised herself that as soon as this was over, she'd design an outfit that was both utilitarian *and* fashionable. Of course, she knew it was silly to worry about looks at a time like this. But appearances could be very important. They affected morale, after all, and if she had to bother with saving the world, she darned well was going to look good while doing it. She finished checking herself over, giving her shoelaces one last, savage tug, distinctly irritated at her father for causing her so much grief. She tried to focus on that anger. Better to be angry than scared out of her mind.

Finally, Madam Barrington motioned them over and they gathered in a tight knot.

"Remember, the goal is to overpower and stun him, but if things take a turn for the worse…" She sighed and pursed her lips. "We must think of our own safety and that of the people who have and will suffer at his hand." She looked at Lily while saying this, and Lily gave a small nod of assent, expression grim. She didn't want her father dead. In fact, the very idea made her heart ache with grief. But he'd already dug his own grave, so to speak. A phrase she'd once read summed it up nicely: Whatsoever a man soweth, that shall he also reap.

"Right, so shoot, but only after you've tried clubbing

him over the head." Sebastian said, a bit sarcastic as he fiddled with the newest addition to his wardrobe—a ward ring. It had once belonged to someone in Madam Barrington's family and so wasn't personalized to him. But it was powerful and certainly better than no protection at all.

Lily pursed her lips, deciding against a biting response. They were all tense. There was no need to make things worse. "Just leave my father to me and Ms. B., Sebastian. I doubt he'll be alone, so I'm sure you'll have plenty to keep you busy."

He nodded mutely, rubbing the tattoo on the back of his right hand. She kept meaning to ask him why he didn't hide it anymore. After the first time she saw it when the demon attacked them in the museum, it hadn't gone away, though it only glowed green when he held the staff it summoned in his hand. Perhaps it was related to the strange things her sight was doing these days, like when she could see Grimmold but Madam Barrington couldn't. Another question for another time, she reminded herself. One of these days she really did need to nail Sebastian down and have an in-depth talk with him about the fae.

There wasn't much else to say, so Lily and Madam Barrington went to work casting invisibility glamour on them all. It wasn't true invisibility, of course, at least not the sort of thing you read about in novels. Using the personal wards as the anchor point, it was a temporary spell that mimicked the surrounding scenery. When perfectly still, you were nearly invisible. While moving, an observant person could detect your outline. Yet, without a permanent anchor, it would only last thirty minutes or so until it started to fade, so as soon as they finished they hurried across the dark lawn toward the twinkling lights of the manor house.

Mr. Fletcher was expecting them and opened the front doors without a word at Lily's soft knock. He couldn't really see them, but he nodded gravely as they passed in a quiet shuffle of footfalls. Henry and Ursula were nowhere to be seen—as requested, Henry had not informed his wife of their plans, simply retired upstairs and taken her with him. All these precautions were, of course, necessary, since they had no idea what other listening or seeing spells John Faust had left behind, beyond the ones in his workroom.

The workroom door had been left open, and they filed through it in a silent line, tiptoeing up the landing stairs to gather in front of the boarded-up door to the rest of the second story. They were about to find out if Lily's theory was correct, or if they'd gone to all this trouble for nothing. Madam Barrington, being the more experienced wizard, took the lead. While Lily couldn't see her expression in the darkness, she could faintly see the outline of her hands tracing the lines of the doorframe, made of newer wood whose lighter color contrasted with the darker paneling of the rest of the house. After a few long moments, she stepped back and nodded to Lily, confirming her suspicions: The newer wood wasn't just a random renovation project. It was covering active runes infused with magic. The traces were faint, and Lily wouldn't have known to look for them if it weren't for the differing color of the wood. But Madam Barrington confirmed what she'd guessed, that the hidden runes controlled a portal which, they believed—hoped, really—led to wherever John Faust was hiding away. It was the same sort of spell as the portal to the Basement hidden in the library's archive broom closet. While they wouldn't know where it led until they stepped through, it made sense that John Faust would want a way to get back and forth to his base of operations easily and without detection. Perhaps he'd left it in case he wanted to return to his family estate undetected, or needed an escape. All they had to do was activate it, since its destination would have already been set into the magic when it was created.

Madam Barrington did the honors, though she wouldn't be the first to step through. They'd argued for a long time about that. Sebastian had wanted to go first, claiming he was the "most expendable," though Lily suspected it stemmed from his swiftly developing overprotective streak. He'd had the temerity to suggest she stay behind to "guard their backs," a badly disguised attempt to keep her out of harm's way. She'd given him the tongue lashing he deserved—not only was she better able to protect herself than he, but John Faust was her father and therefore her responsibility. Madam Barrington backed her up, and he'd let it go, though not without a grumble and a dirty look at Sir Kipling, who he seemed to think should have taken his side. It quickly became obvious why he hadn't, since the cat then proceeded to explain to Lily why *he* should go first: he would be the last thing John Faust would expect. When Lily related this to the group, they'd grudgingly agreed that it made sense. If John Faust had set up precautions, it would most likely be to protect against other wizards, not cats. By that same logic, Sebastian had finagled a place second in line—being a mundane, not a wizard—with Lily third and Madam Barrington bringing up the rear to ensure that the portal spell functioned properly.

With their plans already made, no words were needed as Madam Barrington quietly activated the magic and stepped back. Just like the Basement's broom closet, the portal wasn't visible to the naked eye, but Lily could sense its magic. She bent down, feeling around until she found her beloved feline's silky back. She picked him up and gave him a gentle squeeze, putting her ear to his chest and stealing a moment of peace as his purr vibrated through her body. Then she set him down and watched in silence as his outline trotted to the doorframe, looked back at her, then seemed to disappear into the solid wood door.

The plan was for him to scout what was beyond the portal and report back after a few minutes. In the event that he didn't reappear they would have to simply follow and be ready for anything.

Lily's heart pounded in her ears as the seconds ticked by. If anything happened to him…the mere thought made her eyes sting.

After five minutes, he hadn't reappeared, and Sebastian touched her shoulder, indicating it was time to move. He gave her an awkward side-hug. Not the most satisfying farewell, but under the circumstances, she was grateful all the same. She felt the warmth of his body disappear as he moved past her and through the portal, his shape appearing to melt into the door just as Sir Kipling's had, hand raised in readiness for whatever would greet him on the other side.

Lily took a deep breath, suddenly shaking. She closed her eyes and took a slower breath to steady herself—she had to be calm and focused, or her spells would suffer. Madam Barrington's bony hand settled on her shoulder, giving her a reassuring squeeze. Lily nodded and stepped forward, defensive spell ready as she moved toward the door.

Since she was used to walking through the back of the broom closet to get to the Basement, stepping through what looked like a solid door didn't bother her. But what she found beyond did.

***

Lily emerged from the portal to find herself in a wrought iron cage. She stopped dead in her tracks, body trying to cope with the shock of her surroundings as well as the uncomfortable aura of so much iron. Her invisibility glamour fizzed and faded, the spell disrupted by the iron—the only known material able to repel magic. Surrounded by such a cage, she would be hard pressed to cast any spells, though it wasn't as bad as if the iron were touching her bare skin. Fortunately, its dampening ability was less effective on spells anchored by dimmu runes, so her personal ward should still work.

Looking around, her formerly bungee-jumping stomach sank like a rock into her boots. Sebastian stood to the side, fists clenched and body shaking as he glared through the bars of the cage at her father's disgustingly smug face.

Well, she thought, this was just as lovely as a field of daisies in summertime. They'd walked straight into a trap. Yet, since nobody was shouting or flinging magic, she took a moment to glance around, taking stock.

They were in a large room with low ceilings, brick walls, and no windows—most likely the basement of a building. There was one door across the room from them and the space between was filled with tables, books, boxes of clutter, vials, papers, and various strange-looking devices, including the chair from the landing in John Faust's old workroom. This was obviously his new magical laboratory, and Lily felt a sense of ironic relief that at least their guess about the portal had been correct. Turning to look behind her, she saw the runes for the portal set into the brick wall, but the magic was weakened by the iron. She had no desire to find out what would happen should she try to step back through. Even as she watched, Madam Barrington emerged, taking in the situation with a swift look and turning back as Lily had, as if to retreat.

"I wouldn't try that, if I were you, Ethel. Your death would be an incalculable loss to wizardkind. Besides, you've only just got here, and we've been expecting you. It would be quite rude to put all my hard work to waste." He grinned at them. "You wouldn't believe how difficult it was to lug that blasted lump of iron down here."

"We?" Lily asked, genuinely confused but also hoping to keep her father talking. The longer he talked the longer they had to figure a way out of their dire predicament.

"Ah, forgive me, I remember now that you've not been properly introduced. Caden, Trista, come here." At his words, a tall, young man stood upright from where he'd been crouched behind some boxes, fiddling with something. It was the same wizard who'd fought Madam Barrington at Allen's house, though he now sported a trio of scratches across his fair cheek. As Lily puzzled over this, she noticed a shadow detach itself from the wall and come over to stand by John Faust. The light revealed it to be a young woman, lithe, muscular, and most definitely mundane. Lily started, realizing that this must have been the black-clad, ninja-like fighter who had tried to ambush her in her room. She'd assumed it had been a man.

"You both remember Lilith, don't you?" John Faust said, putting an arm around Trista's shoulders as he held out a hand, beckoning Caden to come closer as well. "I'll admit, the last time we all met we were rather distracted by unnecessary squabbling."

"Squabbling?" Lily exclaimed in disbelief, ignoring her fellows as she stepped forward, only stopping as the nearness of the iron bars made her flinch. "You broke into our house, assaulted us, and kidnapped my uncle!"

"All of which would have been entirely unnecessary if you'd listened to reason in the first place instead of running around like a spoiled child thinking they know better than their parents," John Faust said, annoyance showing through his smug expression. "Caden and Trista, on the other hand, know better. You would do well to learn from your siblings' example."

Lily snorted in derision, opening her mouth to retort when the implication of his words stopped her brain like a car hitting a brick wall. "My what? What did you say?" she said, voice wobbling and body going cold. Unthinking, she grabbed the bars of the cage, straining forward for a better look at the two young people. It only took a few seconds for a dull ache to spread through her hands as her fingers went numb, but she ignored it.

"Lilith, meet your half brother and sister. While I certainly wish I could have had more children with your mother, you can't imagine I was going to let her foolish betrayal stop me from doing my duty, can you? None of the others had your mother's pedigree, of course, but, as I'd hoped, my genes were strong enough to carry the weight. My children are a credit to the LeFay name. Some of them, anyway," he said, eyeing her critically.

Lily had no words. Literally no words. She didn't even know what to think. She was almost grateful for the iron bars she clutched so hard her knuckles and fingers had turned white. The ache distracted her from the sharper, piercing pain inside. Yet another knife her father had stabbed into her and twisted with abandon. She wasn't even sure if she had any heart left to break. How could he? Had he ever loved her mother at all, or was she simply a tool, a piece of breeding stock? What did that make her? She'd never felt so degraded, so ashamed of her very existence.

With a new shock of horror, she suddenly realized her father hadn't been *kidnapping* wizard children all these years, he'd been *breeding* them. The realization made her recoil, stumbling back to be caught and steadied by her mentor. As her mind reeled, she searched her siblings' faces, trying to see into their heads, their hearts. How did they feel? Were they loved and cherished by her father as she had never been? Or did he treat them as tools, too?

"You, LeFay, are the most contemptible creature I have ever had the misfortune to lay eyes on." Madam Barrington's cold voice came from behind Lily, who couldn't tear her eyes away from her half siblings, their resemblance to John Faust and each other now all too clear: the same dark hair, the same chiseled, patrician features. "I am ashamed that I ever taught you, and I will forever wonder where I failed in my instruction, as you obviously never listened to a word of it."

"Oh I listened, dear Ethel," he sneered. "'Wizards are a noble breed,' 'it is our duty to use our gift to benefit wizardkind,' 'mundanes can not be trusted.' Any of that sound familiar?"

Lily felt Madam Barrington sigh wearily behind her, her proud stance sagging as her shoulder stooped.

"Everything I do, I do for us. For our future," John Faust continued, spreading his arms to encompass his children, his prisoners, the whole room. "The power and knowledge I seek will save our race. A far worthier goal than you ever strived for with your quiet, passive, worthless life among those who would see us extinct. Mundane laws are meaningless except to keep their own kind from anarchy and self-annihilation. They don't apply to us. We have a higher calling, and it is extremely *vexing* that you insist on disrupting it." His last words were said with contained savagery, the anger showing only briefly before he resumed his mask of smug triumph. "But we are done with such unpleasantness. Now that you are here, you can either join me, or watch. Either way, you're going nowhere any time soon."

In the ringing silence that followed his words, Lily heard a muffled yowl.

"Shut your face you worthless pile of dog droppings and let me out!"

"Kip!" Lily exclaimed, straining forward, trying to see where the yowl had come from.

"Ah, yes, the cat," John Faust said with a sour look. "That thing is much more trouble than I have time to deal with. Caden, take it out and dispose of it."

"What? No! Stop! Don't you touch my cat!" Lily screamed, beating against the metal bars and rattling the door.

Caden didn't look at her, simply returned to the boxes and picked up a solid metal container shining with complicated spells. As he lifted it, it rattled, swaying while violent hissing and spitting came from within. Lily could now see that his hands and arms were covered in scratches, and she wished Kip had managed to scratch out his eyes in the process.

Trista eyed her brother, her face unreadable as she leaned toward her father and spoke quietly. Lily could only just hear them.

"Is that really necessary? It's only a cat, after all."

"It is a pest and will be dealt with like one. But what does it matter to you? You sound as soft-hearted as your sister. It's unbecoming."

Trista withdrew, face as stony as it was before. She moved away to lean against a table, once more taking up her watchful stance. John Faust flicked his fingers at Caden, who had hesitated, awaiting his father's command. Now the young wizard headed for the door.

Lily renewed her clamor, yelling after him and threatening unspeakable things if he so much as touched a hair on her cat's head. She even tried to throw bolts of energy at him, not caring if they burned him to a crisp. But they withered and sizzled to nothing mere feet from the bars, her grasp on the Source severely limited within the iron cage.

When the door closed on his retreating form, Madam Barrington took hold of her shoulders, half holding her back, half holding her up as she broke down sobbing.

"Please, Father, call him back," she cried, humbling herself to plead for Sir Kipling's life. "I promise, Kip will be no trouble, I'll tell him to behave. Please!"

John Faust moved away and to the side of the room, returning to his stool and whatever task he'd been attending to at his table. Back turned to them he said: "Daughter, you must learn that actions have consequences. You have defied me at every turn, and so have only yourself to blame. Perhaps you'll learn not to cross me in the future."

At that, Lily really lost it. She didn't know what she was shouting, but it probably would have earned her a lifetime of mouth washing with soap. It was only her mentor's and Sebastian's strength combined that held her back, and Sebastian finally gave up and grabbed her in a bear hug, pinning her arms to her side so she would stop beating against the bars of the cage.

"Hush, Lil, hush," he whispered soothingly in her ear. "I got this, just calm down, will you? I've got a plan." He had to repeat himself several times before his words percolated through her blind rage and grief, but finally she subsided, going limp in his arms.

He carefully set her down and stood up, visibly steeling himself for something. It was only then that she noticed his whole body was shaking and he was covered in sweat. She remembered weeks ago how he'd told her that iron hurt those with any connection to the fae. With the amount of fae magic he used, she wondered how badly his proximity to the iron was hurting him. Based on his body language, quite a bit.

She had no idea what he had planned. Beat his staff on the door until it broke? Normally she would use magic to trip the lock, but everything was made of iron. She wouldn't be able to get a grip on the latch, much less move it.

Even as the half of her brain still functioning considered escape methods and the other half curled up and cried, Sebastian made his move. Before their very eyes, he walked out of the cage. Its bars passed through his body as if he'd become incorporeal, though he screamed in pain as they touched him, oozing burns appearing on his skin as the air filled with the smell of singed flesh. But in less than a second it was over and he was out, running full tilt at John Faust, glowing staff materializing in his hands.

Before he could swing at the man, Trista intercepted him with a spinning kick to the chest. Sebastian stumbled, barely keeping his feet as he gasped for air. He lost his grip on the staff and it disappeared, but he immediately called it back, swinging the dangerously spiked end toward Trista's head. She dodged the blow, ducking smoothly inside his swing and double punching him in the chest, again driving the air from his body.

He stumbled back, staff disappearing again and not returning as he gasped loudly for air. But Trista didn't let up. She followed him, methodically striking at nerve clusters and muscles as she systematically took him apart. He landed a few solid punches, but Trista's lithe body pivoted with the blows, negating their strength. Her next strike was a knife-hand to the neck, and the blow seemed to stun him. He swayed unsteadily, then collapsed in a heap on the floor, groaning.

With a clearing of the throat, John Faust stood up, visibly shaken but doing his best to hide it. "Well, it seems Mr. Blackwell has all sorts of tricks up his sleeve. No matter. We'll soon find them all, once I have him strapped down. Good work, Trista. Tie him up. Thoroughly, mind you."

She did as he asked, trussing up the groaning form like a turkey at Thanksgiving. Lily watched, numb, unable to do anything to help her friend. Her throat was already raw from yelling, and it didn't help in any case.

Excitement over, John Faust turned back to his worktable. Trista left Sebastian lying on the floor and she went to the boxes, rummaging through them in search of something. Since both their backs were turned, neither saw Sebastian casually sit up, shrug off the ropes as if they were wet noodles, and begin creeping toward her unsuspecting father.

But Lily saw it. She had just enough time to glimpse the triumphant "Ha, suckas!" look in her friend's eye before he leapt on John Faust, attempting to put the older man in a stranglehold.

He might have been successful, too, if Trista hadn't been so incredibly fast. Whipping around like a striking cobra, she threw whatever was in her hand like a ninja star and it struck Sebastian in the back of the head with an audible clunk. The blow dazed him, and before he had a chance to recover the young woman had already closed the distance, scooping up the discarded rope as she went and leaping on his back. In the blink of an eye the rope was around his neck and tightening as Trista pulled with all her might. Lily screamed, watching Sebastian flail and desperately gasp for air as he tried to get a hold on his attacker. But he couldn't, and as each second passed his movements grew weaker. Finally, he sank to his knees, then forward onto his hands, then slumped to the side, unmoving.

John Faust, standing back and rubbing his neck with a hate-filled glare, motioned to Trista, who unwound the rope and stepped away, impassive once more. Lily held her breath, willing Sebastian to get up, to breathe, anything.

Her father must have noticed her fearful stare, because he gave a coughing laugh. "Don't worry, Lilith dear. He's just unconscious. I have a great many plans for this boy. I wouldn't allow him to escape so easily. A quick death is too good for a Blackwell."

This time he gave Trista special shackles to use on Sebastian, which she fastened securely before stepping back to let her father cast some spell. At his words Sebastian floated up in the air to hover, limp, a few inches from the ground. Weak with relief that her friend wasn't dead, Lily's interest was momentarily piqued, curious to know what words John Faust had used to shorten and simplify the usually complicated process of creating a neutral gravity bubble. However he'd done it, it enabled the much smaller Trista to maneuver Sebastian's unconscious form toward the door with minimal effort.

"Put him in one of the cells, I'll deal with him later. Don't damage him, mind you," he admonished as she accidentally banged Sebastian's lolling head against the door frame, "Oh, and bring Allen back with you. It's time we got started," he finished as she disappeared up the stairs.

"Allen?" Lily asked, prompted to words. "He's alright?"

"More or less," John Faust said dismissively, bending to pick up his overturned stool and sitting back down at his worktable.

"What have you done to him?" Madam Barrington demanded, turning from where she'd been examining the flickering portal at their back.

"Nothing life-threatening. He didn't, after all, kill anyone, only stole my research and destroyed years of sweat and tears, not to mention expensive and valuable equipment. I simply helped him to…*understand* my pain."

Though his back was turned to her, Lily could hear the venom in his voice, and she shuddered, feeling sick. The iron didn't help. On top of everything that had happened, her proximity to such a large quantity was making her feel nauseous.

"What are you going to do with him?" Lily asked, hoping to distract him.

"Finish what I started. If your friends hadn't interfered last time, we'd already be on our way to finding Morgan le Fay. I could use you, still, of course. But I think it more fitting for Allen to have the pleasure, since he stole my research in the first place, which prompted me to invent this location spell."

"But if you have Morgan's diary back, then why would you need to use the spell still?" she said. "I thought you said it was dangerous. You can't do that to Allen."

"Allen will be fine, child. The side effects are not life-threatening, and he can't possibly get any crazier than he already is."

"No! You can't do this! Please, why not use the diary?"

Her father waved a dismissive hand in her general direction. "I had only just managed to translate it when Allen took it. I haven't even properly studied it and there's no guarantee Morgan's vague ramblings point to her final resting place. I've wasted enough time preparing the last twenty years. Now is the time for action."

Just then she heard the sound of footsteps accompanied by a whimpering sound. Caden and Trista appeared through the basement door, supporting Allen between them. The poor man was trembling and pleading in broken sentences. Caden turned and locked the door behind them, then all three headed toward the middle of the room.

"Where is Kipling?" Lily yelled at Caden, roused to life once more. "Where is my cat? What did you do to him?"

"Be quiet, girl! Or I shall find reason to make Allen's stay here much more uncomfortable." John Faust's irritation was evident, but he paid her no more mind as they manhandled a weak and struggling Allen into the device, strapping him down.

Lily quieted, but with her whole body already aching and nauseous, the thought of her beloved companion lying somewhere, bleeding, dead…her stomach heaved and she threw up, making a mess all over the floor of the cage.

The sound made all three of her captors look up, and John Faust shook his head impatiently. "Good heavens, Lilith, what is the matter? Are you ill?"

"The iron," she gasped, leaning against the brick wall as far from the cage walls as possible. An idea had come to her. She began to groan loudly, holding her stomach, dry retching a few more times for effect. Madam Barrington started forward, looking concerned, but Lily waved her back.

Her father sighed. "Ah, I had forgotten. It affects you more strongly. Well, with a few assurances of your good behavior, I suppose you can observe from somewhere else in the room. Caden, get the shackles. No, the regular ones. And a gag."

Her half brother came over to the cage and threw a pair of what looked like thick hand-cuffs into the cage. As she'd hoped, they were not made of iron.

"Put those on," Caden said, his voice higher than his father's but with that same smooth quality.

Lily did as instructed.

"Now come over here. You in the back, if you cause any trouble, she stays here, no matter how sick she gets. Got it?" Madam Barrington nodded, standing calmly as Lily went to the door of the cage and waited as Caden unlocked it and pulled her roughly out. As soon as he'd locked it once more, he took a strip of cloth and gagged her tightly, so she couldn't cast spells. Finally he led her over to a chair on the other side of the room, near the door, and sat her down, using some lengths of rope to tie her to it. "Cause any trouble and you're back in the cage, understand?"

Lily nodded, noticing that even though Caden's voice sounded like his father's, his speech was less refined and lacked the subtle hint of British upbringing that was no doubt a result of John Faust's youth spent at boarding schools in England.

Checking the ropes one last time, Caden left her, returning to his father's side and helping him with some adjustments as Trista looked on, trying to stand where she could keep an eye on everyone in the room. Unfortunately for her, Madam Barrington and Lily were now on opposite sides of the room, with the device in the middle. She appeared to consider the situation, then turned toward the cage, gauging Madam Barrington as the greater threat and only glancing occasionally over her shoulder at Lily.

So far, so good, Lily thought. The next part would be the hardest.

She closed her eyes and tried to calm herself. It was

difficult. Everything still throbbed, her stomach felt like it was in freefall, and she was on the verge of tears, fighting to keep horrible images of her companion's lifeless form from her mind. Not ideal conditions. But she couldn't give up. Not now. Not ever.

She pinched her arm, the sharp pain giving her something else to focus on besides her fears. She used that focus to bring her mind under control, ignoring what was going on in the center of the room, ignoring her grief for Sir Kipling, ignoring her worry for Sebastian, ignoring her hatred for her father. With every fiber of her being, she focused inward, feeling the strong pulse of the Source with relief and summoning it to her will.

Though she hadn't yet managed to cast without words, after weeks of practice she thought she understood what Allen had been trying to teach her. Magic wasn't like a hammer or saw, a tool separate from herself that she didn't need to understand, just know how to use. Magic was supposed to be instinct. A part of her as familiar as an arm or a leg. You didn't tell your limbs what to do, you just decided and they followed along. It was like the difference between doing math on your fingers and in your head. When you didn't understand math, hadn't internalized its functions and variations, you needed physical and visual aids to control it. But once you understood how it worked, had made it a part of your subconscious, it was a simple matter of instinct.

Tuning out the world around her, she let her head droop, as if in defeat. In reality she was looking at the shackles around her wrists. They were heavy cuffs, but the locking mechanism looked to be a simple turn latch. She focused on that latch, visualizing it vividly and imagining it turning, seeing every detail of its turn in minute detail.

When she was ready, she opened her mind to the Source, summoning it to her in the calmness she'd practiced during meditation. She let it flood her mind, feeling its energy, and directing it toward the latch until her whole body coursed with it. Concentrating so hard that her temples began to throb, she *knew* the words of power and forced her magic to fill them, follow them, bring them to life. It was sluggish to respond, but she bore down, keeping her visualization front and center until the magic flowed the direction *she* wanted.

Slowly, the latch quivered, then shifted, then finally clicked, and she felt the left shackle loosen. She didn't stop there, despite the beads of sweat trickling down her forehead and neck. Renewing her efforts, she slowly, laboriously unlocked the other shackle, holding onto her newfound control by the skin of her teeth as shouts and cries from the center of the room threatened to distract her. In a last gasp of concentration, knowing she didn't have the skill to untie the knots behind the chair, she went for a less tidy, but still effective, solution: heat. Singed, the strands would be easy enough to break.

A scream finally broke her concentration, scattering her thoughts like shards of glass as her head came up. Sights, sounds, and feelings came flooding in and she became hyperaware of the whole room. With effort she blocked out the flood of sensation, focusing on the middle of the room. Allen was screaming. John Faust must have activated his location spell, because the device was alight as his power coursed through it, through Allen. Her uncle was rigid, eyes shut and mouth wide open as the veins in his neck and arms stood out. Caden and Trista watched, mesmerized, and Lily knew it was now or never.

With a mighty heave—well, mighty for her at least— she flexed her arms, twisting away from the chair. She could have wept in relief when she felt the ropes give way. Moving as little as possible, so as not to draw Trista's observant eye, she carefully disentangled herself and put aside the now-open shackles, removing her gag. Her eyes were fixed on the key to the iron cage lying on a worktable behind the group watching Allen. All she needed to do was sprint over, grab it, and free Madam Barrington before they had a chance to stop her. With John Faust distracted, they might have a chance of disabling her siblings before they could react.

She was gathering what remaining strength she had, preparing to sprint, when a voice echoed in her head. It was like a thousand bells all ringing at once in one, massive toll of pure noise.

Unlock the door.

She clapped her hands to her ears in pained shock, but the voice was gone as suddenly as it had arrived. It felt like the same presence that had spoken to her and Sir Kipling at the museum. The same presence that had helped them, had put its magic into her ward. But what did it want her to do? She was already going to unlock the door to the cage. Wait, what if it had meant...

She looked to the side at the door to the stairs leading up to the ground level. The doorknob slowly turned, as if someone on the other side were trying to open it on the sly, but was foiled by the lock.

Wincing in sympathy at Allen's continued screams, she inched over to the door and turned the key Caden had left in the lock. The door opened a crack and she peered through. Sebastian's brown eye peered back.

"Lily?" he hissed, jumping in surprise at her sudden appearance.

"No time!" she whispered back. "I'm going to go get Madam Barrington out. Cover me!"

Not waiting for a reply, she turned and sprinted for the worktable. Trista saw the movement out of the corner of her eye and whipped around. Expecting to feel a blow on the neck or back, Lily ignored her, grabbing the key and heading straight for the cage. She heard Sebastian shout Trista's name, but didn't have time to look back to see what was happening.

Fortunately, Madam Barrington had been alert the whole time, watching Lily from the other side of the room as things unfolded. She was already speaking, preparing a spell as Lily slammed into the bars of the cage, not bothering to slow as she shoved the large, heavy key into the lock and turned it, pulling the door open with numb hands. Madam Ethel Mathers Barrington strode out of the cage, eyes alight with righteous anger and hair standing on end, crackling with magic just waiting to be unleashed. And unleash it she did, straight at Caden. Not as observant, or quick, as his sister, he was only just tearing his eyes away from his father's pulsing form when the magic hit him. The young wizard dropped like a rock, stunned by the massive bolt. If he'd been a mundane, it would have killed him. But Madam Barrington knew he was wearing a ward and in no real danger.

Pushing herself away from the dampening influence of the iron, Lily joined her mentor as they prepared to attack John Faust. Just then an ear-splitting yowl rang out and her heart leapt at the sound, threatening to burst from her chest in joy. Forgetting everything, she spun, searching desperately for the source of the noise.

There, in fine feline form, was Sir Kipling, leaping back and forth at Trista as he and Sebastian tag-teamed her. Lily realized he must have slipped in with Sebastian. Over the commotion she also heard high-pitched squeaks and realized the tiny flashes she saw were two pixies circling, diving at Trista's head. Lily's half sister might be inhumanly fast, but with a cat-shaped buzz saw, two miniature dive-bombers, and an angry witch attacking from all sides, she couldn't defend herself. Lily wanted to rush to their aid—it looked as if Sebastian was limping—but instead she turned away. They had things under control but wouldn't for long if she didn't do something about John Faust.

Madam Barrington had moved ahead and Lily hurried to catch up. They approached her father carefully, but he seemed not to notice, still in the throes of his spell. Allen had long since lost consciousness, but he didn't seem to need to be awake for whatever John Faust was doing. Lily and Madam Barrington looked at each other, and Lily saw her own uncertainty mirrored in her eyes. Should they interrupt the spell? Would it hurt Allen? Would John Faust lose control and kill someone, even himself?

Fortunately, they never had to find out. At that moment her father stumbled back, catching and supporting himself on a nearby table as he shouted hoarsely. "Yes. Yes! It worked!" Despite his triumph, they could see the spell had taken a toll on him. He was covered in sweat and his skin had a grayish tinge. He looked around, dazed, as if only just seeing the room for the first time.

Though the battle between Trista and Sebastian was the loudest thing in the room, John Faust's eyes went straight to Caden, laid out on the floor. "What have you done to my son?" he cried, rushing to the young man's side and kneeling, checking for a pulse.

"What have you done to Allen? What have you done to the other children?" Lily yelled at him, anger coursing through her veins as both she and Madam Barrington advanced. Now was the time to take him, she knew, when he was weak. Yet the sight of him on the ground cradling Caden's head brought a fresh stab of anguish to her heart. How she wanted him to cradle her like that, to show her even a smidgen of the care he had for her half brother. And her poor brother. Kidnapped as a child and raised by this monster through no fault of his own. He was to be pitied more than she, having endured a life her mother had saved her from.

"Caden. Caden! Wake up!" John Faust pleaded, ignoring them as he shook his son. The young man groaned in response, raising a weak arm to hold his head. Sighing in relief, his father stumbled to his feet and faced them, glaring at Madam Barrington. "You'll pay for this, woman. You've meddled in my family long enough. You've poisoned my daughter against me, even convinced my father to turn his back on my cause. You're no wizard, you're a meddlesome witch," he said, spitting out the epitaph like a curse.

"Do not be a fool, LeFay. You have only yourself to blame. You have twisted what I taught you and used it to justify your own selfish schemes. Whatever happens here is squarely on your shoulders. Now give up before someone gets hurt. You are already near collapse yourself. There is nowhere to go."

John Faust laughed, a chilling, twisted sound. "I'm not your student anymore, Ethel. Don't begin to imagine you know the limits of my strength. I don't delight in pain or death, but they are necessary tools for the greater good. I suggest you go back to your cage before I use them on you."

There was a moment of tense silence, broken only by the yowls, curses, and sparks of the fight unfolding on the other side of the room. Then all three wizards attacked at once. The magic met in midair, clashing in a huge wash of energy that threw them all backward off their feet. Lily was first up, casting an extra shield between them as John Faust aimed another spell at Madam Barrington. The battle was furious, but swift. It was clear, despite his words, that her father was weakened. Caden was little help, stumbling to his feet but barely able to form more than a basic ward, much less attack. Lily and Madam Barrington pounded at John Faust's defenses, trying to stun him. If they could only knock him out for a moment, they could use a pair of iron shackles on him and be done with it.

They might have done it, if not for one crucial mistake. They had come at John Faust from the direction of the cage, with the exit unblocked behind him, instead of circling and trapping him between them and the wall. As they fought he backed up, shouting at Trista to get her brother and go. The young woman appeared in Lily's field of vision, covered in small, bloody scratches and sprinting for the door. She grabbed Caden under the armpit and hauled him up, supporting him as they headed up the stairs.

As John Faust reached the bottom step, he spoke through gritted teeth while still concentrating on maintaining his defensive spell. "It doesn't have to be like this, Lilith. You're on the wrong side of history. Don't throw your life away fighting for them. I'm only trying to help our people survive."

Lily hesitated, the spell on her lips dying as pain and longing stabbed through her chest. Despite everything he'd done, she still craved his approval. Yes, his methods might be reprehensible, but he *was* trying to preserve the wizard race, a legitimate problem that no one else had even begun to acknowledge, much less address. There was so much good wizards could do in the world if only they'd come down from their lofty pedestals. Maybe she would be more help to wizardkind, to humanity as a whole, if she were at her father's side. Maybe all he needed was a conscience, and she could provide that.

At that moment Sebastian ran up behind her, panting, and they were joined by their various four-footed and winged allies. Sir Kipling came to stand between her legs, hissing at John Faust, and that's when she remembered what he'd ordered done to her cat. Good grief, who was she fooling? She had to stop pretending and start dealing. Her father was an unrepentant, incurable git, no matter what his goals were. If she wanted to help wizardkind, she had to start by putting him away where he would do no more harm.

"Thanks, but no thanks, Dad," she said, giving him a mirthless smile. "I don't trust people who don't like cats." With that she prepared to renew her attack, but John Faust turned tail and ran, taking the stairs two at a time.

"You two check to make sure Allen is alright," Madam Barrington ordered in a voice that brooked no argument. Then she turned and followed John Faust, moving surprisingly quickly for her age.

Lily hesitated, wanting to follow, but distracted by Sebastian pulling her into a bone-crushing hug. Once she realized he wasn't trying to strangle her, she returned it with equal fervor. As he released her and ran to the center of the room, Lily bent and picked up Sir Kipling, squeezing him so tightly he protested with a meow of alarm.

"Hey! I'm not a stuffed animal, you know."

"I thought you were dead," she murmured, voice muffled as she buried her face in his fur.

"Me? Oh you of little faith. What an absurd thing to think. I'm a cat, after all. Don't you know we have nine lives?"

"But how did you escape?" She asked, putting him down and hurrying to join Sebastian. As they gently unstrapped Allen and lifted him off the chair, Sir Kipling explained that Caden obviously had no idea how to kill a cat. He'd tried a few spells, all of which Sir Kipling's ward collar protected him from. But the cat had craftily played dead, and since his long fur mostly hid the collar, and the young wizard only nudged him with a foot to check for life, it was easy enough to fool him. As soon as the wizard left, Sir Kipling ran and found Sebastian. He was distinctly vague on how he got Sebastian out of his cell. Lily suspected it was a combination of his own unique cat magic and whatever had enabled Sebastian to escape the iron cage.

Laying Allen out on one of the cleared-off tables, they checked his pulse. It was weak, but steady, and he was breathing. "I don't think we can do any more for him right now. He's probably just exhausted. Come on!"

Their group ran for the stairs, Sebastian in the lead since he'd already been to the floor above once. The stairs led up to a white hall with tiled, linoleum floors. It looked eerily like an old-fashioned mental ward, with small cracks in the wall and some of the tiles missing corners. Lily didn't have time to wonder where they were, however, as Sebastian sprinted off to the left. They passed the unconscious form of a very large, very square-looking woman, slumped against the wall. She wore the clothes of a caretaker of some sort and had a ring of keys on her belt.

"Who?" Lily stammered as they passed.

"No idea." Sebastian shouted, jumping over her outstretched legs as he ran. "She tried to stop me and I gave her the ol' one-two."

Lily went around the unconscious woman rather than jump over her but didn't have time to wonder further as they heard a cry from up ahead. Rounding the corner, they saw the entrance of the building, a high-ceilinged foyer with double bar doors leading out into the night. Trista, Caden, and John Faust were just disappearing out of them, but she barely noticed. Her eyes were drawn to the crumpled form in the center of the floor.

"NO! Ms. B.!" Lily screamed, skidding to a halt by her mentor as Sebastian barreled through the doors after her fleeing family. The pixies followed Sebastian, but Sir Kipling halted between Lily and the doors, taking up a defensive stance and keeping an eye on the room around them as Lily forgot all else but the woman in her arms.

Madam Barrington's skin was ice cold, and at first Lily couldn't find a pulse, her hands were shaking so badly. When she finally did find the artery on the side of her mentor's neck, she couldn't tell if it was pulsing or not. But holding a finger in front of her nose she thought she could feel the faintest brush of air. With frantic motions she checked Madam Barrington's whole body, looking for injury. But she found none. No blood, no burns, no sign of damage. And yet her mentor was so cold, as if in death.

She was scrambling at her pocket, on the verge of calling for an ambulance, when a weak voice behind her made her jump.

"Is sh—she alright?"

It was Allen, and Lily cried out in relief to see him upright. At least, mostly upright. He looked terribly weak, with barely any color in his skin at all. But at least he was talking in coherent sentences. Lily supposed she should be grateful her father preferred mental and emotional torment over physical harm as a form of retribution.

"You survived!" Lily cried, gently laying her mentor down on the floor and running to help Allen.

"App—pp—parently so," he said, stuttering worse than ever. "Th—though I th—think I may n—need some time to, w—well, recover."

"Is anything hurt? Do you need a hospital?"

"A psy—psychologist perhaps," he attempted a chuckle, but coughed instead. "N—n—no, I j—jest. I o—only need r—rest, I think. B—but let me l—look at Ethel. Oh, J—Johnny, what h—have you done?" he muttered, lowering himself painfully to kneel at Madam Barrington's side. He felt her forehead, neck, and wrists, then checked under her eyelids and in her mouth.

"C—c—cursed."

"What?" Lily asked, alarmed.

"S—she's been c—cursed. D—doctors will d—do her no good."

Lily felt a stab of fear. "Will she be alright? Can you fix her?"

Allen sighed. "I w—will try. F—for now we m—must keep her warm, and h—hydrated."

With a bang, Sebastian burst back in the front doors, skidding to a halt and taking in the scene with a glance. "Allen, you're alright! What's wrong with Aunt B.? Is she hurt?"

"Allen says John Faust cursed her," Lily said, trying to keep the tremble out of her voice.

"That bastard!" Sebastian exclaimed, punching a fist into his palm.

Lily suddenly remembered he'd gone after them. "Where are they?"

"Gone," he said gloomily. "Jumped in a car and raced away. Who knows where to."

"Oh, this is a disaster," Lily moaned, burying her face in her hands. Madam Barrington was hurt, John Faust had gotten away, presumably with the knowledge of Morgan le Fay's whereabouts, and they were no closer to stopping him than they had been before.

"Hey, hey." Sebastian knelt at her side, putting a

comforting hand on her shoulder. "We saved Allen and busted Mr. Fancypants's operation wide open. We'll sweep the place, hide anything we need to, and call the cops. John Faust won't have anywhere to go. He's on the run. We'll figure this out, don't worry."

"But Ms. B.," Lily said, on the verge of tears. "What if she—what if she, d—dies?"

With strong hands, Sebastian helped her stand and she turned to bury her face in his neck, fighting to hold back the tears. Madam Barrington was like a mother *and* a father to her. She'd been the one and only person who understood her and helped her discover who she really was. The thought that she might die, that Lily might lose her strength, wisdom, and support, was almost more than she could bear.

"Shhh," Sebastian whispered into her hair, holding her tenderly. Tentatively. "It's going to be okay. You're not alone."

Lily clung to his words, and a numb sort of peace came over her. She felt the crushing weight, the tightness in her chest, ease. Now was not the time to break down, she knew. She had to be strong. There was still work to do, and with Madam Barrington gone, it was up to her to take the lead.

Taking several deep breaths, with only a few sniffles in-between, she pulled back, giving Sebastian a grateful look before turning to Allen. "Before…" her voice caught, but she pushed on. "Before all this Madam Barrington showed me how to cast a temporary portal back to the Basement at McCain Library. It will be a safe place for you and her to rest while I sterilize this place of magic. Sebastian and I will carry her. We need to get her downstairs where I can cast the portal."

"Sebastian." She turned to him. "Once Ms. B. is safe, call Richard. He's expecting it. Do you have any idea where we are?"

He shook his head. "Nope. Still in Georgia, probably.

The foliage looks familiar. But I can find out if you'll lend me your phone. Mine's dead again." He gave an apologetic shrug.

Lily nodded, remembering how she used to fuss at him for not charging his phone. He would always laugh her off, calling her a worry-wart. That time seemed so long ago, when all they had to worry about were normal, run-of-the mill adventures like ghosts and time loops. There was no mirth in Sebastian's eyes now, only worry floating on the surface of a deep, smoldering pit of anger.

Lily had no time for worry, or anger. She would have to process all this later. Right now she had a job to do, and she intended to do it.

Epilogue

I T TURNED OUT THEY *HAD* BEEN IN AN OLD MENTAL WARD, LOCATED ABOUT AN hour and a half southeast of Atlanta, near Macon. The facility had once been state-run but was decommissioned several decades ago and purchased by a private trust.

They found this out after the fact, of course. The FBI lost no time in showing up, forcing Lily to focus her efforts on the basement as she hurriedly threw books, charts, notes, and unapologetically magical items through the portal she'd cast to the library Basement. There was nothing she could do about the large device in the middle of the room. It was worthless without John Faust, of course, and there were enough dimmu runes all over the place that she couldn't hide them all.

She got everything hidden just in time, deactivating the portal to the Basement and wiping away the aluminum paint as the sound of sirens approached. She'd already checked and seen that the portal in the cage had faded to nothing. The runes were still there but couldn't be reactivated, not surrounded by the iron cage. She would have to recommend to her grandfather that he tear out and replace that doorframe in John Faust's workshop.

When the FBI arrived, SWAT team in tow, the first thing they did was a sweep of the building, something Lily and Sebastian hadn't had time to do. The first floor contained what had previously been exam rooms, now repurposed as storage, an office, a schoolroom, and a gym. The kitchens were still functioning, and they also found what must have been John Faust's bedroom. To Lily's relief, he hadn't left anything magically incriminating in it, having kept all his books, devices, and supplies in the facility's basement.

Then the sweep team headed up to the second floor. There, each locked in their own individual room, they found the children. There were seven, ranging in age from three to sixteen. The youngest, only a toddler, looked about with wide, frightened eyes. The older ones had blank expressions and were silent as the grave, not answering any of the policemen's questions. None of them looked abused. In fact all were the picture of health, with bright eyes, rosy cheeks, and strong bodies that clearly got plenty of food and exercise.

Lily was conflicted, wanting to talk to them, to tell them she was their sister and that she would help take care of them. But she knew that was out of her hands. Child protection services had sent several people and the children were taken away, presumably to be treated and then returned to their families.

Though she couldn't care for them, she did warn Richard that they might have...odd ideas and behaviors. There was no telling how John Faust had raised them, isolated here their whole lives with only him and the square woman as parent figures. Richard assured her they would all go through a thorough psychological evaluation and be treated as victims of a cult.

That prognosis certainly wasn't difficult to come by. Richard hadn't even needed to float the idea himself. The FBI agents took one look at the basement and declared John Faust a loony of the highest degree. They'd already sent people after him, putting out an APB on John Faust and the car. Since, according to Richard, Caden and Trista were about twenty years old and legal adults, they were being treated as accomplices rather than victims.

After EMTs took the squarish woman away on a stretcher—Sebastian had given her quite a knock—Lily and Sebastian gave statements, Richard and his partner, Agent Meyer, presiding. They kept it simple: Being suspicious that John Faust was up to no good, they had come to confront him and he fled, leaving them and the younger children behind. Lily had to explain her own less-than-friendly relationship with her father. But, being seen as a victim herself by the FBI, and with Richard running interference, the questioning didn't go too deep.

Sir Kipling stayed out of sight throughout, knowing not to reappear until it was time to go. The pixies, of course, had long ago been thanked and dismissed. Lily wondered how much alcohol they would be getting for their aid.

Once their interview was over, they were told they could leave. They didn't have a car, of course, and had to call a taxi to get home, hoping against hope the driver could find their address, since they'd already claimed a taxi was how they'd gotten there in the first place.

Richard assured Lily they'd surely found more than enough evidence to put John Faust behind bars for life—if they ever caught him, of course. Lily pulled him aside for a moment to explain how iron worked on wizards, warning him that nothing else but constant sedation could keep John Faust under control. She wasn't sure if Richard took her seriously, but he wrote it all down and promised to pass it on to the appropriate people.

After that, Sebastian got some burn cream and bandages for where the iron cage had left minor burns on his skin, and the two of them were left wrapped in blankets and sitting on the bumper of an ambulance. They waited there thirty minutes before their taxi finally arrived. An hour and a half, and a *lot* of money later, it deposited them at Madam

Barrington's house, where they retrieved Sebastian's car. They would have to wait to get Lily's car back from the LeFay estate some other time.

It was well past midnight, so they had to sneak into McCain Library, dodging a few campus security guards. When they finally stepped through the broom closet and into the Basement, Lily felt ready to collapse. But she stiffened her spine and did what needed to be done, helping get Madam Barrington comfortable and finding some food and water for Allen. Tomorrow they would need to figure out a way to sneak her mentor out of the basement and drive both her and Allen back to Savannah. Allen insisted that's where she needed to be if he were going to treat her properly. Plus, during Allen's captivity, John Faust had boasted about how he'd infiltrated the townhouse's defenses, so Allen knew what to shore up to prevent any further "disturbances." In any case, he doubted John Faust would bother them anymore.

"He's h—headed off to England, y—you can be sure," he said, his stutter having improved with a blanket, hot tea, and some digestives Lily kept in her office. "H—he wouldn't have fled so readily if he, well, hadn't already g—gotten what he was looking for: Morgan's l—location. Remember, my brother is not exactly, um, malicious, s—so to speak. If we s—stay out of his way, I believe he will, hm, s—stay out of ours," Allen finished, bringing his cup of tea to his lips very slowly and carefully. Despite the improved speech, he still had a bad case of tremors along with intense nerve pain in his extremities, most likely caused by the extreme amount of magic his body had been forced to channel. They were hopeful time would heal his wounds, but who knew if he would ever be the same.

Lily agreed with Allen's assessment of John Faust, though

it made her heart ache to know Madam Barrington would be so far away from home. Allen promised she could visit anytime but insisted he needed no help in nursing his patient. Personally, Lily thought his flock of enchanted hands would do a better job of nursing Madam Barrington than he ever would. She silently resolved to have her mother look in on them regularly, once she and Sebastian left for England.

For that was where they had to go.

Sebastian was skeptical at first, but even he couldn't deny that they'd come too far to simply give up. If John Faust had gone to England to find Morgan, they would have to follow. Either to stop him, or to find her first. Thanks to Madam Barrington's foresight, they had the copies of the diary and John Faust's translation that she had made their first night at Allen's townhouse. The originals, along with John Faust's eduba, were mysteriously missing from the mental ward. Lily could only assume her father had taken them when he fled.

There was much planning to do, but all agreed it could wait until tomorrow. Everyone was dead on their feet. Lily made sure Allen was as comfortable as possible. He insisted it would do Madam Barrington more harm than good to be moved that night, so he would be staying with her in the Basement.

Sebastian drove Lily home, chuckling for the first time that night when he opened the car door and Sir Kipling bolted out, bounding joyfully up the apartment steps to scratch at the door and meow at them to hurry up.

He supported Lily as they made their weary way up to join her cat. At the door Lily fumbled with her keys, dropping them with a curse.

"Here, let me do that," Sebastian said, stopping her from bending over to retrieve them. He was probably afraid she wouldn't be able to get back up.

Ignoring her half-hearted protests, he accompanied her inside, helping her to the bed and taking off her shoes when she just stared blankly at the floor, too weary to do anything at all. Pulling back the covers, he made her lie down and tucked her in, gently running his soft fingers across her cheek as he brushed her hair out of her face. Sir Kipling jumped up on the coverlet and picked his way over the lump of her body to curl up in his proper place: nestled against her chest where his purrs would lull her to sleep. She was already half unconscious by the time Sebastian switched off the light and turned to go, but she caught his hand.

"Don't leave," she mumbled. She didn't really think about the request, she just knew she didn't want to be alone. Not after tonight.

Sebastian hesitated but then gave in, lying behind her on top of the covers so he could curl his body around hers, head close and breath warm on the back of her neck. It took a few moments, but he finally seemed to work up the courage to put a protective arm around her, holding her tight. Sir Kipling didn't protest the invasion of his space. In fact, he purred even louder, if that was possible.

"I'll always be here," Sebastian whispered in her ear, "for as long as you need me."

"Promise?" Lily mumbled into her pillow, eyes heavy as she started to drift off.

"I promise."

Lily sighed contentedly, nestled between Sir Kipling's purring warmth and Sebastian's solid strength. Maybe things would be alright, she thought. After all, where could she go wrong with these two? It was her last thought before she fell asleep, dreaming of double-decker buses, men in tall fuzzy hats, and lots and lots of tea.

Glossary

aluminum - a metal favored by wizards for its usefulness in absorbing large amounts of magic because of its high energy density potential. Safer and more stable than lithium, it is widely used in crafting spell anchors (see dimmu runes) either as a raw material or an inlay. While spells can be cast onto any substance but wrought iron, aluminum better absorbs the magic fueling the spell, thus making the spell more potent and long-lasting (as long as it is cast in conjunction with the proper dimmu runes and sealing spells).

angel - one of the three species of magic users (human, fae, and angel/demon). Spoken of in myth and lore, their origin, powers, and purpose are largely unknown to modern wizards. It is said that they are the stewards of heaven and the most powerful of the three species.

Basement, the - the magical archive beneath the McCain Library containing a private collection of occult books on magic, wizardry, and arcane science, as well as an assortment of artifacts and enchanted items. Created in 1936 during the library's original construction, it is accessed through a secret portal in the broom closet of the library's own basement archive. At any point in time, the Basement has a gatekeeper, the wizard tasked with its maintenance and protection and upon whom rests the control of its magic. This collection of knowledge was bequeathed as a public resource to wizardkind, but, because of the decline of wizards in modern society, has been very little used by anyone but its gatekeeper. Lily Singer is the current gatekeeper, with Madam Barrington as her predecessor.

battle magic - a dangerous form of quick casting requiring an intuitive mastery of Enkinim along with an adroit enough mind to shape magic on the go. To battle cast one must react largely on instinct. Without as much time to carefully control and constrain the magic used, there is much higher risk of accidents or backfires.

construct - a crafted being, usually built in the likeness of a man or animal, enchanted with abilities. Though complex to make, they can be crafted out of almost any material. While they can be built to act and respond in a very lifelike fashion based on the parameters of their controlling spells, they are not alive in the biological sense and can't be killed. Their magic must be broken or altered for them to stop working. Used for everything from manual labor to mobile wards, messengers, guardians, and spies, they can be created to respond only to certain people, commands, or circumstances.

crafting - the art of creating and enchanting objects. Such objects, once made, can exist and operate separate from their creator or even magic in general, as the controlling spells are anchored to dimmu runes carved, inlaid, or otherwise affixed to them. To craft properly, you must not only know the properties of your materials, but also the dimmu runes needed to attain the desired result.

demon - greater - a fallen angel. They are those who rebelled and were cast down from heaven, their magic corrupted.

Each has their own unique name by which they can be commanded, if one is brave enough to speak it and powerful enough to master its owner. They are creatures of great power, hate, and thirst for destruction.

dimmu - [dim + mu = {dim = to make, fashion, create, build (du = to build, make + im = clay, mud)} + {mu = word, name, line on a tablet}] the Enkinim word for runes of power, the script used to write Enkinim, the language of power. In and of itself, this script is not magical, and a mundane could write it all day without achieving anything. Dimmu runes are used by wizards to anchor their spells. Infused with magic from the Source, these runes enable and guide the carrying out of the desired enchantment and can preserve the enchantment's effect long after the spell is cast.

ebony staff - a fae staff made of twisting ebony wood belonging to Sebastian Blackwell, a gift from the fae. At the top the branches, as of the roots of a tree, flare out to twist around a glowing green gem embedded within in the wood of the crown. With the abilities he was given, Sebastian can summon it from the fae realm at will, but as soon as he releases it, it disappears back from whence it came.

eduba - [e + dub + a = {e = house, temple, plot of land} + {dub = clay (tablet), document} + {a = genitive marker}] the Enkinim word for library, used by ancient Sumerians to indicate the houses where their clay writing tablets were kept. To a wizard, however, it describes a book containing their personal archive of knowledge. Similar to the mundane notion of grimoires, edubas are full of much more than simply spells. They accumulate centuries of history, research, and personal notes as they are passed down, usually from parent to child or teacher to student within powerful wizard families. The knowledge in them is magically archived, such that you must summon the desired text to the physical pages before it can be read. This allows for vast stores of information to be carried around in one physical book.

elwa - fae word of greeting. It carries deeper meaning, however, than a simple hello. It is a request to commune with or share the presence of the named fae. The request may be denied or ignored, in which case the supplicant must withdraw. It is considered extremely rude to ask a second time.

Enkinim - [Enki + inim = {Enki = Sumerian god of creation and friend of mankind} + {inim = word; statement; command, order, decree}] words of power, the language of magic by which wizards control and direct the Source. Named after the Sumerian god Enki, who, it was said, taught mankind language, reading, and writing.

fae - one of the three species of magic users (human, fae, and angel/demon). Myth says they were created to help steward the earth, and that long ago they worked side by side with man to nurture it. But they have long since disappeared from sight and memory of mundanes and are now the subject of fairy tales. Wizards know of their existence and have some lore pertaining to their habits and home in the fae realm, but most of it is theory and conjecture.

fae glamour - a type of fae magic by which fae disguise their true shape. They also use it to create illusions or temporarily change the appearance of inanimate objects. While wizards can cast their own type of glamour to achieve a similar effect, their scrying spells can not see through fae glamour. It can be defeated using a seeing stone, something only fae can make. A fae can see through another fae's glamour.

familiar - a companion creature, being, or entity of some sort. Used in different contexts for witches and wizards. A witch familiar is usually some kind of spirit or creature with which they've made a bargain and formed a partnership. Some such beings can take the form of animals to avoid detection, thus the stereotype of witches having black cats. These dealings can be dangerous, however, and often lead to the practitioner changing, knowingly or not, by simple association. "Something given, something gained" is the witch's way. Most wizard familiars, on the other hand, are nothing more than loyal pets wearing enchanted collars. In rare cases, however, a skilled wizard could create their own familiar by crafting a mechanical body and enchanting it with abilities. These construct familiars were used for everything from manual labor to acting as mobile wards, messengers, protectors, spies, and more.

Grimoli'un - a mold fae befriended by Sebastian Blackwell, who calls him Grimmold. The *'un* of the name denotes masculine character. Grimmold has a sense of smell so good he can track things across dimensions. He has a weakness for specially aged pizza (Sebastian's usual bribe in exchange for Grimmold's services) and is very allergic to soap or cleaning fluids of any kind.

human - one of the three species of magic users (human, fae, and angel/demon), and the only one of the three with a direct connection to the Source. Whereas fae and angels/demons were created with a set amount of magical power proportional to their status, humans have no innate limit. They are limited only by their own will, discipline, and skill, as well as the frailty of their mortal bodies. Also, not all humans can use magic. While all fae and angels/demons are innately magical, only certain humans descended from the wizard lines manifest the ability to access the Source and manipulate magic. It is thought the difference is genetic and inherited, but no one yet knows how or why.

initiate - a term traditionally used to indicate a member of a wizard family who is not a wizard. Because not all children born to wizards or wizard-mundane couples could use magic—yet were still raised within the magical community with knowledge of its secrets— there arose the need for a distinguishing word for someone not magical, yet not ignorant like a mundane. Because these mundane children of wizards often became the butlers, valets, housekeepers, etc., of wizards, the term initiate has come to mean someone who works for a wizard family, caring for them and keeping their secrets. It is an old-fashioned term, generally used by the very traditional. Most modern wizards simply call all non-magic humans mundanes, whether they know about magic or not. With the decline of wizard families and magic use in general, along with society's general acceptance of, rather than fear of, magic, the existence of initiates in the traditional sense has all but disappeared.

iron: salts - the common name for ferrous sulfate, a range of salts with high iron content used in various industries as well as a health supplement to treat iron deficiency. It has also long been used by wizards as a natural remedy for certain magical maladies, such as magic poisoning. If a wizard is not trained to properly control, channel, and withdraw from the Source when magic is not in use, the body can become overstressed and, in extreme cases, become catatonic. Also useful to counteracting certain magic-based poisons and potions.

iron: wrought - a metal which repels magic. Spells cannot be anchored to it, affect it, or pass through it, and it dulls the effectiveness of any magic in its vicinity. Because fae and angels/demons are beings of pure magic, it is poisonous to them. It will burn them on contact, its presence weakens them, and it will kill them if ingested in large quantities. A wizard wearing iron or standing near iron will be hampered or completely prevented from casting, depending on their strength and skill. Iron does not, however, hurt wizards in any way beyond a slight weakening effect that is a result of blocking their access to the Source. Only wrought iron has this ability. Other mixtures of iron alloy such as steel have little or no effect.

Jastiri'un - an elemental fae befriended by Sebastian Blackwell, who calls him Jas. The *'un* of the name denotes masculine character. Jas can control light and sound (mechanical and electromagnetic waves). Like most pixies, he has a weakness for alcohol, which Sebastian often trades him for various services.

McCain Library - the library of Agnes Scott College, a private liberal arts women's college near downtown Atlanta. Built in 1936 to replace the smaller Andrew Carnegie Library constructed in 1910, it was originally still called the Carnegie Library, then later renamed the McCain Library after the college's second president in 1951. Complete with four main floors, a grand reading room, and three attached floors dedicated to the stacks, this building is Lily Singer's workplace and domain. She is the college's Archives Manager, and her office is located on the library's main floor. The basement floor contains the library's archives as well as the portal to the secret magical archive of which Lily is the gatekeeper.

mundane - a term used by wizards to denote non-magical humans. Generally, mundanes are ignorant of the existence of magic, the notable exception being witches. Other enlightened mundanes include members of wizard families who were born without the ability to use magic. These non-magical members of the wizard community were traditionally known as initiates. Historically, the term mundane was derogatory and insulting. Accusing a wizard or initiate of being "mundane" was paramount to calling them ignorant fools. The wizard community looked down on mundanes and considered them little more than animals. The fact that mundanes regularly executed anyone they suspected of using magic helped to solidify wizards' negative attitude toward them. That attitude has largely disappeared with the advance of society, though there still exists a lingering feeling of superiority among wizards.

Oculus - Meaning eye or sight in Latin, this is the name of John Faust LeFay's construct familiar crafted in the form of a raven.

Pilanti'ara - a plant fae befriended by Sebastian Blackwell, who calls her Pip. The *'ara* of the name denotes feminine character. As a plant fae, Pip has a certain area she is responsible for. Within that area she cares for all growing things. Like most pixies, she has a weakness for alcohol, which Sebastian often trades her for various services.

pixie - any fae that are small, quick, and flighty. This is purely a human term and has no relation to actual fae taxonomy (naming and classification). However, it is true that most pixies are energetic, fun-loving, and have a weakness for alcohol, which they can metabolize in vast amounts compared to their body mass without getting drunk. Of all the fae, they are the ones most familiar to, and seen by, humans because of their curiosity and lack of fear.

power anchor - a crafted object—usually something small and wearable like an amulet, necklace, or ring—that wizards use to focus and amplify their magic so as to cast more precise and powerful spells. For particularly powerful spells, wizards can create a one-time-use, secondary power anchor which they might draw or carve on the floor to further channel their magic.

runes of power - also known as dimmu runes, these are the symbols used to write Enkinim, the language of power that shapes magic. They are similar in appearance to the cuneiform script used in Mesopotamia during ancient times.

seeing stone - traditionally a triangular stone with a hole through it, though the stone can be any shape and still work. In ancient times these stones were made by the fae and given to certain humans so they could look through the hole and see past fae glamour. Few were preserved and passed down and so are rare today, for the fae have long since withdrawn from contact with humankind and give no more such gifts as they did in times past.

Source, the - the place from which all magic comes. While many creatures and parts of nature are innately magical, filled with the Source's power, wizards are the only beings in the universe born with an innate connection to it and the ability to draw on it at will. The Source is not sentient, only raw power. Magic drawn from the Source has to be shaped and directed by the caster's will using words of power (Enkinim). Incorrect use of Enkinim or poor control over a spell can cause backfires or spell mutations, resulting in a different outcome than intended and sometimes causing the injury or death of the caster. Though many known, reliable spells exist, the power of the Source is, in theory, limited only by the willpower and knowledge of the caster. Though safe to use within limits and with the proper training, many wizards over the years have died from overestimating their own strength or attempting dangerous spells which they did not properly understand. Thus, use of magic by modern wizards is in decline. With the rise of mundane technology, many wizards feel magic use is not worth the trouble or cost.

spell circle - a simple line or mark on the ground providing a visual aid and anchor to the casting of any sort of circle, such as a shield circle or circle of containment. Spell circles can be permanently engraved or carved into a surface accompanied by dimmu runes that add to the stability and effectiveness of whatever casting is being done.

spell: curse - a category of complicated and dangerous spells that are always meant to harm. Curses require an immense amount of magic to cast, but once the initial spell is completed, they are able to self-sustain by virtue of their complex if-then structure. Because of their strength, they are very difficult to break. Either their effect must be counteracted, or they must be unmade by knowing the exact parameters of the if-then structure. The most effective defense when it comes to curses is to not be cursed in the first place.

spell: portal - a risky yet useful means of transportation not completely understood by wizards, but which is assumed to take advantage of whatever space other magical creatures travel through to and from the human realm (such as fae and demons). The origin of the spell is unknown, but its specific formula has been preserved. Historically, any experimentation with or deviation from the formula has resulted in permanent disappearance. At its most basic, portal spells connect two specific, geographical locations. Because the space between realms is outside the dimensions of time and space, travel is instantaneous. A portal cannot be cast without knowledge of the exact location of its counterpart.

spell of: compulsion - used to control another human. Only works with the initial willingness of the subject, usually gained through subtle suggestion or trickery. Once the subject has been compelled for the first time, however, they are particularly susceptible to it again even if they try to resist. Traditionally a type of magic used only on mundanes, as it is social suicide to compel another wizard. If discovered, the offending wizard will be ostracized and mistrusted by his community.

spell of: containment - a kind of spell circle used to contain magic. It is usually cast as a safety measure when doing spell work.

spell of: conveyance - a type of spell that can transmit sensory input, whether audio, visual, or tactile, from one item to another, even over great distances. Variations of this spell class can be used for many things, even a wizard version of the mundane cell phone.

spell of: invisibility/cloaking - a type of glamour spell that helps conceal the subject from sight. Not true invisibility as mundanes understand it, but rather a spell that mimics the surroundings. When perfectly still, a wizard can be nearly invisible; while moving, a visible outline can be detected with careful observation.

spell of: shielding - a kind of spell used to shield the caster from magic. One type—a barrier through which magic cannot enter—is often cast as a spell circle. Another type—a selective spell that blocks only incoming active or targeted magic—is commonly used in personal wards.

steward - a member of any of several semi-formal wizard conglomerates, grouped nationally by country, who attempt to preserve knowledge of magic and resolve disputes between their fellow wizards. Traditionally, wizards keep to themselves and do not accept the oversight of any formal body, preferring to deal with things internally within their own family units. Stewards are more caretakers and mediators than enforcers. There is no formal international wizard political system. Attempts were made several times throughout the nineteenth and twentieth centuries but always came to naught. A steward's authority is largely based on how formal and structured its conglomerate is, which varies by country. Britain has one of the more stable conglomerates because of their long history and strong traditions. America, in contrast, has had several conglomerates during its short history. Their size, nature, and authority are often in flux. The only universally agreed-upon rule among wizards is: never meddle in mundane affairs. The second, unspoken and assumed, rule is: don't reveal magic to mundanes.

Thiriel - the fae who gave Sebastian Blackwell his ebony staff.

truth coin - a silver coin given to Sebastian Blackwell by his father. It is inscribed with dimmu runes and enchanted to grow warm in the presence of lies. The degree of warmth is directly proportional to the degree of the lie.

twilight, the - the space between the fae and human realms, existing outside normal time and space. Known only to the few wizards who have been friends of the fae over the years. Only fae can enter, navigate, and exit it safely, though they can bring other beings with them without harm.

ward - magical protection of some kind, usually cast into an anchor such as a bracelet (personal ward) or into runes set in/around a location (stationary ward). Ward spells can be customized to do a variety of things. Personal wards usually contain a combination of a shield spell along with various minor spells that help protect the bearer from weariness, sickness, or other physical harm. Stationary wards put up around a house or created to protect a certain location or object, can be set to protect against specific things (just wizards, or alternately, just mundanes, for example). They can also be customized to prevent the passage of physical objects, sound, light, etc.

witch - a mundane who, through trades, favors, and alliances with other beings, gains magical power or the service of said beings. "Something given, something gained," is the way of a witch. While uncommon, the other two magical species (fae and angels/demons) have been known to form alliances with humans, mundane and wizard alike. Besides directly gaining other beings' magic, witches also often trade for the services of various supernatural beings. Many witches favor demonic pacts, as demons are the most eager for contact with humans. Such pacts, however, usually end badly for the witch, or else the witch is irrevocably changed, sometimes tricked or forced into subjugation to whatever demon they were trying to control. Spirits in their various forms are one of the other more common partners of witches. But since they are incorporeal and have no need for physical things, they can be hard to bargain with and, by nature, are unstable. Fae, while shy of humans and largely unknown to them, do occasionally form pacts. Historically, witches who allied with the fae were known as druids, but the term has largely fallen out of use because they are now so rare.

wizard - a human with the ability to access the Source and manipulate its power. The ability is thought to be genetic, as it seems to be passed from parent to child. Legend says magic was given to Gilgamesh and so only his descendants inherited it. Like most inherited genes, it can be diluted by mixing with normal human genes. So a wizard marrying a mundane is less likely to produce wizard children than a wizard-wizard union, though even those are not guaranteed to have all wizard children. A wizard's abilities are not instinctive, they are a skill that must be taught and mastered to use effectively.

words of power - the language (Enkinim) used by wizards to control their magical power. Passed down over the centuries, these words help shape and direct a wizard's spells, both activating and limiting their effects. Though many set spells exist, new ones can be discovered and old ones customized. The stronger a wizard's will, the more adroit their mind, and the better their understanding of Enkinim, the more they can do with magic. Magical experimentation can, however, be extremely dangerous.

Check out this preview of Lydia Sherrer's
fourth Lily Singer Adventures book

LOVE, LIES, AND HOCUS POCUS: LEGENDS

Now in paperback and ebook

Chapter 1
A Hop Across the Pond

LILY SOMETIMES WONDERED WHY HEALTH INSURANCE DIDN'T COVER THE COST of cat ownership. It really ought to, since cats were one of the leading contributors to stress reduction and overall happiness in households across the nation. They were one hundred percent natural and had no harmful side effects—well, if you ignored the hair. She supposed, to be fair, it should cover dog ownership as well. But dogs didn't purr, so they were at a distinct disadvantage in the stress-reduction department.

At the very least, she thought she should get some sort of premium discount, since Sir Edgar Allan Kipling—her snarky, obstreperous, talking cat—was solely responsible for preventing a variety of health complications over the past twenty-four hours. Heart attack. Anxiety attack. If-you-do-that-one-more-time-I'm-going-to-kill-you attack. The therapeutic effect of burying one's face in a fuzzy cat tummy knew no bounds.

Not having a heart attack was a good thing, since the fate of wizardkind currently rested on her shoulders. Being a socially awkward introvert didn't help, and she'd long ago admitted she needed all the friends and allies she could get. Which brought her back to the heart attack. It was an understandable concern, considering that her most powerful ally lay near death, afflicted by an unknown curse.

Madam Ethel Barrington was Lily's friend, mentor, and instructor in the wizarding arts. Though the woman was more than a hundred years old by Lily's best guess—wizards aged well, she didn't look a day over seventy—she'd always been a pillar of wisdom and stability in Lily's life. Now she lay cold and ashen as the grave, and Lily was trying very hard not to panic.

Lily sat by her mentor's sickbed in her uncle Allen LeFay's townhouse situated in the heart of historic Savannah, Georgia. Though one of the more modest of Savannah's historic homes, it was nonetheless an impressive example of antebellum architecture with its high ceilings, wood-paneled floors, and plaster walls complete with crown molding. Madam Barrington's room was clean and well lit by sunlight streaming in from four tall windows, two each on the east and north walls. Privacy was preserved thanks to a handy spell that made it appear from the outside as if the curtains were drawn. Allen didn't like mundanes nosing about, and there were plenty in this city full of curious tourists.

Despite the sunlight, however, and copious layers of warm blankets, Madam Barrington's hand was still deathly cold as Lily gripped it between both of hers, keeping silent vigil beside the bed. Her heart felt as cold as the hand she clutched, and just as immune to the sunlight. Back aching, limbs stiff, and eyes stinging with weariness, Lily tried not to think too much as she watched the slow, almost imperceptible rise and fall of her mentor's chest. But with nothing else to occupy her thoughts, like iron to a magnet they inevitably gravitated back toward the cause of this whole mess: her father, John Faust LeFay.

It had been less than twenty-four hours since their…confrontation. Though to call it a confrontation was a bit of an understatement. If you asked her best friend, Sebastian Blackwell, he would have described it as an epic battle between good and evil. Which was why she rarely let him explain things: he liked to exaggerate. She supposed he deserved a break in this instance, however, since he *had* gotten his butt soundly kicked by her half-sister Trista. The young mundane was a veritable expert in armed and unarmed combat and had unfortunately been brainwashed by their father to help him in his grand plan to "save" the wizard race and bring about an age of "benevolent" wizard rule. So from Sebastian's perspective she supposed it had been an epic battle. He'd had to use every bit of his fae magic—acquired in a trade, as was the witches' way—along with his own natural wiles to eventually run her off.

And that was the other reason Lily preferred to think of it as a "confrontation." They hadn't won. Oh, they'd rescued Allen and freed the other wizard children John Faust had been raising as his brainwashed minions. And John Faust had fled, along with Trista and her wizard half brother, Caden. But they hadn't won. Madam Barrington had been almost killed by one of John Faust's curses, and their adversaries had escaped with knowledge of Morgan le Fay's location. Morgan was one of the most powerful wizards from the past two millennia—and Lily's ancestor. There was no telling what kind of power John Faust might obtain from her, whether she was still alive or not.

What with John Faust getting a head start, her mentor being fatally ill, and knowing she had to go to England and fix it all, alone, it was a testament to the power of Sir Kipling's purr that she hadn't lost it already. Alright, so, not quite alone. Sir Kipling would be coming, and then there was Sebastian.

"How's she doing?"

The soft voice behind her made her jump, and she turned to make shushing motions at Sebastian's bright-eyed, boyish face as it poked around the door into Madam

Barrington's sickroom. Turning back to the bed, she gently released the ice-cold hand she'd been holding and laid it on the covers, trying not to think how like a corpse her mentor looked. It was the blue lips and grey skin that did it, and the fact that her breathing was so shallow it seemed nonexistent. To make Madam Barrington more comfortable, Lily had taken down her strict bun and combed out the grey hair to cascade over her shoulders. It was the first time Lily had ever seen the older woman's hair down. It made her look more vulnerable. More human.

With a sigh she moved away, pausing to pet Sir Kipling, currently stationed in a catloaf on the older woman's chest, where his warmth and purring would do the most good. Then she slipped out of the bedroom—the last room at the end of the hall—giving Sebastian a weary shrug as she quietly answered his question. "I can't see any change yet. Allen seems sure his antidote will at least get her conscious, but I can't help worrying. What if she doesn't wake up? I can't bear the thought of leaving before we know she'll be okay."

Though she fought to hold it back, moistness formed in the corners of her eyes and threatened to spill down over her cheeks.

"Hey, hey. It's gonna be fine." Sebastian assured her, giving her shoulder a comforting squeeze, then leaving his hand there. While its warmth was not unwelcome, what she really wanted was to·wrap her arms around him and bury her face in his collar. That was out of the question, of course, so she compromised by leaning forward slightly to rest her forehead on his chest and taking deep, slow breaths to calm her emotions.

While she was eternally grateful for his friendship and knew she couldn't have gotten this far without him, he did create his own set of problems, though not exactly the ones you'd expect. The fact that he was a witch was a non-issue, even though witches and wizards were traditionally rivals. Being born with magic, wizards tended to distrust and look down on witches for their wheeling and dealing to acquire magic for themselves. But Lily and Sebastian had long since decided to ignore the traditions of their elders. The fact that he was a ne'er-do-well who considered rules to be more like guidelines was, surprisingly, not a major problem, either. He had a good heart and always meant well, even if he drove her crazy.

No, the biggest problem was that she had finally, sort of, almost admitted that she loved him. She hadn't spoken about it openly, but the fact that she had progressed from denial to semi-acceptance was a huge step for an awkward, controlling, up-tight introvert like herself. Of course, the most sensible thing to do would be to ignore her feelings and get on with the task ahead. The problem was, she didn't know if she wanted to be sensible anymore.

Staring at the polished wood under her feet, she felt Sebastian's chest rise and fall in a sigh of his own, making her uncomfortably aware of how close they were. Raising her head and stepping back, she turned to stare out the hall window that looked over the busy street below, giving absent, one-word answers to Sebastian's concerned queries.

The whole relationship issue was made more complicated by this life-threatening adventure they'd been sucked into, clouding her judgment with worry and fear. Everything depended on her. With Allen recovering from his own injuries while simultaneously nursing Madam Barrington, Lily was the only wizard with the necessary knowledge to track down Morgan le Fay before John Faust. They might already be too late. Who knew how long it would take them to puzzle out her location from their copy of the ancient journal Morgan had left behind? John Faust, on the other hand, had already discovered her resting place, using a location spell he'd devised. A spell he'd channeled through her Uncle Allen, almost killing him.

They'd "confronted" John Faust too late to stop him using the spell, but at least they'd survived the encounter intact and had deprived her father of his base of operations. The old mental ward he'd been using as a magical laboratory was now an FBI crime scene where Agent Richard Grant—their contact in the agency—was busy leading the investigation against his illegal activities. Not that the FBI knew anything about John Faust's larger plans. They thought he was just some crazy cultist wacko. Lily wished it were that simple.

The worst part was, she agreed with her father. Not with his methods, of course. They were deplorable. But his goal to repopulate the wizard race was a noble one, especially since most wizards were in denial about their slow decline and eventual extinction. Even her father's vision of ruling mundane society, putting an end to their petty wars while using magic to make people's lives better, was a laudable goal. Supremacist, racist, arrogant, and wildly idealistic, but still, laudable. If her father hadn't been such a miserable excuse for a human being, she might have been tempted to join him. But having already been held captive by him and experimented on herself, she'd thoroughly and irrevocably burned those bridges. Her father was wrong. The ends did *not* justify the means, and no amount of future good could justify present immorality.

Lost in her own dark thoughts, she became aware of Sebastian again only when he gripped her by the shoulders and gave her a gentle shake. "Hey. Hey! Are you hearing me, Lil? You're gonna be fine. You know why? Because I'm going to help you. And so is Kip, and Allen, and your mom, and everyone else. You're not alone. We'll figure this out together, okay?"

Lily took a deep breath and nodded. She opened her mouth to say something bracing that she didn't feel when she heard a weak, halting voice from inside the bedroom.

"Hello…Mr. Kipling. I do n't suppose…you could… fetch some water…could you?

Thanks so much for picking up this book and joining Lily, Sebastian, and Sir Kipling in their adventures. We hope they brought you laughter and maybe a tear or two. If you enjoyed the story and want to see more published please take a moment to leave an honest review. Book reviews help authors write better and sell more books and are a great way to show your support. Thank you!

If you'd like to stay up to date with Lydia's newest publications, sign up for her newsletter at lydiasherrer.com/subscribe. This is where you can get behind-the-scene sneak peeks, freebies, book giveaways, and chances to get involved in the story-making process.

You can also connect with Lydia online!

Read all about Lydia and her books: lydiasherrer.com/about

Like her page: facebook.com/lydiasherrerauthor

Follow her on Twitter: @LydiaSherrer
twitter.com/lydiasherrer

Follow her on Instagram: lydiasherrer
instagram.com/lydiasherrer

Listen to her ocarina music: youtube.com/c/lydiasherrer

ABOUT THE AUTHOR

Award-winning and USA Today-bestselling author of snark-filled fantasy, Lydia Sherrer thrives on creating characters and worlds you love to love, and hate to leave. She subsists on liberal amounts of dark chocolate and tea, and hates sleep because it keeps her from writing. Due to the tireless efforts of her fire-spinning gamer husband and her two overlords, er cats, she remains sane and even occasionally remembers to leave the house. Though she graduated with a dual BA in Chinese and Arabic, after traveling the world she came home to Louisville, KY and decided to stay there.

49604426R00207

Made in the USA
Columbia, SC
24 January 2019